Land of Dreams

Land of Dreams

E. J. DENSMORE

ISBN: 0692458468
ISBN 13: 9780692458464
Library of Congress Control Number: 2015943883
Carroll Publishing, Oak Forest. IL

One

Sometimes the weight of everyday life was so crushing that all Ellie Purnell could do to escape it was run. How perfect and metaphoric. *Run and save yourself while you still can!* Run.

She snuck quietly out of the bedroom every morning at 5:00 a.m., avoiding the creaky spots on the wooden floor like she was performing the delicate routine of a cat burglar avoiding laser-beam security. Creeping slowly down the stairs, she rested at the bottom step to lace up her well-worn shoes, relief already beginning to wash over her. Soon she would be alone, navigating the blackness and engulfed by the stillness of early morning. In some seasons, she would welcome the sun and the blissful song of jubilant robins and the persistent call of cardinals, but those mornings were few and far between.

It didn't matter. Even in the darkness of fall and winter, she would brave the weather greedily, desperately seeking at least forty-five minutes of tranquility and clarity. *I am alive. I am alive. I am alive.* This was the mantra repeated silently with each footfall, nothing but the sound of her own steady breath and her shoes smacking the ground. And then suddenly, her mind would go blank. The meetings, the obligations, the week's schedule (bring Jordan to soccer, pick up food for a work function, buy paper towels, finish grading essays) would simply vanish. In front of her—nothing but the rhythmic sound of her feet hitting the pavement, lulling her into a meditation. No one to demand or need things from her. No one insisting anything. Just her and the sound of her own heartbeat. And then, of course, the rush of peace, the adrenaline that would cleanse her of everything.

This particular morning, she would not see the sun. Those glorious mornings were near enough, though. Something to anticipate. It was the beginning of spring in southern Wisconsin, the brisk mornings heating gradually into temperate afternoons if one was lucky.

Spring here could be brutal and cold, keeping everyone in their fleece coats and the flowers hidden deep in the earth until the middle of May. But it was only just the end of March, and this year, the crocuses were already rearing their heads. Daffodils had started to peek out from beneath last year's brush piles. Spring was going to be sublime. Ellie could feel it in her bones. It was what kept her going.

The air was thin and cool, hinting of wet earth as she set off down the steps of her home, down the long gravel drive out to the county road. Spring was always full of possibilities, with students returning from midterm breaks and preparing for the final push of the school year. It also meant an easier summer term was ahead, somewhat a break from the monotony—new students, new faces, daylight, and sunshine. It meant that Ellie had time to travel, plant, and, of course, run. Half a mile down the road, she would reach town, running past the dilapidated rows of cheap college housing where oftentimes the inhabitants had just settled down for the night. Occasionally she might run past some kids who were still on their front porches with their plastic cups in hand. And occasionally one would recognize her through his stupor and wave, saying "Professor Purnell!" It didn't bother her. She was used to being the town celebrity.

Anger was what fueled this morning's run. Ellie was aware of it and silently willed herself to take it slow. She had to resist the urge to burst from the house like a racehorse from its gate.

Slowly. Don't hurt yourself. The calm will come.

She started out at a forcibly controlled trot.

Fuck him!

No, slow down. Focus.

Feet beginning to move themselves rhythmically, trot, trot, trot, trot, her face relaxing, she breathed in the coolness, mentally repeating another mantra—*Be a funnel, not a vessel. Be a funnel, not a vessel. Be a funnel, not a vessel*—and trying to relax her clenched jaw and squinched-up forehead, the ever-deepening line between her eyes. *And let's face it*, she thought, *at thirty-nine, I can't afford more years on my face. Relax. Take it out of your face.* And like magic, she did. Trot. Trot. Trot. Her face became impassive, unreadable. This was the mask she had perfected over time.

By the time she reached the town square, she had accelerated to her full speed, the speed she would run for the rest of the distance. She absentmindedly passed the post office and the tiny town library, which was really no more than a historical building since most people used the university library, if any library at all.

Damn Internet could never replace the dank but beautiful smell of an actual, tangible book in hand.

Good. An errant thought.

This was the beginning of the transition. She waited for her mind to still. The anger persisted. *Come on!*

Past the only diner on the town square where old Will Miller would soon be arriving to open shop. Past the Black Bear Pub. Past Andy's Bar and Grill, a favorite of the students, where even the pavement outside smelled of stale kegs and vomit. That thought made her even angrier. *Come on!* No use. She couldn't control the replay of last night's events.

"I am done," she had told Alec. She knew it was a risk even as she said it, but she didn't care. He could be unpredictable when he was drunk. Would he just laugh at her? Would he blow up, call her a fucking bitch, wake up Jordan? (This was unlikely. Alec had become a much nicer drunk as he aged). Would he even remember what she had said? Perhaps not. And what did she mean, anyhow? Hadn't she said exactly that a million times before? How many times had she threatened to leave her marriage in the past fifteen years? Certainly too many to count. And did she ever? No. Alec probably secretly laughed at her threats every time he twisted the cap off another bottle, making love to his mistress, Jack Daniels. The thought nearly made her laugh.

"I don't know why you always have to be so uptight," he slurred. So he was going to make one of his usual arguments: "You're just a stick in the mud," which was not to be confused with, "A man works hard, and he should be able to drink whenever he wants," or Ellie's

5

all-time favorite excuse, "You are such a bitch. You drive me to drink."

"I'm uptight?" Ellie asked with contempt. "Let's say for argument's sake that's true." She was building herself up into a fury. The only satisfaction she had was making herself sound superior to Alec in his drunken stupor by presenting an argument that he couldn't possibly follow. "The sun also rises in the east. I am a woman. You are a man. We are standing in a house. So what? Do any of these facts affect the truth that you drank too much *again*? What does me being uptight—assuming I am, in fact, uptight—have to do with the fact that you are stinking drunk? God, I can't even take you to a work function without you totally embarrassing me." She threw her hands up in utter disgust and made her way down the hall to their bedroom, hoping desperately that he would pass out on the sofa in the living room.

"That's just like you. Making some professor's argument about everything," he called after her. "Why don't you write an essay on it?" he snickered, obviously pleased with himself. "The only fact I know is that you don't know how to have a good time. Whatever, Ellie. The only person who has a problem with my drinking is you. I got along fine with everyone there!"

It was too much for her to let go. She stormed back down the hall.

"Maybe you did, Mr. Good-Time Drunk, working the crowd, thinking you're so fucking charming, but

I'm the one person who should matter. It's *my* opinion that should matter. Tomorrow I'm going to have to go into work and smile and nod when everyone says, 'Your husband enjoyed himself a lot last night'—wink, wink. Before we left for the restaurant, I specifically asked you not to drink too much, didn't I?"

"Oh my God. You sound like my mother. Why don't you just loosen up? You're so uptight."

No, Alec, your mother is dead, and she would never have reprimanded you for drinking too much, she thought bitterly but was wise enough not to utter. "I guess I had to be uptight enough to drive us home because *God forbid* you should stay sober enough to do that. By the way, it was an important dinner for me. The security of my job may depend on it. Thanks for fucking it up."

Surely this fight would be yet another bitter memory.

Or maybe not.

Alec's drinking had become such an expected way of life that few experiences stood out anymore. The memories that were most hurtful were the ones at the beginning of their marriage, when Ellie still held onto some hope. When Alec's behavior could still shock her. Before she felt so jaded. Maybe tonight wasn't so bad after all. I mean really, what had he done? Talked a little too loudly? Gushed over her in an obviously over-the-top, drunken manner while he was still feeling all warm and sweet ("She's so smart, this woman. I don't know what she's talking about half the time, but I still love her! She's brilliant")? Slurred his speech? Not so bad. Stopping to unzip his suit pants to piss next to the car so everyone coming out of the restaurant could see?

That was bad.

The humiliation Ellie felt.

That was bad.

Alec struggled over his middle-aged belly to reach for his shoes, pulling one off with a pop and tossing it onto the rug. "Yeah, you may be smart, but you're boring. Boohoo. Your husband had a fun night out, and you didn't. Loosen up," he baited her. She could feel the anger and disgust rising in her. How had Alec become this man? This thing? He used to be so beautiful. Now he disgusted her.

"I'm done." It came out of Ellie's mouth as a slow, quiet promise. An oath. "I can't do this anymore. I am done." Alec responded with a dismissive laugh, tugging his other shoe free and walking around Ellie to get to the liquor cabinet in the front room. Every muscle in her body tensed as she resisted the urge to hit him when he went by. As the words "I am done" formed again on her lips, she stopped. It wasn't worth the taunting. Something had finally died in her. Whether or not Alec believed her, she was done with caring about his drinking and maybe even done with caring about him. She certainly was done fighting about it. And all hell would freeze over before she would bring him to another work-related function. Was she done with their marriage? That was more complicated.

Something cold and wet brought Ellie out of her trance. A drop of rain? Then she realized she was sprinting. It was sweat that stung her eyes, a surprise in this weather. She usually didn't blind herself with perspiration except in the humid months of summer. She had inadvertently pushed herself to her physical limits, purging herself. And now here she was, drenched in sweat. Forget the fact that her lungs felt as though they might burst. She consciously slowed herself to a run again. The university quad, the dorms, the nineteenth-century buildings that housed the administration offices, and the library were far behind her. She even managed to pass the liberal-arts building, where her modest office sat overlooking the quad. She had run past without noticing her home away from home.

At a steady, manageable pace once again, she made note of the darkness beginning to lift. It was time to turn down the next county road and make her way back, past the local farmers' fields, tranquil and still, past the rocky creek that split the land, partially hidden by cottonwood and pine trees. How many times, as a kid, had she swam in that creek, liquor concealed in water bottles, sneaking cigarettes? She wondered idly if Jordan had yet begun to do the same—the cigarettes, not the liquor, of course. Jordan would not be sneaking any liquor and live to tell about it.

Ellie slowed once again to a trot past the few scattered farmhouses that dotted the open road. Movement in the fields hinted at a pack of coyotes, but they were certainly more afraid of her than she of them. Their presence was actually a comfort to her, a reminder that she was never really alone, no matter how much she pitied herself at times. The birds, the trees, the coyotes, and the deer were all a part of something bigger. That was why she endured the punishment of running outdoors. She imagined herself as some creature of nature for whom the events of life were without value. The birds could not choose their fate, nor could the coyotes or the deer. And yet they survived. They managed the rough winters or they didn't. They scrounged enough food to eat or they didn't. They lived and they died, and it wasn't worth noting. The rest of the pack or the flock continued on.

Maybe that was really how Ellie should look at her life rather than beating herself up for choices she did or didn't make in the past. Five months short of her fortieth birthday, she found herself toying with this philosophy. Certainly, as an English professor, someone who had studied literature and written critical essays about it her entire adult life, she had thought about the meaning of life before. But it was different now. Somehow musing over one's mortality was different at thirty-nine than it had been at eighteen. At eighteen, the world seemed to lie before her like a land of dreams; at thirty-nine, the path seemed closed. Her choices had been made. What opportunities were there now? And what difference did it make, really? Perhaps, like the wildlife around her, she was just meant to survive.

Ellie slowed to a brisk walk up the gravel drive to the house. To her surprise, she could see a light on in the upstairs master bathroom. Was Alec really getting up this early or just making a frantic dash to the bathroom? Maybe he had meetings this morning. Ugh. That meant navigating around him, the delicate dance of avoidance that Ellie and Alec had perfected over the years. He would certainly be too hungover to deal with Ellie shaming him again. She had run out of steam, though. Why ruin the endorphin rush by having another futile argument over Alec's drinking? Whether or not he remembered it, Ellie had already said what she needed to say the night before. If they avoided each other this morning, then they could both pretend like nothing happened. Life could continue on as it had for years.

The landscape lights still lit up the front walk as she made her way to the stone steps, pausing to stretch her calves. It was a beautiful house by anyone's standards, built especially for her. Alec insisted that they use only the best materials, and no expense was spared.

Whether or not that was a gesture for Ellie's benefit or Alec's ego was debatable, but the end result was the most perfect house that Ellie could imagine. Best of all, the architects incorporated the surrounding forest, removing as few of the trees as possible while clearing a site for the building, and preserving a grove of black locust trees surely a hundred years old. In a few weeks, they would burst into gorgeous white flowers, framing the roof. The wraparound porch extended all the way around the house to a back patio, where a bench was built around a majestic Sunset Maple whose leaves turned the most breathtaking fire-lit orange and red in autumn. In the early days, the tree made Ellie think of Penelope and Ulysses's bed in *The Odyssey*, a reference Alec surely could not appreciate. Ellie herself had planned the landscaping, something she was particularly proud of. Because it was such a large property, the maintenance kept her very busy, even with the hired gardeners. That was OK. Busy was good.

Ellie hesitated as she pushed slowly down on the handle of one of the double doors. She could see no light through the decorative glass, but she steeled herself for a possible confrontation anyhow. Stepping into the open air of the expansive foyer, she realized she was holding her breath. There was still no sound in the house. She was safe. *Get into the shower as soon as possible.* Jordan would be up soon, and she would be momentarily safe from a possible fight with Alec.

The thought saddened her. Poor, sweet Jordan. If he could see into her mind, he would be destroyed. At fourteen, he still worshipped his father. Could both Ellie and Alec be lucky enough to be spared the punishment of teenage insolence? To Jordan, Alec was Christlike—perfect, infallible. Even so, how much had Jordan witnessed over the years? Didn't he ever wonder why his father chose to sleep on the sofa so many nights? Jordan must surely recognize the stench of stale liquor on Alec's breath. Certainly alcohol was part of the work events, family parties, and get-togethers with friends that the Purnells had hosted in their home over the years, but did Jordan, by chance, ever observe just how much more his father consumed than any other human being who walked through the door of their home? It was hard to say. Jordan was so small and immature for his age, mostly due to his illness. Even if he was the most astute teenager in the world, even if he could recognize the signs, Ellie doubted it would make a difference to Jordan that his father was an alcoholic. Jordan and Alec had a father-son relationship that was enviable. It was possibly the only reason Ellie hadn't left her marriage. She remained in her big, beautiful home and held up the façade. How could she crush Jordan's soul? Especially after he'd been through so much.

Never mind these musings—she needed to get ready for work quickly and quietly if she wanted to begin her day devoid of drama. As she had done many times before, she snuck back up the stairs toward the bathroom.

~う

An hour later, Ellie maneuvered her black Jaguar slowly into her assigned parking space in back of the liberal-arts building, pulling down the visor to check her lipstick in the mirror. Smoothing back her long chestnut hair, she stared back at her reflection with wide, hollow, brown eyes. Despite her best efforts, she still looked tired. She would sit a moment longer and wait until Mozart's forty-first symphony finished, concentrating on getting her headspace right. Then she could go into this morning's meeting with Dr. Long, the English department chair, feeling calm, the melody still rolling around in her head. Last night's events were almost forgotten now, and she was feeling more optimistic about starting her day. She had seen a chipper, blissfully ignorant Jordan off to school this morning and avoided a snoring Alec. Now the bright spring sunshine blinded her through her windshield, and all was good—as long as she could dodge any quips about Alec pissing next to her car in the restaurant parking lot.

"Hey!" A voice and a fist pounding on her window startled Ellie out of her contemplation. "You're already beautiful! Stop trying to fix yourself!"

"You just scared the hell out of me!" Ellie blurted angrily at the sight of her closest friend, Marta.

Marta put her hand up to her ear jokingly. "Eh? I can't hear you. Get out!" She lifted the strap of a large, brown leather tote, overflowing with papers, over her tiny shoulder. "This bag is killing me! Hurry!"

Ellie rolled her eyes and began gathering up her handbag and her own black leather tote, opening the door and sliding out as carefully as possible in her tight-fitting pencil skirt and heels. "Good morning, Id," she said dryly to Marta, using the Freudian nickname.

"Look at you!" Marta teased, appraising Ellie, eyeing her platform pumps and sleek outfit slowly. "Fancy."

Ellie laughed. She liked clothes, had a huge walk-in closet full of very expensive things (after all, what better way to cheer oneself than to shop?), but today she had outdone herself. Perhaps she was overdressed for a regular Friday spring morning at the university, especially when most of the professors dressed like Marta— well, not exactly like Marta in her frayed jeans and ratty Birkenstocks, but casual nonetheless. Ellie didn't care, though. Being impeccably dressed gave her a sense of control. It was part of the persona. You know, the woman whose life is perfect. Professor Purnell, the town prodigy, graduate of the University of Chicago, ageless, brilliant, witty, reserved, and without flaw. Being better dressed than the students inspired a level of respect that Ellie also needed. The longer she taught, the less she could tolerate the dozing off, the "note-taking" that was really surfing the Internet, the texting that some of these students did openly. As crazy as it was, when she walked into a lecture in a $500 pair of shoes, the students listened. Her clothing commanded respect.

"Yeah, fancy for Long," Ellie explained.

"Ahh, Long Duck Dong." Marta snorted, rubbing her nose ring. "I'm so disappointed that I couldn't make it last night. I bet that dinner was a hoot." She brushed her long burgundy bangs out of her eyes, revealing an impish blue. For a woman in her late thirties, she neither looked nor acted a day over twenty.

"Well, it was a free meal. That I can say for sure," Ellie replied

"Really? The university could afford that? I thought we were supposed to be there bowing and scraping to defend our jobs because 'there ain't no money, ma'am,'" Marta drawled with joking contempt.

"Long paid, I'm sure. Not the university. You didn't miss much. We tossed around some new ideas for summer class offerings. He had some idea for a foreign-exchange program offering, like a study abroad in England. It would take the place of two British lit credits. He was really vague about it. He said he's just trying to drum up enthusiasm for the English program—show the university president that our program is progressive and—"

"Blah, blah, blah. Why did you have to go out to dinner for that? Isn't that what we're going to discuss this morning?"

"Yeah, I suppose…collegiality?" Ellie guessed, and then added bitterly, "But if we didn't have the dinner, then Alec wouldn't have had the opportunity to get drunk and piss in the restaurant parking lot."

"That's excellent!" Marta had to stop to toss her head back in laughter. She genuinely thought Alec entertaining. "I am going to have to give him shit about that. That's perfect!"

"Please don't." Ellie looked serious.

"You don't see the comic value in him pissing in the parking lot?" Marta asked, looking confused, and then laughed again. "I bet Long had a heart attack."

"Oh, God. I hope Long didn't see."

"Please, it would have been worth missing my date to see Alec pissing in the parking lot. Classic!"

"You had a date?" Ellie asked, surprised.

"Yeah, I had a date with my girlfriend, Mary Jane! I think I'm in love. You're welcome to come over for a threesome any time you want," Marta joked.

"Don't tempt me," Ellie replied seriously.

Marta stared back at her with exasperation. "Give me a break. Half of this staff is on Xanax. Hell, half the world is on Xanax. What's a little weed?"

"Escapism," Ellie admitted.

"What do you think your dancing is?" Marta shot back, and then brightened, saying, "Speaking of that, I think we're due to crash some parties soon."

Ellie smiled widely. "Really? You have some good leads? I could definitely dance."

"That's my girl!" Marta exclaimed. "I'm looking into it. You know, I've got my sources. This next one may call for a road trip!"

"Nice," Ellie exclaimed but then added darkly, "I could use a road trip. A road trip far away from here."

"What's wrong?" Marta suddenly looked at her seriously, concerned.

"Nothing new," Ellie said resentfully. "I'm just stressed, I guess. I'm worried about what crazy plan Long is going to come up with. I have a stack of essays a mile deep that I still have to grade, and I have that critical piece that I still haven't finished writing. My heart just hasn't been in it lately. I haven't published anything since last year. I don't know…" Ellie trailed off as she and Marta made their way up the faded carpeting of the liberal-arts-building staircase, toward their offices. The building was yet to be swarmed by students who casually made their way to class with their earbuds stuffed into their ears, backpacks slung over their shoulders, coffee in hand, looking like they had just rolled out of bed, still clad in their sleep clothes. Oh, the nonchalance of youth! Even unshowered, hungover, and sleep deprived, they seemed to Ellie to have more energy than her. Their plump faces still looked fresh.

"I just don't feel like I have it together," she lamented. "I have this unbearable urge to escape."

"Sounds like spring fever to me."

"Yeah, I guess," Ellie easily agreed. She didn't feel like talking or thinking about Alec anymore. Even though Marta was her closest friend, Ellie would only confide in her so much. Maybe she still had the loyalty of a wife, or maybe it was that she secretly believed that Marta couldn't possibly understand. Maybe Ellie was afraid she would not like what Marta would have to say about Alec and Ellie's disputes; after all, Marta herself had never been married. What did she know about men? She was gay! She didn't have children. She had no one to take care of but herself, and there was no one to let her down.

Marta thought Alec was harmless, funny even. Maybe he was. Maybe all of Ellie's anger and resentment was self-imposed. Maybe she overreacted. Maybe *she* was really the problem. It was just this thinking that kept their marriage together for so long. A little distance made last night's fight seem ridiculous. Anyhow, Ellie was too busy to spend much time fretting over it today. Dealing with her true feelings could wait until she wasn't so busy at work. This was the cycle. Work. Avoid. Work. Avoid.

"I'll find you after my eight o'clock. We can walk down to Long's together," Marta offered as she rounded the corner to her office.

"Sounds good," Ellie answered, heading three heavy wooden doors in the opposite direction. A few feet before reaching her office, she noticed bright sunlight through her open door. Someone was in her office.

"Ellie!" John Long surprised her.

"Oh my God, John! You scared me," Ellie blurted. *What are you doing here?* Her boss sat perched precariously on the edge of her desk, all rosy and rotund, looking full of uncharacteristic mirth. He nearly rubbed his hands together with delight. Ellie tentatively set her bags down on the floor next to the open door she was so confounded by the sight of him in her office.

"I didn't mean to scare you!" He laughed, again oddly uncharacteristic for someone usually so dour. "I just needed to share some very exciting news."

"Wow." Ellie faked a smile as her stomach tensed. "I was just with you ten hours ago! What's transpired since then? You've been busy!" She winked disingenuously, a gesture Marta would have guffawed at.

"Well," John Long said, leaning in conspiratorially, "this has been in the works for a while. I just wasn't sure whether or not we'd get approval. I didn't know anything for sure until four this morning."

Ellie's fingers began to tingle. Was she going to faint? *Sit down.* She could sense something big was coming, and she was suddenly terrified. Again faking enthusiasm, she cautiously pulled out her leather chair and eased herself into it. Professor Long had sense enough to move from her personal space in order to face her. He paused to look quizzically at a poster of Morrissey that Ellie had hanging on the far wall and then he made eye contact with her. "We are going to do a debate series!" he burst out.

Ellie looked at him blankly. Surely he'd had had too much coffee. What was so exciting about a debate series? "That sounds lovely, John. Tell me more."

"Oh, Ellie, where to start?" Long mused gleefully. Ellie consciously fixed her face into an impassive stare, even as she felt the corner of her right eye begin to twitch. "Do you know the literary critic Liam Curran?"

Ellie searched her mind in vain. The name was familiar, but there were too many thoughts swirling around in her head for her to pinpoint where she had read his work. She was too anxious for Long to continue his explanation. "I think I've read some of his essays," she lied, trying not to sound too impatient. *God, just get on with it! Tell me already.*

"Yes, he's actually an American literature scholar who's written several monographs on the Harlem Renaissance and Ellison's *Invisible Man*, but his early work included major English works like *Frankenstein.*

21

He's British—well, both Irish and English—his parents—well, that's not important. The point is that he's coming here."

Oh, God. I'm losing my job. Oh, God, I'm losing my job.

"He's coming as a guest! He's not taking a position here," Long explained suddenly when he saw the blood leave Ellie's face. Then he burst into laughter. "*He* wrote to *us*! He actually requested a debate series here as part of his study-abroad program. It's not costing us anything, but we are going to benefit greatly. He's bringing fifteen students with him. They are all studying American literature and want to spend a semester in the United States. The university will get the tuition for these students, but most importantly, we'll get some much-needed publicity and respect for our program among our academic colleagues. It's a win-win. We draw attention to our program, and we get to host *Liam Curran*!" Long had a curious flush. He was flustered! Was he in love? Ellie still groped for meaning. What was he saying? A long, strange silence followed.

"So this debate series…" Ellie probed.

"Well, he wants *you*," Long blurted.

"Come again?" Ellie spit out, and then silently chastised herself for being so obviously cynical.

"He requested a debate series with *you*!" Long answered with enthusiasm.

Again an awkward silence ensued. Ellie chose her words carefully this time. "Well, that is quite flattering."

The minute it came out of her mouth, she knew it didn't sound convincing. She was having a difficult time trying to make sense of what a debate series meant for her summer schedule. Could this news come on any worse a day?

"Well, yes, it is quite flattering," Long agreed, oblivious to Ellie's dark mood and sarcasm. "He says he is quite a fan of yours. He says he's read all of your essays. Yes, he claims to be an expert in the critical style of Elizabeth Purnell! A big fan, Ellie."

"Yet he wants a debate series?" Ellie asked suspiciously.

"Well, I'm sure a debate in the most collegial manner," Long offered.

"Yes, I suppose." Ellie paused, choosing her words carefully again. "But how entertaining will it be for people to watch my biggest fan praise me and my brilliant work for an hour?"

"Minor details." Long said dismissively "We can talk about all that later. We haven't worked out details on the topics of debate. I just wanted to share the *fantastic* news with you first! When we meet with the rest of the English department this morning, I'll tell everyone where his students will be placed and which classes he'll coteach and observe."

"He's going to coteach?" Ellie smiled wryly. Marta was going to just *love* that. And certainly Marta would be affected. She had the lion's share of American literature classes at the university. Ellie exclusively taught

British literature. Why didn't Curran want a debate series with the American literature professors? Why Ellie?

"Yes, he will probably work with Marta," Long said, confirming Ellie's suspicions. Ellie's mouth curled into a genuine smile now. Boy, the shit was really going to hit the fan. Marta didn't play nice with others. Was it wrong to be happy that Marta would share in the misery? Ellie didn't care—she felt relieved that someone else besides her would be inconvenienced. She would revel in Marta's inevitable rant.

"Well, I guess we had better read up on Dr. Curran." Ellie faked enthusiasm.

"Oh, I have all his books." Long jumped on the suggestion. "I'll bring some of the more obscure ones to the meeting today, but I know you've read *American Mask*."

"Oh! I have," Ellie answered genuinely for the first time. "Yes..." She paused midsentence as she tried to remember exactly when she had read the book. It was right at the same time Jordan had become ill or at least when they discovered he was ill. Everyone in the English department was buzzing about the book. Right around the time of Hurricane Katrina, this Dr. Curran published a book critiquing pre–Civil Rights American black literature that perfectly predicted the plight of the poor black citizens of New Orleans. It *was* brilliant, Ellie had to admit. The book was so eerily prophetic that for a few months, every literary critic in the United States was making reference to or interviewing Liam Curran. The release of the book couldn't have happened at a more relevant point in history. At a time when nature had turned the outside world upside down, Ellie's inside world had imploded also. Liam Curran's acclaim was but a blip in her memory.

"*American Mask* was published around the time of Hurricane Katrina. I seem to remember that year was a tough one for you," Long offered.

You don't know the half of it, Ellie thought.

John Long was surprisingly astute at this hour in the morning. Funny. Ellie had never really considered him the most sensitive person. It was surprising that he remembered how stressed she had been during that time. She tried not to let herself think too much about it. The specter of it still haunted her, yet another thing to run away from every morning.

"It was," Ellie finally answered. Long sensed the heaviness in the air and made a move toward the door.

"Well, I'll leave you to your work."

"Yes, I have class in a half hour. Meeting at eleven?"

"Eleven o'clock! I'll share the exciting news! Do you think Marta will be agreeable?" Long was again being astute.

"Oh, I think so," Ellie lied. She didn't feel like defending Marta right now. Better to lie. Let Marta sulk and pout to Long herself. It wasn't going to change anything anyhow. Ellie believed Long and Marta secretly enjoyed the constant bickering that went on between the two of them; it created workplace drama that both of them seemed to relish—Marta because she loved to "stir the pot" just to get a rise out of Long, and Long was so terribly dull that disagreeing with Marta was the highlight and excitement of his day. They thrived off each other! Ellie had to admit that it was usually very entertaining to watch, like a petulant teenager and her father disagreeing on everything just for the sake of disagreeing.

Long nodded absently and waved a weak good-bye as he ambled out the door, leaving Ellie at her desk, temporarily confused as to what to do next. She set her purse in front of her and let her hands simply rest on top, scanning her office as if searching for an answer. What had just happened? She suddenly felt so fatigued. She had slept fitfully because of her anger the night before, overcome by that gnawing feeling that Alec would burst into their room at any moment and reignite their argument. Now this unexpected news from Long—she could barely process what it all meant. She reached into her desk and pulled out a pad of sticky notes. "Liam Curran" she scribbled onto a note, pulling it off and pressing it onto her laptop. Later she would have to make a point of googling the infamous Professor Curran. Right now, she had to get to a lecture—the lecture she was supposed to be giving.

Game on, sister. Time to pull it together.

Grabbing her laptop and a manila folder with pre-sentation notes that she wouldn't ever reference, Ellie made her way downstairs again to the lecture hall.

At five minutes to eight, the small auditorium was still largely empty except for a handful of students huddled in the back of the lecture hall and Ellie's current teaching assistant, a second-year doctoral fellow named Megan. It perturbed Ellie to no end; she found nothing ruder than students scrambling into her classes late.

Most of the time, it was just too much of an effort to reprimand them publically (even though they deserved it), but certainly it would be reflected in their grades.

Little assholes. Don't expect a break from me with your final papers!

She didn't feel very charitable toward kids (adults?) who stumbled into class late and unprepared after a night of drunken debauchery, still reeking of sex and liquor. It was just disrespectful. Ellie recognized that lately she harbored an unusual amount of animosity toward most of her students; her patience had all but worn out. Sometimes their limited understanding of the texts and their banal, one-sided interpretations annoyed her. In retaliation, she would entertain herself by humiliating them with questions that were so far beyond their understanding that they would ramble like fools as they vainly groped for answers. This was especially fun when she knew they hadn't done the reading at all. Oh, English majors! They could be so overly confident with their ability to bullshit. Arrogant kids.

Sometimes Marta would sneak into Ellie's lectures, sit at the very back, where no one but Ellie could see, and roll her eyes, mouthing things like "Duhhh!" when a student said something stupid. Even though it was quite funny, and it kept Ellie from losing her temper at the students for being unprepared, she also felt a deep sadness. At what point had she lost her passion and her patience? Her students seemed so very young now. And so simple. So very simple. Ellie doubted their ability to even grasp what they were reading sometimes.

Today she was to discuss *Frankenstein*, ironically written by Mary Shelley when she was just an eighteen years old herself. Ellie suddenly felt a pang of disgust for the author. Certainly Mary Shelley was more mature in 1790 than these modern kids who spent every free moment mindlessly glued to some form of media. Self-educated in philosophy, history, and literature, Mary Shelley was in a completely different league than these contemporary students. Imagine Mary Shelley watching the Kardashians or *Say Yes to the Dress*! Compared to Shelley, these students were imbeciles.

And yet, an eighteen-year-old in 1790 still looked like an eighteen-year-old now—fresh faced with a plump neck and breasts. Facial skin that didn't look like a jack-o'-lantern three days after carving. Mary Shelley may have been better educated or more "mature," but she was still so young when she wrote her first and most famous novel. Maybe that was why Ellie felt such disdain toward the students lately; she felt resentful due to her own futile fight against time. Trying to battle aging was like running up a downward escalator. There was no way to stop the inevitable march toward middle age. Every year, Ellie got older, and her students stayed the same age! It was a constant bitter reminder that she was one year closer to becoming invisible while beauty and youth would always surround her.

"Dr. Purnell," Megan interrupted Ellie's brooding, "what part of today's lecture would you like me to handle?" Megan, tall and blond, looked more like a runway model than a candidate for her doctorate in English literature. She was almost obscenely pretty, but did nothing to flaunt it. Megan could show up at study sessions in jeans and flip-flops with her hair in a ponytail, her skin scrubbed and shining, and look stunning. And although she was completely aware of the power her appearance had over people, she used it usually for humor.

Megan entertained Ellie and Marta at the Black Bear Pub more than a few times by playing the "stupid blond girl" act. The three would laugh and laugh when Megan would string along the most pitifully drunk boys, who would literally fall over themselves just to talk to her. Little did they know they were being made the brunt of the joke by arguably the most brilliant student the school had ever had. Ellie felt humbled to be Megan's mentor, much like she did when she unofficially mentored Marta as an associate professor. But Megan was different than Marta; she had a drive and ambition about her that Marta had never had. Ellie would never say as much, but Marta could probably sense it. Because of this, there seemed to be a weird animosity growing recently between Megan and Marta.

"Megan, why don't we coteach today? I can start, and you can jump in at any point. I know you composed lecture notes, but we can be less formal if the class discussion seems to being going well," Ellie suggested. Even though Ellie had dressed up, she felt a sudden urge to run a casual class this Friday morning. Actually she felt the sudden urge to conduct class from a chair with a glass of wine in her hand!

"That's fine. I'll start up your laptop," Megan offered. "There's a chai latte on the front table for you."

"You're awesome!" Ellie knew there was a reason she loved this girl! God, it was so nice to have someone think of *her* for a change. Too bad she couldn't drag Megan with her to be the assistant at home too.

Within moments, droves of students filed into the lecture hall and settled into their seats. Ellie stood near the door and greeted them with the most gracious smile she could muster while Megan took care of setting up. By nine o'clock, class was in full swing. Ellie had already covered two of the five discussion topics she had planned and was moving to the third when she saw a flash of Marta's burgundy hair through the thin glass panels of the wooden lecture-hall doors. Then Marta's impish face pressed up against the glass; Ellie nearly burst out laughing. Marta signaled her frantically through the door.

Uh oh! She must know!

"Go ahead," Megan whispered, obviously seeing Marta also. Megan knew Marta well enough to know that Marta wouldn't be deterred. "I'll take it from here."

"Miss Groll will finish this first half. You can break at half past nine," Ellie announced and then headed toward the door. Marta must have let her class break early.

"Hi," Ellie said tentatively as soon as the heavy door eased to a close behind her. "Don't you have class right now?"

"I let them go."

"You let them go?"

"Yeah, it's Friday. Half of them didn't show up for class today anyhow. I let them go early."

"Long is not going to be thrilled about that."

"I already talked to Long." Marta's face was unreadable. "He doesn't care what I do today. He's whistling 'Zip-a-Dee-Doo-Dah' out of his ass, he's so happy!"

"Really?" Ellie played dumb.

"Oh, don't be coy, Elizabeth!" Marta finally grinned. "I know you know. I came to make sure you hadn't jumped in front of a car or tried to slit your wrists with an envelope opener!"

"Is this true sympathy? You seem awfully glib for someone who's going to end up with a forced teaching partner this summer."

"It's Liam Curran!" Marta burst out, uncharacteristically girlish. Ellie stood looking, perplexed. Marta cocked her head to the side, shrugging her shoulders, equally confused that Ellie did not understand her enthusiasm. Finally she grabbed Ellie's hand. "Come on." She practically ran Ellie back up the stairs toward her office. Being herded up the stairs by Marta was so unexpected, Ellie couldn't help but feel amused. It was certainly better than anger.

Marta's office looked much like Marta herself. She had band posters and pictures of poets covering every inch of the tiny space. A copper lamp with a funky crimson velvet shade, fringe and all, sat perched on her desk among piles of unkempt papers. Next to an antique, leather, claw-footed chair sat a small end table draped with some hippie-looking multicolored fabric swatch she must have found at one of the many flea markets she haunted. It was an eclectic mess.

"I let my students go right after I noticed Long loitering outside my classroom. It's like he was begging me to confront him. How could I resist?" Marta explained breathlessly.

"Yeah, he was apprehensive about your reaction," Ellie admitted.

"I knew it! He couldn't resist telling you first. I can't believe you didn't let me in on the gossip!"

"I didn't know how you'd react. I hate being the bearer of bad news."

"It's stellar news though, Ellie! This means all I have to do all summer is sit back and relax while this guy charms everyone with his intelligence and wit. Who knows, maybe I'll actually learn something new too."

Ellie burst out laughing. "Oh, now I see. I was concerned that someone had abducted my best friend and replaced her with some eighteen-year-old groupie. You're really just happy because you think you'll have less work to do."

"No!" Marta clarified impatiently. "I'm not being facetious, Ellie."

Ellie felt perplexed again. "I don't get what you're saying, Id."

"Watch a couple minutes of this," Marta replied as she turned her laptop around to face Ellie. Marta moved the cursor to the play icon on a YouTube video that was already cued up. It was an interview. On the screen sat two men, the one conducting the interview looking like most of the men Ellie knew in the academic world—middle aged, balding, heavy glasses, and clad in tweed.

The other man was striking. Ellie leaned in. Transfixed, she instructed Marta, saying, "Turn it up." She eased sideways into the leather chair, not taking her eyes from the screen. The younger man, in his late thirties—maybe forty—who was being interviewed, wore jeans, a fitted button-up oxford, and a black jacket. He laughed easily, at one point touching the arm of the interviewer in a friendly, comfortable gesture. He tossed back his head to laugh genuinely, sending a mess of wavy brown bangs across his forehead. Was that an English or an Irish accent that Ellie heard? It seemed an odd combination of both. Whatever it was, the slow, steady depth of it hypnotized her. Ellie wasn't paying attention to what was being discussed so much as the demeanor of the man being interviewed.

"Liam Curran?" Ellie asked with raised eyebrows.

"See?" Marta laughed. "I don't even like men, and even *I* can appreciate *that!*" Ellie only replied feebly with some little sound in the back of her throat. "It doesn't hurt that his books have been hailed as groundbreaking." Marta stopped talking in order to wait for a response. "Do you really not know who Liam Curran is?" she finished impatiently.

"I guess I've been really self-absorbed. I guess I *should* know him. But..."

"Well, he obviously knows you."

"So says Long." Ellie looked back at the graceful image on the computer screen. "I don't know if I should feel flattered or apprehensive."

"Maybe a little bit of both."

Two

The water of this river flows backward,
Reinfecting me
With the muddy
Taint of you,
(It's not the Seine, you say)
I laugh.
A defense.
What else can I do?
Give in to the grayish black
Of a Wisconsin Ganges,
Washed infinitely
In guilt.

—JAMES LAWSON, "THE RIVER"

"You can't step twice,"
You swear,
But the whole house
Moves to you—
Waits your return from the

Baptismal spring,
Your river running red
With guilt,
A backward current
Carrying all truths toward
Your bed.

—AVERY VAUGHN, "SAID RIVER"

In John Long's infinite disorganization, he had planned and publicized the first debate for Thursday, May 23. Liam Curran and his crew of fifteen were not to arrive until Wednesday night. *Welcome to America. We have no manners.* Surely the professor would be exhausted. Ellie put her hands up to her face to cover her annoyance when Long told her.

"It probably would have been nice to let him become acclimated to the campus before we threw him in front of an auditorium full of people, John," she suggested as gently as she could; Long was already beside himself.

"Oh, I've made a terrible impression already," he lamented.

"It'll be fine. I'll go easy on him!" Ellie joked in order to cover up her own apprehension. The pit of her stomach felt hollow and queasy when she thought about stepping onto a stage without some sort of debate preparation. She had never even met this guy and had only the vaguest idea where the conversation would lead on stage. She and Curran had exchanged courteous e-mails two months ago when Long first informed Ellie about the debates, but that was the extent of their contact:

> *Dr. Purnell,*
>
> *I am looking very forward to our discussions. Might we apply psychoanalytic criticism to* Frankenstein*? Dr. Long said this is part of your regular curriculum and would be quite valid.*
>
> *Yours,*
> *Liam Curran*

> *Dr. Curran,*
>
> *Yes, a psychoanalysis of Mary Shelley would be a very familiar topic for me. Have a safe trip over. I look forward to meeting you also.*
>
> *Sincerely,*
> *Dr. Purnell*

She had hit send before she realized that she had signed as Dr. Purnell instead of Ellie. *Did it sound too stuffy? Oh, why am I worrying so much? What difference does it make?*

Now the debate day had come, and she couldn't help but feel resentful toward Long for screwing up. How much more relaxed she would feel if she'd had the opportunity to meet with Liam Curran to "size him up" a bit before walking onto a stage. Long had at least given Ellie the courtesy of providing her with the list of questions he would ask as the moderator. The problem was that Ellie had no idea what Curran's positions were in regards to psychoanalytic theory. If this Dr. Curran had really read all of Ellie's critical work, he would be at a great advantage; he would already know how she would likely answer questions. Despite what Long had said, she hadn't come across any essays of his specifically dealing with Mary Shelley. Ellie didn't know what to expect, and she hated not knowing what to expect.

Take it out of your face.

She realized she was clenching her jaw.

"Just treat this like a regular lecture, Ellie," Long reassured her. "Think of Dr. Curran as a slightly contentious student with really thoughtful responses. You're an expert on Shelley. Just answer naturally."

"Thanks, John. I will try to keep that in mind." *My students aren't usually awake enough to be engaged, let alone contentious, but I'll keep that in mind.*

E. J. Densmore

"Would you like me to wait and walk down with you?" he offered.

"I'm going to be a moment," Ellie said, brushing him off. *I need to find my center, and I can't do that with you hovering over me.*

"Very well. We'll meet in the lobby outside the auditorium. Are your parents coming?"

"Yes, my father wouldn't miss this for the world."

"Excellent! Everyone in the department will be thrilled to see him again," Long chirped happily as he made his way out the door. "I have a good feeling about tonight!"

Ellie waited until Long was safely down the hall and then eased the door silently shut. She felt slightly nauseous and flushed as she closed her eyes, pulling her palms into a prayer, taking a long breath in. She breathed it out slowly. Boy, if anyone ever caught her in the midst of her little rituals, they'd think she was a weirdo. Arms up over her head, legs parted, she gracefully swan dived down until her folded arms swung nearly to the floor where she hung comfortably, rocking back and forth slowly. If she couldn't put her gym shoes on and run out the door to relieve stress, then the next best thing was yoga. No wonder everyone in her department had a private stash of Xanax. Ellie feared that if she ever took that route, she might never turn back. That escapism was Alec's way. Ellie refused to use substances as a means to destress, so instead she spent a good deal of her life in downward dog.

Before she left her office, she readjusted her camisole and smoothed her dress. No bra straps sticking out. No lipstick on the teeth. Her long, brown hair looked a little tousled from hanging upside down, but it wasn't an unflattering look. There was no more procrastinating. It was time to make an appearance. Everything was going to be fine. Marta would be in the front row, keeping Ellie amused. Ellie's father, a former professor of English himself, would be looking on reassuringly. Even Ellie's mother and Alec said they would come in support of her, even though, to them, a debate about Mary Shelley and psychoanalysis was probably akin to watching paint dry. Yes, everything was going to be fine. *Time to do this.*

Ellie walked absently through the English section of the liberal-arts building toward the auditorium. Through a windowed corridor, the sun was just beginning to set, casting an ethereal pink light over the lawn of the quad. Her thoughts became lost in the waves of cottonwoods that canopied the old building, their leaves tingling like bells in the spring breeze. Why couldn't they have this debate outdoors? Being outdoors would have set her at ease. Next time, she would suggest that. She would be more at peace if…

If.

She stopped dead in her tracks.

At the end of the corridor stood a group of twenty or more people. They seemed to spot her at the very moment she noticed them. As if on cue, nearly everyone turned to look at her as silence fell upon them simultaneously. She continued forward even though her instinct was to halt; she felt her skin turning pink as she struggled to make sense of the awkwardness. Then Marta sprung from the crowd, looking every bit as flustered as Ellie suddenly felt.

"Ellie!" Marta sounded strange, like a teenager who'd been caught by her parents doing something scandalous. "This is Dr. Curran." The people of the group, who Ellie now recognized as Long, the other English professors in the department, Megan, and a gaggle of Curran's students, stepped aside, parting a sea of bodies. The eerie light of the setting sun flooded the space between them as a man stepped forward with an extended hand. Even in heels, Ellie had to crane her neck to look into this face.

What she saw there was unnerving and beautiful. His green eyes never left her face as his massive hand enveloped hers in a gentle but firm shake that was just slightly too long to be unfamiliar. She was surprised (and mildly intimidated) by his size. The video footage of Liam Curran had not done him justice. He had to be at least six-feet-two, all broad shoulders and long, graceful neck. His hair, a lighter brown than it was on video, was combed back neatly but hinted at an unruly wave. Surely he was an athlete of some sort; no man his age could be so fit without doing something rigorous. Simply put, he was stunning. Ellie gawked blankly. Did he say something? There was a ringing in her ears. She was stupidly overcome.

"I am thrilled to finally make your acquaintance," he said, leaning in confidentially. There was the suggestion of something salacious in his tone, but then he smiled broadly, an innocent, disarming smile that made Ellie question her initial instinct.

"Likewise," she answered, trying to sound ambivalent. *Likewise? That's a stupid thing to say.* But he never took his eyes from her. He was studying her. Certainly everyone else could see that he hadn't turned away from her gaze, their eyes still locked as everyone looked on. Ellie felt like she'd been frozen in time. Again a deep flush spread from her cheeks to her neck. She was simultaneously conscious of the scrutiny of the onlookers and yet indifferent about any conclusions they might draw. Liam Curran's stature was commanding, but it was the intensity of his attention that held Ellie firmly in her spot, unable to utter another word. Being within his gaze was like basking in sunlight.

Or maybe just like being a deer in headlights.

"I'm sorry this debate is so soon after your arrival," she offered, glancing quickly over at Long and regretting instantly that she'd called attention to the scheduling snafu. Luckily Long seemed to be lost in his own reverent thoughts while gazing dreamily at Curran's back. "I promise I won't be too fierce."

"Oh, I hope you shall!" Curran answered, again flashing a disarming smile that Ellie could not decipher as either genuine or devious. It made her feel uneasy.

"Have you had the opportunity to settle in at all?" she continued the empty small talk that she so despised.

"We have. My students have settled into their dorms, and I am off campus, not too far. Thank you for asking. I'm very eager to observe some classes in the next few days or so. Marta has invited me to begin planning also." He motioned to Marta as she scurried up alongside Ellie, her tiny, bared arms covered in tattoos, looking suddenly awkward and nervous. What spell had this man cast over everyone?

"Yes, let's start planning right after the debate at the Black Bear," Marta suggested.

Noticing Curran's quizzical expression, Ellie added, "It's one of the bars up town."

"Oh! I think that's a fine plan!" Curran agreed. "I'm anxious to know the town. It would be good to unwind properly."

"Oh, Marta will see to that." Ellie lightened. "Tomorrow morning, you just might regret getting so unwound!"

"Unlikely," Curran laughed, a deep and genuine sound that escaped him easily. "I hope you'll come too."

"She will," Marta answered, emphatically sensing Ellie's hesitation to answer.

Damn that Marta! Making plans to go out and drink when the debate hadn't even begun yet. All these distractions.

"Very well." Liam Curran placed his warm, lingering hand at the small of Ellie's back. "Elizabeth, shall we begin?"

The sound of her proper name stopped her suddenly. Coming from this man she had just met, it seemed less formal than deeply intimate. Elizabeth Purnell was the name she published under, but barely anyone besides her mother occasionally called her by her given name. Ellie actually hated the nickname "Ellie," but it had stuck with her since childhood. Even though it was a ridiculous thought, Ellie fancied this Dr. Curran could sense her disdain with the immature moniker. It was like he could read her mind. She again looked into his face for an explanation, but he was unreadable. Everything about his friendly demeanor should have set her at ease, but she still couldn't shake the feeling of being off balance. She allowed him to lead her into the auditorium toward the stage.

When they entered, the room exploded into applause. It was a small lecture hall, and nearly every seat was filled. Ellie wondered if the other professors, like her, had offered extra credit to their students for attending. How else would the university have packed them in like this? People in the front row eagerly stood to shake Dr. Curran's hand. God, maybe Ellie really *had* underestimated this man's influence. She fully expected to see people handing him books to autograph. Women would be throwing their bras soon! A sudden wave of contempt washed over her. *I didn't know I would have to share the stage with a rock star! Give me a break.* She searched the crowd for her parents and finally located them at the far right of the auditorium, first row in front of the stage. The seat they had saved for Alec was still empty.

She made her way toward them, feeling suddenly relieved. Her father always had that effect on her. "Hi, Daddy." Ellie hugged him.

"Don't be nervous," he whispered knowingly into her ear.

"Do I look nervous?" she asked with discontent; she wanted to appear calm and together. She was working *desperately* to look calm and together.

"You don't look nervous at all except when your vacant eyes start scanning the crowd like you're planning your escape!" He tilted his head back slightly as he laughed. Her father was always laughing at his own jokes. It made Ellie laugh too. He was right. "Don't worry. I won't tell," he assured.

"Won't tell what?" Ellie's mother broke in. She decided to get up from her seat to join the conversation. Maggie Lawson had cleaned herself up for the occasion, trading her work boots and riding gear for a pair

of dress pants and a modest blouse, but her manner-
isms still set her as the opposite of her cultured, mild-
mannered husband.

"Nerves, Mom." Ellie smiled feebly.

Her mother looked at her doubtfully and tilted her
head. "Ellie, please. I've never known anyone as quick
witted as you—or as sharp tongued. You could eat him
alive." For a moment, Ellie thought she saw sentimentality in her mother's face, but it quickly vanished. "Stop
sniveling!"

James Lawson gently elbowed his wife. "Enough."
He turned to Ellie. "You'll be fine." As he was finish-
ing his encouragement, Dr. Curran approached the
three, silencing Maggie Lawson completely. Amazing.
The great and powerful Liam Curran could even make
Maggie Lawson shut up.

Ellie luckily remembered her manners enough to
make introductions. "Dad, this is Dr. Curran."

"Please call me Liam, sir. I am so honored to meet
you." Curran shook James Lawson's hand earnestly.
Again Ellie looked into Liam Curran's face. At that instant, he was flushed and childlike, beaming at the introduction. "I am a great fan, a great follower of your
work, sir!"

"Thank you, Liam."

"I have read your poetry for decades. During my
undergraduate studies, I once wrote a critical paper
comparing your work to Robert Lowell."

Ellie's father looked pleased. Since his retirement, he hadn't spoken about literature nearly as much as he would have liked. Maggie Lawson now had him all to herself to muck out stalls and run menial errands for her horse-breeding business. It was hardly preferred work for a poet. James Lawson favored riding the animals, admiring their stateliness, and leaving the work to someone else. Buried deep within that mild-mannered, quiet exterior was probably somewhat of an ego maniac, though. He would have loved to talk about himself and his writing with Dr. Curran. Only the fact that the debate was soon to start kept him from engaging the younger professor in a three-hour discussion on philosophy, poetry, art—whatever topic an old English professor might ponder, might yearn to discuss, as he begrudgingly cleaned up horse shit. Instead he conceded, "I'm flattered. Thank you. While you're here, we must have you out to our farm."

"I would enjoy that." Curran nodded gratefully.

John Long summoned Ellie and Liam up to the stage and quieted the audience. After lengthy introductions that included both professors' accomplishments, the debate started. Dr. Curran, as the guest speaker, was given the opportunity to present his ideas first. Ellie scribbled mindlessly on a legal pad in front of her—small swirls, big swirls, swirls inside of swirls.

So, as it turned out, this Liam Curran was a graduate of Oxford *(of course he was)* and had published three books in the past eight years. He also spoke five languages *(of course he did)* and had spent much time traveling the world either as research for his books or for lecture appearances. Curran wrote from all schools of criticism too. *My God. Is there anything this man doesn't know?* Sitting up at the front table with the merciless lights searing her forehead, Ellie felt woefully unprepared. She had read only one of his books all the way through. Only one. In her deep and prolonged sulk during the past two months, she hadn't researched his background much at all. She had been planting her flower beds and fighting with Alec! The extent of her knowledge of Liam Curran came from the glossy inside cover of *American Mask*, his most renowned book, the one that John Long had given to her to read.

Luckily the first half hour passed uneventfully. John Long seemed so taken with Liam Curran that he just continued to ask for clarification and redirected him without so much as acknowledging Ellie. Much of what was supposed to be a "debate" turned out to be more an interview with Liam Curran, guest speaker. Curran graciously obliged by speaking at length—easily, fluidly. He was a pleasure to watch, obviously so in his element. His voice could lull one into a trance. *Damn it!* Again so distracted. Ellie glanced over toward her parents. Even her mother looked engaged. Alec's seat was still empty. It figured.

Her legs had almost gone numb she was so relaxed. Then it happened.

Like a slap in the face.

Ellie snapped back up into the present as Dr. Curran's words registered. "The problem I have with Dr. Purnell's psychoanalytic interpretation of *Frankenstein* is not that it differs from mine, but that she, in fact, changes her own perspective." There was an audible rustling from the audience. Had they also snapped awake, ears perking up at the sound of a challenge?

"Within which essay, sir?" Long probed.

"Within several essays," Curran accused, leaning in closer to look Ellie directly in the eyes. She felt her heart literally skip a beat in her chest. What was he referring to? Would she seem completely absentminded enough to ask? A sense of panic started to rise in her.

Keep your face calm. Take it out of your face.

As if sensing her confusion, Curran continued, saying, "As an undergraduate at the University of Chicago, Dr. Purnell published one of her first essays titled, 'Mary Shelley and the Search for a Father Figure' under her maiden name, Elizabeth Lawson." Ellie's mind scrambled frantically, searching for a recollection. Nothing. *Nothing.*

What did I write?

"Almost a hundred years ago," Ellie teased, trying to stave off her panic. The appeased crowd lit into laughter.

"Well, then, you are quite well preserved, Doctor," Curran returned, tipping his head.

Ellie was not put at ease by the flirtation; he was still poised for attack.

He continued, saying, "Your original essay posits that Mary Shelley created the character of Victor in the likeness of her father that she worked through the grief she felt over her own mother's death and her sense of abandonment by writing *Frankenstein.*"

"Yes, Dr. Curran, I do recall that essay," Ellie admitted. She *did* suddenly remember the essay. Too bad it really did seem like a hundred years had passed since she'd written it. Who was this guy? How in the world had he even found that essay? Ellie doubted *she* could find it; it was probably stuck on some hard disk in a cardboard box somewhere in the crawl space of her parents' house.

"Do you recall, then, a second essay written three years later, titled, 'Victor Shelley, Percy Reborn'?" Liam Curran once again looked at Ellie directly. His face was blank. There was no hint of malice or of triumph. She felt herself getting angry.

"I do recall that essay, Professor. I believe it was one of the last essays published during my fellowship at the University of Chicago. I argued that Mary Shelley subconsciously created Victor in the likeness of her husband, Percy Shelley. Victor's character is generally read as someone to be admired and pitied. I argued that he is really the true villain."

"And that Mary Shelley subconsciously wrote him that way."

"Yes."

"So you not only demean one of the greatest known love affairs in literary history—that of Mary Shelley and Percy Bysshe Shelley—but you also contradict your original theories?"

Ellie failed to suppress a bitter laugh. "Yes, I suppose I do. And with all due respect, Dr. Curran, I would hardly interpret Percy Shelley's leaving his pregnant first wife to run off with seventeen-year-old Mary Wollstonecraft as a great love story."

"As I suspected," Curran countered. A long, uncomfortable pause followed. He waited for Ellie to defend herself, but she still wasn't sure what he was implying. "So really, a reader of your essays should be just as concerned about *your* subconscious and its effect on the interpretation of a novel as they should about the subconscious of the author's at the time of writing it?"

Who is this guy? Has he been reading my essays with the intention of figuring me *out? Good luck.*

Now Ellie leaned in. "I'll grant you this: that is certainly an interesting theory, but really, doesn't every author's personal experience influence what he or she writes, Dr. Curran? Doesn't our personal experience influence, either consciously or subconsciously, everything we do? So of course, it colors our interaction with a text! It certainly dictates what subject matter we critique."

"How can a criticism be unbiased then, Dr. Purnell?"

"Critical theory isn't unbiased, Dr. Curran. It's not absolute. It's theory. That is how it can change. And that, I suppose, is how my interpretation of *Frankenstein* changed." Ellie glanced into the crowd to see Marta shifting uneasily in her chair.

"Life experience?" Curran pressed.

You have no idea, sir.

"So a reader of your essays should expect, above all, a study of *your* subconscious over the course of time?"

"I suppose a reader of my essays can expect whatever they wish." Ellie cut off the line of questioning before it became any more personal than it already had.

An awkward titter burst from the crowd. Did he want her to stand up in front of an auditorium full of people and pour out her sad little soul—the woeful story of her youth and why she had grown to hate the idea of Percy Shelley and all that he stood for? Should she tell the crowd what happened between her years in undergrad and her doctorate that made her change her mind? Ha! Not likely. Ellie felt her hands steady again. She had regained control of the situation.

"Anyhow, Dr. Curran, if we are really to talk about love affairs, I much prefer the correspondence of the Joyces." The audience roared with laughter again in her reference to the lewd sexual letters written by the author James Joyce to his wife. It was an easy joke for an audience of English professors and students.

Liam Curran, too, grinned widely, an easy laugh escaping him also.

He was beautiful.

Ellie decided she hated him.

The remaining few minutes of the debate were icily civil. Ellie completely avoided even glancing in Liam Curran's direction. Nothing she explained further in defense of his accusations seemed to come as a surprise to Professor Curran. He was obviously intimately acquainted with every single word she had ever written on the subject of Mary Shelley. It seemed he had no further intention of challenging her publically.

John Long finally ended the torture by thanking the two professors and approaching the table to shake their hands.

Fuck you, John Long. And fuck you too, Professor Perfect. And fuck you, Alec, for not showing up.

Ellie put on the most convincing smile she could fake and nodded to the audience, taking Long's hand into hers and shaking it firmly. Oh, if she could but reach up and scratch out his eyes! It was John Long, after all, who had set this whole thing up. Then she turned to Dr. Curran, extending her hand once again. Was that contrition in his face? He looked ashen. For a moment, Ellie suppressed a wicked, nervous laugh. Maybe her face betrayed her?

Could he read her contempt? Hadn't she perfected the "fuck-you smile"? Perhaps not.

As soon as John Long reached for Curran's hand, Ellie turned to exit stage left. The crowd had already begun to talk and stir. People were moving from their seats. Eyes were no longer on her or the stage. Was it rude to walk out? Probably. But Ellie didn't care. She didn't care that she had left her parents dumbfounded in the front row without a proper good-bye. She didn't care that Marta was bursting at the seams, wanting to share her tantalizing observations and surely a scathing critique of the debate. The truth was Ellie rarely allowed herself a moment of self-indulgent pouting; Marta and her father would understand.

Even though Ellie knew it would look terribly rude and juvenile not to stay to talk with guests and faculty who had come to the event, she didn't stop herself from walking out. Relieved that she was the first person to exit the auditorium, she quickened her pace, resisting the urge to run—the urge that seemed to be overwhelming lately. As soon as she came to an outside door, she opened it and disappeared into the shadowed courtyard. Her body was working independently of her good judgment. Once she was out of sight, she slowed her conspicuous pace. No one from the auditorium would be able to spot her now. There was still a warm breeze that carried the scent of lilac bushes over the campus, and it calmed Ellie as she pulled off her heels to walk through the cool grass. She didn't know where she was heading. Her office was in the opposite direction. Her purse, keys, and cell phone all sat inside her desk drawer.

The farther away from the auditorium she got, the calmer she became, and the sillier her actions seemed to her. Stopping underneath the darkness of a weeping willow, she leaned against the trunk for a moment, shoes in hand, to think.

Why had she gotten so angry after all? This Dr. Curran was just doing what one does in a debate, right? He was challenging her.

Well, maybe she was just sick of being challenged all the time! Maybe it was the constant tension between her and Alec that just made her bitter. Maybe she just couldn't take any more contention. Maybe she was just having some sort of midlife crisis. Perhaps she had reached the end of her rope of patience—her bullshit threshold, if you will.

She laughed. Yes, she had to be going crazy! Years of maintaining this persona of someone so civil, patient, and polite had finally driven her mad when, deep inside, she really lived an emotional hot mess— the sort of person who would gladly lash out at you for the smallest insult. And now, in order to save face, she would have to make up some stupid excuse for walking out after the debate. Damn it. She hated backpedaling.

After weighing her options for a few more minutes, she ruefully made her way back through the courtyard toward her office in the liberal-arts building. If anyone asked, she would fib and say she had had an emergency call from Jordan that she had to return. That was kind of cheap, but no one would question her further about it. It was too believable a lie.

She took her time walking through the courtyard, past the library and the freshman dormitories. Besides the distant laughter and voices that carried through the open windows like faint echoes, the campus was still, abandoned and ghostly. Most of the students had left after finals the week before. The only remaining students were the small fraction who had stayed behind for summer term.

By the time Ellie reached her office, the rest of the building was black. Everyone had left. Thank God. She opened the deep side drawer of her desk and pulled out her purse, rummaging through for her cell phone. Seven text messages:

Jordan:
I'm home. Andy's mom gave me a ride home from practice. Ate what you left out. Love u.

Alec:
Have to take emergency conference call at six. Sorry. Good luck.

Marta:
Freak! Where r u?

Alec:
Marta is looking for you.

Marta:
Dobbs has your drink waiting. Shake off the salt and get up here.

Marta:
Shall I spank the mean professor 4 u? Stop sulking.

Marta:
S.O.S! Don't leave me here alone with Long Duck Dong.

Ellie laughed out loud. *Fine, Marta. You'll get your way.* She texted back.

To Marta:
On my way. Wine better be chilled.

To Alec:
Having drink with staff. Make sure Jordan is in bed before midnight.

~⁀

A t the Black Bear Pub, a large enough crowd had gathered that no one noticed when Ellie slipped in. As she entered, the dank odor of stale beer and cigarettes assailed her, the smell of smoke still permeating the paneled walls. At first glance, the bar was a dive, but Joe Dobbs was savvy enough to carry the best craft beers and the most varied wine selection in town. So although the décor was typical Wisconsin chic—animal heads, mounted fish, and all—the establishment had a trendiness about it. On any given night, there were people of all ages—students, professors, and locals—who frequented the bar. It had become a hub of intellectual gatherings and discussions, no longer attracting the typical beer-chugging coeds that many of the other local establishments did. "The Bear" (as Marta fondly referred to it) had a string of great musical acts play regularly. Sometimes Ellie even reserved space for her students to do poetry readings. She and Marta spent a good deal of time there and knew Joe Dobbs, the owner, well.

As Ellie bellied up to the bar, her glass of sauvignon blanc and a bottle of water sat waiting for her. "I love you!" She mouthed to Joe as he popped the caps off a couple of beers for a waiting customer. Ellie downed half the glass in one gulp. That would take the edge right off. She was such a lightweight that one glass of wine would make everything in the universe just right. At the end of two, she was the wisest person in the world. Three glasses—she had better be dancing!

Joe came around the bar to greet her with a warm embrace. Just a few years older than Ellie, he appeared much more weathered. He worked hard, and he looked it. "Where have you been, stranger?" he asked, holding her an arm's length away to look at her, his face that of a concerned older brother.

"Busy grading finals. No time for fun," Ellie complained.

"You can always grade your essays here," he teased amiably.

"The grades would be much better if I were drinking!"

"But your handwritten comments would look much worse!"

"True." Ellie laughed. "How are the kids?"

"They're good. Amy graduates high school next week and is going to UW Madison in the fall." He returned behind the bar and began wiping it with a cloth. "Adam is going to be a sophomore next year. He's playing a lot of baseball this summer. The bar is sponsoring his travel team."

Ellie then asked about his wife. "What's Jan been up to?" Joe paused strangely.

"Well, she moved up to Greenbay."

Ellie didn't quite understand what he meant, "For work? That's awfully far…" She stopped midsentence.

"Not exactly." He searched for the right words and then said, "We're getting divorced."

"Oh. Joe…I'm sorry."

"It's OK. I mean, I'm fine. We're all fine."

"Did you…"

"I wasn't surprised," he interrupted. "It was a long time coming. It's really all for the better."

"And the kids?"

"They're staying with me. They seem to be OK, I guess. How can I know? I've never done this before." He laughed dolefully.

"So Jan was OK with them staying here, huh?" Ellie could never understand how a woman could leave her children. An army would have to pry her kicking and screaming or carry out her dead body before she would ever agree to leave Jordan behind.

"Well, the kids are old enough to decide where they want to live. They don't want to leave their friends, what's familiar. And Amy, she will have enough changes in her life next year. When she comes home from college, she wants it to be home, you know?"

"Yes, that makes sense," Ellie agreed. A line was forming at the other end of the bar. "I'm glad you seem to be all right."

"Just keeping myself busy…" Joe trailed off as he left to take care of the other customers.

E. J. Densmore

Ellie propped her foot on the bar's brass foot rest and leaned into the counter, lost in thought. The familiar calming effect of the wine began to make her feel flushed and warm. She downed the second half of the glass and took a long swig of cool water. When Joe looked up, she raised her empty glass. He nodded back at her knowingly.

"I offended you," a deep, unfamiliar voice said from above her head. Ellie immediately turned to see Professor Curran come around her right side, so close their arms brushed.

Immediately she felt sheepish. She waited for him to explain himself further before protesting and lying ("No, I wasn't offended. Why do you think I was offended? I didn't just run away like a bratty child. I had to call my son."), but she thought better of it. Against her will, she felt a smile spread across her face. She was a shitty faker. If he could tell she was offended, then she may as well own it. She neither confirmed nor denied.

"You are not quite what I expected, Dr. Curran."

"Nor are you, Dr. Purnell."

"Please, just call me Ellie. I think you've earned that much after publically calling me out."

"I'll call you Elizabeth. I don't think Ellie suits you."

"Really? And why is that?"

"Too juvenile." He took a swig of his beer without taking his dancing eyes from her. "You are obviously a seasoned fighter. Ellie sounds much too innocent."

"I do have a lot of fight in me, Dr. Curran."

"I would bet on it. Please, call me Liam."

"I will call you Dr. Curran since a man with such a fan following deserves that deference."

"And perhaps you might be a fan, too, had you done your research, Elizabeth."

Ellie's mouth gaped open in surprise. By now, everything in the universe felt A-OK. The first glass of wine had done its job. Instead of feeling offended, she was deeply amused. "You're very direct for an Englishman."

"And you're very inhibited for an American."

"I suppose we should make a balanced pair, then, Dr. Curran."

"I've always thought so, Elizabeth."

"Always?" she snapped back quizzically.

Was that a flash of embarrassment in his eyes? What did he mean by "always"? Ellie decided not to press and let the moment pass. "How did you find that first *Frankenstein* essay I wrote?"

"I looked for it." He winked. "I research, remember? That's what I do best. Why do you think I have such a fan club?"

"Dr. Curran, look at you." Ellie fanned her hand across him from his face to his feet. "I know why you have a fan club, and I doubt it's your research." The wine was now doing the talking.

Feigning insult, he put his hand to his heart. "You cheapen me, Professor. I *am* really quite good at research."

"I don't doubt it, Dr. Curran. Only a genius could have located that first essay on Shelley."

"I've read everything you've ever published. Your prose is inspiring." He set his half-empty bottle on the counter and straddled the stool next to her. "Do you write poetry?"

The question came as such a surprise that Ellie couldn't decide how to answer.

"Not for publication," she lied.

"I'm surprised," he said, although he didn't look it. Was he toying with her? Had he really read *everything* she'd ever published? The thought was disconcerting.

"I wrote quite a bit when I was younger." She continued with half-truths. "But I always felt I was in the shadow of my father. Critical writing came much easier to me." Curran didn't look convinced, but he let the air settle comfortably between them while he seemed to ponder what she'd said. He took a final swig of his beer and then quietly studied the label.

The *whole* truth was that Ellie wrote poetry prolifically. It was a compulsion, a catharsis. Like running, it was a cleansing. She had written poetry from the time she was old enough to write, and although she had, as a younger woman, felt intimidated by her father's legacy, she had long since outgrown that insecurity.

Ellie was not her father, though. She could not openly reveal the rawness of her personal experience to the world through her poems. It felt too much like walking around naked. Her father never seemed to mind that the entire world knew about his numerous affairs and his doubting God and his grappling with the meaning of existence. Ellie couldn't live that publically, the inner workings of her psyche laid bare for all the world to dissect.

She wrote poetry because she needed to. In order to survive. In order to avoid implosion. She wrote and confessed the most intimate events of her life. She just did it under a pseudonym. Avery Vaughn. It was a combination of the names of two great-grandmothers, one from either side of her family. It wasn't until recently that "Avery" had much of a following, and now with social media and the Internet, there were fan pages and blogs. The sometimes scathing, brutally honest poetry of Avery Vaughn was all over the web. And it was completely autobiographical—completely confessional—because it could be. After all, Avery Vaughn didn't really exist. Ellie worried that she might not be able to maintain her anonymity much longer, which frightened her. She couldn't continue to write authentically if she couldn't maintain a public distance from her own personal narrative. It was just too painful to be that candid. She was too private a person.

Easily Ellie's biggest secret, the poetry had never even been seen by Marta. Ellie kept a leather-bound book hidden deep in the stacks of the university library in a tiny, mildewy room that no one ever entered but her. For years now, she would retreat down there, four floors into the cave of the library basement, and pour out her soul, old-school style with pen and paper like she did in undergrad. The organic process was part of the catharsis. She would write her first drafts, cross out, edit, revise, and then revise again, all in the solitude of the library where barely anyone ever ventured to go. Once it was perfect on paper, she would birth it into the twenty-first century by typing it up and sending it out into cyberspace.

"Dr. Curran…" Megan approached Ellie and Liam at the bar. "Your students were just sharing stories of your climb up Everest. Come tell us more," she entreated, stepping between them without so much as acknowledging Ellie. Ellie felt deep annoyance.

Good to see you, too, Megan. You traitor.

She'd seen Megan's come-hither act many a night before, but this was no act.

Joe, ever observant and efficient, brought Ellie a second glass of wine and set a new bottle of Bass next to Liam. Liam nodded to Joe and stood.

"Tell them I'll be right back," he said, dismissing Megan. She flashed her radiant smile and sashayed back to the table, her long, golden hair bouncing behind her as she left. Ellie felt a tug at her heart. It was a strange, unexpected feeling that left her suddenly sad. Liam caught her watching Megan move back to the table and set his hand on her shoulder. "You're not upset?"

"About what?" Ellie asked, surprised. She was more surprised, though, by her internal reaction to his warm hand resting on her heavily. It was comforting and familiar. She hadn't realized she needed any comforting.

"Our first debate?"

"Not at all, sir." She smiled warmly, possibly her first genuine smile all night. His hand lingered. "Everest, huh? Sounds interesting."

"A man must do other things besides research, Professor."

"Indeed," she said, nodding.

"Very well." He hesitated to leave her at the bar, but she made no effort to move.

"I'll be over soon," she assured with no intention of moving too far until the second glass of wine was gone. Again Ellie was aware of her antisocial tendencies, but it wasn't enough incentive to move just yet. She was finally feeling relaxed and didn't want to put effort into banal small talk. She'd rather just observe from afar. She turned to watch Dr. Curran leave. There was certainly nothing wrong with the view from behind! Nothing wrong at all.

Marta made her way toward Ellie, smiling at Liam in passing, and took the seat that he'd left empty. "Well?" she questioned.

"Well, what?"

"Well, I see you're here finally. Little breakdown, eh?"

"You're not the only neurotic around here, Id."

"You're scaring me with this news! I depend on you to be the stable one!" Marta teased. "You didn't look rattled at the debate. You sounded pretty cool actually, but I knew you were upset."

"Oh, yeah? How's that?" Ellie asked, wondering.

"The way you clawed into the table when you said "I hate Percy Shelley'!"

"Shut up! I never said, "I hate Percy Shelley'!"

"You were starting to go all feminazi over what a philanderer he was." Marta snorted.

"Whatever! Feminazi is your job."

"That's right, and don't forget it!" Marta waved Joe down. "Can a girl get a drink in this place?"

"Sure, where's the girl?" Joe teased. Ellie let out a blast of laughter.

"Just get me some liquor, man!" Marta ordered. "You can call me whatever you want as long as you get me another beer!" Joe set off to dig up another Red Stripe for Marta. "Seriously, Ellie, the audience was pretty impressed. Long is ready to propose to Liam Curran, he's so happy. I talked to your dad for a few minutes afterward, and he thought the debate was fascinating. You should call him tomorrow. He was really proud of you."

Ellie felt a pang of guilt for running out without saying good-bye. "I'm a heel for running off stage, aren't I?"

"It's all good," Marta reassured. "I don't think it was too noticeable to anyone besides us. The audience was really energized by your chemistry."

"What do you mean?" Ellie's brows furrowed.

"I don't know. It's tough to explain." That was a first—Marta at a loss for words. "I just had the sense that I was witnessing something dynamic—special. Even your dad said so."

"He is perplexing, isn't he?" Ellie motioned again to Liam who, by now, had the group at the table enchanted, hanging on his every word as he motioned widely, obviously telling some fascinating tale.

"I don't just mean him; I mean both of you. Together. At one point, it was like watching a choreographed dance—then it was a cage match!"

Ellie chuckled. "I have no explanation for what happened up there on stage! One moment, he's so serious and formal, and the next I feel like…" She didn't know quite how to finish. Or maybe she felt she was being too honest. Even with Marta, sometimes being honest was uncomfortable.

"I can see how you feel." Marta was serious, and then added with finality, "I have decided that I like him."

"That's very soon for you."

"I know, right?

"He should consider himself very lucky then."

"Yes, he should," Marta agreed.

Joe finally returned with Marta's beer. "Your highness." He flipped off the top and handed it to her with a flourish.

"You're awesome, Joe," she called after him as he returned to the register, and then turned to Ellie suddenly as if she'd just remembered something. "Want to take a road trip next weekend?"

"I would love to! Where are we going?"

"Chicago. Tony is DJing an invite-only warehouse party in the city."

"Yay!" Ellie clapped her hands like a child.

"Dust off your dancing shoes. This is supposed to be a great party. A lot of my friends from Miami are actually going to come up for this."

"I'm not staying in any shit room," Ellie said.

For years, she and Marta had snuck off to all-night events, usually ones hosted by people Marta had gone to graduate school with down in Florida. The trips were Ellie and Marta's dirty little secret. Ellie went to dance. Marta went to party. No questions asked.

"Book a room then, princess. I'm not sure where I'll be sleeping."

Isn't that the truth?

"It's a deal," Ellie cried blissfully. Besides running, there wasn't anything else Ellie would rather do than dance.

Three

July of Ellie Lawson's Twenty-fifth Year

She met us at the door,
Fresh from the shower,
Smelling of soap and loose powder,
Her hair wrapped neatly into a bun,
White cotton blouse rolled loosely at the sleeves,
Unbuttoned down to her navel.
She ushered me in with a smug laugh,
Eyes narrowed to slits,
Black mascara crushing her eyelashes.

My face went numb
Under the weight of her stare.
I laughed uneasily.
She said nothing,
Leaned over both of us
Braless
To reach for an ashtray.

You smoked your cigarettes
To the base of the filters.
Looking sheepish,
Looking scolded,
Holding back a scream.
I kissed your face.
You flinched.
A hole developed
At the base of my neck.
The knocking began to ache.

When I walked home alone,
Past the cemetery, slowing to look
Beyond the metal gates,
The streetlights threw an undignified
Light over the headstones.
But the silence was liberating.

I walked home that night, climbed
the stairs to our room,
Undressed and laid awake for hours,
Staring at my reflection in the mirror,
Reassuring myself.

I lay awake for hours, staring at our picture,
Balanced precariously on the shelf.

—AVERY VAUGHN, "HOLDING BACK A SCREAM"

*E*llie struggled to open her lids, slowly becoming aware that her heavy face was plastered to the mattress by drool and hair. She tried lifting her arm and found it asleep, pinned under her hipbone. *Rough night.* Maybe she would just lie here for a moment and wait for the rest of her body to wake up. What was the rush? It was Saturday, and she was going to be holed up inside all day finishing that damn essay anyhow. What were a couple more minutes? Breaking her arm free, she reached up to wipe the drool from her opened mouth. Attractive. *Glad no one had to see that.* The air conditioner labored loudly from the living-room window, but it hadn't done much to cool the old apartment. The ceilings were just too high. The humidity, smelling of Freon and mildewed wallpaper, hung heavily in the air.

Ellie rolled over to look at her fiancé, still blissfully asleep. God, he was beautiful! His angelic face framed by his long, blond hair, he looked much younger than twenty-five. He always looked younger when he was asleep. Ellie woke before him most mornings, and it wasn't uncommon for her to watch him as he slept, marveling at her good fortune, imagining how beautiful their children would be some day. Well, maybe. If they decided to have children. Maybe. After her doctorate was done. They had too much traveling planned and Dylan's band. That wouldn't be much of a life for a baby. Ellie looked down at her naked breasts and the concave basin between her hipbones. Not ready for children.

They lived on the top floor of an old brownstone that Dylan's parents owned as a rental property, and, of course, there was no air conditioning except the one pitiful machine that hummed angrily from the front room. It figured. This summer was brutal. Chicago had seen seven consecutive days over one-hundred degrees, and the heat was not predicted to let up any time soon.

Ellie surveyed the room sleepily. The view from the floor was strange. She and Dylan had dragged the mattress off their bed and into the living room where they hung sheets as best they could from the doorways to block off the rest of the apartment and seal in the cool air. Their living room looked like the type of sheet-tent hideout that kids dream of. It was kind of cool.

And, well, it was definitely kinky. That wasn't the intention, but it sort of played out that way. Maybe she would reach under the thin sheet that covered them both to see if Dylan felt well enough for another round. Finishing that Frankenstein essay could wait a while longer if it meant having him in her again. She was insatiable lately. Just seeing the tiny triangle of light-brown hair directly over his heart made her stomach queasy with desire. She brushed her lips against his pink nipple and placed her hand on his stomach. Dylan stirred as he tensed under her touch.

She had a sexual need lately that was bottomless. Maybe it was all the stress of writing. Maybe it was simply being alone too much. Really alone. Inside-her-own-head alone. The silence of the university library and the art museum where she would often write drove her to near madness sometimes. She would sit for hours, nearly motionless save for the frantic movement of her cramped right hand, furiously scribbling thoughts across notebooks full of cross outs, arrows, and side notes, absorbed in her own theories—existing in a world only of her own creation ("I have known the inexorable sadness of pencils"). Studying English had always proved to be a desolate and isolating choice of major, but never so much as it seemed now during the final push of her doctorate. Ellie felt that perhaps she was running out of energy. Lately all she wanted to do was live. When could she stop reading and theorizing and just live?

Dylan (and everything about Dylan) made Ellie feel alive. His cutting wit and cynical observations of the world always amused her. He was completely unconventional. He made her laugh with his ridiculous spontaneity. Instead of dutifully going to work for his father's accounting firm after college, Dylan instead pursued his love of music (much to his parents' ire), tirelessly promoting his alternative band until he had amassed a very large and loyal local following. In the three years that Ellie and Dylan had been together, she had watched him progress from a little-known opening act to a renowned headliner who played almost every major small venue in the city. Rumor had it that his band might be offered a record deal soon. Certainly

Dylan had acquired a vast network of contacts through his promoting over the years, but really, the band was just plain talented. Ellie was biased, of course, but it was true. The band was really great and deserved a chance at a larger audience.

"You're Samson," Ellie often teased Dylan (his power was in his hair.). It was a joke, but it was also the truth. His long, golden tresses were his trademark; they made him difficult to miss and difficult not to admire. Ellie, mildly dismayed, had observed more than a few women stop to gape at Dylan in the convenience store, at the El stop, or on the corner hailing a cab. And the concerts? Those were the worst. Dylan on stage, under the spotlights, shirtless, sweaty, jeans hanging loosely from his pelvis, leaning seriously into his guitar, a look of passionate concentration furrowing his brow, and his hair let loose from the ponytail, half stuck to his wet face. It was raw and sexual. It made Ellie heartsick.

And, really, if she was going to be totally honest with herself, maybe *that* was the cause of her desperation. The tedious hours alone made her just the smallest bit paranoid. What did Dylan do with all his time besides practice? They lived rent free in the brownstone apartment that his parents owned, so it wasn't like he was out working a real job. She couldn't even guess at all the people Dylan knew through his gigs and his travel.

No. She wasn't going to succumb to her insecurities. She wasn't going to check up on him. She had her life, her responsibilities. He had his. But when she came home at the end of the day, after grueling hours of grading essays and creating lesson plans as a junior slave (aka teaching assistant) for the great Dr. Messing of the University of Chicago English department, she would fly at Dylan, who until just recently, was more than eager to be the recipient of her unchecked sexual desire. Lucky boy. How many blow jobs had he received recently in the middle of the kitchen, Ellie's purse and book satchel still hanging from her shoulder?

The feeling of unease was irrational, though. Wasn't it Dylan, after all, who was so overprotective and jealous that he insisted Ellie always take a spot on the balcony where he could see her during the entire show? After every song, he would make eye contact with her and often wink. Sometimes he would mouth, "Bear," which was his pet name for her. It was Dylan's own unique public profession of love. He refused to ever leave her alone with his bandmates, jokingly (or not), calling them "vultures" and "opportunists," and he worried incessantly that Ellie would get pulled unwillingly into a mosh pit again, as she once had, severely bruising her leg. Better to be safe on the balcony, if there was one. If not, Ellie stood to the left of the stage where Dylan could always see her.

"You belong to me," he told her before every show. "I don't want anyone else to love you." It was fierce and sincere. And hot. How could Ellie refuse his wishes?

E. J. Densmore

She would have agreed to being locked away in a box if that was what he wanted. He owned her, body and soul.

Ellie made sure she returned his sentiment, proved her loyalty to him, her unquestionable devotion, as often as she could, but especially before concerts. The rest of the band members snickered at Ellie and Dylan's unofficial ritual and the fact that Ellie had probably seen the inside stall of the men's restroom in every club in Chicago. They were probably just jealous that their girlfriends weren't as willing. It ensured that she sent Dylan onto the stage sated, and, in turn, she was calmed by the inevitable soreness between her legs. It was both painful and comforting, the residual throb reassuring her of their physical and emotional bond.

"Dylan," she whispered into his ear, running the tips of her nails over his abdomen. She started to move her hand lower.

"Stop!" he whispered back, suddenly grabbing her hand to halt her. Startled, she jumped, but he held her hand tightly, bringing it up to his lips to kiss her fingers. "Naughty girl. Aren't you tired still?" He turned onto his side, pulling her arm around him, forcing Ellie to spoon his naked backside. It was almost too much to bear.

"I'm never too tired for you," she admitted.

"I'm dying," he moaned. "Just lay here with me?"

"Really?" Ellie felt disappointed. "Too much to drink or just tired from playing?"

"Both," Dylan mumbled. "Maybe you wore me out yesterday too."

"Guess we should work on your stamina."

"Not now, Ellie," he replied firmly, sounding just the slightest bit annoyed. Ellie kissed the muscular space between his shoulder blades and rested her head sideways against his back, trying to overcome the sting of rejection.

Stop being so sensitive. He's just tired.

She lay motionless with her arm locked in his, listening to the muted sounds of traffic vaguely discernable under the deafening white noise of the air conditioner. Through the floor, she could sense movement from the apartment below. Madison, the cute, blond college undergrad, must be up and about. Dylan's parents rented the two other apartments in the brownstone to students from DePaul. Below them lived Madison, with two other profoundly shallow girls, Lisa and Liz, and some guy named Nathan who was easy on the eyes but dumb as a box of hair. Dylan and Ellie often mused about the relationship of the four.

"Maybe he's really their pimp!" Ellie exclaimed.

"No," Dylan said, disagreeing. "He's far too stupid for that."

"Maybe stupid is just an act. I mean, they can't be that stupid. DePaul is a difficult school to get into."

"He's their sex slave!"

"Really? You think they would choose him? He's not *that* cute. Do you think he could handle all three?" Ellie doubted.

"I don't think so. Maybe he's really gay and just lives there to give them fashion advice because they're so lame."

"No way. If Nathan were gay, he'd have way better taste in clothing. And music."

"Yeah, you don't ever hear any Morrissey coming out of that apartment."

"Shut up, Dylan Ross. Not only gay men listen to Morrissey!"

"I'm not criticizing Morrissey. I'm just saying it would be much better than Shania Twain…Wait. It *is* a sign of his gayness. 'Man, I feel like a woman!'" he sang sarcastically.

Ellie and Dylan's debates would always end with side-splitting speculation over what topics of conversation occurred in the apartment below: "Blue eye shadow or no eye shadow—discuss!" or "closed sandals vs. peep-toe sandals—which are better? Go!" or "comb vs. pick." Ellie did the best imitation ever: "So I found this stuff…this really awful, like, stuff, inside my belly button. I was so, like, disturbed by it. I mean ewww, where did this come from and who put it there? Do we all have this fuzz in our belly buttons, and if so, why is there no product to remove it? Oh my God, I could totally develop a product to remove it! I'm going to be so totally rich and famous!"

"Who is that?" Dylan snickered.

"Madison. She's the most vacant by far."

Ellie smiled faintly, remembering these exchanges. Finally Dylan's breathing grew deep and steady. He was asleep once again. She shut her eyes for a moment. Could she fall back to sleep? Probably not. May as well just get up and head out to the museum to write. After a few more minutes with her face buried into his back, submersing herself in his heavenly scent, she gently wiggled her arm free of his grasp.

Thirty minutes later, she slid out the door as silently as she could, her waist-length hair in a wet braid trailing down her back. She had thrown a banana, some pencils and notebooks, a water bottle, and several copies of critical essays she'd printed off the university's research database into her bag. She couldn't bring herself to return to the library at the university again today. She needed a change of scenery. Today it would be total immersion therapy.

Ellie headed for The Art Institute where she would spend an hour or so roaming the European collection and looking for inspiration. She often sat near a painting by Jean Baptiste-Camille Corot titled "Interrupted Reading," which featured a girl in her corset and skirt looking very put out. Presumably the painter was disturbing her reading by painting her likeness. Ellie could relate. Today this painting would help Ellie slip into Mary Shelley's historical space. She needed to be among the art that was created during the same time period as the literature she critiqued to see the colors and the landscapes, the expressions, and the clothing of the subjects so the works of art could transport her. She would then be able to write there for hours on end, oblivious to the date, time, or outside world.

Heading toward the brownstone's outside door, Ellie passed the downstairs apartment. Yes, the band of idiots was up. Were they doing aerobics? Some repetitive thumping was coming from a boom box near the door accompanied by the sound of footsteps moving up and down inside the apartment. Ellie moved more quickly toward the exit so as not to be caught in some awkward, disingenuous exchange. She wasn't good at hiding her true feelings, but she took no pleasure in being unkind to a person's face (much more fun to do that behind their backs. After all, they couldn't help that they were so stupid!). It was just easier for Ellie to avoid people she didn't particularly like. If she were ever cornered into an unsavory interaction, who knows how she might behave? Better to avoid it.

Even though the halls of the brownstone were not air conditioned, opening the door to the outside felt like stepping into hell. The air coming from the street vents appeared in odd little distorted waves; everything seemed eerily still except for the underlying electric buzz of window-unit air conditioners, which seemingly appeared overnight in every window in the neighborhood. Even the leaves on the trees drooped miserably. The heat was obscene. Ellie hesitated for a moment on the front sidewalk. Should she bring a cardigan? All she had on was a pair of cut-off jean shorts and a T-shirt. It could get really cold in the museum. If she was sitting still…She glanced back at the door tentatively. No. Too lazy to go back up the stairs. Decisively she headed down the block.

It was noon already, and the sun sat high and relentless in the sky. Not surprisingly, few people were out for a Saturday. Usually the streets were much busier. Ellie observed a little Hispanic woman scurry onto her porch to attend to the sagging flowers in her window boxes with a red watering can. Then she quickly disappeared to the shade and safety of her air-conditioned apartment once more. Not even the birds moved. No angry sparrows aggressively fighting one another for stray crumbs. Ellie took the baseball hat out of her bag and pulled her impossibly long braid through the back of it. Sweat beaded at her forehead already, and she hadn't even reached the bus stop yet.

"Shit!" she cursed, stopping directly in the middle of the sidewalk. She had forgotten the paperback copy of *Frankenstein. Damn it!* How was she supposed to write an essay without the primary source? What to do? Walking all the way back to the apartment in this heat seemed like an intolerable option. Too bad she didn't have enough money to hail a cab back the five blocks she had walked. Maybe if Dylan was up, he could meet her halfway with it. Even if he wasn't up yet, Ellie was sure he wouldn't mind throwing on a hat and walking two or three blocks to bring her the book. He never complained about helping her out. She looked around for a pay phone. Luckily there was one at the entrance of the corner deli half a block away. What was the rush now? She leisurely made her way over to the phone, digging through her bag for a quarter.

"Dylan! It's Ellie. Are you up?" Ellie begged into the answering machine. He wasn't picking up. Maybe he couldn't hear the phone over the roar of that blasted air conditioner. "Dylan, I forgot my *Frankenstein* novel. Can you meet me at the corner of Webster and Halsted with it? I don't want to walk all the way back. It's too…" The machine cut her off. Maybe he was in the shower.

Great. Just stellar.

She turned toward their apartment and unenthusiastically started her trek back in hopes that Dylan would hear the message and meet her halfway. When she was a block from the apartment and Dylan was still nowhere in sight, she gave up all hope. *Oh well. I guess I am going all the way upstairs and doing this walk all over again.* Had the temperature increased by ten degrees since she left the first time? It sure felt like it.

Once she got inside, Ellie dropped her bag at the bottom of the stairs. No use in dragging that up again.

She labored up the steps, hanging onto the handrail as she went. As long as she was here, she would splash some cool water on her face in the kitchen before she headed back out again. Maybe she could put some ice in a baggie and set it on her neck as she walked. That would look super stupid, but at least it might keep her from fainting! She paused a moment on the stairs to catch her breath. Looking up to the landing, she noticed their apartment door was open a crack. In her attempt to be quiet on her way out, she must have failed to shut it completely.

Panting slightly, Ellie pushed open the door. Momentarily dumbstruck, she stopped instantly where she stood. Her mind scrambled to make sense of what was directly in front of her eyes, directly in front of her on the front-room floor, on the mattress on the front-room floor, directly in front of her. A woman's bare back and a head full of blond, wavy hair. A woman's head, full of wavy, blond hair tossing seductively. A woman's arched back. A woman's rear end writhing up and down rhythmically. And beneath her, a set of legs. A man's legs. And his feet. And his pelvis moving up to meet her. Had Ellie entered the wrong apartment? The woman didn't stop. They didn't hear Ellie. They didn't see her standing there. They didn't hear Ellie begin to hyperventilate. She grasped the doorjamb to steady herself and that's when she saw the trail of clothing— shoes, shorts, underpants.

"Oh my God," Madison screeched. In one swift move, she rolled off Dylan and grabbed a sheet to cover herself from the waist down. One small breast protruded from underneath a clawed-at sports bra. Dylan was left uncovered, a lewd and tragic comedy. Naked, bare, and exposed. He drew his legs up beneath him as if he could hide what he had done.

"Ellie," he lamented.

What was happening? Ellie was starting to see stars. *Don't you dare pass out. Don't you dare pass out! Keep it together. Don't you dare look like a bigger fool than you already do.*

No sound came from her mouth. Mute. As if she were in a coma, observing passively from somewhere inside her head, she watched Madison scurry around the room, trying to hold the sheet over her bottom while picking up her clothing. Madison picked up one shoe and dropped her shorts, picked up the shorts and dropped the other shoe. Ellie turned to flee, and then something deep inside halted her.

She would stay.

She would stay and watch the shit show unfold. Dylan, eyeing Ellie cautiously, didn't move. He must have sensed what lived within her.

When Ellie's breath returned to her, she charged crazily into the room, knocking Madison over with two opened palms. Pushing the "sheet wall" aside, she headed straight for the kitchen. *Bottom drawer on the left next to the sink.* In one swift move, she yanked open the metal drawer, sending half of its contents crashing violently onto the kitchen floor. What she needed was still there, gleaming brightly at the bottom. She grabbed the handles in her right hand and pivoted toward the sheet again. As if possessed, she tore through the sheet, knocked Dylan onto his stomach by kicking him squarely in the back with a flat foot, and straddled him. Taking a handful of his hair in her left hand, she began cutting with her right.

"Fuck you, Samson. Fuck you!"

"Ellie, stop!" Dylan struggled. She nicked his scalp as the first chunk of hair fell onto the mattress.

"No, Dylan, you stop. You fucking liar. You stop!" She was frantic, unstoppable. Madison looked on, horrified, scrambling backward toward the far wall. Ellie was able to grab another huge handful of hair and chop before Dylan finally knocked her off. Flying sideways, she hit her face on the corner of the end table, so high on adrenaline that she didn't even notice she was bleeding.

"Get out! *Get the fuck out!* Both of you!" Ellie screamed insanely as she struggled to stand. She waved the scissors ominously. Dylan and Madison both looked horrified; Dylan, his hair a bloody mess, and Madison still half naked. An unnatural silence fell over the room momentarily as all three eyed one another, waiting for someone to make the next move. Something in Ellie vaguely relished the momentary sense of control. It made her suddenly burst into laughter.

"Her? Really, Dylan? You fucked her? Madison? Idiot savant. Sorority girl wonder! That's the best you could do?" She waved the scissors again at them, leaning in for effect, causing them both to flinch as Dylan continued to clutch his gushing head. Ellie laughed some more, a bitter, crazy sound, and then she stopped as suddenly as she had begun, the cut on her upper lip bleeding down her chin. She clenched the scissors tightly and wiped her face with the back of her hand. In one final act of defiance, she whipped the scissors at the window. The old glass cracked but did not shatter.

Explain that one to your parents, Dylan.

In a daze, she stumbled absently toward the door.

"You're the one who's an idiot," Madison whimpered almost inaudibly from her spot on the floor. Then her voice grew more confident. "This isn't the first time."

"Shut up, Madison," Dylan pleaded.

"It's been going on for months!" Madison got louder as Ellie entered the hallway. "Months! And I'm sure I'm not the only one!" She called after Ellie.

Ellie descended the steps numbly, pausing to lift her bag back over her shoulder. It had only been eight minutes from the time she returned to the time she now left, but it felt like a lifetime ago. It *was* a lifetime ago. Everything had changed.

I t was dark when Ellie returned to the apartment that evening. She couldn't be sure how much time had passed. At some point during the afternoon, she had found herself underneath the El platform, thinking she might escape somewhere, but she was overcome by confusion, a sense of panic, almost like she'd lost control of what was real. And really, there was no place to escape to anyhow. She couldn't get away from what she had seen. She couldn't get away from the pit of nausea in her gut and the ache of her clenched jaw.

The earsplitting roar of the El train had actually been a comfort somehow; the sound absorbed her, made her invisible. Roaring in and out like nuclear waves. The rattling tracks, the earth flying, the hot wind whipping up, the dust, the sound of tramping feet, people going about their lives all around. Coming and going. Where was *she* going now? *Oh, God. Oh, God.* What was she to do? She had sat, clutching her bag in front of her for hours, searching faces. As it had gotten dark, she found herself heading back home. "Home." Her bag still felt very heavy. Her water bottle sat full at the bottom.

But even as Ellie opened the door to the apartment and found it strangely empty—air conditioner silenced, mattress moved back into the bedroom, window taped up—there lingered in her a sense of hope ("Hope springs eternal in the human breast"). He must still love her, right? She didn't do anything to deserve this (or had she?). If he still loved her, he would come back. Right? He would come back.

"Get the fuck out!" she had said. But it was in the moment. She didn't really want him to leave. She didn't really mean it. Maybe he was angry that she had cut his hair. Maybe she should have just turned and walked out instead of going all batshit crazy on him. *Oh, God. I didn't really want him to go. I didn't mean to hurt him. I just wanted him to love me like he said he did—like I believed he did.* She just wanted to undo what had been done. To unsee what she had seen.

Ellie dashed for the bedroom and pulled open the top drawer. Dylan's clothes were gone. His side of the closet had been emptied. His pillow was no longer on the bed. Everything else in the room was intact— pictures and concert ticket stubs stuck in the mirror, Ellie's hairbrush, a couple of hemp bracelets. Only Dylan's belongings had disappeared as if by magic (or evil spell), and for the first time all day, the finality began to sink in. Wasn't it just last night that they had ridden home from the concert on the El together, Dylan lovingly, protectively cradling Ellie in his free arm as he balanced his guitar case in the other? ("So short a time to teach my life its transposition to this difficult and unaccustomed key.") The minute the apartment door shut behind them, they were on the front-room floor, devouring one another ravenously. Three in the morning, but it didn't matter.

The phone rang. Ellie sprang from the bed and ran toward the front room. A second ring. She nearly fell over the arm of the couch, grabbing the receiver and sending the rest of the phone crashing to the floor.

"Hello?" her voice was thick and dry.

"Ellie." It was Dylan.

"Why did you take your clothes?" she asked desperately, not waiting for an answer. "Is your head OK? I'm so sorry I freaked out. I didn't mean to hurt you. Where are you? Are you OK?"

A long silence hung between them as Ellie felt the panic begin to rise in her. Why wasn't he saying anything?

"I'm so sorry, Ellie," Dylan's voice, thin and ghost-like, answered finally. That was all it took to unhinge her. The tears finally streamed silently down her face in unrelenting torrents as the day's shock gave way to humiliation.

"Why her?" Ellie wondered pitifully. Again all that ensued was silence. "I have always been faithful to you, Dylan. I could never love anyone but you." Ellie began to work herself into a sob. "I don't understand. Why? Why did you have to sleep with Madison?"

"Ellie, listen to me," Dylan's voice grew insistent. "Ellie. Ellie, you're too good for me."

"What?" she asked, confused. "What are you talking about? I love you! Just come home. We can talk about this in person. We can sort through things. I forgive you, Dylan. Just come home." She had to move the phone away from her face so that he wouldn't hear her choking.

"Ellie, I can't."

"Why, Dylan? Why can't you? Just come home!"

"Ellie, it's like I wanted to get caught or something. It's like it was meant to happen. I almost feel relieved."

"What do you mean, you feel relieved?"

"I can't be faithful to you. I can't be tied down. I mean…maybe I'm a horrible person who is cursed, meant to be alone forever. But I can't live this lie anymore. It's killing me."

"Dylan, what do you mean?"

"Ellie, stop it. I know you know what I mean."

"Know what?" Ellie continued to place her hand over the receiver to mute her weeping. She needed him to be direct.

"Madison is not the only girl, Ellie." Dylan stopped to wait for a reaction, but Ellie couldn't get the phone back up to her face to answer. She wept so convulsively that for a moment, she had to place the telephone receiver on the sofa.

"Ellie?" she heard Dylan ask loudly. "Ellie?" Placing the receiver back to her mouth, all she could produce was the guttural moan of a wounded animal to let him know she was still listening. "I am afraid of commitment. I don't really think marriage can work for anyone. I know that I can't be faithful. I really do love you, Ellie. I just can't love you the way that you love me."

"Tell me what I did!" Ellie demanded pitifully.

"You didn't do anything, Ellie." Dylan sounded genuinely sad. "I should have let you go a year ago. We never should have moved in together. I just thought I could change."

"You don't love me?" Ellie's strangled voice was barely audible.

Silence.

"I will always love you, Ellie. I just can't be the person you want me to be. I'm sorry I hurt you."

"Why can't I be enough?" She no longer hid her weeping. *Why can't I be enough? Why?* Dylan said nothing on the other end of the phone.

"You can stay at the apartment until you find another place."

"Will I ever see you again?" Ellie sobbed.

"I don't know."

Ellie placed the receiver gently down in its cradle, slumping onto the floor next to the sofa. Grief assailed her as she rolled into a ball on her side, unleashing primal howls into the stiflingly still air of the apartment. Nobody would hear her over their air conditioners, and no one could help her even if they did. She was completely and utterly alone. *"Madison is not the only girl, Ellie."* How many others had there been? How many? When? Where? Was it always here in this apartment?

A fresh wave of humiliation and self-pity washed over Ellie as she imagined coming home from school just minutes after another woman had left, the smell of sex—it's energy—still lingering in the air, undetected only by a fool.

No. It wasn't always in their apartment. It was everywhere. *May as well be honest with yourself now, fool. No need to pretend you didn't know he was cheating.* There was that Asian girl at the party last summer (some friend of the drummer's) who seemed overly interested in talking to Ellie. Initially Ellie thought maybe the girl was attracted to *her*, but then Ellie caught her following Dylan around the room with her eyes, some strange, inexplicable expression of sadness only thinly veiled.

Then what about the time they were both invited to that party in Wrigleyville? Dylan's "friend," Jamie, a girl he'd grown up with, had just gotten married and moved into a new apartment ("Come see where I live!"). Oddly enough, when they arrived, the husband was nowhere to be found. Jamie spent the entire night sizing Ellie up through narrowed, heavily made-up eyes. An unexpected, sickly pit had formed in Ellie's gut, always her intuitive gauge even when her mind went into denial hyperdrive.

And did everyone else know? Was that why Ellie always had the sense that people avoided her ("They are opportunists!")? Was that why Dylan was so overprotective? (Sit up in the balcony where I can watch you so you don't accidentally run into someone I've slept with. Don't go into the women's bathroom to overhear girls trading stories about their sexual encounters with the infamous Dylan Ross.). Was that the real reason Dylan never left Ellie alone with his bandmates? After all, Dylan couldn't guarantee that anyone but him could keep such a devastating secret for so long.

Ellie laid her cheek against the cool floor. Her crying stopped. She was too exhausted to cry any longer. Maybe she would just lay here for a while and shut her stinging eyes. *This is how I began today.* The thought nearly crushed her, sending a fresh stream of tears sliding down the outside corners of her eyes without sound. An inexorable sadness had burrowed deeply into the center of her chest, leaving an open, festering wound. She had no control of her emotions.

As much as she wanted to just sleep, she could not quiet her mind. Maybe there was some alcohol somewhere. That would help her rest, but she was too weak to look for it. Exhausted. *Maybe I will just close my eyes for a moment until I feel strong enough to get up.* The sheets still hung from the doorways, but they were completely still. No air conditioning to stir them. *Too tired to move.*

"Ellie, I love you." Dylan held Ellie's face in his hands. It was winter as they stood on a busy street corner, people passing all around, but all Ellie saw was Dylan. And his look of complete adoration. The twinkling lights of a Christmas tree

flashed in the background. Dylan's face seemed to be framed in evergreens. "Marry me!" he entreated. Ellie leaned in to kiss him, when suddenly his face morphed into a black ram, huge horns wrapping around wildly and then disintegrating into dust and blown away in the wind.

Ellie snapped awake, her heart beating irregularly. She was thirsty but too tired to move. Without the air conditioner blowing, she could hear the sound of traffic on the street outside. Was it Saturday night? Early Sunday morning? The apartment was in complete blackness except for light from a streetlamp shining through the open blind of the patched window.

There was movement in the apartment below. Madison. Ellie felt a pang of shame. *"It's been going on for months."* How long had Ellie been the joke? This must be God punishing her for her arrogance. God. Karma. Whatever. She was being punished for laughing behind Madison's back, for thinking she was so much smarter. *Elizabeth Lawson, University of Chicago scholar, the joke is on you. Ha! Ha! The fucking joke is on you!* Did Madison and Dylan have sex on Ellie's pillow, her side of the bed, and then laugh about Ellie's blind trust? Did Dylan laugh about Ellie the way he had laughed about Madison? No. No one could be that wicked, that cruel, that malicious. Or could he be? *"I just can't be the person you want me to be."* It was too much to contemplate.

Too weak.

Tears involuntarily began to stream down Ellie's cheeks again. She hated herself for being so gullible. How could she believe that anyone could love her completely—forever? She wasn't so very perfect. Her face was just slightly too narrow, her nose too long. She was pretty but not breathtaking. Her hair was thick and long but a mousy color of brown. Her eyes were nothing remarkable. She often wished she could be more "cute." Cute and blond and petite and bubbly. Ellie was always too serious. She laughed easily, but it was usually an ironic laugh, not easy and friendly and, well, cute. What made her so worthy of Dylan? His presence sucked the air out of a room. He filled up the space with his radiance. His beauty. Ellie's chest hurt, thinking of his playful laughter. She would never hear that sound again. She wrapped her arms around herself but chose not to get up. Maybe she would just let herself die here on the living-room floor. What did it matter?

Hot light beamed through the broken window where Dylan had lifted the blind to patch the glass. It lit a blistering path across Ellie's arm, onto the floor beneath the curtain leading to the kitchen. From the floor, Ellie watched dust dance through the light path. A fly buzzed somewhere in the room.

"Ellie, wait!" Dylan yelled to her from the beach. Her horse galloped ahead.

"Just follow me!" Ellie instructed Dylan as her white stallion headed for the ocean. Ellie had flowers braided into her flowing hair. She seemed to be almost floating. She was floating! The horse had gone into the water so deep that it had to swim. She wrapped her arms around the horse's neck and leaned in, laughing. It was wonderful. She felt so carefree.

Out of nowhere, a huge metal structure rose from the water, its gray surface glistening from the sun and reflected off the tiny beads of water. It resembled some massive metallic Picasso sculpture.

"Hurry, Dylan!" Ellie urged. His horse still stood on the beach as Dylan looked on. He was tentative. Unable to resist the urge, Ellie jumped off her horse to swim toward the metal leviathan. Water rippled gently around it. She felt safe and content as she began to ascend the structure effortlessly, her dress miraculously dry. Dylan urged his black horse toward the water, but it bucked in protest.

"Dylan!" Ellie beckoned him.

"I can't!" he explained as he tried once again to coax the black horse into the water. Suddenly the horse bucked up, sending Dylan face down into the sand. He didn't move.

"Dylan!" Ellie screamed frantically from the top of the metal structure. "Dylan!" She couldn't leave him there. Letting go, she plunged toward the water. It turned to ice as she slammed stomach first.

A vicious abdominal cramp seized Ellie, wrenching her awake. *Oh my God, I have to get onto the couch.* But when she struggled to move, a violent wave of nausea knocked her back. Her weak arm reached behind to search vainly for a pillow. Finally. Pulling it off the couch, she attempted to slide it under her head. *Oh, God. I'm going to be sick.* She stopped moving in an attempt to still the spinning. *Just lay still.* The nausea passed momentarily.

~

E llie gradually opened her eyes. The apartment was dark again except for a curious blinking light in the corner of the front room. From where Ellie was laying on the floor, she could see the red flash, flash, flash, reflected off the ceiling. It was mesmerizing, soothing. She shut her sore eyes once more. The answering machine was blinking. She must have missed a call. She would check it in a minute. As soon as the nausea passed.

~

"E llie" *Her mother's stern face loomed huge in front of her. "What's going on?" Ellie attempted to speak, but no sound came out of her mouth. She struggled to explain, a vague fear in her. Can't disappoint mother. Better answer her. Her mother's face grew larger, contorted. Bright white light surrounded her mother's head. It moved away and then popped back into focus. "Oh my God, Jim, help me!" Her father's giant face flashed past her, yellow and orange trails like kite tails behind him. Something grabbed her foot.*

"No!"

It was a snake wrapping around Ellie's ankle. She was so hot. The icy snake wrapped around her wrist and whipped across her forehead, leaving the sting of dry ice.

"Ellie, wake up! Ellie! Elizabeth!"

"Elizabeth!" Maggie Lawson laid her forearm against her daughter's scorching forehead. "Jim, call nine one one. She's burning up. Ellie, how long have you been laying here?"

"Mom."

"Elizabeth Lawson, how long have you been laying here?"

I don't know. Ellie's throat was a desert. A charley horse crippled her leg, sending it jerking involuntarily. Maggie Lawson looked on with horror. Without waiting for her husband's help, she lifted Ellie by the shoulders and began dragging her toward the bathroom.

"Jim, she's got heatstroke. Get me some ice. She needs a glass of water. A bottle of water. Whatever you can find. Bring it fast."

"Mom!" Ellie tried to protest. The apartment started spinning as Ellie's head bobbed, chin hitting her chest. Intuitively her mother stopped in time to prop Ellie into a sitting position so she could vomit, very little, onto the black and white kitchen tiles. Within moments, the deafening roar of the bathtub faucet, frantically pouring out its freezing contents into the basin of the claw-foot tub, echoed through the bathroom. In one seemingly effortless move, Maggie Lawson lifted her daughter and dropped her into the freezing water, clothes and all.

"Ahh!" The primal screech of torture that escaped Ellie took all of her remaining energy, her head collapsing against her chest as shock knocked her out cold.

~~~

Ellie crept across the wooden planks of her childhood bedroom and placed her ear against the door. She could hear her parents' hushed voices in the kitchen below, but it was too difficult to make out what they were saying. Her mother had ears like a dog. Should she risk opening the door to stand on the landing in order eavesdrop? Surely her mother would hear her.

Unbelievable. You're twenty-five years old. Stop acting like a captive child.

Weird that her mother still had the ability to make her feel like a kid. Defying her better judgment, she snuck noiselessly down the hall to the top of the staircase, careful to stay obscured. Maggie and Jim Lawson milled about the kitchen in their usual morning routine. This was probably the second pot of coffee, which meant Maggie Lawson was properly fired up.

"What did you tell Dr. Messing?" she asked her husband.

"I told him the truth," he answered absently.

"Well, what exactly did you say?" she said, searching.

"I told him that Ellie had heatstroke. That's the truth, isn't it?"

"Well, it's believable enough. Even if it's only part of the truth."

"She didn't try to kill herself, Maggie, if that's what you're implying."

"Shhhh!" she scolded him. Then in a lowered voice, she said, "How do *you* know that, Jim?"

"I just do…" he said, trailing off. "I just do." He sounded unsure.

"Why didn't she turn on the air conditioner then? She was only a few feet from it. Why didn't she drink anything? She must have been laying on that floor for a couple of days. In one spot."

"Maggie, I don't know. She's obviously depressed. People deal with depression differently."

"Like by giving up on life? And not drinking or eating anything for days at a time? I suppose you would know," her mother added bitterly.

James Lawson refused to acknowledge her last comment. "I don't think she purposely stopped eating or drinking. I refuse to believe that she tried to kill herself." The more her father denied the possibility, the more convincing he sounded to himself. "She's tough like you, Maggie. She wouldn't give up so easily."

Ellie cringed. She was nothing like her mother.

"What did Messing say? How long will they allow her to be gone from school and still keep her fellowship grant?"

"As long as she needs." Jim Lawson sounded uncharacteristically adamant and protective. "She'll be back as soon as she is well enough to be back. She almost died for Christ's sake. She hallucinated in the hospital bed for an entire day before finally coming around. Dr. Messing can run his own classes for a while. I'll help her finish that *Frankenstein* essay if need be, but if I know Ellie, she'll be too proud to ask for help anyhow. Again like someone else I know."

"I don't think we should baby her for too long."

"Go easy though, Maggie. Give her some time. We don't even know for sure what happened. If it weren't for Dylan's mother calling us, we wouldn't even have checked up on her."

"Whatever. That woman is just trying to assuage her guilt for raising such a no-good liar of a son. I'll tell you what, if that boy so much as even tries to contact Ellie again, I'll kill him with a pitchfork."

Jim Lawson laughed heartily. "I don't doubt it. Be fair, though. We haven't heard from Ellie...."

"What do you want to know?" Ellie stood, looking over the landing into the kitchen. Startled, her parents gazed up at her from the center island. Long, wild hair trailing down her back, Ellie descended the stairs and took a seat at the counter. She hadn't been down from her bedroom in five days and felt spitefully gratified by her parents' surprised silence. Neither parent knew how to start questioning; each was too afraid to upset her. "I caught him cheating on me with the girl who lived in the apartment beneath us," Ellie offered almost defiantly. Then unexpectedly, her cheeks grew hot with humiliation.

You're done crying. Don't you dare start now.

"I knew it!" Ellie's younger sister, Becca, appeared in the doorway, fresh from riding. "That piece of shit!" she exclaimed.

Ellie laughed into her hands, her mercurial emotions getting the better of her.

Thank you, Becca, for saving me!

"Becca Renee Lawson, boots off in this house! That's what the mudroom is for," Maggie Lawson scolded harshly.

"Oh, I couldn't resist the drama of it all, Mom! They're clean." She lifted up both boots one at a time to reveal only dust. It was a good distraction. She rushed to Ellie and threw her arms around Ellie's back, hugging her from behind. Setting her head on the back of Ellie's shoulder, she whispered, "I never liked that arrogant, entitled asshole! He thought he was better than everyone, but he was never good enough for you."

"Well, he had me fooled." Ellie sighed regretfully, looking down at her hands. Her parents stood at the other side of the island, waiting expectantly for more elaboration. "I know what you're all thinking, and you're wrong," she started defensively. "I didn't try to kill my-self," she finished. Both Maggie and Jim Lawson seemed to exhale. "I was in shock. I caught him sleeping with some other girl. In our apartment. And I freaked out and left. I just sat outside all day because I couldn't think straight and didn't know where to go. I didn't want to go back to the apartment because I told them to get out, and I didn't know if they would still be there…It was just so hot. I guess I didn't realize how hot it was."

"Why didn't you call us?" her mother lamented.

"Mom, I was in shock. I don't know why I didn't call anybody."

Because I didn't want to talk about it, Mom, that's why.

"I'm going to give you a pedicure," Becca announced, coming to the rescue again. "Let's go sit on the porch. It's not too hot yet. I'll get a bowl of water to soak your feet in." She grabbed Ellie's hand and led her out of the kitch-en toward the front door. Both parents looked as if they might protest her leaving but thought better of it; Ellie would talk more when she was ready. Best not to rush her.

"We love you, Ellie," Jim Lawson called after his daughter.

"I know, Daddy," Ellie answered.

As Ellie sat on the porch swing overlooking the Lawson's horse ranch, Becca gently placed Ellie's feet into a bowl of warm water she'd carried out from the kitchen. The late morning sun was already scorching the dirt of the two outdoor arenas. The wise horses moved slowly, careful not to use too much energy swatting at flies, small dirt clouds swirling around their hooves. At the far end of the ranch, a handful of hired workers repaired a fence. Becca inspected Ellie's cuticles thoughtfully through the water.

"You haven't had a pedicure in a while," she observed.

"No, I guess I haven't."

"Want to tell me what happened?" Becca looked up patiently at Ellie from the floor of the porch.

"I cut his hair."

"Yeah?" Becca grinned widely. Ellie knew Becca understood without any more explanation. It was a long, satisfying moment. "I bet that made you feel a little better."

Ellie nodded with just the slightest twinge of guilt. Becca lovingly removed one of Ellie's feet from the water, drying it on an old towel, and set to work pushing back the cuticles.

Even though Becca was the baby of the family, Ellie's only sibling, she was the one who always took care of Ellie. Their father called Becca the "old soul" and the "animal whisperer." And it was true. Becca never got angry, never held a grudge, never judged, charmed every living thing she ever met, both man and beast, and was clever and smart as a whip to boot. She had a way of defusing any family argument that ever erupted in the Lawson household simply by way of her angelic presence. She was the yin to Ellie's yang. And even though the two were so completely different, Ellie couldn't help but be in love with her little sister, the Zen master, who could read Ellie's thoughts before she even uttered them. This summer was Becca's last spent at home before starting veterinary school. *No slackers allowed in the Lawson household.* Delivering her first foal at age ten, veterinary medicine was Becca's destiny.

"I caught Dylan sleeping with Madison, that skank who lived in the apartment beneath us, and I totally lost it! I jumped onto his back and attacked him with scissors!" Ellie laughed ruefully. It was all she could do to keep from crying again. "Of all the people he could have been with, it had to be her. I hated that girl, and now I hate her even more."

Becca nodded her head as she worked in order to let Ellie know she was listening. A wave of relief washed over Ellie as the words began to pour out in torrents. "You know, I suspected he was cheating on me long before this. I felt suspicious. I felt it in my bones; I was just too afraid to check up on him. Or maybe I was just too afraid to feel like I do now. Completely let down and stupid and humiliated."

She stopped suddenly before she quietly admitted her worse fear. "Maybe I will never love anyone again."

E. J. Densmore

Her chin began to quiver. She looked out over the ranch, the still oaks majestic and constant. Those trees had been there forever. The thought comforted her, keeping her from crying. Some things never changed. Some things were still beautiful.

Becca stopped what she was doing to place a comforting hand on Ellie's knee, her compassionate hazel eyes wide and patient as she looked up from under a wisp of sandy-blond hair. "I've never really been in love before, Ellie. I've never even come close, so I don't know if I have any real advice for you."

"That's OK, Becca," Ellie said, excusing her sister while staring off quietly toward the distant group of men working on the far end of their property.

"It seems like being in denial about him cheating all that time was probably a self-defense mechanism of sorts. How was your brain supposed to accept something so unimaginable when he had once asked you to marry him? To love him forever. To spend a lifetime with him."

Ellie's hand flew up to her mouth. The words were too poignant.

"Oh, Ellie, I'm sorry," Becca said, apologizing immediately. "I only meant that you shouldn't be so hard on yourself. Why would you want to believe he was capable of something so dishonest?"

Ellie only shrugged her shoulders and mutely shook her head. She felt slightly nauseous again.

"Ellie," Becca said suddenly, "did you ever consider that maybe Dylan is not the person you are meant to be with?"

Ellie looked down to meet Becca's direct gaze. What did she mean? Ellie *loved* Dylan. Even now. That's all she knew for sure. She hadn't contemplated what was "meant." All she knew was the profound emptiness she felt now that Dylan was gone, and the nagging, urgent need to fill that void. What exactly did Becca mean?

"I think…" Becca hesitated as she allowed her thoughts to form. "We all have the capacity to love several people. Maybe even an endless number of people! But there is only one person you're meant to be with. Forever. And maybe Dylan is not that person."

The idea sent a hot spear of grief through Ellie's chest. The thought of Dylan "belonging" to someone else, destined for another woman, not meant to be Ellie's, was almost too much to contemplate.

"Like a soul mate?" Ellie asked.

"Sure," Becca agreed.

Ellie laughed woefully. "That doesn't make me feel better, Becca!"

"Oh, I'm sorry, Ellie," Becca apologized. "I want it to make you feel better! I want it to give you hope! Think about what this means: happiness is out there waiting for you still! Dylan was not *the one*. He wasn't."

"Ellie." Their mother appeared at the screen of the front door. "When Becca's done with your feet, I want you to take this out to the workers." She pushed the screen door open with her behind and carried out a tray of glasses and lemonade, setting it on the small porch table next to the swing.

"*Why not, Becca?*" began to form on Ellie's lips when a flash of realization hit her. "OK, Madam Defarge." Ellie sneered, comparing her mother to the scheming character in *A Tale of Two Cities*. The reference was lost on her mother, but Jim Lawson's burst of laughter could be heard from just inside the door. "Sure, I'll bring it out to the workers. I'll even do it now!"

"Ellie!" Becca said, laughing and allowing her sister to go. Ellie snatched the tray from the table, much to her family's amusement, and set off down the long dirt driveway in her sleep shorts and tank top, wet feet, and untamed mane of hair straggling behind her. She would really need a pedicure now. Poor Becca!

In the heat, it proved to be a long walk down the driveway. Why hadn't her mother just given her a cooler or jug? This stupid tray and pitcher were cumbersome. She'd be coming out here all day to replenish a pitcher.

Oh. Of course! That woman!

As Ellie got nearer to the group, all but one of the men continued to bend over their work, unaware of the wild specter of Ellie Lawson bearing gifts.

Stopping to watch her approach, he leaned against his post-hole digger, with bare, tanned arms crossed over the top and the broad, smooth muscles of his shoulders flexed. Sweat poured down his shirtless chest to the waist of his jeans as he rested one foot on the fence he was fixing.

"Hi." He smiled broadly as Ellie searched awkwardly for someplace to set the stupid tray. His deep-brown eyes watched her curiously, amused. Two adorable dimples graced a boyish face. He looked younger than Ellie but held himself solidly self-assured. Ellie felt suddenly self-conscious. *What for?* He stood there covered in dirt, sweating profusely, and she had literally just gotten out of bed. They appraised one another.

"This is for you." She held out the tray. The man looked around him, still openly amused.

Yes, it's a pitcher.

"Thanks," he said and took the pitcher off the tray. Lifting it to his mouth, he drank down half the contents as Ellie looked on, annoyed and surprised. Nice body and cute, but now she'd have to come out with more lemonade for the rest of the group. He handed the pitcher back to Ellie and swiped his forehead with the back of his dirty hand.

"You live here?" he asked.

"Yeah, my mom's horses." Ellie motioned with her head toward the stables. "I'm Ellie Lawson."

"Nice to meet you, Ellie," he answered. "This is my crew." Mimicking Ellie, he motioned with his head toward the rest of the men who were still busy at work. "I'm Alec Purnell."

Four

July-August of Ellie Lawson's Twenty-fifth Year

"Are you sure this is the place he said to meet him?" Becca looked around the gravel parking lot doubtfully. The tiny tavern that Alec Purnell had invited them to sat very isolated on a county highway nearly fifteen miles from the Lawson farm. Most of the cars in the lot had seen better days, but it was the motorcycles lined up twenty deep in front that really intimidated her.

"I'm sure it's fine," Ellie said reassuringly. What had she to lose? She had almost died alone on the front-room floor of her Chicago apartment a week before. A handful of harmless bikers in a Wisconsin tavern didn't frighten her. She was in a reckless mood anyhow. Feeling well enough to get good and drunk. And well, she deserved it.

Becca swung her white Ford Probe next to an old Chevy pickup and put it in park. She turned to look at Ellie, "You're sure you feel like being out?"

"Oh my God, yes! I feel like being out," Ellie insisted. "If I have to stay one more minute in that house

113

with Mom and Dad, I'm going to go crazy! Besides you thought he was kind of hot, didn't you?" She felt strange talking about someone besides Dylan in that way, almost disloyal. A pang of guilt struck her, but she buried it immediately.

"Alec?"

"Yeah."

"Yeah, he's totally cute."

"So? Let's just go have some fun. Maybe he has some cute friends."

"I'm just concerned about you," Becca admitted.

"Nothing to worry about as long as you promise to be the driver tonight."

"Sure. I'll drive while you watch the line on the road and let me know if I'm swerving!" Both girls laughed as they exited the car. The Lawson sisters had more than once spent the night "sleeping it off" in a car. If that was what had to happen tonight, well, then so be it.

Even before they pulled open the awkward glass doors with "Ray's County Seat" embossed in burgundy lettering, The Rolling Stones could be heard lamenting, "You can't always get what you want." They entered into a dark, low-ceilinged dive, the familiar smell of cigarettes and stale beer assailing them. As Ellie and Becca's eyes adjusted to the darkness, they realized that most of the people in the bar had turned to see who had just walked in. Luckily Alec stood only a few feet from the door with a pool stick in his hand, a beer in the other.

"Hi!" he grinned boyishly. His smile was adorable, charming even. "You found it OK, huh?" The rest of the patrons turned back to what they were doing.

"Oh yeah. No problem. I just never realized this was here," Becca answered.

"This is my friend, Josh." He motioned to a much taller guy with blond hair at the end of the pool table. Josh held up his hand to signal hello. Nodding back, Ellie recognized him as one of the Alec's workers. "Some of my other friends are in back by the juke box, but I pretty much know everyone here. What do you want to drink?" Alec set his pool stick on the table.

"Oh, I'll get it," Ellie replied. Alec gave her a strange look, pursing his lips and shaking his head in disapproval. "Rolling Rock," she said, giving in with a smile. This felt weird to her. "Becca, what do you want?"

Becca eased into a barstool by the window a few feet from Josh. "I'll have a Rolling Rock too. And a shot of Jägermeister." She winked at Ellie. "Make that two. One for me and one for her. We're celebrating tonight."

"Oh yeah?" Alec asked.

"Yeah, a rebirth," Becca joked.

"Hold that thought!" Alec commanded as he headed for the bar. Ellie watched him go. He was only a few inches taller than her but had broad across the shoulders like a wrestled. He was also barrel chested and tan with thick, wavy brown hair that was so dark it looked black in the light of the bar. Either he spent a lot of time lifting weights in a gym or the sort of physical labor he had done at the Lawson's farm the day before kept him looking like he did. Ellie was used to dating lanky musician types like Dylan. Alec was a totally different species.

What would those arms feel like? I wouldn't mind... She realized she was staring. As Alec reached the bar, Ellie locked eyes with the woman behind the counter, blond, ratted hair, probably in her forties, likely once a pretty face now lined by time and cigarette smoke.

"Mom, can I have two Rolling Rocks and two shots of Jägermeister? Josh, you want anything?" Alec yelled back toward the pool table. Josh held up his Budweiser.

Mom? Had he really just called that woman "Mom"?

Ellie smiled feebly. Should she walk over? Awkward. No. She would just stay put. Walking over seemed awfully presumptuous. After all, this guy had simply asked her to meet him at a bar. It wasn't a marriage proposal. For a moment, Ellie nearly burst into laughter at the absurdity. A week and a half ago, she was engaged to Dylan Ross, son of Gerard Ross, who ran one of the largest accounting firms in Chicago. The Ross family of Oak Park. Old money. Tonight she was meeting up with a fence-post digger and his bartending mother in a shit-hole bar in Wisconsin.

No, that is just snobbery. That's why you ended up being the fool.

True. Dylan's superior upbringing certainly hadn't made him any more decent a person. The fucking liar.

"So what do you mean rebirth?" Alec returned, handing Ellie and Becca their beers. Becca eyed Ellie tentatively.

"I just broke off my engagement," Ellie announced boldly. She had the sense that she was watching herself from outside of her body; saying the words felt foreign, like a hazy dream.

"Really?" Alec eyed her as he took a swig of his beer. "I guess I have some lucky timing then?" He flashed a perfect smile.

"I guess so," Ellie said flirtatiously. She took the shot off the table where Alec had set it and slammed it down, relishing the familiar burn. "Your mom works here?"

"Yeah, that's my mom. Sorry if that's kinda weird… She's cool. This is where I usually hang with my friends, so I just figured I'd tell you to meet me here."

"No. It's cool. My mom drives me crazy right now. I think it's sweet that you don't mind being around your mom."

"No, I don't mind at all. I actually took a semester off school to come back and help her make her bills. My asshole stepfather just walked out on her."

"Oh." Ellie frowned. She didn't really know what to say. That sort of thing was unfamiliar territory to her. Her parents had been married for what seemed like a hundred thousand years. And certainly there was nothing as passionate as a fight going on in the Lawson household. Maggie Lawson was certainly all business and as little drama as possible. "Where did you go to school?"

"I was at UW Madison studying engineering. That was two years ago. I had every intention of returning to school, but then I started my business, and it's been doing so well."

"So the fencing business is yours?"

"Yeah. I'm actually working on getting a patent right now for one of my fence designs."

"Oh, right. My mom was saying something about that the other day when you guys were out working on our farm." Becca jumped into the conversation. Ellie had no idea what she was talking about. She had probably been lying in bed, trying to sleep off her sorrow.

"Yeah, that's the fencing I installed for your horses. Your mom's farm is kind of my experiment. She was really encouraging. If it works well, I can use your mom *and* my work there as a reference."

"So you're good at building things?" Ellie knew it sounded stupid the minute it came out of her mouth.

"Yeah, I guess so." Alec laughed. "I restore cars too. Maybe if you're lucky, I'll give you a ride in my '67 Camaro later," he offered playfully, not breaking his gaze.

Maybe if you're lucky, I'll let you give me a ride in it!

"Do you live with your parents?" he asked.

"God, no!" Ellie blurted. Becca almost choked on her beer.

"No, she abandoned me nearly seven years ago!" Becca complained.

"I've been at the University of Chicago since I was eighteen," Ellie explained. "My undergrad major was English. I finished my Master's last year, and I've been slaving away at my doctorate since then."

"So what are you going to do with an English degree?" Alec wondered. Becca again laughed, knowing full well how irritated Ellie would be with such a question. "I'm sorry," he immediately apologized, realizing his misstep. "I guess I just…"

"I'm going to be a professor like my father," Ellie answered rather proudly. "Have you ever read anything by James Lawson?"

"No," Alec admitted.

"He's a pretty famous poet. I'm surprised you didn't study him at Madison."

"Maybe we did in Comp one-oh-two or something. I'm a math guy," he offered contritely. Changing the subject, he blurted, "So why'd you give this fiancé the boot?"

Wow, he is bold.

Becca seemed to be enjoying just listening to the exchange. She wasn't coming to Ellie's rescue tonight.

"He was a dick. That's why." Ellie took a long swig from her bottle of Rolling Rock. "He was a guitar-playing prick! It turned out he was playing me too. I was his fiancé, but he also had several girlfriends." She laughed a little too ruefully at her own wordplay.

"Ahh, I see," Alec replied knowingly. "Those musical guys get all the chicks!" He saw that Ellie had grown uncomfortable. "He's an idiot if you ask me." He set his hand on her forearm for a moment to show his sincerity.

"Yeah, I think so too," Ellie agreed, finishing the rest of her beer.

"Another?" he offered.

"Please."

Alec returned to the bar, again the perfect gentleman, taking care of his guests. Ellie was impressed. He seemed to possess a politeness not many guys their age did. Something about him was so grounded and mature. Not like Dylan who refused to get a "real" job working as an accountant, even though that was what his parents had paid for him to learn to do at DePaul. Alec obviously wasn't afraid to work hard—just look at the way he had slaved at her parents' house. Dylan had always had a sense of entitlement. Even though he was a brilliant musician, Ellie doubted he ever worked hard a day in his life. Everything came so easily to him. He was beautiful and talented and wealthy through no effort of his own, and apparently he also got more ass than a movie star. Ellie's heart stung at the thought. Now that she knew what Dylan was capable of, she was beginning to see him for who he really was—immature, selfish, eccentric, and narcissistic. All those qualities that she once found endearing seemed hateful to her. She hated *him*. She hated him for carving out her heart and leaving her broken. The more she had to drink, the more she hated him, and the more she vowed to forget him.

Four beers later, Ellie and Becca had become pool players extraordinaire through Alec and Josh's tutoring. Ellie had stopped worrying about whether or not Becca was having a good time and fell completely under Alec's spell.

"Meet me by the bathrooms," Alec whispered in Ellie's ear. Her stomach flipped with excitement followed by a sudden sense of unexpected anger. Was he asking her to go into the bathroom with him? *Wow. That's pretty forward.* But she went back there anyway, curiosity getting the better of her. She'd make him wait, though. She slipped into the restroom and splashed some water on her face, starring into the mirror at her shiny face. Her makeup was a mess. Why bother when it's one-hundred degrees outside? She fumbled for a piece of toilet paper and wiped off the rest of her lipstick, replacing it with Chap Stick from her purse. When she exited the bathroom, Alec stood waiting in the narrow hallway outside the door.

"I want to show you something." He eagerly grabbed Ellie's hand and led her out the back entrance of the bar and into the thick, still heat of the night air, crickets deafening in the blackness. Ellie could barely see in front of her. He led her farther from the back door and into the parking lot. "This is the car I just finished restoring," Alec said proudly once they stopped in front of what appeared to be a black or navy car with two white stripes on the hood. Ellie didn't know very much about cars. She had never even owned one herself.

"It looks great!" She searched for another encouraging phrase to say. Her head was swimming, and it was still so hot outside.

"I know it's hard to see out here in the dark, but this is the first time I've taken it out, and I just wanted to brag!" he exclaimed sweetly. It was too much. Ellie grabbed his face with both her hands and kissed him on the mouth. She'd been dying to do that all night, and the alcohol had finally given her the courage.

Alec's arms went slack for a moment in shock. Ellie stepped back from him, bumping gently into the car, but it was impossible to make out his expression in the dark. What possessed her? Had she moved too quickly? Suddenly he leaned into her, pressing her against the driver's side door, his face an inch from hers.

"I'm trying to be good tonight," he breathed slowly, pushing Ellie's hair away from her face with his nose. His splayed hands, pressed against the window, rested on either side of her, pinning her to the car. He brushed past her cheek slowly until his face was buried in her hair, inhaling deeply. Then she felt his mouth on her neck behind her ear—small, chaste kisses—and then his tongue, smooth and warm, moved downward.

"You don't have to be good." Ellie reached up to feel Alec's flexed arms, his shoulders. Oh, God. Those shoulders. Slipping her hands under the short sleeves that bunched over his biceps, she lingered for a moment, lost in the sensation of his mouth on her neck and his tensed muscles under her hands. His mouth met hers intensely as he gathered her in his arms, pressing his pelvis hard into her abdomen, causing Ellie to moan. He was a passionate kisser, with wide, soft lips just aggressive enough to make her completely aroused. His hands caressed her back, her behind, up her arms to her shoulders, where he let his fingers play over the straps of her tank top. Her hands traveled to his hard chest and then down his taut abs to his belt. She was aching for him.

Their kissing deepened and then slowed. Her hands lingered at his belt buckle. His hands halted at her shoulders. They both stopped. This wasn't the place or time.

What am I doing? Oh my God, he must think I'm the biggest slut.

Alec braced himself against the car again, resting his head on Ellie's shoulder. His hair smelled heavenly.

Catching her breath, her chest rose and fell as she exhaled all of her pent-up sexual energy.

"I'm sorry," Alec apologized.

"What for?" Ellie took his face in her hands again. "I kissed you, remember?"

"Yes, it is your fault!" He laughed. "See what you do to me?" He stood up, smoothing his shirt and straightening his belt. He bent down again to kiss her lightly on the lips. It took all her self-control not to pull him toward her again. The beer had temporarily dulled any sense of judgment or remorse. Had they been anywhere else besides a steaming, dark parking lot infested with mosquitos and crickets behind the bar where his mother worked, Ellie would probably have sealed the deal and worried about her reputation later. She took another deep breath.

"I guess we should go back in," she suggested.

Looking somewhat guilty, they went back inside, returning to the tables near the window and finding Becca still lost in conversation with Josh, who looked completely smitten. The room had started to clear out. It was nearly two in the morning. Alec's mother watched coolly from behind the bar. *I guess now would definitely not be the time for introductions.* His mother didn't seem very friendly.

"So where did you and Alec disappear to?" Becca pressed as they drove toward home.

"He wanted to show me his car," Ellie explained. She felt an unfamiliar emotion rising in her chest. Her face got hot. "I kissed him," was all she could say before she stopped suddenly; if she continued, she might burst into tears.

"Ellie, you can't cry! You're supposed to be watching the road!" Becca scolded, recognizing Ellie's curt answers as a sign of her impending tears.

Ellie laughed instead. "I know. You're doing fine, I think. Don't swerve to the left so much." But her heart felt heavy. She had kissed another boy. Really kissed him. She would have gone all the way too if he hadn't sensed that it was too weird and too soon. She had been ready to tear off his Levis right there in the parking lot. What was wrong with her?

Yeah, what is wrong with you? You should have torn his belt right off his hot little body, you dumbass! You're a free woman. You can do whatever you want.

Hooray. She never wanted to be free of Dylan. He's the one who didn't want her. Hot, quiet tears rolled from the corners of both Ellie's eyes despite her best efforts to stop them. She continued to look out the window, not wanting Becca to see. She didn't want to talk about it.

When they pulled stealthily into the long gravel driveway of the Lawson farm, Becca cut the lights. She knew it was futile, though. Maggie Lawson would be at the window, waiting anxiously for her girls. Once she saw them drive up, safe and sound, she would return to bed for a few hours at most. The girls liked to joke that their mother, like the horses, slept standing up.

Ellie crept noiselessly up to her room, slipped off her shorts, and lay in bed facing the window. The moon cast a long shadow across the armchair, onto the floor, and over the bedspread at Ellie's feet. Somewhere Dylan slept under the same moon. She wondered where he was at that very moment. She couldn't remember the date since she'd left Chicago for this Wisconsin vortex—gone from being an adult in Chicago, nearly married, back to being a captive child in her parents' home. Did Dylan have a show this weekend? Where was it? She couldn't remember. God, that stint in the hospital had fried her brain. Everything was so foggy, so surreal.

Ellie's thoughts wandered to Alec. He *was* really hot. She couldn't help but be attracted to him. She just felt so guilty. Regardless of Dylan and his infidelity, should she be ready and willing to sleep with someone so soon? What did that say about her? Shouldn't her heart—her body—still long to be faithful to Dylan?

Maybe he is not the one you're meant to be with.

So if Dylan was not who Ellie was supposed to be with, who was? Did she now have freedom to choose? Could she craft her own destiny? She had never really thought before about what qualities the perfect man should have. Dylan was the only boy she'd ever loved.

Now that he'd betrayed her, all she knew was that she wanted someone she could trust. She wanted to be with someone she could believe.

No, I want someone the exact opposite of Dylan. I want someone who is nothing like Dylan at all. Someone kind and responsible.

Could she be the master of her own fate instead of being tossed around by circumstance? The possibility comforted her as she fell into a fitful, drunken sleep.

"Ellie," her mother called from the kitchen below. It couldn't be much past ten in the morning.

Why does she hate me? Ellie's pulse beat miserably in her forehead like a mallet against stone. *I will never drink again.*

"Ellie, Alec Purnell is on the phone," Maggie Lawson bellowed up the staircase. Ellie's heart skipped a beat. She fumbled with the covers and hobbled to the door as quickly as she could without vomiting.

Her mother looked surprisingly pleased as she handed Ellie the phone. "Hello?" Ellie answered, turning her back away from her mother and wandering into the front room.

"Hi." Alec sounded surprisingly energetic. He could obviously handle his liquor much better than she could. "What are you doing today?"

"Nothing," Ellie answered far too quickly. *Did that sound pathetic? Too eager?*

"I'm coming to get you then."

"OK. Can I have an hour to get ready?"

"Sure. Be hungry. I'm going to make you lunch."

"OK." She hung up, feeling a wide grin spread across her face. She was startled to see her mother standing a few feet behind her when she turned back around.

"Going out?" Maggie Lawson asked.

"Alec is coming to get me."

"Good," her mother replied thoughtfully. "Good. You need to get out. This is good," she said again as if she were unsure. Ellie pushed past her mother toward the stairs. She felt too queasy and annoyed to be interrogated.

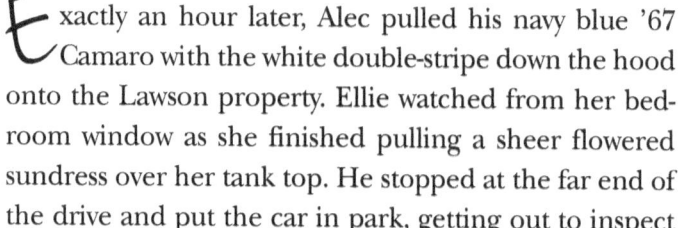

Exactly an hour later, Alec pulled his navy blue '67 Camaro with the white double-stripe down the hood onto the Lawson property. Ellie watched from her bedroom window as she finished pulling a sheer flowered sundress over her tank top. He stopped at the far end of the drive and put the car in park, getting out to inspect his handiwork with Maggie Lawson, who, of course, just happened to be outside near the newly installed fencing.

He strode around the back of the car confidently, extending his hand to her mother. They spoke seriously for a moment as Maggie stood with her arms folded, nodding emphatically. Then she laughed, tossing her head back just slightly. She liked him. Alec Purnell had the seal of approval from Maggie Lawson. *That* was really saying something. Who could resist that boyish face though, that intense, unblinking, genuine gaze? And he looked even better this morning than he had last night, wearing a snug, white V-neck T-shirt and a pair of khaki shorts and flip-flops. Ellie found herself hurrying to get outside.

"Hi." Alec smiled playfully, not allowing his eyes to leave Ellie as she made her way past the oak trees down the Lawson driveway toward him and her mother.

"Hi!" She smiled, squinting in the sun. The ibuprofen had started to kick in, vastly improving her mood.

"I was just telling Alec how pleased I am with the job he's done. This fence is more than I'd hoped," Maggie explained, running her hand over the top rail of one of the sections of fence.

"I'll take your word for it," Ellie responded snidely. She was relieved that her mother liked Alec, but she didn't feel like talking fences. "Where are we going?" she asked Alec.

"Well, I promised you food, but let's take a drive first! I haven't had the car out during the day yet." He was visibly excited, glowing like a child. "Good-bye, Mrs. Lawson." He extended his hand again. After shaking, he went to Ellie's door and opened it to let her in.

She ducked into the tiny front seat as Alec rounded the car and got into the driver's side. The car started up like a Harley, the deafening roar of the muffler engulfing them. Alec gingerly turned the car around in the driveway, careful not to leave Maggie Lawson in a cloud of dust, but once he pulled onto the two-lane highway in front of their home, he set his foot firmly on the gas. Ellie suppressed a squeal of satisfaction as she watched her mother, who was shaking her head, through the passenger side mirror. Alec glanced over at Ellie with a devious grin.

With the windows open and the engine screaming down the highway, it was too loud to talk. That suited Ellie just fine as she sat back, simply enjoying the view of the Wisconsin countryside. The sky was a bright blue with puffy, cotton-candy clouds floating happily across the horizon like a Magritte painting. The stifling heat had finally broken. The weather forecast had predicted a perfect summer day in the eighties. Alec flipped through radio stations, finally stopping at an Oasis song that blared through the speakers.

They drove through town, past the university, past the river, and around the bend of the highway toward the neighboring town. A breeze had kicked up, sending a thousand grateful leaves swaying on the branches of the maples and hickories that lined the county road. Even the prairie grasses on the side of the road seemed relieved that the heat had subsided.

Alec made a sudden turn down a long, winding road to nowhere. Small, neatly kept ranch houses set back on sizable forested plots dotted their path. They drove on for another five minutes or so until the car slowed. "This is my house," Alec nearly yelled over the engine as they eased up the long asphalt driveway of a slate-blue ranch with white shutters and a small front porch. The landscaping was immaculately kept. The house sat clear of a forest of pines that surrounded it on both sides. Alec parked the car just short of the garage.

"What do you want for lunch?" he asked as he took the keys out of the ignition. "I can cook just about anything, assuming I have it in the refrigerator."

"I'm not picky," Ellie claimed. The truth was that she didn't know whether or not she could stomach food yet. She didn't want to be rude by not eating. Maybe she could just talk him into a diet Pepsi. Alec opened the front door, letting Ellie into a house that was sparsely furnished but clean. The air reeked of stale cigarettes though, which instantly made Ellie's stomach lurch.

Oh my God, I'm going to be sick.

Alec moved quickly past Ellie into the small, galley kitchen.

"Mom!" he scolded before Ellie turned the corner, "Not in the house!" Ellie followed behind Alec just in time to see his mother snubbing out her cigarette. His mother looked up, unpleasantly surprised as it dawned on her that she'd been reprimanded in front of some stranger. Some dumb girl. An awkward silence hung in the air with the putrid smell of the cigarettes.

"Mom, this is Ellie Lawson," Alec offered. Ellie's arm lifted partially to extend a hand when she realized Alec's mother had no intention of shaking it. Thankfully Ellie had read the cue before embarrassing herself and instead lifted her hand into a silly, childish wave.

"Hi." She smiled as sweetly as she could. It felt like the most disingenuous thing she'd ever done in her life.

"Your mom's the one with the horses?" his mother asked strangely.

"Yes. My mom breeds horses." Ellie struggled to make sense of the conversation. Where was she going with this? "Alec and his crew installed new fencing at our farm a couple of days ago. That's how we met."

"Do you ride the horses?" she asked.

"Yes, but not much lately. I've lived away at school since I was eighteen. But I grew up with horses."

"I always loved horses," his mother went on dreamily. "I never did ride them, though. I had a lot of horse things when I was a kid, like a horse blanket and a horse calendar. You know, like a calendar with all these horse pictures on them?"

"You are welcome to ride our horses any time." Ellie felt like she was talking to a child.

"Mmmm," his mother replied cryptically, turning to reach for the coffee pot. She wore a pair of cut-off shorts and a tank top without a bra. The back of her hair was matted. Had she slept in her clothing? She reached into the cupboard for a coffee cup and absently knocked it onto the floor with a crash. "Oh, God, I'm sorry," she cried, looking up at Alec as she bent to pick up the pieces.

"It's OK, Mom. I'll get it." He rushed to pick up the broken chunks of ceramic cup before she stepped on them with her bare feet. Then it dawned on Ellie.

Oh my God, she's drunk!

Alec worked quickly to clear the mess. "Mom." He put his arm gently around her. "Why don't you go back to sleep for a while? You don't have to work tonight, do you?"

"No, not until I have to go back to the plant on Monday," she answered, rubbing the side of her face. Ellie wondered at her age. Her small, thin body did not look much older than forty-five, but her tired, puffy face told a different story. Alec led his mother into the other room, leaving Ellie standing in the kitchen. Through a wide back window, she could see into their yard behind. Unfenced, it went on for acres. Out back stood a huge pole barn, probably Alec's workspace. It was a nice property, especially for someone so young.

"Sorry." Alec returned, looking slightly embarrassed. Ellie shrugged. "She's been having a pretty tough time lately," he explained.

"It's OK." Ellie didn't think it was any of her business.

"I wish she didn't have to work at all. She works during the week at the canning plant and then bartends on the weekends. I told her I would take care of her now that my stepdad is gone, but she's too proud."

"Maybe she likes working, Alec. Maybe it's better to be busy than to be alone." *Isn't that the truth?*

"I never thought of it like that," he said pensively. "Maybe you're right. I can't help myself from worrying about her, though. I just want to make enough money to live comfortably, you know? To be able to take care of the people I love."

"Well, it looks like you're doing a good job. Your house is really cute. It looks like you have a lot of land too."

"This is nothing." Alec batted his hand. "You should see the plans I have for this property. Let's take a walk."

"You have any diet Pepsi?" Ellie asked hopefully.

"Sure."

Alec led Ellie out the back patio doors into a wide open space that did, indeed, extend for countless acres past the pole barn.

"You didn't grow up around here, did you?" Ellie asked. It was close enough to her parents' ranch that she figured she would probably have run into him at some point earlier if he had.

"No, we moved around a lot when I was a kid. My mom's been married a few times. I was born in Ohio, and then we lived in Florida for a while, but I went to high school up near Greenbay. My mom moved down here while I was in college in Madison so she could work at the plant."

"No brothers or sisters?"

"No, just me and my mom. After I left school, I started the fencing business. I was able to buy this property just a couple of months ago. You see all this?" He motioned to a line of black locust trees nearly ten acres from where they stood. "This is all mine."

"Wow!" Ellie was genuinely impressed.

"Come on," he said, grabbing her hand. He led her through a field of tall grass and wild flowers toward the grove of locust trees. "We should have worn better shoes," he said, apologizing. Ellie maneuvered cautiously through the field until they stopped to survey the land from the shade of an enormous maple tree. Ellie looked up, admiring the tree. A soft breeze kicked up again, sending the leaves sailing on their stalks.

"This is a sunset maple!" she exclaimed.

"Oh yeah?" Alec asked.

"Probably the biggest one I've ever seen," Ellie explained excitedly. "This tree must be a hundred years old! Do you know what color this will be in the fall?"

"No." He laughed.

"The most brilliant orange-tinted burgundy you'll ever see in your life. You can't even imagine a color so beautiful!" She looked up at it appreciatively.

Alec smiled, admiring her sudden enthusiasm. "How do you know so much about trees?"

"My dad," Ellie answered. "He's the romantic in our house. When Becca and I were growing up, my father was all about teaching us to observe and appreciate what's beautiful in the world. He has an artist's eye, you know? He taught me everything I know about nature— trees, flowers. He taught me how to garden too."

"He sounds like a great guy," Alec said.

"Yeah, he is," Ellie said fondly.

"I never knew my father," Alec confided. He sat beneath the maple, motioning for Ellie to follow. She found a soft, dry spot next to Alec where she sat down cautiously, pulling her knees up to her chest and wrapping her arms around her ankles. "I hope to be like your dad," Alec continued. "Someone my kid can admire." He absently plucked the white flower of a weed from the ground and twirled it between his forefinger and thumb. Reaching over, he tucked it behind Ellie's ear. "You're really different from any girl I've ever dated," he said suddenly.

"Yeah? How so?" Ellie asked playfully.

"I don't know. You're not as shallow, I guess. You're a better listener…You are really beautiful too."

Ellie felt herself blush.

"When you walked down the driveway in your pajamas the other day, I thought I must be dreaming!"

Ellie laughed nervously, remembering how bold she had been. Moving to kneel on his heels, Alec leaned forward to kiss her, balancing awkwardly on one hand. In anticipation, she tilted her head upward slightly to meet his lips. His mouth gently lingered for a moment, softly kissing her bottom lip until his tongue parted her lips completely, passionately deepening his kiss. She reached up to run her hand over the faint stubble of his face, his tensed neck and shoulder, resting her hand finally on the flexed arm that supported him. She wanted to be closer.

Sensing the strange position, Alec stopped suddenly, looking at Ellie with smoldering brown eyes.

"Here," he offered as he reached behind his shoulder with one hand, deftly pulling his white shirt over his head to expose a bronzed, chiseled belly and two dark brown nipples scattered with light-brown hair. Ellie could barely breathe. He laid the shirt behind her back and gently coaxed her to the ground.

"Better?" he asked quietly in her ear as he lay next to her in the grass, propped up on one elbow. Ellie answered by touching his face gently and placing one finger over his mouth; she nodded her head slowly without breaking his gaze. He leaned over her partially—his warm, bare chest rubbing against Ellie's arm—began kissing her again, and then stopped to watch her face as he ran his hand over her cheek, down her neck to rest at the shoulder strap of her dress. His fingers played over the strap and then slipped it slowly down her arm, freeing one breast, which he cupped in his hand. Ellie realized she was holding her breath.

"You're perfect," Alec exhaled passionately, moving his hand over her nipple, and then leaning down to taste her.

"Ohh," Ellie moaned as his wet tongue circled her nipple and then took her breast into his mouth, sucking hard. She grabbed his shoulders with tensed fingers and then ran her nails down his exposed back. She was so aroused that she ached. He moved to her other breast, kissing, sucking, teasing.

Ellie couldn't bare it. She pushed herself under him, the weight of him hot and hard on top of her. The veins in his arms popped out under the stress of his restraint. Ellie groped desperately at his belt, this time not hesitating to unbuckle him. She needed him inside of her. She needed to cure the throbbing ache between her legs.

Finally she succeeded in undoing the belt, reaching in to find him more than fully ready. Alec gasped at her touch, pushing her dress up to get at her panties.

In one deft move, he pulled her underwear down and freed one leg, parting her first with his fingers and then resting just the tip of himself inside her.

"I want you," Ellie begged.

"I know." Alec moved in just the slightest bit further.

"Please," Ellie demanded.

"I want you too." Alec inhaled, burying himself completely. Ellie cried out. The sound seemed to urge him on—his tongue searching her mouth as he set a slow, sensual rhythm with his hips that Ellie met thrust for thrust.

For several sublime minutes, they lingered in this bliss, exploring each other's bodies between the slow, heavenly meeting of their hips. Ellie's hands traveled all over Alec's broad shoulders, down the muscular hollow of his spine, and all the way to the small of his back. Her legs began to shake as she moved closer and closer to climax.

Oh, God, not yet. I could feel like this forever. Alec slowed, sensing that Ellie was near.

"Do you want to come?" he asked between kisses.

"Yes," Ellie moaned.

"Are you sure?"

"Yes!"

He quickened his pace and then slowed again until she begged for closure by wrapping her legs around him completely and grinding into him with all her force, her body seeming to move independently of her wishes to prolong the experience. Alec moved in and out again and again until Ellie finally exploded around him. He let himself go too, emptying into her with an animallike bellow and then collapsing onto her chest, his face lying against her naked breasts. Her entire body felt swollen and hypersensitive when she felt his warm mouth kissing her breast again.

"I couldn't resist!" He laughed, looking up at her through beautiful, black lashes. They lay there for a moment longer, the soft summer breeze still rustling the prairie grass in the open field next to them.

When they moved to redress, it felt surprisingly like the most natural thing in the world. Being naked midday, making love under this maple tree. The feeling of guilt that Ellie had battled last night was nowhere to be found.

In the moment, she was happy.

For six more weeks of summer, Ellie stayed at her parents' house, lost in some strange flux between the life she had left seven years ago when she first went off to college and the life in Chicago that had halted abruptly when she caught Dylan and Madison on the living-room floor. Was she eighteen or twenty-five or sixteen again? She had no sense of reality. Her parents tiptoed around her gingerly, not wanting to disturb her delicate state of mind, which meant she had free reign to be as irresponsible and unambitious as she pleased.

She wasn't working, she wasn't going to school, and she wasn't writing. She spent every waking moment she could with Alec—eating, going to movies, playing pool at the bar, riding horses. Drinking. A lot. Having sex. A lot. Everywhere. Several times a day. She knew she had to return to Chicago at some point, but for those six weeks, she put it out of her mind completely. It was the only way to heal. When her father came into her room one day at the end of August and sat at the end of her bed, sighing heavily and saying, "Ellie, I don't want to see you throw away all you've worked so hard for. I think it's time you considered returning to school." Ellie knew her hiatus was over.

The view from Ellie's dorm room was dismal. She felt like she'd been condemned to prison, having to return to the dorms, this ten by ten cellblock. *Only four more months.* Then she could leave. She could go "home," wherever that was, or she could look for work as a full-time professor. Six weeks ago, she had hoped to stay on at the University of Chicago. Now, looking out her cellblock window, she couldn't imagine staying in this city. Everything she had once loved seemed anathema to her now. She couldn't shake this feeling of paranoia closing in on her; Dylan was everywhere in this city. Ellie's fear of running into him or seeing him somewhere began to illogically consume her. She was afraid of having to confront him. What darkness might she spiral into if she were to see him again accidentally? Jim Lawson humored his eldest daughter by agreeing to take Becca to the brownstone with him in order to gather Ellie's belongings and move her into the dorm. Ellie had hysterically refused to ever go near there again.

Then they brought Ellie up to her new exile at the University of Chicago and left her there alone, choked by the smell of institutional disinfectant, the room bare except for a plastic-covered mattress, a cork board, and a rotary phone. At least as a doctoral candidate, she was given her own room. In the grips of confused despair, Ellie set her pillow on the bed and lied down to sleep, the afternoon sun still blazing through the uncurtained window.

The first week back was not as lonely as Ellie had expected. Dr. Messing kept her busy all day, and the *Frankenstein* paper she still had to complete kept Ellie busy at night. She had taken a much different approach in regards to a psychological analysis of Mary Shelley—Ellie no longer admired the romance of Mary and Percy Shelley and Percy Shelley's influence on his young mistress. Surely Mary Shelley knew he was a cheater and a liar. Ellie would skewer that cheating son of a bitch, Percy Shelley, any way she could and make the paper more about him. Her anger kept her focused on writing. Anger felt better than melancholy.

And Alec *did* call her every single night. After she spent hours working on her essay or cathartically writing poetry in the library, she would go back to her room to wait for his call. There wasn't very much to say, though. She just missed being near him. Feeling wanted. Their relationship was so physical that it was difficult to get a sense of comfort through the telephone. And she had felt so ill since she'd moved back. The fact that she hadn't been eating much probably didn't help. Ellie secretly wondered if she felt ill because she hadn't eaten or if she hadn't eaten because she felt too ill. Was she so tired because she was depressed or because she was sick? Physically, she just didn't feel like herself. Physically, something had changed.

The second Friday after coming back to Chicago, Ellie found herself returning to her dorm room with absolutely no plans for the weekend. All her friends in Chicago were Dylan's friends too, and she wasn't ready to reach out to anyone, to reenter their circle and risk running into him. A profound sadness settled over her as she made her way toward the front desk to retrieve her mail. She would just go upstairs and lay down. She was exhausted and nauseous anyhow.

The girl at the front desk handed Ellie her mail. There was only one letter. Ellie knew the handwriting

143

immediately. Her heart skipped a beat in her chest. Should she even open it? Should she do that to herself? She took the elevator up to her room, shut the door behind her, and sat absently on the bed, staring at the white envelope that she'd laid on her lap. Curiosity got the better of her. Tentatively she tore it open.

My beautiful Ellie,

The past month and a half has been pure misery without you. I'm sure your mother never gave you my messages or bothered to tell you I called, but I did.

I'm so sorry for what I've put you through. Since we've been apart, I've had time to think, and I've realized that I just took you for granted. I just took for granted that you'd always be around and you'd love me no matter what. And I was selfish thinking I could have you and every other woman too.

But I realize now that I don't want anyone else. I just want you. I know that now. I know I don't want to live without you. I know that you've always been faithful to me. I know now that no one will ever love me as much as you do. I can't go on like this another day.

Thinking of you being with anyone else is driving me crazy. I love you with my entire being.

Please forgive me. Please. I'm begging you to give me another chance. I promise I can be a better person. I promise I will be the person you thought I was. I can change. If you just give me another chance, I promise I will change.

We can still have the life we dreamed of, the life we had planned.

Yours forever,
Dylan

Ellie's hands trembled as she finished reading the letter, but no tears surfaced in her eyes. *Too late, Dylan. Much too late.* She felt sorry for him and sorry for herself, but there was no going back now. The life they dreamed of was dead. All that remained was a sense of inexorable disappointment, a quiet resignation that all was lost. She still loved him desperately, and maybe she always would, but she could never trust him again; their relationship was tainted. A life with him would mean a life of looking over her shoulder constantly. And, well, she hadn't exactly stayed "faithful" either—not in the

E. J. Densmore

sense that he probably assumed she had. She hadn't sat around pining after him. She had drowned her sorrows in sex; perhaps she wasn't who he'd thought she was either.

Ellie ripped the letter in half once, then again, and again, and again until it was shredded into a pile of tiny pieces. She gathered it up in her hands and placed it gently in the bottom of the garbage.

Cutting through the silence came the shrill ring of the phone. Ellie literally jumped, her heart beating rapidly. She almost laughed at herself. It was certainly Alec.

"Hello?" she sounded winded.

"Hi, beautiful!" Alec's enthusiastic voice lit up the phone. "You sound tired."

"I am. It's good to hear your voice, though." She sat back down on the bed, emotionally drained. "I think maybe I'll go to sleep."

"Really? Why so early? It's only five."

"It's been a long week, and I haven't been feeling very well."

"Do you think you could stay awake for just a little while longer?" Alec inquired hopefully.

"I guess," Ellie said, confused. "Why?"

"Because I'm in the lobby right now! I missed you too much. Surprise! Can I come up?"

"Of course you can!" Ellie nearly cried. He immediately hung up the receiver.

Minutes later, the two stood in Ellie's open doorway, locked in a desperate embrace. Ellie buried her face in Alec's chest, the top of her head resting perfectly under his chin, her arms wrapped around his waist. She was never so happy to see someone in her entire life. Sensing how emotional she was, Alec made no attempt to move. He ran his hands over her back and down her hair, silently offering what comfort he could.

"I'm happy to see you too," he whispered, kissing the top of her head. Ellie stepped back from him, looking up slightly to meet his concerned gaze. For what seemed like ages, she searched for the proper words.

"I think I'm pregnant."

For a moment, Alec did not move.

"Really?" His hands still rested on Ellie's shoulders, but his face, the tone of his voice, were indecipherable. He dropped suddenly to his knees in front of Ellie and hugged her waist, placing his face against her stomach. Then, as if the news had really just sunken in, he asked, "I'm going to be a father?"

Looking up at Ellie with such an unexpected joy, he had rendered her speechless.

"I promise you I will be the best dad! I promise you I will give this baby everything!" He kissed her stomach over and over and then rose to kiss Ellie's face. "Marry me!"

Five

"I celebrate myself and I sing myself
And what I assume, you shall assume,
For every atom belonging to me
As good belongs to you."

—WALT WHITMAN, "SONG OF MYSELF"

Ellie was taking her own sweet time getting to work on the Friday morning a week after her first debate with Dr. Liam Curran. She had had a good, long run in the sublime freshness of a summer dawn. Like a natural morphine drip, it had set her so at ease that even Alec, in his usual morning snit, could not drag her down into a foul mood. Unfortunately those endorphins from running had also sapped any sense of time or urgency. She hummed softly to herself as she put on her makeup and dried out her hair. All Ellie could focus on was the fact that in a few hours, she would be escaping with Marta to Chicago for a weekend of dancing. Secretly. To the rest of the world, they would be attending some boring English conference, when really they would be hiding out from reality for two days, lost in a dark, anonymous world of hard-driving bass. Ellie was high with anticipation. God, she needed to let off some steam!

"Where are you going again?" Alec asked as he fumbled for the coffee pot.

"Chicago," Ellie answered, shoving her laptop into its protective sleeve inside her leather bag. She glanced up at the clock. Shit! She was feeling so complacent, so relaxed, that she hadn't noticed the time. Ten minutes behind her normal schedule! She hated being late.

Who cares? Marta is probably still in the shower. If she bothers to shower!

It was true. Why did Ellie care? Marta was always late, and anyhow, Megan would start class if need be. Ellie avoided taking advantage of her assistant, though. Too much bad karma. Her days as Dr. Messing's "go-to girl" were still fresh (but not fond) memories.

I do not want to be Dr. Messing.

"Jordan is camping with Andy's family tomorrow?" Alec confirmed.

"Yes. I left his schedule on the refrigerator." She walked over and pointed to the sheet of paper, making sure Alec eyed it, committing its location to memory. This certainly wasn't the first time that Ellie had left her fourteen-year-old son, but she always wrote express instructions anyhow. Not that they were followed—don't eat too much takeout (They always had a feast of junk food while she was away.). Don't let him stay up too late (Jordan always appeared exhausted and hollow eyed when his mother arrived home.). Call me if you need me (No one ever called.). Ellie always left home feeling a bit guilty and worried but returned to a house that was still standing and a child who was still alive.

Well, usually.

Except the one time.

Ellie forced that memory from her head. Too happy to think about that now.

"Jordan should bring his cell phone," Alec suggested.

"Of course he'll bring his cell," Ellie snipped. She was irritated at the obvious suggestion when she was running so late. She didn't have time for a discussion.

"I'll give him his allowance money early," Alec stated as he turned to lean against the kitchen counter. It was an invitation to argue.

"He didn't finish cleaning the garage yet!" Ellie pointed out in frustration.

"I know that's what you told him he had to do, but he won't have time with soccer practice, and he needs the money for this weekend," Alec explained.

"Listen, Alec, you are going to create a spoiled brat with a sense of entitlement if you keep handing him money without making him earn it. I don't appreciate you undermining my authority with him either." She scowled. "Give him the money on the condition that he finishes cleaning the garage. It's a loan."

"I'll give my son money whenever I want. Give me a break. He's not spoiled."

"I didn't say he was spoiled. I said he's going to be spoiled if this continues!"

Damn. I am doing exactly what I didn't want to do. Standing here arguing with him.

"It's not like we don't have the money to give him," Alec continued.

"That's not the point!" Ellie felt exasperated.

"Why are you always so adamant about making the kid suffer? I wasn't a child of privilege the way you were. So sue me if I want to give my son everything I didn't have."

Ellie could barely contain her surprised laughter. It was true that her childhood was not marked by constant moves or a revolving door of stepparents the way Alec's was, but she would hardly call mucking out stalls and working on a farm a "privileged" upbringing. No one lived in Maggie Lawson's house without earning his or her keep! Ellie gathered up her bags, her bottle of water, and her purse and headed toward the door. Such an ignorant comment didn't even dignify a response. Alec knew what buttons to push to engage Ellie ("making the kid suffer" and the "you're a crappy mother" insinuation), but she wasn't going to bite. She and Alec couldn't agree on anything lately, so why bother?

"I'll check in on him tomorrow," she added.

The door slammed blissfully behind her, effectively freeing her from the unbearable weight of contention that seemed to be crushing her and Alec lately. Her troubles were sealed off at the closing of the door. Maybe she would just get into her car and drive and drive without ever looking back. Maybe she would just drive until the road ended at the sea. The idea made her smile to herself as she set her laptop and a small overnight bag in the back seat of her car.

Well, at the very least, the car would stop at Lake Michigan tonight, windows down, speakers thumping! She waited until she pulled the car onto the county road and then pressed the accelerator down with authority, blaring the song "Cocktail Queen" at a near-deafening volume. It was Marta and Ellie's road trip anthem. Marta actually got the lyrics tattooed around her ring finger during a trip to Miami. (*"This is my only devotion," she joked.*) Marta was married to partying. Fitting.

Ellie's smile broadened. Today was going to be a good day.

At 10:00 a.m., Ellie found herself watching the clock anxiously. She wasn't really engaged in the discussion she was supposed to be leading: the WWI poetry of

Wilfred Owen. Too heavy for today. Maybe she should let Megan handle it. Maybe she should just sneak out for a bit. She scanned the small group of people who bothered to show up for a nine o'clock class on Friday. There were seven or so exchange students of Dr. Curran's in the class. Ellie wondered what they were telling him about her lectures. Would it make her look bad to leave class?

Oh my God, he's not your boss! Why do you care what he thinks? Why don't you go sit in on his class?

Yes! That was a brilliant idea! She would go sit in the back of *his* lecture today. Wasn't that the agreement after all? Weren't they to learn from one another? Wasn't he supposed to sit in on Ellie's class too? And yet, he hadn't visited once in this past week since the debate. *Well, that's being sort of unfair. He's been settling in, planning with Marta.* What better time to pay a visit then? Maybe unnerve *him* a bit. Anything to pass the time faster than being in here.

"I'm going to drop into Marta's lecture," Ellie whispered, leaning in to Megan.

"To see Dr. Curran?" Megan's look of jealousy was thinly veiled.

"To size up the competition," Ellie explained. *Don't look so smitten, Megan. It's pathetic.*

"OK," Megan agreed pitifully. "I'll finish the class."

"Thanks." Ellie exited quickly, feeling only the slightest bit guilty for pulling a Dr. Messing. It was a justifiable distraction and had to be more interesting than leading a dreary discussion about war poetry. Ellie, feeling very pleased with her clever plan of work avoidance, nearly skipped down the stairs to the lower-level lecture hall. At the very least, she would be able to student watch at the back of Marta's class, observe the "natives" in their natural habitat. Learn something of the fucking-off habits of her own students. It wouldn't be time wasted. Just time more entertaining.

She brought a pad of paper and a pencil with her to take notes, if need be. Not dragging that laptop into a lecture. That would be rude. Too much temptation to surf the Internet. The students in her classes always thought they were quite clever with their technology—like they were so covert and so discreet—but Ellie always knew when they weren't engaged.

You're so bored sitting here listening to me? Imagine how I feel repeating myself for the twelfth year. No, she wouldn't be that rude to Dr. Curran or to Marta. She would actually listen.

Ellie snuck into a seat at the back of the lecture hall as inconspicuously as she could, entering noiselessly through a back door.

The hall was packed. Packed! On a Friday morning? During the summer?

She took one of the only open seats near the back corner, as high up as she could sit. Scanning the room, she noticed several other professors sitting with their classes.

No wonder the hall was so full. It was practically the entire English department. Had they arranged to come in and observe? *Thanks for leaving me out of the plans!* Had they not asked her because they thought she wouldn't want to go or was it expected that she should have professional courtesy enough to think of it herself? Damn! Why was she always so self-absorbed that she couldn't foresee what was socially proper? Now she felt like an ass. Unconsciously she slouched down into her seat.

No, this must have been impromptu. Marta would have told her about it if had been planned. That thought made her feel more at ease again.

Yes, Marta would have told me. I wasn't purposely excluded.

As it was, not a single person turned to acknowledge movement in the back of the room when she entered. She had safely slipped in undetected. By everyone. Except...

Liam Curran locked eyes with her from the front of the room. It was so brief that Ellie almost questioned whether or not he had really seen her. A small smirk played across his face. Her heart skipped.

Damn! He *had* seen her. Damn. Damn. Damn. Now she would have to acknowledge that she had been there, had snuck in late. That looked worse than not coming at all.

Marta, looking perfectly at ease, leaned against the wooden table that supported the projector, her bare, tattooed arms folded over casually, her burgundy hair its usual unruly mess. Ellie absently wondered if Marta was stoned. To look so calm all the time. Ellie leaned in a bit and squinted. Maybe she could send Marta a psychic message: *Look up here!* But Marta, like the rest of the audience, was engrossed in Curran's presentation. The huge overhead screen read: "Walt Whitman— Buddhist Visionary?"

A girl toward the middle of the hall raised her hand. "So do you think that Whitman was aware that his poetry resembled Buddhist theory? Was he consciously writing a spiritual manifesto?" she asked once Professor Curran had nodded to her.

"That's an excellent question," he pondered as he rubbed his chin in thought. He walked across the front of the hall slowly and then leaned next to Marta at the table for a moment, obviously contemplating what the girl had asked. His stature dwarfed Marta, shoulders as broad as a basketball player's but so comfortable in his size that he was almost graceful. He wore a pair of jeans and a fitted oxford, looking at once professional and comfortable, the reading glasses poking out of his breast pocket—the only nod to his age.

"What do you think?" he redirected to the audience. *Nice. Very Socratic.* Asking his class before influencing their interpretation with his own opinion seemed a sincere gesture, not forced, but practiced and natural. Hands shot up.

"Yes?" he pointed to a male student in front.

"I think Whitman was simply experimenting with Eastern thought. I think there were too many other things going on in America at the time he was writing for him to be confident enough to write a spiritual manifesto."

"Interesting." Professor Curran did not move from the table. The audience waited anxiously for him to weigh in, to confirm. "I do agree with you." He addressed the student. The boy looked pleased. "We can't ignore that the very first lines of 'Song of Myself' are 'I celebrate myself and I sing myself, and what I assume you shall assume, for every atom belonging to me as good belongs to you.'"

"I'd like to assume some of his atoms," the girl sitting in front of Ellie whispered to her friend. Ellie choked with surprised laughter. The girl glanced up suddenly, crimson.

Professor Curran continued. "The fact that he opens such a lengthy poem with lines that confirm the interconnectedness of all living things is impossible to ignore. After all, here is his thesis, yes?" The group nodded in assent. "Rather, I like to read 'Song of Myself' as a spiritual stream of consciousness. Whitman wants the reader to contemplate what he would have called 'oriental' concepts of spirituality just as he himself was doing, I imagine."

"But in the way that Thoreau contemplated the practice of Eastern meditation by choosing to 'live deliberately' in the woods in *Walden*," Marta offered.

"Absolutely," Liam Curran agreed emphatically. He was obviously charged by the line of questioning and the interest of his audience. Ellie found herself lost in his words, like the rest of the students, fascinated by him. His enthusiasm was contagious.

"Walt Whitman, like Thoreau, like all of us, seems to be on a spiritual journey. With all the tumult of his generation—the violence of slavery and the American Civil War and the assassination of President Lincoln—one should not be surprised that an American poet would be so preoccupied with the origin of his existence. Life after death. The very meaning of life, of suffering." He stopped suddenly and walked up a couple of steps into the audience. Every set of eyes in the hall followed his movement.

He launched into a verse by memory as the audience sat transfixed. "A child said what is the grass? Fetching it to me with full hands; How could I answer the child? I do not know what it is any more than he. I guess it must be the flag of my disposition. Out of hopeful green stuff woven, Or I guess it is the handkerchief of the Lord…And now it seems to me the beautiful uncut hair of graves."

Waiting quietly, he allowed the group to contemplate.

"So back to your question." He motioned to the girl who first raised her hand. "Was Whitman writing a manifesto?" He walked up several more steps, stopping directly next to Ellie's shoulder. She stopped breathing. *Keep looking at your hands.* Marta finally made eye contact with Ellie. Some flash of understanding passed between the two of them. Was that a laugh Marta suppressed? Liam Curran did not move, his smooth British accent resonating deeply above Ellie's head. Even his voice was lovely.

"I believe that Whitman was on a path toward spiritual understanding, enlightenment. One might argue the entire writing of 'Leaves of Grass' where 'Song of Myself' appears was part of that journey—his rambling style, the vacillation between uplifting poems and elegies. Whitman is verbally meditating—taking the reader on a journey of both physical sensations and of sweeping existential questions. Consider the difference in passages from 'Song of Myself,' such as the infamous nude men bathing in the river, all very sensual and visual. Compared with a passage where he asks, 'What is grass?'—in other words, 'What is life?'—and then ultimately posits that 'the smallest sprout shows there really is no death.'" He paused again to let the audience absorb what he had said.

"Certainly very Buddhist in its appreciation of the present while simultaneously acknowledging the perpetual continuation of life through nature. Rebirth? Reincarnation?" Again he paused for a minute or two. "Through this stream of consciousness, this meditation, if you will, Whitman searches for meaning just as the reader searches for meaning. He forces the reader to be mindful of the present, what is…"

"Not what is meant." It was out of her mouth before Ellie realized she had said it aloud. She put her hand up to her mouth in surprise, making it even more conspicuous.

Liam Curran looked down at her, his bright-green eyes hinting at a smile. "Perfectly stated, Dr. Purnell. Whitman urged his readers to be mindful and appreciative of what truly is as opposed to obsessing over what is meant." All eyes focused on Ellie, but she had no more accidental words to offer. She wanted to disappear into the fabric of her chair.

"Perhaps what is and what is meant are one and the same," he added without turning away and then changed direction, "Let's analyze some specific passages." Saving Ellie from any more unwelcome attention, he turned to walk back down the steps of the lecture hall. The audience shuffled their notebooks and novels, iPads and laptops fired up, ready to take notes.

Ellie sat engrossed, like the rest of the audience, for the next hour. Dr. Curran was both insightful and humorous, entertaining and thought provoking. Ellie found her thoughts drifting to her childhood, her first introduction to Whitman. Her father would often quote Whitman: "I am the poet of the Body and I am the poet of the soul. The pleasures of heaven are with me and the pains of hell are with me." Then when she or Becca would get into trouble, Jim Lawson would say jokingly, "Don't be the pains of hell!" Maggie Lawson would roll her eyes at her husband's self-amusement. The girls soon came to understand his vague literary references and could quote any number of authors, although the true meaning of the words was lost on them. It was strange and invigorating to sit in Curran's lecture and contemplate this very familiar literature with a fresh perspective. *Wow. What an unexpected reaction.* Ellie had to admit that this Liam Curran was, in fact, living up to his hype.

"I am so grateful for such a warm and welcoming reception." Professor Curran ended the class nearly an hour and a half later. "Please return at any time. I'd be honored to have you again attend my lecture." The crowd broke into enthusiastic applause.

Ellie stayed seated while people gathered their belongings, turned their cell phones back on, checked their text messages. Then they started filing out. The hall began to clear except for a large group that had gathered around Curran at the front table. Marta began packing up, shutting off the projector, signing off her laptop.

Ellie thought she should go up and shake Liam Curran's hand, tell him how much she had enjoyed the discussion. Maybe she should explain why she had walked in an hour late. No. That would be lame. It was completely innocent after all. Making excuses would just make her look guilty.

Marta waved to Ellie and then pointed at her watch and motioned toward the door. It was the unmistakable "let's get the hell out of here" cue. Ellie looked tentatively at Dr. Curran and his crowd of admirers and hesitated. Should she wait? No. She exited the back door she had come in.

Several hours later, both Ellie and Marta stood at the window of their suite in The Four Seasons Hotel, admiring the view of Lake Michigan. The sun was setting behind the opposite side of the hotel, sending blinding, brilliant bursts of light reflecting off the glass of the surrounding skyscrapers, creating at once a scene both surreal and serene. Looking out at the beach, the tops of trees, tiny cars, and people scurrying below, Ellie felt oddly at peace. She had a complicated relationship with the city, her old home. A lot of conflicting emotions. In this moment though, standing inside The Four Seasons hotel, somehow erased all the misery of her younger experiences in Chicago.

She walked over to the refrigerator and took out a chilled bottle of wine. *Let's drink to making it out alive!* Marta brought her a corkscrew and two glasses.

"You're going to miss this view if you don't come back here tonight!" Ellie teased. Ellie and Marta usually stayed someplace upscale when they snuck out of town, but this was by far the biggest splurge Ellie had ever made. And so what? She was nearly forty, and she could afford it. Again it was a far cry from her days in Dylan's parents' brownstone.

"I'm not saying I won't come back with you, I just don't want to make any promises," Marta explained, handing Ellie a glass. They both stood at the window, sipping their wine, watching dusk begin to drag long shadows between the buildings. "What do you have planned for tomorrow?"

"I don't know," Ellie admitted.

Maybe I will venture out to the Art Institute.

Maybe. If she felt brave enough. Wander the halls again, maybe visit her old friend, "Interrupted Reading." "What are *your* plans?"

"I'm planning to get laid," Marta announced definitely. Ellie nearly choked on her drink.

"So sure of yourself, are you? Is this the reason for the costume?" Ellie pointed to Marta's uncharacteristically feminine dress—an innocent-looking black poplin mini, with spaghetti straps and a button-up ruffled front that she had belted around her tiny waist.

"Aww! That's cruel, Ellie!" Marta smacked her on the shoulder playfully. "Is it bad?"

"No, you look adorable, Marta.

"Good! I'm trying for cute." Marta tilted her head and batted her eyes as she curtsied.

"Very convincing." Ellie raised her glass.

"And I see you mean business tonight as well." Marta was referring to Ellie's skinny jeans and Chuck Taylor's.

"Old girl is going for a workout!" Ellie kidded. When she went to a party like this, it was to dance. And dance only. She wasn't there to drink. She wasn't interested in the drug scene. She wasn't there to socialize—it was too loud to talk anyhow. She had no interest in being hit on, on making an impression. She didn't want anyone's attention. She just went to dance. To be lost in the impossibly deep, soul-thumping beat of a constant bass, the ecstasy of constant movement, the meditation of all-encompassing sound, where she could disappear into the writhing crowd and become invisible.

And so she dressed properly—a black spaghetti tank and flat shoes that she could dance in for hours. She had straightened her dark chestnut hair so that it fell several inches beneath her shoulders but wore a hairband around her wrist. Tucked into her back pocket was a knit cap just in case her hair became hopelessly drenched.

She had teased Marta about her appearance, but in reality, Ellie's outfit was more a costume than her best friend's. Ellie had the appearance of one of her students, a woman much younger—the complete opposite of the guarded, polished professor she usually masqueraded as. To Ellie, the transformation felt exhilarating.

She turned to Marta thoughtfully, "Did you know the entire English department was going to show up to your lecture on Whitman today?"

"Not exactly." Marta looked surprised. "Liam and I went over my syllabus a couple of days after he got there. I told him I usually spent two class periods on 'Leaves of Grass,' and he asked if he could have one of those days to present his theories. I said 'Hell yes! Please teach my class for me while I watch!' All I did today was stand up there and add my two cents, but he did all the talking. I told you this was going to be a good gig for me!"

"Well, I wish I had known I was supposed to be there." Ellie shot Marta a disdainful look.

"Don't look at me! I didn't invite anyone in. That was probably his doing," Marta surmised.

Ellie suddenly felt slighted. It hadn't even occurred to her that Professor Curran was the one who had done the inviting and that he had left her out. "Do you think he purposely didn't invite *me?*" Ellie wondered out loud.

"No," Marta answered quickly and then stopped to ponder her initial response. "I don't think he's like that. Honestly, Ellie, he's been nothing but genuinely polite."

"He's British, Marta. Of course he's polite…unless you're facing him in a debate."

Marta laughed. "Yes, unless he's harassing you about contradictory Mary Shelley essays you wrote seventeen years ago."

"I know! Weird, right? Do you remember what you wrote seventeen years ago?" Ellie asked.

"I barely remember where I *was* seventeen years ago, let alone what I was writing about in undergrad!" Marta agreed. "He does seem to know a lot about you, Ellie."

"Yeah, like what?" Ellie asked, surprised.

Really? What is there to know and why would anyone care?

"Well, for instance, the day we looked over my syllabus, we sat and talked in my office for almost two hours."

"Really?" Ellie felt annoyed. "I can't believe you haven't said…"

"We sat and talked about you, and I didn't want you to feel self-conscious," Marta admitted.

"What do you mean? What did you tell him?" Ellie's hands felt sweaty suddenly.

"It was nothing personal, really. He just asked me about certain essays you'd written; he wanted to know if

I'd read them, too—what my opinions were. He could quote several passages, list many of your theses, knew your dissertation from the University of Chicago. I mean, it was all very professional."

"Great. He probably wants to use what you told him against me in the next debate," Ellie lamented.

"It wasn't like that, Ellie. He seemed..." Marta trailed off as she searched for the proper adjective. Ellie waited sourly. "He seemed...sincere. I didn't get this competitive vibe from him. Honestly he's probably one of the most laidback people I've ever met."

"Maybe he's medicated!" Ellie laughed.

"I don't think so!" Marta replied emphatically. "I offered to smoke with him, and he refused."

"You did not!"

"I did! Right there in my office. Too bad Long wasn't there to share. He could use some weed!"

"Shut up!"

"I swear to God! I lit up with Liam sitting there, and he could have cared less. Didn't bat an eye. He just wanted to talk about your writing." Marta clapped her hands together suddenly as if she'd just remembered something important. "Oh yeah, and he asked me if you have ever published poetry. He said he found it odd that someone with such a legacy never 'tried her hand' at writing poetry. He said that someone with such a 'lovely poetic style of prose must certainly write poetry.'" Marta attempted to imitate his accent.

E. J. Densmore

Ellie's heart sank. Maybe that's what this was all about. The master researcher had somehow located Avery Vaughn. God, if he could find her undergrad paper on *Frankenstein*, he could, in fact, find anything. What could his angle be though? What could he possibly gain in revealing that Ellie published under a pseudonym? She would have to beg him not to reveal her identity if this was his plan. It would ruin everything. She might never be able to write authentically again.

"Well?" Marta asked.

"Well what?" Ellie played coy.

"Why so quiet now? I just told him I'd never seen you write poetry. And I would know, right?"

Ellie felt just the slightest bit guilty lying. "Yes, you would know."

"Did you ever write creatively?" Marta wondered.

"Sure. Don't most English majors experiment with something creative?" Ellie tried to redirect. "You've published some stories, haven't you?"

"Nothing very good," Marta admitted. "I've written a lot of hate poetry in my life, but that was basically personal therapy."

"It's all personal therapy, Marta. Haven't you ever read my father's work?"

"Yeah, I just like to believe a lot of his confessional stuff is made up. No offense, but the picture of your father getting it on with multiple mistresses kind of creeps me out!"

"Me too," Ellie admitted. "Maybe it *was* all made up. I'd like to think that it's *mostly* made up, but who knows?"

"So are we ready to do this?" Marta downed the last of her wine.

Ellie knew Marta was avoiding anymore discussion and agreed to change the mood. "Yeah, let's go."

Their cab pulled up in front of an unassuming brick façade located somewhere in the heart of the Back-of-the-Yards neighborhood, not too far from Ellie's college haunts. The couple of glasses of wine Ellie had enjoyed at the hotel made for a mellow ride, but now, driving through this part of the city, she had a strange sense of déjà vu. Maybe it was their proximity to the University of Chicago or the hot, still air that smelled vaguely of sewer and exhaust. And something else. Rain. Ominous clouds hung east over the lake. Something felt oddly familiar. Ellie was aware that all these years, she hadn't been in Chicago during the summer. Maybe that's all it was. Her memory of the heat. All her memories.

"Do you know where the entrance is?" Ellie laughed when the cab halted.

"Let's follow them," Marta suggested, pointing to two men in jeans and a woman wearing a scandalously short skirt and freakishly high platform shoes. Or maybe that was a man in the skirt and platform shoes. Who could tell? When Ellie wasn't dancing, people watching was always deeply entertaining. There would be beautiful shoes and sequins and wigs and skin. A lot of bare skin. Intricate tattoos and piercings and leather. And sometimes feathers. It was a fascinating scene, a conglomeration of those, like Ellie, who wished to escape, to go unseen, and those who wanted to be part of the show. The vibe was always positive, though. Ultimately people came to dance. What could be happier than that?

Ellie handed the cabbie a twenty and slid out of the car. She and Marta followed the other three people down a well-lit alley where the sound of drums, harsh ghostly whispers, seeped through the bricks. A door opened, allowing sound to escape like a sudden blowhorn. Ellie dug into her back pocket to get the invitations Marta had told her to hold. She thrust them into the hand of the hulking man at the door, who then quickly ushered them in.

Sound immediately enveloping them, they were transported into a fantasy world inside what must have once been some sort of factory space. The soft glow of white candlelight that lined the walls from mesh sconces on the floor created a strangely romantic glow that softened the cold metal appearance of industrial staircases and cement floors. Flowing white fabric hung from entryways. The fifty-foot ceilings were covered with white, iridescent helium balloons. The effect was spectacular. Ellie felt as if she were floating, lost in a very serene dream.

"Wow!" she mouthed to Marta, who looked equally overcome. This was by far the most elaborate decorating they'd seen at a party. Marta's friend, Tony, had finally gotten his big break last year, releasing his first commercially successful CD. His collaboration with a Southside rapper on one of the songs had brought him back to Chicago to promote. This visual masterpiece had to be the work of his record label.

Marta and Ellie had the good fortune to be invited to this event with VIP access to Tony, of course. Such success couldn't have happened to a nicer guy. As it turned out, the Cuban Adonis, the desire of every woman in the room, was as educated and talented as he was attractive. Over the years, Ellie had met Antonio only a handful of times, but she sensed the admiration wasn't only one sided. There was a playful flirtation between her and Tony. And when she came to dance? Well, he made it worth her while. Oftentimes, she felt as if he played the entire night just for her. He jokingly called her "Commander," after a song that he claimed captured her personality on the dance floor.

Ellie and Marta ascended a metal staircase, which led them to an open platform overlooking the wide expanse of warehouse space. Another DJ, the opening act, worked a dance floor that was still fairly empty.

"I'm going to get a drink!" Ellie yelled.

Marta shook her head. "We're VIP! Let the waitress do that!"

Ellie shrugged in agreement. The back of the platform actually led to a second floor, a set of small rooms that had been fashioned into sitting areas behind the DJ equipment, furnished with plush burgundy settees that looked turn of the century, an interesting contrast to the modern feel of the sconces and the curtained entryways. The effect was warm and dreamlike. Looking down onto the main floor from above, Ellie noticed several other similar sitting areas had been constructed against the walls, each with partially curtained entries, allowing observers only a glimpse of what was inside. Waitresses scurried in and out carrying trays.

Ellie smiled to herself. *Very sensual touch. People watching might prove even more interesting this evening.* Already the elaborate hairstyles and feather boas were making a smattered appearance.

"Beauties!" Antonio held out his arms to Marta and Ellie as they located his curtained space. He rose from a settee where he sat surrounded by several young women, all skin and glitter. *Disposable girls.* It was a shame really. Someone of Antonio's intellect and talent couldn't possibly be interested for too long in women so shallow and obvious.

But I bet they're a lovely temporary distraction.

It reminded Ellie of the college bars. Same scene. Different place. Young women as desperate as the young men to hook up. Groping for some physical connection to validate their worth. Flesh. Emptiness.

Tony hugged Marta and then kissed both her cheeks. Turning to Ellie, he grabbed her shoulders to assess her and then took her into his arms, "You've come to dance, I see!" he breathed happily into her ear. Kissing her on the forehead, he exclaimed, "I've got new stuff for you! You won't be disappointed!"

"I can't wait!" Ellie exclaimed. Tony's beaming face reminded her of Jordan, ecstatic to share what he'd created, anticipating her certain approval. It was endearing. Tony motioned to a waitress. "What you want to drink?" his Cuban accent emerged. "The usual?" Ellie and Marta nodded. He ordered their drinks and the waitress scampered off. Bored, his group of admirers looked on, unable to hear the conversation over the pounding music.

"I thought you had another friend coming, no?" Tony asked, confused.

Ellie shook her head. "No, just the two of us!" She looked to Marta for an explanation when a flash of sequins caught Ellie's eye.

From behind the curtain of the adjoining room slinked a curvaceous Latin goddess, unnaturally tall due to her platform thigh-high boots. Clad in the quintessential club clothes, sequined bodysuit, and hoodie, her hair spiraled out from her head, a wild, sensuous mess. Ellie's eyes narrowed as the woman approached, wrapping her long, brown arms around Marta from behind, her blood-red nails playing over Marta's chest. Marta reached up to grab her hands, leaning back into the woman, a look of childish joy lighting her expression.

Unbelievable! Ellie fumed. *That Marta! She knew Lilliana would be here the whole time!*

Lilliana. Marta's ex.

Lilliana. That sneaky, dirty whore. Ellie hated her. God, she hated her. It was too late to check herself—she shot Marta a questioning glare. But that was enough. Marta would understand everything that look contained, the "Really?" and the "You hate yourself that much?" and the "You said you'd never speak to her again!" and the "Don't you remember what she did to you?" But Ellie already knew the answer to all of those questions. After all, the answer stood in front of her, whispering into Marta's ear and giggling. Ellie's relationship with Marta was predicated on the motto, "No judgment. No questions asked."

I'm not staying up all night with you this time, Marta. No vomiting and wishing for death between passing in and out of consciousness.

Ellie sighed. What was the point in anger or lecturing? Marta wouldn't respond to it anyhow. Sometimes being near her was like watching a train wreck unfold, setting a toddler free in a room full of knives. She was bound to hurt herself somehow, and there was nothing Ellie could do to stop it.

Lilliana kissed Marta's neck behind her ear and then looked up innocently, as if she had just noticed Ellie standing there.

"Ellie!" the name rolled beautifully off her tongue, but Ellie wasn't fooled for a moment. Lilliana extended her long, thin hand.

"Hi, Lilliana! What a nice surprise! I didn't know you'd be here," Ellie said, emphasizing "here" as she looked Marta right in the eyes.

"Marta didn't tell you?" she feigned hurt, placing her hand on a cocked hip. "Naughty as usual!" She ran a red nail gently along Marta's cheek.

Gross. God only knows what lives beneath those nails.

Marta and Lilliana had lived together for several years while Marta worked on her Master's and doctorate in Miami. Supposedly it was a serious, monogamous relationship, but Ellie doubted Lilliana could ever commit to just one person. It was doubtful she could survive with just Marta's attention, even with as doting and devoted a scope of attention as it must surely have been. In fact, Ellie doubted that Lilliana was even gay at all. She was just the sort of woman who would have used being gay as a ploy to entice men, using their juvenile fascination with lesbians to attract attention to her. Lily needed everyone, men and women, to notice her. She was the embodiment of everything Ellie hated in a woman—shallow, vain, mean, dishonest, stupid, and promiscuous.

"Those are some dancing boots!" Ellie couldn't resist the urge to be snarky.

"I'll leave the dancing to you, love," Lilliana replied. "You're obviously dressed for it!"

And, Lilliana, I'll leave you to do what you're dressed for, hooker.

"Yes, I *am* ready to dance!" Ellie said aloud, smiling at Tony, who had been standing idly by the entire time. "I have no one to impress but him!" she nodded to Tony. He hugged Ellie to his side affectionately.

At once, the current DJ announced Tony to the wild applause of the crowd.

Tony hugged Ellie good-bye as he whispered in her ear, saying "Have fun tonight!"

"I will! Good luck!" Ellie bade and then turned to Marta expectantly.

"Go dance!" Marta mouthed, so she set off down the stairs to find her place on the dance floor.

Once again, a strange, unsettling sense of déjà vu set in, much like following Dylan around years ago on his quest to make connections for his band. The memory of that compared with the reality of this moment was actually empowering, though. Here, now, Ellie had nothing to lose. She was no longer afraid of being alone. Not like when she would have to claim Dylan in the bathroom before every show.

Ridiculous. How sad and desperate I was. Fifteen years later, Ellie didn't care that Marta would disappear with Lilliana for the night. She didn't care that Tony would return to his entourage behind the DJ booth. She didn't even care what Alec was doing back at home in Wisconsin. She had achieved a comfortable numbness that effectively shielded her from any human being.

As makeshift curtains opened from the side rooms, emptying their contents, the floor swelled with people. Ellie felt her phone buzz in her back pocket. She pulled it out. One text message.

From: Marta
Come back up! Need you!

Not a chance, Marta! Suffer.
Ellie put her phone back into her pocket and disappeared into the crowd, absorbed into a mist of bouncing bodies. She searched for some space for her sometimes wild elbows. Now that she had finished her third glass of wine, she hadn't a care in the world. Her limbs moved of their own free will, her head pivoting on her neck, her hips swaying. There was no stopping it now. Tony

deconstructed a song, down to just the bass line, adding in synthesizers, a second drum line, a hook. Ellie was familiar with this song, which sounded so much like a cross between Depeche Mode and Nitzer Ebb with a modern electronic twist. Everything old became new once again. Certainly Tony knew his musical influences, and this was a nod to his youth. She doubted many people here could appreciate the similarities. She could, though. It made her feel eighteen again.

Her phone buzzed in her back pocket again. She stopped to look at the text.

From: Marta
Seriously. Need you upstairs.

Sorry, Marta! No way.
Ellie moved deeper into the crowd. She wasn't looking at her phone again. Drunkenness had set in, and the music was taking over. She was going to "celebrate herself and sing herself"! *That's right. I am celebrating my damn self!* And the idea cheered her. Made her completely lose herself. Before she knew it, she was dripping with sweat, which meant, considering her cardio stamina, she had been going at it for a while. Blissfully possessed by the music that moved through her like a current, shaking her bones from the inside out, she was unaware of anything but the present moment. The flashing lights. The people moving around

her. The periodic vibration of her cell phone against her rear end, which she consciously ignored. The energy of the crowd urged her on, infected her. She was completely one with this gyrating, chaotic mass. It was hypnotic.

"This is especially for Ellie!" she heard Tony yell into the crowd over the beginning of the next song, which transitioned seamlessly from the last. But Ellie recognized the song as something different. Tony had remixed one of Ellie's favorite Kaskade songs. A woman's slow, whispering voice sang out over a gradually increasing beat until the synthesizer worked into an explosive crescendo. As the tempo grew faster and the bass grew louder, the crowd answered with movement that mirrored the music in perfect synchronicity. Everything about the song—its lyrics, its sentimentality, the longing in the woman's voice, the demanding tempo—spoke to Ellie's mood. She was completely and utterly lost in the moment.

Songs later, her phone buzzed in her back pocket again. Feeling more sober and terribly dehydrated, she decided to take a break for a couple of minutes. Down a bottle of water. Maybe watch the crowd. Maybe check her texts. She pulled the knit cap from her back pocket and put it onto her head as she shimmied through the crowd toward the nearest bar. As she approached, she got a glimpse of her reflection in the mirrored backdrop. Her bare neck and chest were glowing. Her makeup gone, her face looked flush and fresh. The knit cap she wore gave her the appearance of someone very young. *Good.* At that moment, she was feeling very young.

It occurred to her that years ago, she never could understand the appeal of boys (and sometimes girls) throwing themselves into a mosh pit in front of Dylan's band. It seemed the stupidest and most dangerous thing in the world. But now she finally understood. Being out there alone at the center of the dance floor. Being lost in the moment. Being absorbed by the energy of the crowd. Searching for some life-affirming experience that would take away the monotony of everyday existence. Something that would make her feel again like the world still "seemed to lie before her like a land of dreams." How weird it was that life ran full circle. How strange and unexpected that entering middle age felt so similar to the angst of being a teenager.

Ellie ordered a bottle of water and leaned against the bar, drinking half of it down in one gulp. She wiped some from her chin as she scanned the crowd. A lot of beautiful people. She wondered what they did for a living. Did they have children? Were they here with their spouses? Girlfriends? Mistresses? Where did they return at the night's end? Were they trying to run away too? She finished the rest of the bottle of water and set it on the bar. Pulling out her phone, she checked the time. She had been out there for two hours! Fifteen texts from Marta. *Oops.* She tapped to open them.

"I like you much better without the hat," a warm voice breathed very close to her ear. Ellie turned. She was rendered speechless.

Liam Curran, wearing an amused grin, a half empty pint in hand, stood directly next to her at the bar.

Six

July of Ellie Purnell's Twenty-seventh Year

Ellie shot up in bed, startled from a light sleep. Something had woken her. Was it the baby? She swung her legs out from under the covers and then stopped to listen in the blackness. Nothing. The digital clock on the dresser read 2:37 a.m. Then she heard it again. The pitch was about the same as a baby's cry, but it was laughter.

A woman's laughter. Drunken, stupid laughter at that. *Unbelievable.* Did that woman ever stop drinking and just go to bed? Ellie lay back down on top of the comforter listening for Jordan, just to be sure. Frustration crept over her scalp and into the beginning of a tiny crease that had sprouted between her eyes over the past year and a half. *When will I ever be able to sleep again?* Really sleep. Eight hours of uninterrupted sleep. Would that day ever come? Ellie ran her hand over the cool, empty space next to her on the bed, pulling Alec's pillow toward her. If she weren't so exhausted, she might actually miss him, miss having a real person to hug instead of just a pillow. It seemed this month that he was gone more than he was home.

She supposed she should be grateful that he had so many meetings with out-of-town investors, but Ellie was just too tired and too lonely to think rationally. Her day-to-day life seemed so distant from Alec's. While he spent most of his week wooing potential investors, fulfilling customer orders, or overseeing production of materials, all she knew was the constant cycle of taking care of a toddler (mostly alone)—nursing, changing, bathing, playing, nursing, sleeping, waking—all in what seemed to be one endless day that transitioned into an endless night marked by sleeping done only in spurts. At fifteen months, their tiny bean of a son was running around and jabbering happily but still didn't sleep more than three hours at a time. He still nursed constantly, refused to take even a sippy cup or bottle, and projectile vomited most solid foods.

"He's fine." Maggie Lawson would say, dismissing Ellie's incessant worry. *"If there was something wrong with him, he wouldn't be walking so well and talking like he does. Look at him! I've never seen such a precocious child. Just keep nursing him. He will ween when he's ready, just like the horses."*

Just like the horses, Mom? *"But when will he sleep?"* Oh, God, when would he just sleep?

"I suppose when he's ready," her mother would sigh.

And yet, here he *was* asleep. And Ellie was awake. It was Linda Purnell who woke Ellie this time. Even through the walls of the pole barn that Alec had painstakingly transformed into a beautiful apartment for his new family, Ellie could hear her mother-in-law's shrill voice. *She must be outside of the house.* Sure enough, the laughter rang out again, followed by the deafening start of a motorcycle engine.

Just pull out of the driveway. Hurry, before...

Too late. Jordan screamed out and then hesitated momentarily before working himself into a wail. Ellie waited before dragging herself off the bed toward his room. Maybe he would stop. *Maybe that fucking motorcycle will pull out of the driveway, and we can all just sleep soundly. For a few weeks straight.*

No luck. Jordan continued.

As she lifted him from his bed, Ellie decided she would just let him sleep with her tonight, "bad habits" be damned. Alec wasn't home half the time anyhow. Anything to get some sleep. She would have climbed into the crib with Jordan to get him to stay asleep if she could fit.

The motorcycle still idled defiantly in the driveway. Ellie put Jordan to her breast to quiet him and lay back down on her bed. Tomorrow Alec would be home. She would tell him about the motorcycles, and the constant noise, and the partying, and the people coming and going at all hours of the night. She would tell him, and *he* could deal with it. The thought of Linda Purnell being put in her place made Ellie's face relax. She drifted off again into a half sleep with Jordan cradled in her arm.

⁓

"Have you been eating?" Maggie Lawson stopped grooming one of her mares to look her daughter over more closely. "Turn around." Ellie did as she was told, Jordan perched happily on her hip, reaching out for the horse's face with his anxious, meaty, little hands.

"Horsey!" he squealed.

"I *have* been eating." Ellie defended herself truthfully.

"How much do you weigh right now?" her mother demanded suspiciously.

"I have no idea, Mom!" This time she lied. She knew she was fifteen pounds thinner than her normal pre-pregnancy weight, but it wasn't because she wasn't eating. On the contrary. She couldn't eat enough. Jordan nursed every calorie out of her, and well, she was haggard. It was the lack of sleep. Her body never rested. As she woke four times a night, it used up every last bit of energy from any food she might have ingested. Her clothing hung off her like a scarecrow.

"Well, you don't look healthy. I'm making you lunch today. Then you're going to take a nap. Jordan can play outside with me. Right, sweet boy? You want to play with Grammie?" Maggie Lawson kissed her grandson on the forehead as she walked around the front of the horse to lead it back into its stall. Ellie watched her silently for a moment.

"Thank you, Mom. I don't know what I would do if I couldn't come here during the day sometimes. Just a change of scenery makes me feel so much better." The words even surprised Ellie as they came from her mouth. *Sometimes the isolation is enough to drive a person mad.* Her mother said nothing in response as she closed the door of the stall and secured it with a lock. Maybe Maggie Lawson was relishing the moment, enjoying the rare appreciation from her usually surly daughter. Ellie meant what she had said, though. Being at the farm was a welcome change from the solitude of their apartment, even if it meant sharing the company of her overbearing mother.

"There's really no preparing yourself for motherhood." Maggie Lawson answered finally. She stopped a moment, wiping the dust from her hands onto the front of her jeans and then resting her hands on her hips. "No matter what age you are when you have your first child, you never feel quite competent enough." She laughed thoughtfully as if she were reminiscing. "Then when you think you have things figured out, your child starts changing again and challenging you in different ways you never even expected." She nodded toward Ellie. "And some children are more challenging than others!"

"You said I wasn't colicky like Jordan though!"

"No, but you were difficult. Demanding. Not like Becca, who was content just to follow you around."

"How did you manage two of us *and* the business with Daddy gone all the time?"

"Well, your Daddy wasn't gone so much once you were a little older." Now it was Maggie Lawson's turn to lie. She turned toward the house. Ellie and Jordan followed, out of the relative coolness of the stables and into the unrelenting July sun. Ellie had a vivid recollection of her father being gone to promote his books quite a bit during her childhood. He traveled the United States and Europe, always returning with some exotic doll or fascinating little trinket for each of his daughters.

"Sometimes it was actually easier without your father here," Maggie Lawson admitted absently, as if it were an afterthought she voiced only to herself. "I was too busy to be lonely, and your grandma helped me out a lot. It's what women do."

They entered the house through the back door where Maggie could remove her boots in the mudroom off the kitchen. Ellie scanned the room before letting Jordan out of her arms to start his manic exploration of every surface and shelf within arm's reach. Once down, his tiny bowed legs carried him lightning speed, a tottering little hobbit, across the length of the house and back before Ellie could stop him. Perhaps that was why she was so thin! Ellie followed behind Jordan, not daring to stop him from his quest, for if she picked him up, he would surely arch his back and scream out in protest. She attempted to continue her conversation with her mother from the far side of the living room.

"Did you hear from Becca this week?" Ellie asked loudly as her mother rummaged through the refrigerator.

"Yes, she has exams, but then she's coming home for a week or so. She's anxious to see you and Jordan. And her horses!"

"I bet," Ellie acknowledged fondly. She missed her sister terribly. Becca was nearly done with her second year of veterinary school, and their lives couldn't possibly be any more different. Ellie had never before felt so distant from her younger sister, whose life was school, studying, and exams. Getting married and having a child had completely disconnected Ellie from the academic world.

Hell, it had completely distanced Ellie from *any* world.

She felt as though she lived outside of society. The thought depressed her. Then she felt guilty. Shouldn't she want to be home with Jordan? What was wrong with her? There were women who would kill to stay home with their babies.

Soon after Ellie and Alec were married, Alec was granted the patent for his fencing design. Jim and

Maggie Lawson lent him start-up money to create a formal business plan, hire more employees, and open a modest plant to assemble materials. In addition, Maggie's referrals and connections helped the business prosper locally. Ellie didn't *have* to work. She was completely taken care of. Something inside her felt empty and incomplete, though. And it wasn't just a sense of exhaustion. It was a sense of being unfulfilled. She craved the mental stimulation of discussing literature. Philosophy. Psychology. God, something other than *Sesame Street* or *Go Diego Go.*

And then, of course, having to deal with that white-trash imbecile of a mother-in-law who once hissed spitefully in Ellie's ear, "I know you trapped my son. I know your type." Ellie had to steel herself from bursting into a bitter laugh. *Yes, you're right. I trapped him so that I could live alone in a pole barn next to the likes of you! You've discovered my brilliant plan for the perfect life!* What type did Linda Purnell think Ellie was? The type with her doctorate who just so happened to get knocked up? Doubtful.

Guilty. Again. Those thoughts aren't fair to Alec. Or to Jordan. Ellie took a seat at the bottom of the steps where she could block Jordan from climbing. Her mother worked busily assembling sandwiches in the kitchen.

"Your father is going to retire at the end of next school year."

"Really?" Ellie was genuinely surprised. She didn't think her father would ever retire, even though he was nearing sixty. Some professors taught well into their seventies or eighties.

"He said he just wants to write. To finish this last book finally. I think he's just sick of grading essays."

"I can understand that," Ellie commiserated.

"Daddy wants you take his position at the college. He said John Long has been asking about you and that you're a shoo-in."

Ellie's heart skipped a beat. Two years ago she would have scoffed at such a suggestion. The last thing she had wanted to do was to stay in the small town where she grew up and take over her father's teaching job. Before catching Dylan cheating, Ellie and Dylan had made plans to backpack through Europe as soon as she was done with school; they would teach, write, and tour. Live like artists. Obviously that dream had died. And now that things were so different…now taking her father's job seemed like a way out of her isolation. Now it was a beacon of hope.

"That's wonderful!" Ellie squealed with unchecked enthusiasm. Her mother stopped suddenly to observe her daughter. What a reaction! Ellie was more despondent than her mother had suspected.

"The college will make you submit a letter of application, your transcripts, and your published works.

I'm sure they'll make you come in for an interview too, but it will all be just formalities according to your dad."

"I don't care what I have to do! I just need to be among books again. And adults."

"Well, it won't be until next summer, but that will give you some time to prepare."

"Just the thought of reentering the world, having some sort of a schedule, having intellectual conversations…" She trailed off. Her mother knew what she meant. Maggie Lawson nodded, pleased that her daughter seemed hopeful.

After gratefully eating her lunch, Ellie climbed the stairs to her old room, allowing her mother to take Jordan outdoors to play. Though Maggie Lawson was the least sentimental woman on Earth, she also had no interest in redecorating. Ellie's room therefore remained a time warp, exactly as she had left it almost nine years prior. Canopied twin bed. Worn patchwork quilt. Walls adorned with band posters and handwritten copies of poems. The angst-ridden words of Anne Sexton and Edna St. Vincent Millay. Ellie paused to read some yellowing papers tacked to the board near her old desk. She laughed to herself. How could she have possibly appreciated such poets at seventeen? Their words were now so much more poignant through the lens of life experience. Ellie pulled back the covers and crawled into the time capsule of her old bed. This was the most relaxed she had felt in a long while. With the happy thought of returning to university life still fresh on her mind, she fell deeply and blissfully asleep.

How is my beautiful wife? Dylan's hands moved slowly up Ellie's back to her shoulders and then down her arms and back up again. *I missed you.* She felt the mattress sink down as Dylan spooned her, his warm, hard body enveloping her. He draped his arm over her torso, hand searching the bottom of her shirt for an opening, and then a strong wide hand across her bare abdomen, resting just above the top of her panties. Skimming her stomach with long, agile fingers. Gently moving back and forth across her sensitive skin.

"Wake up, sleepy!" Alec whispered lovingly into Ellie's ear. Ellie drowsily came out of her dream, eyes blurry, straining to focus, lost momentarily between the past and present, struggling to remember who lay next to her—Alec or Dylan. How old was she? Where was she? Warm breath on her neck, underneath her hair. Kisses trailing down her bare shoulders. She was awake now, but so warm and comfortable she didn't stir. What lengths would he take to wake her? She wanted to savor the moment. "You smell so good," Alec purred in her ear. His hands slid into her underwear. "I know you're awake now." He laughed quietly. Ellie responded by placing her hand over his and guiding his fingers into her. She backed up into him, feeling the strength of his erection against her backside.

"Where is my mother?" Ellie whispered naughtily.

"Busy out back. I snuck in the front door." Alec answered between wet kisses on her neck that increased in strength as Ellie became more and more aroused, using both their hands to stimulate herself. "This isn't illegal now in the Lawson house, is it?" Alec teased as he worked Ellie's pants down and then freed himself.

"No. You're my husband." Ellie reached behind her to help guide Alec inside. She let out a gasp as he entered her and then met his slow, small thrusts eagerly and quietly.

"Oh, God, I missed you," Alec gasped into her hair. "You feel so good."

"I missed you too," Ellie whispered heavily.

"I can tell." Alec's voice was raspy in her ear as he moved just ever so slightly in and out, a controlled, sensual force that had Ellie almost holding her breath with want. She grabbed the free arm he draped over her side, burying her face in his hand, kissing his open palm.

"I wish we could just…" She started to climax. "Lay here like this forever."

Alec pulled her back forcefully against his stomach, burying himself into Ellie as deeply as he could. Hugging her with both arms, his entire body tensed suddenly and released slowly as he rested a relaxed, satisfied face in the damp, soft skin at the back of his wife's neck. They lay quietly intertwined in one another for several long moments.

"We got the Penderson contract." Alec finally broke the silence with little more than a whisper. Ellie moved slightly onto her back so she could look into Alec's face.

"Really?" Her eyes were wide in pleased wonder.

"Yes!" A broad smile spread across Alec's face. He looked tired too. From driving? Worrying? Lack of sleep? Ellie reached up to touch the stubble on his face. "Do you know what this means? We are set. We'll have the revenue now to keep the business solvent for years. We are going to be OK!"

"We are going to be better than OK!" Ellie exclaimed. "I'm so proud of you, Alec! That's wonderful, wonderful news!" She kissed him deeply, running her hands up into his disheveled brown hair. This gigantic commercial fencing contract guaranteed Alec national business and revenue for several years. The news of the contract mixed with the promise of the college professorship almost sent Ellie into rapture. Unexpectedly, hot, persistent tears sprung from her eyes.

"Are you crying?" Alec laughed in disbelief.

Nodding, Ellie laughed back. "I'm just so tired. Or maybe it's hormones. I don't seem to have any control of my emotions. I just feel so much happier now that you're home."

"Me too." Alec smiled. He kissed her again as he moved off the bed to redress. Ellie lay quietly on the bed watching him, knowing, unfortunately, that she would not be able to go back to sleep.

"Now that I've seen my beautiful wife, I want to see my beautiful boy," Alec announced as he stood to tuck in his shirt, straightening himself. "I'll see you at home?"

"Yeah, I just want to rest here a little longer." Ellie rolled back onto her side, curling up her legs.

"All right. That gives me some time to check in with my mom and share the good news," Alec said.

Ellie felt her stomach and jaw tense. *Why ruin a perfect moment with talk of her?* Ellie couldn't bring herself to fake even an ambiguous response. Surely if she tried, it would just come out an angry tirade. She wanted to have a conversation about Linda Purnell, but this was neither the time nor the place to have it. She had to craft a way to broach the topic delicately, diplomatically. Alec, wisely sensing the awkward silence, leaned over to kiss Ellie on the forehead then quickly exited, gently closing the door behind him.

When Ellie arrived back at their apartment two hours later, she was surprised that the house was so still. Empty. No sign of Alec. She had purposely taken her own sweet time leaving her parents' house—figured she'd give Alec enough alone time with his mother. Jim

Lawson had returned from work, and he and Ellie had sat out on the front porch swing for a while, leisurely discussing the possibility of Ellie starting her first full-time professorship the following school year. The presence of her father made her feel safe and calm, happy. She delighted in the view, the late-afternoon sun casting long shadows over the outdoor arena, the oaks near the house blowing lazily in the wind as the horses meandered contentedly near the fence, the endless pine forest that encircled the entire Lawson property. It was the happiest she'd felt in a very long time.

Now this.

A sense of doom hung over her. She looked up at the clock, calculating in her head exactly how much time it had been since Alec would have arrived back here. His work truck with the "Purnell Fencing" logo was parked out front. Setting Jordan down, she went into the bedroom to check for his luggage. None to be found. He must have pulled into the driveway, leaving everything in the front seat, and gone directly to his mother's house. *His house.* Really? He was so anxious to see his mother that he didn't even bother to bring in his things? Ellie felt annoyed.

Well, at least he stopped at your parents' to see you and Jordan first.

She would go inside and give the baby his bath, nurse him, and put him to bed. By then, Alec would certainly be home.

Jordan went down without a fight. His Grammie had worn him out in the fields, chased him on his little legs until he was good and tired enough to go home. Ellie stealthily shut the door of his nursery behind her and stood in the short hallway leading to their kitchen to listen. Still no Alec. Initially she was surprised that he hadn't come home to put Jordan into bed, but now she felt almost a suffocating sense of disappointment.

Damn this emotional rollercoaster. She couldn't help herself, though. All week, she had envisioned Alec coming home—in her head she pictured them making dinner together. Then he would help her with the baby's bath and put Jordan down to sleep. The two of them would spend the rest of the night just curled up together on the couch. Maybe Alec would run Ellie a bath or give her a back rub. They would make love in the tub. Or in the front room. Or both! He would take care of *her* for a change. It was a lovely fantasy that she played over and over in her head to help her get through the long, sleepless nights and the noise of constant party traffic.

Maybe she would just step outside, take a walk down the driveway, see if maybe Alec was outside. Did she really want to face her mother-in-law? Ellie had successfully avoided the woman for a couple of weeks now, which was no small feat considering they lived only several hundred feet from one another. The fact that

Linda stayed up all night and slept most days made it a bit easier, though.

The minute Ellie stepped out the side door of the pole barn, she could smell smoke, though there was no tell-tale drunken laughter or loud voices. *Just wait. It's much too early for that. The motorcycles have not arrived yet.* Maybe they wouldn't. Maybe Linda Purnell would behave better now that Alec was home. She did seem to have fewer "guests" when Alec was not away. Ellie fixed her face and boldly set out toward the smell of the smoke.

"Hi, babe!" Alec reached out his hand to Ellie as she approached from the growing darkness of the side yard. In the uncertain light of dusk, it was difficult to make out the expression on Linda Purnell's face, but the older woman's stiff body language as she shifted her scrawny, malnourished legs hinted at the cool reception Ellie was likely to get once she arrived.

"Where have you been hiding?" Linda asked sweetly. Speech and body obviously did not correspond. Alec pulled Ellie next to him affectionately.

"Yeah, Mom says she hasn't seen you much lately."

"Well, you keep different hours than us, Linda," Ellie answered equally kindly, addressing her mother-in-law directly.

So this was the game Linda was going to play? Wait until Alec gets home and then make trumped-up accusations about Ellie purposely keeping her from the

Jordan. Like Linda really cared. Unless that child came with a bottle of Jim Beam strapped to his back, she could have cared less about seeing him. Obviously the plan was to turn Alec against Ellie.

Bring it on, you tore-up hag. I can play coy. "The baby gets up very early, and you are usually asleep all day," Ellie finished. *Because you are up drinking all night.*

"She'd like to see the baby more," Alec said, reaching up to move Ellie's hair from her face. She flinched involuntarily, on the defensive. Surprisingly Alec didn't seem to notice. Ellie felt a pang of guilt at her instinctual reaction and then realized in disgust: *He's drunk too! He's fucking drunk. Unbelievable!* The guilt she had felt quickly dissipated, replaced by disgust and resentment. She tried to move away from her husband, but he held her firmly to his side.

"Linda, you are welcome to see the baby any time you want!" Ellie continued to play along. *As soon as hell freezes over.* "Jordan and I usually have no set plans. Pop on over if you want. I know you're busy with visitors every night though, so again, maybe during the day would be best. Maybe we could all go for a picnic or something." *But I'm sure you'll only come if you can drink your lunch.*

The idea of a picnic with Linda Purnell was so ludicrous that Ellie almost burst out into laughter. Breaking free from Alec's arm, she casually walked over to the sliding glass doors looking into Linda's kitchen. Sure enough, nearly an empty case of beer sat on the floor next to the garbage. *Could be from last night.* Yeah right. Both Linda and Alec held one in their hands.

"Want one?" Linda offered Ellie mockingly, shrewdly observing Ellie's snooping.

"Yes, I'd love one, Linda. I'd love about twenty actually. But I'm nursing. It's a sacrifice, but that's what good moms do." An icy silence fell over the two. Linda Purnell wasn't nearly as stupid as Ellie imagined. Again Alec seemed not to notice. "Besides," Ellie continued, "I doubt I would find a spare beer in your house, let alone twenty." She turned to Alec. "I don't want to leave Jordan in the house alone. When do you think you'll be in?"

"In a little while," he assured with a slur.

Doubtful.

"Mom and I were just celebrating the good news."

"Yeah, all that money's good news for you, isn't it Ellie?" Linda asked innocently.

"It is, Linda. Good news for you too, huh?" she responded with a sarcastic wink in her mother-in-law's direction. Then turning suddenly, she headed back toward the "barn." The closer she got, however, the less angry she felt—the hot, prickling sense of defensiveness replaced by a pervasive sadness that settled deep within her bones.

By eleven, Jordan was up again, crying to be fed. Or held. Or both. Who could tell? Ellie just obliged her son. What else could she do? Were all babies this way?

Fortunately there were no motorcycles tonight. Thank God for small favors.

After placing Jordan back in his crib, Ellie decided to at least try to lie down. She had given up on Alec returning to their bed that night. It was going to be a bender. He would surely spend the night where he fell. Even stumbling across the driveway would prove to be too much of a challenge for him.

Unfortunately Ellie had more than a few times witnessed her young husband outdrink every person in the room, with the exception of his mother. Which meant the next day he would spend every hour of light buried underneath a blanket on the living-room sofa. Not talking to Ellie. Not helping with the baby. Not taking his family out to lunch. Not going anywhere. Holed up in the house but not present. *Oh well*, Ellie thought sadly. At least he was in a good mood going into this binge. This binge was a celebration, not an escape from stress at least. *Does that make it any better?* Well, tomorrow's recovery might be less hostile.

Ellie realized she was clenching her teeth. Once again, she had vacillated between two emotions. No longer wallowing in self-pity, she felt a slow, hot rage begin to burn within her.

Hours passed as she tossed and turned until finally she heard the click of the front door and the stumble of heavy footsteps. No light. At least he was trying to be quiet. Then the crash of keys on the tiled kitchen floor. Ellie cringed. Would this wake the baby? Her mouth tasted sour with anger. She had to mentally talk herself out of confronting him now. The baby was sleeping, after all. Besides Alec would not be able to have a coherent, rational conversation in his state.

Yeah, but you might feel better if you could swear at him! That might be like waking a sleeping bear, though. Did she dare take that risk?

The footsteps started down the hallway to their bedroom. Ellie decided quickly to pretend to sleep. Better not to have an argument at this hour. She rolled over quickly to face the wall, pulling the blankets over her head. The footsteps stopped short of the bedroom, retreated hesitantly, and then sped away from the bedroom, followed by the sound of the bathroom door crashing against the wall. An agonized choke and then a splash of liquid hitting the bathroom floor echoed into the hall. Another pained moan and choking. Repeated choking. Another splash, this time into water, and then the hollow flush of the toilet. Silence.

Ellie whipped the covers off her in fury and raced for the hall. If he woke that baby, she wouldn't wait for alcohol to do him in; she'd kill him herself. As soon as she entered the hallway, the putrid, acidic smell knocked her back. Looking into the bathroom from the open door, the crime scene was as she suspected. Alec had sprayed a path of reddish-orange vomit all the way from the door, across the mirror, onto the wall and all over the floor where he had ended up on his side, arms covered in stringy puke, cradling the basin of the toilet.

"Are you kidding me?" she hissed at him, forcefully kicking the bottom of his boot as she entered, careful to avoid the mess. No answer. She kicked him in the calf.

"What?" he moaned.

Nothing. She wasn't going to say another word. Suddenly she felt a sense of calm satisfaction. *Fuck you. Sleep in your puke! I'll be damned if you think I'm helping you or cleaning you up.* She shut off the light and closed the bathroom door behind her, leaving Alec passed out in his own filth.

What if he wakes? What if he tries to get into bed smelling like that? She didn't dare lock their bedroom door; that would send him into a rage. Better just to sleep in Jordan's room. The baby was likely to wake her at least once again during the night anyhow. She grabbed a pillow and dragged the comforter off the bed, sneaking into Jordan's room to set up camp on the floor. Before she lied down, however, she made sure to lock the door.

Ellie's shoulder and hip hurt on the unforgiving floor, but she knew she was safer from confrontation if she stayed in Jordan's room. Even while drunk, Alec had the good sense to act appropriately around his son. Drunken rages were usually not the problem, but who could tell how much damage Linda Purnell had done that night by filling her son's head with nonsense? Clever old bitch. Too bad she had gotten to Alec first. Now anything negative Ellie said about the woman would just sound like Ellie was on the defensive.

Was it possible for anyone to be so thickskulled about his mother? Was Alec so blind with love for this woman that he couldn't see her obvious faults? Maybe it was too much like looking into a mirror.

Oh, God. Don't even think that.

Ellie felt sick to her stomach. What had she married into? Was Alec simply destined to be like his mother? *Wasn't he already?* Ellie quickly pushed the thought from her mind.

Ironically sleep was less evasive on the floor of Jordan's bedroom than it had been in Ellie's much more comfortable bed. Once she lied down, she fell right to sleep. By the time she awoke the next morning, realizing in ecstatic shock that Jordan had not woken, midmorning sun flooded the room. She sat up suddenly, a sense of panic overcoming her. Why hadn't Jordan woken up? Her breasts were like rocks. Was the baby breathing? She leaned over his crib frantically, only to see his angelic face sighing peacefully, still in the grips of a deep sleep. Her body willed her to wake him to eat even though she would rather have lied back down to sleep. Scooping him up from his blankets, she sat cross-legged on the floor of his room to nurse him, still listening closely for any sound of life from the bathroom.

Sure enough, the bathroom door was still shut. A fresh wave of disgust assailed her. She would get dressed, put on a hat, and take Jordan out to the farmer's market up town today. Get some fresh corn and tomatoes. Eat something from the outdoor grill. Stay gone until Alec had cleaned up his mess. This idea seemed to cheer her a bit.

Then suddenly bitter disappointment filled her chest. *Wouldn't it be so much nicer if all three of us went?* She filled up a water bottle, grabbed some diapers and wipes, and prepared to head out the door when she stopped short at the kitchen sink. Reaching down, she pulled out the Soft Scrub and left it sitting on the floor in front of the bathroom door. When Alec finally came out, he would get the hint.

She stayed out as long as she could. Three hours. At the farmer's market. At the park. Up town at the library. Finally Jordan had had enough. It was early afternoon, and he was ready for his nap. Ellie had no choice but to return home.

By the time she pulled in the driveway, Jordan was fast asleep. Ellie gently pulled him free of his straps and hauled him into the house. On the way down the hall to Jordan's room, she spotted the bottle of

Soft Scrub, still overtly sitting in front of the bathroom door that was now opened. She glanced into the bathroom. No Alec. He must have moved to find someplace more comfortable to sleep. Something about the thought of him opening the door and consciously stepping over the bottle of cleaner without thinking to clean up his mess incensed Ellie. Her heart began to race in her chest. She set the baby down in his crib as quickly and gently as she could with hands that shook with rage.

"Are you planning on getting up anytime today?" she asked Alec sarcastically as she loomed over him. As predicted, he was curled into a "C" on the living-room sofa, one free arm covering his eyes. He didn't answer immediately. "Well?"

"Yes, of course," he replied nonchalantly as he rolled over to face Ellie.

"Long night?"

"Yeah. You know, my mom was lonely. I just got wrapped up in talking to her," he explained, as if nothing were wrong, as if he had just stayed over there a half hour too long. As if he hadn't defiled their bathroom.

"Your mom is lonely?" Ellie couldn't check her contempt. *I'm lonely, you fucking idiot. I'm lonely!* But she was too proud to say it. Shouldn't a husband want to be with his wife? Shouldn't he want to be with her? Why did she have to beg him to pay attention to her and Jordan? Why did she have to compete with the alcohol and his mother?

Picking up on her tone, Alec slowly pulled himself to a sitting position, "Yeah, she's lonely. Why is that so difficult to believe? You don't ever spend any time with her while I'm away." His accusation stirred Ellie's anger into an indignant fury.

"You're kidding me, right?" Ellie had to steady herself against the arm of the sofa, she was so blinded by disbelief. "Your mother is *not* lonely, Alec, trust me. She has people over there all hours of the night. *Every night!* People who ride in on the loudest motorcycles you've ever *heard*! People who let their motorcycles idle endlessly, keeping me awake! How can a person with a house full of guests every *goddamned* night be lonely?"

"That's bullshit, Ellie," Alec denied.

"Really? I'm making this up? Why would I make this up? How could I even begin to make this up? I'm too tired to be creative!"

"You don't like her."

"Really? I don't like her? Whatever gives you that impression?"

"Give me a break, Ellie."

"No, Alec, really. Why wouldn't I like her? Why wouldn't I like a woman who at every turn accuses me of trapping you?"

"When has she ever done that?"

"Were you so drunk last night that you don't remember her snide remark? 'This money really benefits you, doesn't it, Ellie?'"

"How is that snide?" Alec seemed unconvinced.

"Oh, give me a break. How is that snide? I'm benefitting from all the money you make because I trapped you. That's what she meant."

Alec still looked on cynically. His genuine, oblivious doubt sent Ellie into a near-hysterical tirade. "That woman acts like I couldn't make my own money. Like I *needed* you to make my life complete. Like I *needed* you rescue me from the same pointless, pathetic type of life that she's always had."

Once it shot from her mouth, Ellie knew she had pushed too far, but she couldn't reign herself in. The horse was out of the stall. May as well go all in now. "She must think that every woman on earth is as desperate as she is to hold onto a man. Like you define who I am as a person or something. Like I was nothing before you came into my life. I went to college for nine fucking years!" Ellie worked herself into a fit. "I have a fucking doctorate! I don't need to take shit constantly from some lowlife bitch who cans corn in a factory and spends most of her waking hours so drunk that she doesn't even know what time it is!"

Alec looked eerily calm, but Ellie knew better. He rubbed his face slowly before answering, almost inaudibly, "That 'lowlife bitch' is my mother, Ellie." Then he stood up suddenly, looking down slightly to meet her eyes. "It doesn't matter if she drinks, cans corn, bartends, or whatever else you think is so beneath *you.*

She's still my mom, and I love her no matter what. And you," he said, poking his finger hard into Ellie's shoulder, "better never talk about her like that to me ever again." He turned to walk away.

Ellie followed him down the hall. "Don't walk away from me!" she threatened in a hard whisper.

"I'm done listening to this." He motioned toward Jordan's door as if to imply that Ellie should keep her voice down. The gesture was a calculated slap in her face.

"Oh, please! I shouldn't wake the baby? Why? So your nap won't be disturbed? You don't want to hear him cry? It might inconvenience you?" she returned.

"What are you bitching about now? Where is this even going?" Alec patronized. He pulled the covers back from the bed Ellie had made and got into it, facing the wall away from her. It was too much. She yanked the covers off him and threw them on the floor. It proved to be the last baiting that Alec could resist. Furiously, he sprang from the bed and shoved Ellie into the wall, pinning her by the shoulders. "What do you want from me?"

"I want you to come home when you say you're going to come home!" she admitted, contempt blazing in her eyes.

Don't cry.

"I *did* come home. For Christ's sake, I was in the backyard. You came out and saw me! You could have stayed outside with me and my mother."

"I don't want to drink with you and your mother!"

"That's right, I forgot, you think you're too good for her. Maybe you're too good for me too, Ellie!"

"Yeah, that's what I think, Alec. I'm too good for you," Ellie answered sarcastically. Obviously Alec couldn't understand that she just wanted him all to herself sometimes. Sober. Present. She missed him horribly. She just wanted someone to talk to. Sober. Present. He couldn't get it.

Suddenly she didn't feel so angry anymore. Just sad again. Why was he so clueless?

This argument isn't going anywhere. We just keep going around and around.

"I'm going back to work next year." She shifted suddenly. Somewhere deep inside, she must have known it was the ace in her hand.

"Huh?" Alec stepped back, confused.

"My dad is going to retire next year, and the college is going to offer me his position."

Alec rubbed his face, flustered, unable to make sense of why Ellie was telling him this now. "Why the hell would you go back to work?" he blurted out finally, setting both his hands on his hips. His true emotions were unreadable, though.

"What do you mean?" Ellie acted coy although she had suspected he wouldn't be thrilled about her leaving Jordan. "Why *wouldn't* I go back to work?"

"You don't *have* to work. That's why you wouldn't go back to work. You have a young son. I don't want you to leave the baby!" Alec's earlier dismissive attitude turned into focused anger. Smug satisfaction relaxed Ellie's face. She had gotten the reaction she wanted.

"Jordan will be almost three by the time I go back to work. He can start preschool," she continued innocently. "Besides I didn't get a doctorate to sit *here*," she waved her hand across the apartment maybe just a bit too contemptuously.

"Why are you so fucking hateful, Ellie?" Alec asked in disgust.

"Why are you so drunk all the time?" Ellie stepped forward, daring him to push her again. A wide, slow grin spread across Alec's face. He had regained control of himself and would not be provoked.

"So that is today's theme, huh?" he laughed bitterly. "You are apparently the queen of overanalyzing everything, Ellie. I am *not* always drunk. Yes, I *was* drunk last night..."

"Yes, you were, and the proof is still stuck to the bathroom wall," she said, cutting him off.

"I don't have to ask permission to have a few beers." His voice rose to a yell. "Or to visit *with my mother*!"

"Shut up!" Ellie commanded in a loud whisper, glancing tentatively in the direction of Jordan's room. No crying. Good. The baby hadn't woken.

"I won't shut up," Alec continued less loudly. "You have a son now. You don't have to work. If your life sucks so much, why don't you just write a paper about it? That's what you do anyhow, isn't it? Why don't you write some bullshit essay about how much living in this apartment sucks? How much living next to my mother sucks! Boohoo. I could cry for you!" He held his fists up to his eyes mockingly. "Go ahead and write about it. Who would read it anyhow?"

Ellie was knocked speechless. "Screw you, Alec," she managed to whisper as she pushed past him toward her sock drawer.

What was she doing? She rummaged through her drawer aimlessly as if there were some purpose to her being in there. Finally she managed to pull out a pair of ankle socks and fought clumsily to get them onto her feet. Alec stood by absently watching her, waiting for some type of rebuttal. Were they done? Was "screw you" the end of it? Ellie felt a lump beginning to form in her throat as her face grew red and hot.

Don't even cry.

She pushed past him again toward the bedroom door. "How would you know what sort of 'bullshit' I write?" she asked quietly. "You never even bothered to read my dissertation." Where was she heading? Her body moved as if by instinct toward the nearest escape. A worn pair of cross-trainer gym shoes sat on the floor mat. She scooped them into her arms and jerked open the backdoor.

"Where are you going?" Alec followed her in surprise. She couldn't respond. Fat, hot tears had begun to roll down her face as she hopped down the driveway, struggling to jam her feet into the shoes without untying them.

Hop. Stumble. Hop. Hop. Stumble.

She knew she looked ridiculous, but her wounded pride prevented her from stopping to properly tie her shoes. Finally they were on her feet and she took off like a shot. She ran. Like a racehorse from its gate, she took off, a crazy, disheveled flash of manic color and trailing hair. Alec stood silently at the door, watching his wife from the doorstep. She rounded the corner of his mother's house and was gone.

Down the street, the houses flew by, a dizzying stream of jumbled colors. The afternoon sun peeked in and out of ominous-looking clouds that now traveled quickly across the sky. The wind picked up. The trees swayed vigorously, but Ellie was only vaguely aware. She barely noticed anything but the sense of relief that worked itself out through her limbs with the pound of each foot against pavement. She was free. She was away from *there*. She was away from the feeling of suffocation. She ran.

Maybe she wouldn't go back! Maybe she could just keep running forever. Lost in this moment, awash with relief. The waving summer grasses, rolling hills, ever-darkening sky, the wide expanse of highway stretching out as far as her eyes could see. The hawks floating overhead. The flocks of finches chipping happily in the pines. She could just stay right here! Suspended in time. Never having to go back to the loneliness of that pole barn or the sleepless nights.

Tears resurfaced as Ellie proudly wiped her nose with the back of her hand. She had never run before, but her anguish propelled her ever further. Rounding corners, uphill without stopping. If her body ached, she wasn't aware. She simply ran. And then. Crack! Thunder overhead signaled the opening of the sky. Above her, the clouds had turned gray. Rain had found her. Or perhaps she had run blindly into it. A gentle shower turned suddenly into a downpour, but she didn't stop. She continued, toward nowhere, drenched in mere minutes, her clothing stuck hopelessly to her skin, wrinkling up into pinched pleats under her armpits and in her groin.

Unhindered by the chafing of wet fabric, she continued without a thought in her head. Just the feelings of hurt stubbornly hung on. The disappointment and betrayal and misunderstanding. But she would run them away! She would scare them out of her chest. She would banish them out here in the open fields near the farmhouses—on this country road. She would leave them here if she could. (If only she could.) The rain now came down in sheets around her.

Hitting a slick spot, her ankle buckled beneath her unpracticed foot and sent her down onto one knee.

"Ahh," she cried in agony as she caught herself with one hand before slamming completely to the ground.

Crack! Flash! Now lightning. Ellie struggled to her feet. A stream of blood ran from her knee, coloring the top of her sock pink. Bits of gravel stuck to her hand. The sharp pain in her ankle demanded an end to her run, but she refused to turn back toward the house. By now she was miles away anyhow. May as well continue on. She hobbled away from the street toward a massive burr oak, fully aware that a tree was the last place to hide in a lightning storm. What really were the chances of getting struck by lightning though? The thought nearly made her laugh. Getting struck by lightning seemed like a welcome alternative to returning home.

Could I be so lucky?

She had just reached the tree and awkwardly sat down, somewhat protected from the deluge, when the headlights of a car rounded the highway toward her. The car slowed near the tree, as if unsure, and then screeched to a stop. Ellie made no attempt to move.

"Oh my God, are you OK?" Alec yelled to her from the passenger-side window as it slid down. The cries of a baby escaped the car. Ellie still said nothing. "Get in!" Alec urged. Still she sat. The driver's door swung open.

"I'm sorry!" Alec pleaded as he approached Ellie in the rain, his white T-shirt soaked through by the time he reached the tree. He knelt down on one knee to be at her level. "I'm so sorry, Ellie. I didn't mean to insult what you do."

Ellie finally made eye contact with him. He looked earnest enough, his sweet, brown eyes sad and sincere. "I really am sorry, honey. Please forgive me for what I said. I didn't mean to hurt you."

"I just want us to be a family," Ellie answered finally.

"I know," Alec conceded. "I'm sorry I didn't come to bed last night. I'm sorry I've been taking you for granted. You're a wonderful mom and a wonderful wife. Get in the car please!"

Ellie didn't budge. Alec looked confused.

"I don't mind if you go back to work if that's what this is about," he tried. "I just want you to be happy."

Ellie still sat.

"Listen," he continued, "I was thinking in the car. I was afraid I wouldn't find you. I was really worried!" The sound of pounding rain hitting packed earth began to drown him out. "I was thinking what I could do to make it up to you," he continued desperately. "So I thought I should build you a house! We have the Penderson contract! We have the money to do it now! What do you think? I'll build you exactly the house you want. Away from my mom, OK? Anything you want." He reached out his hand to her. Ellie grabbed it hesitantly.

"Anything I want?" she asked with a half grin. "Away from your mom?"

"Yes, anything you want. I'm sorry, Ellie. I love you. Please! Get in the car!"

"OK," Ellie agreed stubbornly as Alec helped her to her feet. She stepped tentatively from the shelter of the tree into his waiting embrace, rain enveloping them on all sides, a blurred silhouette picture of two people intertwined near a tree, car idling close by.

With an agonized groan, pain radiating from her ankle, Ellie slid into the back seat to comfort her screaming toddler. Hastily unfastening his car seat restraints, she lifted Jordan out of his seat and placed him at her breast. Alec ran around the car, sloshing into the driver's seat as he slammed the door shut. Satisfied, he turned the car around and headed back down the county road toward their apartment, the promise of a new beginning hanging hopefully between them.

Seven

*H*at? Ellie reached up absently to touch the top of her head. This made the illustrious Dr. Curran smile even more widely. He waited patiently for Ellie to make sense of his appearance in this environment; it was something akin to seeing a zebra walking through the middle of the campus quad. He was not part of this schema. This was her secret world. What was he doing here? How did he know about this? Was this some bizarre coincidence?

What is he doing here?

An emotion started to surface out of the confusion as the questions stopped flailing about in her head and began ordering themselves.

Anger.

Marta!

"Dr. Curran." Ellie extended her hand formally. "You've taken me by surprise."

"I see that," he replied, grasping Ellie's hand firmly. His huge palm and long fingers, smooth and cool, completely engulfed her as he leaned in closer. "I presume Marta failed to tell you that I was coming."

"What gives you that impression?" Ellie played coy.

"Your expression!" He laughed as he finished his pint. "You are not very good at disguising your true emotions!"

Really? This guy is a piece of work. He thinks he can read me so well? Doubtful, or you'd know I think you're an arrogant ass!

Or do you?

Ellie smiled sweetly and then waved down the bartender. This called for another glass of wine.

"Do you dance, Dr. Curran?" Ellie asked just a bit sarcastically.

"Tall British men should not dance to music like this, Dr. Purnell!" Again he laughed, amused either by the question or by his own honesty. "I'll leave the dancing to Latin men!"

"So you came to watch?"

"Not exactly, but I dare say I didn't mind finding you out there!" he admitted. Ellie's eyes narrowed. Was he flirting? Suddenly she felt self-conscious, completely vulnerable, her makeup long since washed down her face, her hair in a hat, her chest and back still glistening with sweat. And here he was, standing right in front of her, looking cool and suave as usual. And here she was, out in the open, no longer invisible.

Again she felt the sting of betrayal. How could Marta have told him about this?

Lovely little distraction, Marta. Send in Professor Perfect, and I will simply forget about your tryst with Lilliana.

Well, why give Marta that satisfaction? I'm not going to get mad about her inviting this guy. I am not going to play into that.

Ellie decided on a different tactic. After all, maybe it was not so bad that he was here. It was just... unexpected.

"Well, now you know my secret!" Ellie leaned against the bar, folding her arms.

"That you dance?" Professor Curran smiled. "That's not such an awful secret, Elizabeth."

"Yes, but it's *my* secret. And now..." She put her two fingers on his abdomen and walked them up to his chest, tapping at the hollow between his pecs. "...you have to keep it! Right here."

Now *she* was flirting!

What is wrong with you?

She couldn't help herself. Her anger at Marta was mixed with a peculiar thrill (from being caught, being watched?). Standing in front of Liam Curran, completely "bared," was somehow exciting. She felt in control of the situation suddenly.

"A terrible burden." Liam shook his head. "You will have to repay me somehow for keeping all of this to myself!"

"I'll allow you to escort me the rest of the night! How about that?" Ellie joked. She attempted to pay the bartender for her wine, but Liam stepped in, folding a twenty into the man's hand.

"Thank you," Ellie said before taking a long, healthy sip as he looked on.

"I imagine you'll be better company than Marta's other companions, so I'll take you up on that offer," Liam conceded.

"Since you don't dance, Dr. Curran, let's find someplace to sit," Ellie suggested. To his surprise, she took his hand and led him through the crowd toward the stairs. Ellie felt a twinge of satisfaction at his surprise and his eagerness to follow her. Perhaps subconsciously she had been trying to get near him for over a week now, and it had been impossible. He was always surrounded by admirers, students, or other professors. Now she had his undivided attention.

She spotted a small open seating area obscured by a thin, flowing curtain, lights playing manically against the walls. She hesitated. Did she want to go up the stairs and into the rooms with Marta and Lilliana? No.

"Let's sit here." Ellie turned to look up at Liam, who was standing so close that her chin almost brushed his chest. She had to tilt her head up to look into his face. He leaned down, placing his hand at the small of her back, his mouth brushing her ear.

"I can't hear you!" he said. They were actually closer to the speakers on this side of the club.

Ellie realized she was holding her breath, every nerve in her body alerted. Standing on her tiptoes, she placed her hand on his shoulders to steady herself and then leaned into his ear. "Let's sit here," she suggested again, suddenly a bit lightheaded as she grabbed his hand once more to lead him to the velvet settee. He smelled of soap and summer air. She was sure he could hear her just fine, but she didn't mind the whispering game. It allowed her to touch him. *Innocently of course.* The wine and the setting were making her unusually bold.

"So Id invited you to come out here?" Ellie asked.

Liam exploded into laughter. "You call her Id?"

"You've spent some time with the queen of carnal pleasures, haven't you? It's a fitting name, isn't it?" Ellie laughed.

"I don't know her quite well enough to make that judgment yet," he admitted. "She mentioned that the two of you were coming to Chicago for the weekend and said that I would like the city. She said I should come to this event tonight to meet some of her friends," Liam said, answering the original question. "I've never visited Chicago before, and this seemed like the perfect opportunity."

"So what did you think of her friends?" Ellie smiled, sipping her wine.

"Well, I might say that you two seem an unlikely pair," Liam offered.

"Not so unlikely," Ellie said defensively. "As a friend, I'm pretty low maintenance, which is good because she's pretty low effort."

Liam laughed heartily. "And that works?"

"It does," Ellie admitted. "She makes me laugh. Maybe she makes me not take myself too seriously. She's just…" Ellie paused. Suddenly she felt disloyal. Was she about to divulge too much personal information about Marta? Probably not. After all, Marta had pretty much shown her authentic self to Liam already, smoking weed in the university office, inviting him to this party to meet people like Lilliana. Liam waited patiently for Ellie to finish her thought. "Well, let's just say that I hate to watch Marta self-destruct."

"Sometimes the most gifted people among us are the most self-destructive," Liam mused. Ellie had visions of her father, holed up in his study for days at a time, refusing to come out. Disappearing "to write" for weeks at a time. Returning home exhausted.

"That's true," she agreed. "Speaking of gifted, you gave an amazing lecture today," she offered, changing the subject.

"Thank you," Liam answered sincerely. He took a sip of his pint and then set it on a small metal cocktail table that held several candles illuminating the tiny space. The lightshow of the dance floor filtered through the cheese-cloth curtain, occasionally throwing shadows across the perfect angle of his chin. He leaned forward, placing his elbows on his knees and running his fingers through his thick, wavy hair as if he was contemplating what Ellie had said.

"I wanted to tell you how enlightening I thought your class was and…"

"But then you disappeared," Liam interrupted playfully, placing his hand on Ellie's forearm, a gesture that was both natural and friendly. It was just such interaction that drew people to him; he exuded some sort of benign understanding. Maybe she had misjudged him. Maybe he wasn't arrogant, just intuitive.

"Well, you had several people waiting to talk to you, and I didn't feel like…" She stopped suddenly. He looked at her expectantly but waited for her to finish. "I didn't feel like competing with them for your time." And even as it came out of her mouth, she couldn't believe that she was being so honest. A slow smile spread across Liam's face.

"You don't have to compete with anyone, trust me," he assured her.

Ellie's heart skipped.

How do I respond to that?

"I have never seen a class so engaged before," Ellie said, avoiding a direct response.

"I doubt that," Liam replied. "I'm sure your lectures are as brilliant as your essays."

"Even the *Frankenstein* ones?"

"Yes, even those!" He let out a healthy laugh. "I fear you will never let me live down our first debate. I just couldn't help myself though! You were doodling on a notepad, completely bored, and I needed to get your attention. You were bruising my delicate ego!"

"I'm sorry I'm so rude," Ellie apologized.

"You're not rude, Elizabeth. You're just the most elusive person on earth," he said, suddenly very serious. He looked Ellie straight in the eyes unflinchingly.

He is right. It nearly took the air out of her.

"Well, I'm here now, aren't I?" she asked lightly.

"Yes, here we are," Liam answered, cocking his head to the side.

Suddenly Ellie had the most incredible urge to crawl into his arms. They sat next to one another on the settee for what seemed like several minutes, saying nothing, almost a dare—who would talk next?

"What made you come to Wisconsin of all places?" Ellie finally asked.

"You," Liam admitted instantly. He waited for a reaction, but Ellie was stone faced, unconvinced. "Is it so impossible to believe that I could be such an admirer of your work?"

"I suppose not," Ellie replied with a frown.

"One of your essays deeply influenced my thought. At the risk of sounding dramatic, it was somewhat life altering," Liam admitted sincerely. "Truly. I jest not!"

He smiled, crossing his heart with his forefinger. "I have been a loyal follower of your work ever since."

"Which essay was that, Dr. Curran?" Ellie challenged him.

"Your essay on the true purpose of elegies. You referenced Edna St. Vincent Millay and Ben Jonson, of all combinations! Brilliant, really."

Ellie's face remained blank, giving no indication that she remembered such an essay.

"You wrote extensively about Ben Jonson's poem 'To my First Son,'" he offered, trying to jog her memory. But the memory of writing that essay had not really escaped her. It was a moment in time forever seared into her subconscious and not one she wanted to relive right then.

"That essay almost didn't get written." Ellie confided only that much.

"Well, it was one of the most poignant pieces of critical writing that I've ever come across. Really. It moved me to tears." He stopped to gauge her reaction, to give her a moment to process what he had said. Then he continued to press. "That's why I find it so unbelievable that you don't write poetry." Liam picked up his pint casually, took another sip, and set it back down, never letting his eyes leave Ellie's face.

"And what if I did, Dr. Curran?"

"Stop calling me Dr. Curran."

"Liam."

"That's better. It sounds lovely coming from you."
He smirked.

"Liam, what if I did write poetry?"

"Then I would be a great admirer of that also." He
leaned back on the settee, supporting himself on one
elbow, his forearm flexed against the cushion.

"So you came all the way here to the United States
to debate my essays, which you *so* admire, and to encourage—or harass—me about writing poetry?" Ellie
still pressed.

"I had the opportunity to teach and observe abroad,
and I surmised it might be the most beneficial experience, the most meaningful experience, for my students
to study American literature in America, yes?"

"That makes sense," she conceded.

"I've been to New York City more times than I
can count. I've climbed or hiked most of California,
Colorado, and Washington and the Appalachian Trail
in the east. But I have never been to the hopelessly
flat Midwestern United States until now. And that's
where you are, a writer and professor who I admire.
So here I am! In the Midwest. Are you finally satisfied
with that explanation, grand doubter?" Liam feigned
exasperation.

"Sure," Ellie sighed. "It sounds as though you've
seen more of my country than I have."

"Well, I have probably seen the highest parts of it,
at least," he admitted.

"So you climb mountains?" Ellie rolled her eyes in play.

"Don't change the subject," Liam scolded.

"What is the subject?"

"Your writing," he answered.

"You are far more interesting a topic than that." Ellie batted her hand as if shooing away the suggestion of talking about her.

Let's talk about anything but me! Please.

"Very well," Liam agreed. "We can talk about whatever you'd like."

No sooner had the words left his mouth, a crash of thunder outside heralded several deafening electrical snaps inside. Instantly all sound was sucked completely out of the air like a vortex, leaving only surprised voices and the hush of abruptly still feet. The power had blown out.

"Oh, wow!" Ellie gasped. Liam stood up immediately to assess the situation, protectively shielding Ellie from a possible panic. Luckily thousands of candles inside their mesh sconces still lit the factory space and everyone inside looked only surprised, not frightened. Instantly the atmosphere went from a raucous celebration to quiet confusion. Ellie wondered how long people would stay civil. Could the bartenders continue to placate the masses when there was no music?

"Should we find Marta?" Liam asked. Ellie stood, pulling her cell phone out of her back pocket to finally check her messages.

From: Marta
Stop hating me! Come back for a minute!

From: Marta
Please come back! Just hooking up with Lily 4 2nite! Promise!

From: Marta
Liam Curran is here. I can explain.

From: Marta
Fine. Don't talk to me. He said he will look for you himself.

From: Marta
Sorry. Please don't be mad at me.

From: Marta
Leaving with Lily. I know where to find you.

Ellie looked up, feeling a twinge of guilt. "She left a while ago," Ellie explained. "I ignored all her texts because I was dancing."

"Because you were dancing?" Liam questioned.

"Because I was mad at her for not telling me Lilliana was here."

"Lilliana?" Liam asked.

"Her ex-girlfriend. That cheap…" Ellie caught herself.

Liam burst into laughter. "Such passionate anger! You're protective of Marta."

"Of course I'm protective of her!"

"And she looks up to you."

"I wouldn't go that far."

"I would," Liam continued. "She obviously doesn't want to make you angry."

"This is the extent of my anger," Ellie said defensively.

"Ignoring someone?" Liam raised his eyebrows.

"Yes, I suppose so."

"Is that usually effective?"

"I don't really know." Ellie felt irritated again.

Why are you badgering me? I don't know if it's "effective" in changing someone else's behavior, but it helps me avoid confrontation.

Liam looked thoroughly amused. "Shall we leave here then before this becomes something unpleasant?" he asked. Did he mean the scene or their conversation?

"Sure," Ellie agreed. She wanted to say good-bye to Tony but didn't dare try to find him in this mess. As an afterthought, she decided to text Marta.

To: Marta
Power went out. Leaving with Liam.
Not mad at you. Be smart.

Most of the crowd had filtered from the dance floor toward sitting areas and bars, opting to wait out the power outage in hopes that the music would soon be back. This opened a clear and easy path toward an outside door. When Liam swung it open for Ellie, both were surprised by the sheets of driving rain that assailed them. The street was barely visible through the steam that rose as rain hammered the pavement.

"Come on!" Liam yelled over the deafening white noise of the downpour. He grabbed Ellie's hand and began to run. The hat was no use now; Ellie pulled it off with her free hand, her head instantly soaked through by the rain. Laughing, they ran two blocks down to an SUV that lit up for them as Liam pointed his keyring. Ellie nearly jumped head first into the front seat when Liam yanked open the door for her. In an instant, he had run around the car and was in the driver's seat, little rivulets of water running down the faint stubble of his chin. He turned to her, breathless and laughing, his green eyes bright in the harsh overhead light of the car. Ellie could only imagine she must look like a wet dog.

Here's the real me! No hiding now.

"Where shall I take you?" he asked, starting up the car.

"Marta and I…well, I am staying at The Four Seasons. It's right on Michigan Avenue."

"Very well," he answered, starting up the car.

Ellie felt guilty that Liam had to be her chauffeur, but this sure beat trying to hail a cab in the rain. However, she couldn't imagine sending him back out into this weather, alone in a city he wasn't familiar with. After they pulled up to the hotel, Liam got out to open the passenger door but did not beat the valet, who opened Ellie's door for her first. As Liam came around her side, she had already made up her mind.

"Just stay here tonight," she told him. "It's too dangerous to drive." The valet looked on anxiously. *Is this weird?*

"I don't want to impose," Liam said.

Ellie waved her hand dismissively. "You're safe with me!" she repeated his words, smiling.

"OK," he agreed a bit hesitantly and then quickly grabbed a bag from the backseat. The valet drove off with the car as they went into the building, probably looking as soggy and conspicuous as Ellie felt.

He is a colleague, and you're not doing anything wrong.

Her cold, wet hair stuck to her back uncomfortably as they walked through the ghostly lobby. It had to be close to 2:00 a.m.

This is a lovely view." Liam stood at the window of the suite, looking out at the twinkling lights of the city. Was he referring to the city or their strange re-flection in the darkened window? Ellie handed him a towel as she stood drying the ends of her hair. Even patting his face dry was an elegant gesture. There was something regal about him, composed, beautiful. He was really not like any other man she'd ever seen. Any real man, at least. Maybe a sculpture. But not a real man.

"My hotel reservations are actually quite close to here," Liam murmured. "I think you have the better view, though."

I do now. Ellie smirked to herself.

"You sound exhausted," she said. "I can sleep out here so you can have the bed. I'm afraid you're going to be too tall for the pullout."

"Absolutely not." Liam looked shocked at the sug-gestion and then softened. "I'm not one to be too ter-ribly concerned about comfort. When I'm tired, I can sleep anywhere." He touched Ellie's bare shoulder with a smile, "A sofa bed that is too short is a luxury com-pared to the frozen ground of a mountain campsite!"

"That's true," Ellie agreed, "but I bet that view is even better than this one!"

"Indeed."

"Then good night." Ellie nodded and returned to the bedroom, the imprint of Liam's hand on her shoul-der still warm.

A single brilliant ray of light shot out from between the tiniest break in the two curtains. *Damn my incompetence at closing those tightly!* There was no way Ellie could sleep through the coming of daylight. It was a curse. Years of waking early to a screaming baby, and then, of course, the self-imposed early-morning running schedule had conditioned her body to be up and ready to go, even to its own detriment. This morning, she certainly needed more sleep. What time had they gotten in last night? *They?* She awoke with a start, pulling herself up suddenly from the mattress.

Liam! She had slept so soundly, that the events of last night were temporarily erased from her mind. She crept over to the frosted-glass doors that separated her room from the living area of the suite. Peeking out, she could still make out the outline of his body curled under a thin blanket. He was sound asleep. A surprising feeling of relief washed over her.

Did you think he would be gone?

Was he even real to begin with? This specter. This shadow. This man who keeps appearing from nowhere. And so what if he was?

What if you woke up this morning and he was gone?

Her heart constricted in her chest momentarily. What was wrong with her?

She glanced over at the clock. Eight o'clock. Way too early to be awake, but she knew there was no going back to sleep. She could either go running like she had planned or sit and watch Liam Curran sleep through the glass doors.

Maybe that's not such a horrible idea, the watching part! Although if you do that, you will definitely need a run. And a cold shower.

As she rummaged through her bag for her running shoes and clothes, she caught a glimpse of herself in the bedroom mirror. *Yikes! You look like you've been in a fight.* Her face was so puffy from lack of sleep (and, well, let's face it, age) that she didn't dare go outside without first splashing some water on it to wake herself up a bit. Stealthily as she could, she went about getting ready.

To: Marta
You OK? Going running. Liam stayed on couch last night.

Knowing Marta, she wouldn't be awake to read that text until sometime in the afternoon, but Ellie wanted to check in with her anyhow. (And, if Ellie was really being honest, she was just the tiniest bit worried about her friend). Id, after all, did earn her nickname. If Ellie were to bet, Marta was sleeping off some drug binge and a night of sexual escapades. To her surprise, a trilling bell signaled an incoming text almost immediately.

From: Marta
☺

Ellie felt relieved as she slipped out the door, leaving Liam Curran to a silent, darkened room. She would request that tea and breakfast be sent up to the room when she returned in an hour. *He would drink tea, right? Did the British drink tea in the morning, the way Americans drank coffee?* Well, if not, it would at least be a kind gesture.

Ellie hit the sidewalk with a myriad of other runners, cyclists, and people walking happy little dogs on leashes. People sipping coffee, newspapers in hand, quietly enjoying the early calm of the city. When Ellie and Dylan had lived here, they were never out at this time. Ellie knew the city only at night. Like most young people, they lived like vampires—up all night, sleeping into the late hours of the afternoon. Chicago was beautiful at this time. In the early-morning hours, the day was full of possibilities. The lack of sleep made Ellie feel nostalgic and emotional as she began her run, but surprisingly, the underlying current of that nostalgia was a sense of calm.

Being back here, in the city where she was once devastated, once almost completely destroyed, she felt vindicated. *I'm still here! I'm still alive!* In the past fifteen years, she'd often imagined how her life might have been different if she'd gone through with her marriage to Dylan. At what point would she have realized that he was constantly unfaithful? Would he have "outgrown" his infidelity and eventually succumbed to a monogamous life? What if they had had children together? Would they have ended up in a vicious, bitter divorce?

Would it be worse than your life now?

She pushed that snarky devil's advocate out of her headspace.

Of course it would be worse!

How so?

I worshipped Dylan, that's how. I believed in him. In us.

There. She had admitted it. Dylan was different than Alec. If Ellie had carried that blind faith with her for any longer than she had, being allowed to believe in the fantasy of Dylan—to build a false life with him, one that may have included a home and children—life could certainly be worse than it was now. Alec could never decimate her that way. By the time she had met Alec, she was already disillusioned; that "land of dreams" was muddied.

Maybe she really would go to The Art Institute today. Maybe she would finally stop running from her old demons. After all, those demons had certainly been replaced by new ones. Ones that lived back in Wisconsin. And those demons were manageable. They couldn't hurt her the way she had once been hurt. She wasn't that foolish (she wasn't that in love). She was too jaded to be destroyed.

Ellie had unconsciously chosen a path toward the lake, through Millennium Park, away from the traffic of the Loop. Still, running in such a crowded space, the skyscrapers looming overhead, felt strange. Too many distractions. Ellie was used to running in the solitude of the country where she could mentally checkout, where her feet hitting the gravel road and the rhythmic sound of her labored breath lulled her into a trance. This felt very forced and exposed. People and bicycles and panting dogs whipped by her. She had to focus very hard on where she placed her feet, colors whizzing by unchecked. The sun beat down over the harbor, boats bobbing lazily in the water. A few sailboats dotted the horizon. Ellie kept pushing on, waiting for the adrenaline calm.

Her mind wandered to Alec. Surely at this time in the morning, he would still be sleeping. Probably on the couch, the television looping endless Saturday morning infomercials. Jordan, sweet boy, would undoubtedly come downstairs, after checking his blood sugar, and offer to make his dad some breakfast. He had the generosity of his Aunt Becca. All grace and kindness. Ellie reminded herself of this whenever Alec would go on a bender. Jordan was already perfect (spoken like a true mom). Nothing Ellie and Alec could do would screw him up, right? Everything would be fine.

It will all work out. It will all work out. It will all work out. It will all work out. Ellie's mantra since her rough introduction to motherhood. *It will all work out.* No amount of disdain or disgust toward Alec, even though Ellie tried in vain to veil it, could affect Jordan, right? He would love both her and Alec unconditionally anyhow, right?

Yeah, like you love your parents.

Shut up. I turned out just fine.

She would call Jordan this morning to check on him, to make sure he was packed for his camping trip, and maybe even say something civil to Alec.

Not from your hotel room, you won't.

Liam! The idea suddenly struck Ellie.

Whatever. He is a colleague who slept on the sofa bed.

Her subconscious didn't even bother to laugh. All the voices inside Ellie's head knew damn well it was a strange and inappropriate situation.

Alec would flip out if he knew.

Knew what?

Knew any of it. The dancing. Tony. The party. The man in your hotel room.

Please. You act as if I'm Marta. Drug binges and orgies. I had three or four glasses of wine, danced for two or three hours, and slept alone in an overpriced hotel room with a man on my couch. A man I work with! Not one I picked up at the club. (Well, not exactly, at least.)

Ellie had not convinced herself. A creeping guilt, courtesy of a childhood with Maggie Lawson, started to surface via a vaguely queasy belly.

You lied about where you are.

Oh, so fucking what? It's not like I have ever checked up on what Alec has been doing. All those business trips, all the late nights. At least I can remember where I've been and who I've been with the next morning. Can he say the same? I doubt it. And maybe I need this secret. Maybe I need this so that I can continue to live in that house without anger.

Without anger? That's rich.

Fine! So that I can tolerate my existence.

("Tolerate?" her mother would ask with disbelief. "Easy life to 'tolerate.'")

Realizing how far she had run, Ellie decided to turn around and head back to the hotel. No use spending all this futile emotion on just one half of the run! Put that guilt and anger to work!

She continued to reason with herself: Alec would probably spend the day in the garage (that Jordan was supposed to clean), his head buried under the hood of one of his classic cars, the Sonos system blaring Soundgarden as he cracked countless beers without Ellie's scrutiny. He was probably thoroughly enjoying a respite from her obvious avoidance, a disdain that had created a palpable void between them, an unbridgeable chasm. He could sit on the front porch and watch the gardeners work, even sleep on the porch swing uninterrupted, without the nagging fear that Ellie would come slamming out the front door, flustered, demanding that he do something. Some "menial, bullshit task that she had dreamt up just to get under his skin." Something that had supposedly been on his "honey-do" list for far too long.

So there. Alec is doing what makes him happy, and so am I.

This relieved Ellie of her guilt as she slowed to a brisk walk in her final few blocks back to The Four Seasons.

It was nearly nine on the lobby clock when Ellie decided now would probably be the perfect time to call Jordan so she could avoid having to lie to Alec. Just better this way. She found a complimentary pitcher of cucumber water in the lobby, poured herself a glass, gulping it down voraciously and then retreated to a corner sofa to call. No answer. He was probably still sleeping too. She would just leave him a text.

To: Jordan
Hey! It's Mom. Just checking that you're OK.
Text me when you're up.
Love you.

Regardless of how far away she was or who she tried to pretend to be (or who she wanted to forget she really was), Jordan was never far from her thoughts. He was, after all, the only human being on earth to whom Ellie felt any real connection. For fourteen years, he had been her sole reason for pushing on. Until just recently, everything she did centered around Jordan's happiness, Jordan's education, and of course, Jordan's health.

Her son had finally gotten to the age now when he preferred his father's company over his mother's, where he had "girlfriends" and secrets and didn't need to be hugged all the time. It felt foreign and empty to Ellie. Not being needed. She realized having a child to take care of, to hold and embrace all these years, had filled her need for human touch. Now that was virtually gone. But she refused to be "that mom." The one who was clingy and overbearing. The one who couldn't accept that she now needed her son more than he needed her.

As if it weren't bad enough that her fortieth birthday was imminent, Ellie was also contending with the sense of loss that came with watching her boy grow into a man. And if she were really to be honest with herself, maybe that was another reason for her recent sense of desperation. Soul searching. What was next in life? What was her purpose?

Ellie unlocked the door to her hotel suite as quietly as possible, turning the door handle with the most minute click and easing it open gingerly. Bright sunlight filled the room from the open panoramic windows overlooking the lake. And there, in the center of the floor, cross-legged in a patch of golden sun, sat Liam Curran, face lifted up to the light, his upturned palms resting serenely on his knees. Ellie halted instantly.

"Good morning," Liam breathed quietly without turning around, a hint of amusement in his voice. He had sensed her movement, her surprise at finding him awake. Her desire to leave him undisturbed. Her discomfort at walking in on something that seemed intimate.

"Good morning, Dr. Curran." Ellie smiled. Although he couldn't see her face, she was sure he could hear it in her voice.

"I thought we'd dispensed of that last evening. I believe you can call me Liam now that we've spent the night together," he joked quietly, letting out one last long, barely audible breath, his broad shoulders raising gradually and then lowering. He did not seem embarrassed in the least. Ellie laughed somewhat nervously as Liam unfolded his legs and rose slowly. He was still wearing loose fitting lounge pants and a white T-shirt that clung to his toned arms and abdomen. "Is there no end to your hats?" he kidded in reference to the baseball cap Ellie had worn out running. "Why do you hide such lovely hair?"

"Stop with your flattery, please! There is nothing lovely about my hair right now," Ellie insisted.

"Nonsense!" Liam continued. "You look radiant coming in from your run. Glowing!" He tilted his head to the side slightly, a small smile, the look of sincerity becoming his trademark. He meant what he said.

"You are very charming, Liam, really." Ellie smirked, shaking her head cynically. "I bet that charm has served you well in life. It makes you quite endearing, although I don't believe a word of it!"

A knock came at the door. Liam looked surprised.

"Room service," Ellie explained. "I figured you'd be hungry this morning. I know I am." She opened the door, allowing a waiter to roll in the metal cart with their breakfast—a variety of juices, fruit, eggs, and tea.

"Tea? You are clairvoyant. Thank you!" Liam exclaimed as he saw the contents of the cart. Ellie removed the platters and set them on the table, where she and Liam sat across from one another. "And they even sent milk. Perfect!" He grinned enormously.

"I wasn't sure if you'd drink tea in the morning, but…"

"This is excellent. Thank you." Liam beamed. "I must admit, I still haven't quite adjusted to the time difference. I've been dragging a bit. Nothing a little tea won't fix though!"

"Good!" Ellie felt pleased with herself for having the foresight to order breakfast. Eating something would probably make both of them feel better. "I wasn't sure what to order, so it's pretty standard," Ellie explained in reference to the scrambled eggs and fruit.

"This is perfect," Liam assured her. "I will eat eggs."

"Are you a vegetarian?" Ellie asked.

"I eat fish," Liam answered without looking up from his tea. Ellie watched his long, agile fingers wrap around the spoon delicately, stirring milk slowly into the cup. He gently dunked the tea bag into the milk and water mixture and then leaned back comfortably in his chair to wait for it to steep. When he caught her watching him, a vague look of satisfaction swept over his face. Ellie was beyond caring, even though a faint blush spread across her neck and chest.

I've decided I like you. I don't care if you know.

"I eat fish because I like to fish. It would be an awful hypocrisy if I didn't eat what I caught, yes?"

"You're a fisherman too, Dr. Curran?" Ellie asked, spooning some eggs onto her plate. "You spend a great deal of time outdoors."

"Fly-fishing," Liam explained. "I grew up with a river virtually in my backyard, just like you. Fly-fishing is certainly different than simply putting one's pole into a pond. There's an art to it. A rhythm. Have you ever been fly-fishing, Elizabeth?"

"No, I haven't," Ellie answered.

"I imagine you'd love it," Liam explained. "It requires great patience and concentration, but there's constant movement. Arm and shoulder..." He imitated the fluid movement. "You would probably be quite good at it since you aren't one to sit still for long!"

Ellie laughed. "I suppose I don't."

"Constantly running," Liam added, but it sounded vaguely accusatory.

"I do run a lot," Ellie admitted. *Are we talking about running or running away?* "Do you run at all?" she asked him cleverly in return.

"Not consistently," Liam answered with a smirk, delicately removing the teabag from his cup and taking a long, slow drink from it. He shut his eyes in appreciation, savoring the tea. "I would run with you, though." It sounded like a challenge.

"I'd love for you to run with me," Ellie blurted, at once furious with herself.

What the hell are you doing? You just invited him to run with you, you idiot. You're going to give up your solitude?

"Good, I'll take you up on that offer. After all, there aren't many mountains to climb in Wisconsin!" Liam said cheerily, reaching for some fruit. "A gent must keep himself fit somehow, and I dare say going to the university rec center would become tedious after a while."

Ellie smiled disingenuously as she chewed her eggs, hoping her dismay was not evident. Why had she invited him to come with her? God, he had this way with her. Just like in the debate. It's like he knew just what questions to ask in order to force her into saying what he wanted her to say. And she took the bait! Just like one of his fish. She took the bait every time!

"So you grew up by a river?" Ellie blurted out, wanting to switch the subject back to Liam.

"I did," he answered, happy to talk about his home. "Are you at all familiar with England?"

"A little." Ellie thought about her travels. "I visited London once when I was in college. When I was a kid, my father took us to Devon to see Dartmoor National Park. You know, home of the Hound of the Baskervilles?"

Liam laughed. "Yes, Sir Arthur Conan Doyle, of course!"

"That was really amazing. Haunting. As a kid, I thought it was the coolest place I'd ever seen. It was romantic and spooky and quintessentially British. It was probably that trip that made me want to study English literature. You know, all things British I thought were so cool growing up."

"Like Morrissey?" Liam teased.

"Yes!" Ellie said, surprised.

"I saw the poster in your office," he explained.

"Oh!" Ellie laughed.

"I grew up near the Pennines, the mountain range referred to as 'England's backbone,' in a small tourist town called Ingleton in North Yorkshire. Ingleton sits at the bottom of Ingleborough Mountain. One of three nearby peaks."

"So you grew up near rivers *and* mountains?"

"And caves. It's really a lovely, rugged landscape. I've seen much of the world, and nothing compares to home." He grinned sincerely. "From the top of those mountains, if it's clear, the view would steal your heart." His brows furrowed for a moment, searching for the words. "I always explain to people who've not been there that it resembles the movie setting from 'The Lord of the Rings.'"

"So not even Wisconsin compares, huh?" Ellie joked.

"There are actually some features of your town that remind me quite a bit of home. The weather is fairly similar," Liam explained earnestly. "The rolling hills. But no." He laughed. "Wisconsin does not compare. You also spent a good deal of your childhood outdoors, I presume."

"Yeah, I did a lot of riding. A lot of tending to animals. A lot of grunt work!" Ellie answered. "We are talking about you though! Don't try changing the subject again!" She wagged her finger at him. "Do you ride horses too?" she asked.

"I do indeed ride." Liam waived his hand officially. "My mother raised a proper English gentleman. My father raised a practical Irishman. Both require a knowledge of horsemanship!"

"See, it sounds as though you have a very colorful past, Dr. Curran," Ellie said encouragingly. "Stop holding out on me!"

"I'm not!" he insisted. "I'll tell you whatever you want to know! Yes, I rode quite a bit as a child. We had a large stable on our estate."

"Your *estate*?"

"Yes, our *estate*!" he said, ignoring the implication. "Everyone in that part of the country rides. Really, it's part of the culture. The landscape keeps the local psyche held firmly in the eighteenth century."

"It sounds wonderful," Ellie said dreamily.

"It is," Liam admitted fondly. "You would love it there. You and your romanticizing about all that is British. It is indeed a very English landscape."

"You live in London now though, don't you? Near the university?"

"I have a flat in London where I stay most of the school year. I tire of the city though," he admitted between bites of egg. "My parents still have their home in the country, so I go back often. To be honest, I've traveled so much over the past seven years or so that I don't know I could say exactly where home is."

"On book tours?" Ellie asked. "My father used to travel a lot to promote his books or to give talks."

"Yes, a lot of my traveling has been for lectures or book promoting, but I'm crafty about which engagements I accept. I try to travel to places where I can climb! I won't lie. I've seen some beautiful places. I have to pay my dues by lecturing and then I'm free to explore the natural world!"

"You enjoy lecturing though, don't you?"

"I do. I just enjoy climbing more!"

"How did you find time to do all of that traveling?" Ellie wondered, perplexed. Ellie could barely find the

time to teach, write, and make it to all of Jordan's soccer games.

"I took a leave of absence for a couple of years when
my wife died," Liam answered quietly, looking up from
his eggs.

Ellie stopped chewing, her eyes wide with surprise.
Immediately Liam looked apologetic for the shock of
his honesty. "I thought that was common knowledge,"
he explained.

Common knowledge? Oh, God, I'm such an ass. Was I
supposed to know he had a dead wife?

"I'm sorry. I didn't know," Ellie admitted.

Liam burst into laughter, leaving Ellie mortified
and confused. Was he laughing at her?

"You really dreaded my coming here, didn't you?"
he asked.

Where is he going with this?

"Almost every press release or interview I gave
about *American Mask* makes mention of Katherine, my
wife. She died shortly after the release of the book.
Obviously it was a very difficult time for me; I wasn't really able to enjoy the praise my work was given."

Ellie couldn't bring herself to admit that she'd only
skimmed the pages of his renowned novel in haughty
protest. He was right, of course; she *had* dreaded him
coming here, so much so that she'd hardly read anything he'd written. She had been, and still remained
(as he already pointed out the night of the debate),

woefully unprepared to debate him. Once again, he was eerily accurate in his assumptions.

"There seems to be no use pretending otherwise, Professor," Ellie admitted sheepishly. "I wasn't looking forward to meeting you. Is there anything else you'd like to shock me with this morning? I don't think I feel embarrassed enough yet," she muttered, feeling both shamed and surly because of it.

"I'm sorry," he said, suddenly very serious. He set his hand on her forearm, earnestly wrapping his fingers around her. "I didn't mean to upset you."

Lovely. Now he's apologizing to you *because* you *didn't know about* his *dead wife. How did this happen?*

Liam did not move his hand. His bright-green eyes searched Ellie's face for some clue as to how to proceed. Ellie looked down at her eggs, the beautiful weight of Liam's hand still on her arm.

"Spend the day with me," he said suddenly. Ellie looked up, straight into eyes that were at once sad and imploring. It wasn't what she had expected to see, but it sent such a wistful pang through her that, at that moment, she'd have done anything he asked. "I have opera tickets tonight. Come with me."

"Of course I will." The answer left Ellie's lips before she could even process the request. And then, as if her body moved of its own free will, her other hand set on top of his, holding it in place on her arm, momentarily refusing to let go.

Eight

Oh, you…
Your face so plump, so fresh,
So full of fire,
So fierce.
How dare he interrupt your reading?
Your solitude,
Your dreaming of what lies ahead,
Your suppositions, innocent
expectations, belief in joy,
A world full of what ifs,
You ignorant fool…
If only you knew what I know now,
You wouldn't look so stern,
You wouldn't be wasting your time,
Head buried in a book,
You'd run free,
Feel,
Ache and fuck,
Frantic.

You'd know your time was
Ticking.

—AVERY VAUGHN,
"ADVICE FOR 'INTERRUPTED READING'"

The minute Liam left to check into his own hotel, Ellie tore out her laptop and turned it on. To her frustration, it took forever to connect to the hotel's Internet. She grabbed a pen and paper to jot down the name of his hometown and the word "Katherine" before she forgot. She would try to do a little research so maybe she wouldn't accidentally play the fool again today. See what she could find out.

Or maybe you're just the tiniest bit curious what his wife was like. Maybe that's why you're really interested now.

Finally the Internet connected, and she went directly to Google images, her fingers madly typing in "Liam and Katherine Curran." To her surprise, a virtual collage of Liam's face popped up, interspersed with photos, both individual and group shots, of a striking redhead, with wide brown eyes and perfect china skin, tiny next to Liam. There were several pictures that featured this woman in garish, overdone makeup and elaborate costumes and wigs. Ellie leaned in, squinting, clicking on pictures to make them bigger. This woman had to be Katherine. Ellie felt confused. Was she a stage actress? *A drag queen?* Ellie laughed out loud at the thought. Maybe she was going about this all wrong. She went back to Google and simply typed in "Katherine Curran."

The answer popped up immediately. Katherine Curran of London. Opera diva. *Celebrated* opera diva. A woman born of British "opera royalty" whose parents were world-renowned performers themselves. A woman who died tragically in some accident. Spring, 2005. *Right around the time Jordan got sick.* Ellie searched in vain for details of the accident but could find nothing. She glanced at the upper right hand side of her computer for the time. *Shit!* She had told Liam to give her about an hour and a half before they met up. This snooping around the Internet was eating into her shower time. And God knows after last night's dancing and this morning's run, she needed all the shower time she could get. Now she was going to have to rush.

Ellie was still blow-drying her hair when her cell phone buzzed against the counter.

From: Liam
I'm in the lobby. Do you want me to come up?

Ellie smiled in spite of herself. There was an unexpected thrill in getting a text from him. It was a juvenile and girlish reaction that took her by surprise. How weird to feel like a teenager. *Actually you are giddy, and really, it's sort of nice.*

To: Liam
Sure. Door's open.

Did she have time to straighten her hair? *Yes, just hurry!* She had already put on a simple fitted sundress and a pair of flip-flops. If they were going to the opera later, she was going to have to duck into one of these shops on Michigan Ave and find a nicer dress and a pair of heels. *Hope he doesn't mind shopping.* Alec would sooner shoot himself than follow Ellie into a dress shop. She suspected Liam would be more accommodating.

A few minutes later, she exited the bathroom to find Liam leaning casually against the kitchen counter and taking a long swig from a bottle of water. *God, could he be any more handsome?* He wore a pair of khaki shorts and a heather-gray V-neck shirt, his sunglasses hanging from the collar. As he set the water bottle down, surveying Ellie carefully while she entered the room; he also wore an unreadable expression. Was it amusement? Ellie's smile froze as she noticed her open computer on the counter, a dozen Liam and Katherine Curran photos smiling back at the two of them.

"Finally doing your research, huh?" Liam grinned.

Oh my God! Your stupidity knows no bounds. You left it open on the counter? That is fantastically dimwitted!

"Yes, and I am so suave that I left it open for you to see!" Ellie tried for levity. *May as well own it.*

"So what would you like to know?" Liam offered, folding his arms.

Folding his arms. Don't ask how she died. He's not ready to tell you that.

"Katherine was an opera singer?" Ellie asked tentatively.

"She was. A brilliant singer." He paused, searching for the right words. "It was difficult to believe that such sound could come from a human being. I lie not when I tell you her voice could make the hair on your arms and neck stand on end. Her voice was otherworldly."

"Is that how you met?"

"Through the opera?" Liam asked.

"Yes, did you see her there?" Ellie clarified.

"Oh, no. She wasn't yet done with school. We met very young actually. She was on holiday with her parents near Ingleton, and I led a walking tour they happened to take. I was on university break working, as my father insisted I do."

"You worked in between semesters?"

"I worked during the school year also. My father always feared my brothers and I would become lazy, entitled brats. He was almost obsessive about instilling in us independence and a fierce work ethic. So that's how I happened to meet Katherine."

"It sounds like your father would get along well with my mom." Ellie laughed, hoping the awkward moment had passed.

"Yes, I imagine they would get on well. If not for any other reason than their love of horses," Liam agreed.

"You have brothers?" Ellie continued.

"I do. Two older brothers. I'm the baby. And I'm constantly reminded of that fact!"

"You get teased, huh?" Ellie smiled.

"All in fun," Liam explained. "We are very close, but they band together in their claim that I am Mum's favorite! They won't let me live down the fact that I escaped working for the family business."

"What is that?" Ellie asked.

"Industry. My father founded an inspections and heat treatment company that works mostly with petroleum companies, refineries, and the such." Ellie looked blankly at Liam. He smiled and shrugged. "His company employs over twenty thousand people worldwide with offices in fifty countries. They basically make sure that factories, refineries, and power plants are all in good physical working order by inspecting piping and making repairs."

"And you studied literature?" Ellie began to understand the irony.

Liam laughed. "Yes, Elizabeth. As you might expect, my father was mildly irritated and very much perplexed that I wanted to go to the university to study something so frivolous. But wait!" He held up his forefinger, "My minor was music! I also played the bass violin. Which, of course, regressed into the bass guitar. I drove my father crazy!"

"Very impractical of you," Ellie agreed sarcastically.

"Most impractical of me!" Liam sighed. "My father was a good sport about it, though. I suppose he figured that he already had two sons with MBAs from Cambridge willing to take over the company. He didn't give me too much grief as long as I graduated at the top of my class."

"Which you did?"

"Yes, because I valued my life!" Liam kidded.

"Not because you really are as brilliant as your fan club thinks!"

"Well, I was not a brilliant musician, I assure you. I turned out to be a much better critical writer than I was a bassist."

"I would love to hear you play sometime," Ellie said. "I bet you're really good."

"Maybe you'll get lucky sometime." He winked. It felt like a loaded promise. "I'll play Mozart's twenty-ninth symphony. My all-time favorite."

"Perfect! I love Mozart!" Ellie exclaimed.

"Yes, you certainly have some eclectic tastes in music, Elizabeth." He motioned toward the door. "Shall we?"

"Where would you like to go?" Ellie asked.

"I would love to walk down to the art museum," Liam answered matter-of-factly as he opened the door for Ellie. "The concierge suggested we take a cab, but I think the two of us can manage the walk. It's lovely today anyhow. Not too hot. What do you think?"

"It's a great museum." Ellie smiled weakly. She could do this. "I used to spend a lot of time there when I lived in Chicago," she admitted.

"Then you will have much to share with me," Liam said encouragingly. Again, his choice of words seemed to have dual meanings.

Oh, give me a break! You think he can read your mind?

"Do you mind if we stop to find a dress for me to wear tonight?" Ellie asked almost sheepishly.

A wide grin spread across Liam's face. "Only if I get to pick it out," he answered, cocking his head to the side slightly. Was he joking or was he flirting? "No, I certainly do not mind," he assured her. Shutting the door behind her, he placed his hand at the small of her back to guide her to the elevator—a simple, friendly gesture that felt so sensuous to Ellie that her knees were weak.

I will die if he knows how attracted I am to him. How pathetic and inappropriate would it be—a married woman, a colleague—to fall all over him? Anyhow surely there was no end to the line of available women waiting to "welcome" him to America. Ellie would simply enjoy his company today, the immature satisfaction at being seen with this Greek god of a man, not having to share his attention with a classroom of students or a bevy of gawking, admiring professors.

It was afternoon by the time they made their leisurely way down Michigan Avenue, greeted by a cool summer breeze courtesy of the evening's rainstorm. Throngs of tourists and shoppers ambled along the street in no great hurry. This was tourist Chicago, not to be confused with the bustle of working Chicago. This wasn't a scene Ellie remembered very well. She was always on and off the El platform, walking with a purpose. Funny how the physical city had not changed much, but the feel of it had. *What age and distance will do to your perspective.*

They walked much of the way in silence, Liam's face turning often, his eyes surveying every detail of the architecture. Occasionally he'd ask Ellie about a building or a landmark ("What river is this?") but otherwise, he seemed content to contemplate his surroundings.

"The city is very clean," he observed.

"It is actually," Ellie agreed. "Nice landscaping too. I'm always impressed by how well the trees and city gardens are kept when I visit here."

"Do you garden?" Liam inquired.

"Just flowers," Ellie answered. "But the outdoors were sort of my father's religion. He made sure my sister, Becca, and I could name every single native plant, tree, and wildflower on our property. He was pretty intense about it. Do you garden, Dr. Curran?"

"I do actually. My mother is quite the gardener. Really talented. She is more a landscape architect than a casual gardener. For her, it's an art, not just a hobby. Against my will, I learned much about gardening as a boy by being forced to help her plant and weed. She has always had the most elaborate English garden you're ever likely to see on a private estate. In London, I just grow vegetables. I have a rooftop garden that I manage with my neighbors."

"I bet they'll miss you this summer," Ellie predicted.

"They are getting on OK, I think," Liam responded. "By some great fortune, the house I'm renting this summer had a garden in back. Several of the plants returned from last year, and I was able to put some in this past week too."

"Really? Where are you staying?" Ellie asked.

"Your friend, Joe Dobbs, his mother's home," Liam answered. Ellie knew the house well—a small cottage-like ranch, not too different from the home Linda Purnell once inhabited. Joe's mother had died right before Christmas last year, leaving the well-kept home to Joe. The housing market made it a foolish idea for Joe to part with it, and it was far too nice to be defiled by a bunch of college renters. So there it sat until Liam came.

"What a great idea to let you stay there!" Ellie exclaimed genuinely. "You know, Joe's mom just died this past winter? I'm sure he's thrilled to have someone in the home to tend to it, even if it is just for a couple of months."

"Yes, he has been very gracious. We talked at length the first night I moved in. Had a few bad American beers together!" He laughed. "Obviously his grief is still pretty fresh. He's getting divorced right now, too."

"So he told me," Ellie admitted.

"I'm honored that he trusts me to stay there," Liam mused. "At least I can bring the garden back to life. It will be nice to give him some tomatoes at the end of the summer, maybe some herbs that his mother planted last year. A little reminder that life does indeed continue on."

"That sounds very 'Leaves of Grass,'" Ellie commented with a smile.

"I suppose it does," Liam agreed, quoting Whitman. "'The smallest sprout shows there is really no death, and if ever there was it led forward life.'"

"So you are a true believer of Whitman philosophy?" Ellie asked. "It's not just literary criticism?"

"Entirely," Liam answered, a gentle smile playing over his face as he looked down to meet Ellie's gaze. He was lovely. "Whitman was not the source of his own beliefs. Unbeknownst to him, perhaps, he was a Buddhist. What do you believe, Elizabeth?" he asked suddenly, the question so forward, it caught Ellie by surprise.

"I'm not sure," she admitted quietly, the sounds of traffic suddenly obvious and deafening. "My mother is a staunch atheist, and my father, well, he's a poet!" Ellie laughed. "He's still grappling with God. To this very day, fighting it out. Wanting to believe in something but full of unbridled cynicism." They crossed the street toward the museum, the landmark lions heralding their arrival. "I wasn't exactly raised in a traditional household," Ellie acknowledged as they approached the side of the museum.

"Certainly your parents weren't Buddhists."

Liam let out a bellowing laugh, tossing his head back as he walked. "God, no," he answered. "My father is a strict Catholic, and my mother converted because she loved him. He left Ireland for her, and she left the Church of England for him. It was possibly the greatest compromise ever struck in the name of love!"

"Come here!" Ellie exclaimed suddenly, taking Liam's hand. "I want to show you something!"

Instead of going to the front entrance of the museum, they ducked into a side gate hidden by trees. Right there off Michigan Ave on the grounds of the museum was a reflecting pool and fountain with a charming, unexpected garden.

"I used to spend a lot of time writing here," Ellie said. It felt good to reminisce out loud, to return with Liam as some weird sort of emotional protection. They found a shaded, private spot to sit. Ellie always loved these secret corners of the city, where she could sit unnoticed and watch the world go by.

"So your father left Ireland for your mother?" Ellie dug for details. "Sounds very romantic!"

"He did, but that is a long, complicated story," Liam sighed. "My dad was an Irish nationalist, very involved in The Troubles during the late 1960s. He's never admitted to doing anything truly violent, but I know my father's intensity. Meeting my mother probably saved his life." Liam waved his hand somewhat dismissively, "Do you want to talk Irish history or go look at art?"

I could sit here and listen to you all day. "Oh, fine!" Ellie pouted. "Promise me I'll get to hear more of your life story later, then!"

"I promise." Liam smiled sincerely. "But only if I get to hear more about yours." He allowed her to get up first, smoothing her dress against her abdomen, the innocent action at once becoming suggestive as she noticed him watching her intently. She turned toward the museum, a smirk threatening to surface.

I'll give you something to watch if that's what you want!

She let him walk a few feet behind her before turning to make sure he followed. He was following, all right, his eyes glinting with amused satisfaction. The smile that played across his face confirmed that he knew Ellie's game, but he certainly didn't seem to mind.

For hours, they wandered around the museum quietly together, comfortably near one another, shoulders touching, as they stood to contemplate the works of art. Oftentimes the nearness of Liam's face to Ellie's ear as he read over her, so close she could feel his breath in her hair, was almost too much to bear. She had to consciously resist the urge to back into him, throwing her arms up around his neck so he could clasp her from behind and bury his face in her neck. She amused herself all day by imagining what he might do if she suddenly turned to kiss him.

How near can we get to one another without actually touching?

At each new painting, she would move just the slightest bit closer. Move in. Move in. Just a bit closer. Stop. Just barely close enough to brush naked forearms, elbows, fingers.

And then Liam stopped suddenly. There *she* was. The Jean-Baptiste Camille-Corot painting, "Interrupted Reading." *Old friend.*

Ellie had gotten so wrapped up in her little game that she had forgotten to feel sullen today. *Fuck sullen.* She was actually enjoying the moment. Strange. Instead of brooding about the past, she tilted her face intently toward the picture, allowing a cleansing sense of grateful reminiscence to flow through her.

This young girl's annoyed face had watched her write many an essay.

"There you are!" Liam gestured toward the painting. Ellie looked at him with well-disguised surprise. For a split second, she thought maybe…no.

How could he possibly know? No. I never told him about this painting.

Ellie smiled with confusion.

"The look on her face reminds me of you!" Liam joked. He leaned in to look at the title of the painting. "Hmm, 'Interrupted Reading.' I should guess that is the same look you might give anyone who interrupts you…in anything." He laughed.

Ellie sighed inwardly, relieved. *OK. That's what he meant.* She laughed in response. "I suppose so."

"Yes, she looks quite *stern*, doesn't she?" he asked slyly. "A fierce look, wouldn't you say?"

Ellie's heart stopped.

That was not a coincidence. His choice of "stern" and "fierce" was not a coincidence. He's read your poetry.

"She does look stern, Dr. Curran. If I could talk to her, I might tell her to lighten up some," Ellie said, challenging him.

"Is that right, Professor?" Liam turned to face Ellie, his green eyes dancing with mischief.

"Yes, youth seems to be wasted on the young, doesn't it, Dr. Curran? I would tell her to stop wasting her time reading! Go out and live a little because…"

"Time is ticking?" Liam finished.

"Exactly," Ellie replied as nonchalantly as she could. Trying to turn casually toward the next painting, her heart beating furiously in her ears.

He knows. He knows Avery Vaughn is you.

Oh my God! He had obviously read her poem about this painting. What else had he read? What else did he know?

He knows everything about you then, stupid! He knows about every single fucked-up part of you, how about that?

Ellie suddenly felt naked, ridiculous. She didn't want to be known. She didn't want anyone looking into her soul. She certainly didn't want to explain away the pathetic details of her numb existence. Feeling suddenly as if she might cry, her face tingling and hot, she wandered away toward the other side of the room, pretending to investigate another series of paintings. She dared not turn around for fear of giving away her emotions.

Minutes later, two warm hands rested tentatively on her bare shoulders, an apology of sorts. A truce. A "sorry for calling you out." Liam said nothing, and Ellie didn't move to shake his hands away. It was an oddly intimate stance for two almost perfect strangers.

But then again, this man is really not a stranger, is he? He probably knows more about you than anyone now.

They both stood motionless, statues among statues, absently looking up at the paintings. Consumed by their proximity to one another, flesh on flesh.

So what if he knew she was Avery Vaughn? She would still play stupid. He didn't seem malicious; he wouldn't press her, would he? After all, she didn't press him about his dead wife.

"Shall we find that dress?" Liam asked gently.

"Sure," Ellie answered without turning around. Her face still smarted as if she had been slapped.

They left the museum quietly and walked back down Michigan Ave in silence, Liam patiently waiting for Ellie to extend an olive branch. She wasn't sulking exactly, but trying to make small talk seemed disingenuous. She didn't want to pretend. It took too much work. Luckily she spotted a mannequin wearing the perfect summer dress through one of the shop windows. A deep afternoon exhaustion had hit her, and she was really no longer in the mood to shop. It took no more than twenty minutes for Ellie to duck into the store, try the dress on, and purchase it, along with the same pair of shoes from the display, as Liam wandered about the store amicably, attracting the attention of every woman inside.

"I hope no one at the opera tonight recognizes that I'm dressed just like the mannequin on Michigan Ave." Ellie laughed. "So much for originality!"

"You will bring that dress to life though," Liam assured her. "I'm sure you'll look stunning."

"I'm sure you always have just the right thing to say." She smiled.

"And I'm sure you couldn't take a compliment if you tried," he shot back.

"It's frustrating, isn't it?" She felt just the slightest bit defensive.

"It is," he admitted without smiling. "Let's have an early dinner. I'm starving. That should give us enough time to get changed and make it to the opera by seven."

"Good idea," Ellie agreed.

And it was a good idea. By the time they had finished a bottle of Pinot Noir with bread and salad, Ellie didn't care where they went or what they talked about. It had taken all the fight out of her. She leaned comfortably in her patio chair as they sat under the umbrella at an outdoor café about a block from their hotels. The late-afternoon sun blazed behind nearby buildings, but they were shrouded in the shade of skyscrapers, a temperate, intermittent breeze rustling the tablecloth.

"So what was it like growing up with your father?" Liam asked, casually sipping from his water as they waited for their fish.

"What do you mean?" Ellie asked.

"Well, is he much different than his writing? I am such an admirer of your father's work, but he was not exactly what I'd expected."

"You expected a crazy old radical?" Ellie laughed, clasping her hands together. "Allen Ginsberg, perhaps?"

Liam laughed heartily. "Well, yes, I suppose I did."

"And instead you met someone very normal. Almost invisibly normal. The type of guy you'd pass by at the grocery store without a second glance. The old guy with the coupons!"

"Yes! Exactly!" Liam agreed, amused.

"Well, don't be fooled." Ellie smiled darkly. "My father is a complicated man. He has a wicked sense of humor and loves passionately. I guess he just wears his eccentricities on the inside."

"Such as?" Liam pried.

"Oh, I don't know. He had a penchant for disappearing." It was a strong choice of verb that surprised even Ellie as it came honestly from her mouth. She checked herself immediately. "He was gone a lot. I mean, he traveled a lot when we were kids, for book tours and lectures, and…I guess we just came to accept that was normal. My mother never did much complaining or much explaining." Ellie stopped to reflect.

Honestly since she had become a mother, she had spent much more time contemplating her mother's, not her father's, influence on her development. She had thought at length about how she did (or didn't) want to act as a mother based on what Maggie Lawson had done. But not her dad. Her father always seemed a bit larger than life to her, swooping in with gifts from foreign lands, taking the girls on hours-long walks through the woods, camping out in the barn with them, and letting them stay up as late as they wanted on the rare occasions Maggie Lawson was away. Eating peanut butter out of the jar with a spoon as he quoted Shakespeare in his bathrobe from the front porch. Skinny dipping in the river.

"I don't quite know how to sum him up," Ellie almost whispered. "I always had the sense that my father loved us unconditionally. Isn't that what every kid needs? He wasn't the rock of the house, for sure. That was my mom. But we were in love with our dad."

"Maybe *because* he wasn't around consistently," Liam offered matter-of-factly.

"Maybe," Ellie considered. "When he was though, he was all ours."

"And that was enough." It sounded more like a statement than a question.

"Well, it was all we knew," Ellie answered. "It had to be enough." What did he mean? God, he had such a cryptic way with words sometimes.

I am not falling into your trap, Dr. Curran. I am not divulging too much personal information and then feeling resentful about it.

And yet she couldn't help herself. "Do you mean was I angry that he was gone so much?"

"Were you?" he asked innocently.

"No. I don't think I was. I mean, he was working."

"Was he?"

"I suppose he was. A kid doesn't question those things."

"You've read his poetry though?" Liam asked with a raised eyebrow. "Certainly a teenager, an adult, would question."

"I have, Liam, yes. He's my dad, though. Some things you don't really want to know. I know my dad suffered from depression. He's probably a little bit manic too. I imagine that's why he was gone a lot. Fighting demons, you know? But I don't blame him for his secrets. We all have secrets," Ellie answered defensively.

"That we do, Elizabeth," Liam agreed.

The waiter interrupted their conversation with two steaming platters of salmon and asparagus, setting them down gently on either side.

"Well, I can tell you the narratives of your father's confessional poetry, whether real or fabricated, were plenty to get a young man interested in studying literature."

"So you credit my father with inspiring you to study American literature?" Ellie asked as she took a bite of her meal, grateful to redirect the discussion.

"Well, I certainly enjoyed studying him during my contemporary American literature class while I was working on my first degree. Honestly, it was the great Walt Whitman who really spoke to me. I had to read 'Oh Captain, My Captain' in secondary school, and ultimately that inspired me to focus my master's thesis and my dissertation on American literature. I found everything American fascinating as a teenager. I suppose America had the same appeal to me that England had to you."

"Yeah?" Ellie asked as she broke a piece of her fish with her fork. "What was it you found so fascinating?"

"I guess the whole paradox of America, the fact that this is such a fabled country founded on ideals of equality and rebellion and self-sufficiency, and of course, independence, and yet historically, those things were offered to such a limited few."

"Very true," Ellie agreed between bites.

"The traditional British stance of antimonarchy rebellion seemed all very dull to me. And my father didn't dare involve me in Irish politics, so I found myself very curious about American history in relation to its literature."

"So how did you come to read Whitman's 'Song of Myself' as a religious manifesto?"

"I never used the word 'manifesto,'" Liam denied.

"No, you didn't," Ellie corrected herself, "but you said you definitely believed it to be a spiritual text, a stream of consciousness, almost, a personal search for spiritual answers…"

"So you *were* listening yesterday!" Liam teased as he cut into his food.

"I was hanging on your every word," Ellie replied, just a bit sarcastically.

"Right after you walked in an hour late." Liam smiled ambiguously.

Unbelievable. Nothing gets past this guy.

"I'm sorry." Ellie felt a blush spread across her cheeks. "I had no idea the entire English department was coming to your lecture. No one told me. I thought I was just dropping in casually to observe some class."

"Why did they not tell you?" Liam inquired more gently.

"Perhaps because you were so confrontational at the debate?" Ellie accused playfully.

"Or because you fled the debate in a snit?" Liam laughed heartily, leaning back slightly in his chair, thoroughly enjoying his own joke.

"I did." Ellie grinned sheepishly. "I'm sorry."

"Stop apologizing," Liam commanded. "I find you…"

"Amusing, apparently," Ellie offered sullenly.

"Yes. Not in the way that you think, though," Liam replied thoughtfully, putting another forkful of fish into his mouth as he searched for just the right words. "I find you challenging. Amusing and challenging. And confusing. It's wonderful." He looked down at his food thoughtfully, moving it around with the end of his fork, and then almost to himself, he said, "It is just as it should be."

"What do you mean?" Ellie asked, confused.

"Everything is as it should be," Liam answered. "Everything is as it should be." He repeated it so easily, a mantra of sorts.

"What is meant?" Ellie raised her eyebrows in question.

Liam laughed. "That *is* what you said in the lecture, isn't it? You blurted out 'what is meant.'" He again seemed almost to be talking to himself, and then looking up suddenly, he added, "Yes, 'what is meant.' But I suspect that you mean that in a different way than I do. I suspect you overanalyze everything in search of 'what is meant.' As in 'what is supposed to be?' What is supposed to happen? What is Elizabeth supposed to be doing, thinking, reading, writing, saying? But that is not what I mean."

"You seem to think you know me quite well." Ellie raised her eyebrows as she leaned into the table on her elbows.

"Am I wrong?" he asked incredulously, confident in his assumption.

"I don't know if you're wrong, Dr. Curran. Explain to me 'what is meant,'" Ellie said, gesturing with air quotes, "and I'll let you know if that's how I mean it."

"Consider this, Elizabeth." He leaned in to look at her, serious and intense, narrowing the space between their faces to less than a foot. "Everything that ever happens *is* 'what is meant' simply because 'everything is as it should be.'"

Ellie leaned back in her chair, breaking his gaze to focus on an indistinct spot on the underside of the umbrella, contemplating the difference or the connection between 'what is meant' and 'everything is as it should be.' A slow, ironic smile played across her lips.

"Ahh, see?" Liam asked, tilting his head.

"I do see," Ellie said, really still unsure. "In essence, you are saying that everything happens exactly as it should. There is no use in obsessing over life's events because…"

"Everything is as it should be. Everything has a perfect order to it," Liam explained. "Even what is awful. Or what we deem awful."

"So embrace the present?" Ellie searched for meaning.

"Yes. Be present. Everything is as it should be. It is a comforting philosophy, isn't it?" Liam questioned.

"I suppose," Ellie muttered, unconvinced. "So this is meant?" She waved her hand over the table between the two of them.

"This is *certainly* meant," Liam declared without breaking his gaze.

Something about his intensity made Ellie slightly nervous. His words always seemed to have double meanings, personal inside jokes. And while Ellie didn't exactly feel she was the brunt of the joke, it was disconcerting not to fully comprehend what he meant. *Everything is as it should be.*

"I might have to let this absorb a while, Dr. Curran," Ellie admitted with a playful sigh.

"Fair enough." Liam grinned. "It took me a long while, much of my life, to let it settle in. Accepting this one simple truth is the path to peace."

"Is this the path I'm supposed to be on?" Ellie asked, amused.

"Isn't it the path everyone is supposed to be on?" Liam returned, quite serious. "I imagine that's why you dance. Why you came here to dance."

"I dance because I love to dance."

"Then why is it some secret?"

"Because…" Ellie paused. Why was he always digging? And she let him! Why couldn't she just keep the conversation focused on him? There was no way she was going to explain why she kept these trips a secret. *Spite. Self-preservation. Having a second life helps me to cope.* If he did read Avery Vaughn, he could make inferences, but there was no way she would let the truth come directly from her own mouth. *I am dying inside.* "It's more fun that way, Liam."

"Indeed," he answered noncommittally and then continued to eat in silence. The inquisition was temporarily over.

From: Marta
Back at hotel. Where are you?

To: Marta
Coming back to change now. Are you alone?

E. J. Densmore

From: Marta
Yes.

⁓

"Welcome back to the land of the living." Ellie greeted her friend, who was wrapped in a blanket on the sofa, the lights of the suite dimmed so low they were almost off.

"Just barely." Marta laughed. "Where have you been?"

"Where have *you* been?" Ellie asked. Now she was starting to talk like Liam, answering a question with a question.

"I was with Lily and Tony and a bunch of other people last night. Not at all what you think." Marta defended herself prematurely.

"And where do you think I've been?" Ellie asked with a smug grin.

"Well, I hope you've been with Liam," Marta answered as if it were the most natural thing in the world. As if his showing up weren't strange or unexpected in the least.

"I don't appreciate surprises, Marta," Ellie said resentfully.

"I know," Marta answered dismissively. "That was some surprise though, huh?" She laughed to herself— a hoarse, tired sound full of mischief and self-gratitude.

Ellie stood at Marta's feet, waiting for further explanation. "I thought he'd be good company for you," Marta finally offered with a shrug.

"He has been," Ellie admitted. "He's brilliant to listen to. And, of course, gracious and…"

"Oh my God, please!" Marta cut her off. "That's all you have to say about him?"

"What were you expecting me to say?" Ellie's brows furrowed in disdain.

"Don't make that look. It's unflattering," Marta teased.

"Shut up. I'm pissed at you still," Ellie retorted.

"No you're not. You are dying to tell me about Liam, but you have to act mad about Lily first. OK, OK…let's get it out of the way. Ellie, I am so sorry I had sex with Lily last night. I am also sorry I didn't tell you Liam was coming. Are we good now?" Marta patronized playfully. She was right. God, she had a way of disarming Ellie.

"I just feel weird that he knows about us coming to dance," Ellie admitted finally, picking up Marta's feet and propping them on her lap as she sat under them on the sofa.

"I figured, 'who cares?'" Marta explained. "He lives in London. It's not like he's going to go back and tell somebody what you, the grand Dr. Purnell, does on her weekends. The guy is here for a couple of months and then he's gone. Who cares what he knows? I doubt he's judging you. I think he believes you walk on water."

"I don't know where you get that from." Ellie felt confounded. "He does nothing but give me shit constantly."

"I doubt that," Marta replied. "Look how annoyed you became after the debate, and he was just doing what anyone does in a debate! Asking you difficult questions is not necessarily giving you shit. Besides you're not looking too upset right now. Have you been with him all day?"

"Yeah, we went to the Art Institute earlier today and just finished dinner…"

"See, it was good of me to invite him." Marta sounded pleased with herself.

"…And tonight we're going to see *Otello* at the Civic Opera House," Ellie finished.

Marta sat up, tossing her head back slightly with laughter. "You're having a super shitty time then, huh?"

Ellie's entire demeanor changed suddenly, full of adolescent enthusiasm, "He's beautiful, Marta. I mean, really stupidly attractive," Ellie admitted with dismay. "And fascinating. Just brilliant. And maybe a bit smug and arrogant. I can't really tell."

"So!" Marta nearly squealed.

"So maybe I enjoy his company too much," Ellie admitted. "Maybe that's why I feel mad."

"Stop thinking so damn much," Marta suggested. She laid back down on the couch. "I am going to sleep a little while more, maybe meet Tony out again tonight.

He'll be bummed that you're not there, but I think maybe you're meant to be at this opera."

Yes, "meant" to be there. "Maybe so," Ellie agreed and then disappeared into the bathroom to clean up.

The little black dress Ellie bought may have been the single most flattering thing she'd ever purchased. It was as though it had been tailored especially for her, hiding all of her perceived figure flaws and accentuating her small waist and bust. Her mother's practical voice in her head told her to run back to the store the next day and buy the dress in every color! When she came out of the elevator to meet Liam in the lobby, the look on his face confirmed that she really did look as good as she thought she did.

"You are beautiful," he said sincerely as he held out his hand to her.

"Thank you," Ellie replied quietly, even though her first reaction was to brush off the compliment. "You clean up quite nicely yourself!" She grabbed his hand and allowed him to lead her outside to a waiting cab. He wore a beige linen suit and a verbena green shirt that brought out the color of his eyes.

Am I obviously swooning?

She decided she wouldn't try to hide the satisfied grin that spread across her face. It was, after all, somewhat thrilling to be seen with this man. This man who was impossible to miss. And people would look at them and think they were together. And maybe she would let them think that. And maybe she would enjoy pretending herself. What was the harm in that?

It had been a long time since Ellie had been at Chicago's Civic Opera house. She had forgotten the romance of it—its golden splendor, its regal burgundy staircases, and its elaborate filigreed ceilings. It felt as though she and Liam had stepped back in time 120 years, surrounded by the quiet elegance of this nineteenth-century structure. Liam pulled two folded pieces of paper from his suit coat and handed them to the usher.

"Box level, up the stairs," the usher instructed.

"You bought two box seats?" Ellie looked up at Liam with surprised gratitude.

"It's rude to buy only one." He smiled. "I guess it's good you agreed to come. I would have had to use the other seat for my legs!"

They ascended the stairs to the box-level floor, finding their individually numbered door. Entering through a darkly lit paneled vestibule, which, as Liam commented, resembled a confessional booth, they located their seats.

Ellie laughed as they chose two chairs at the back of the eight-seat box, "It would seem you might need an extra seat for your legs after all! These boxes were obviously made for people much smaller than you!" she teased.

"See how everything is as it should be!" Liam replied as he struggled to get comfortable in the worn, plush, velvet chairs. "You'll be forced to sit very close to me now!"

Several older couples entered the box through the private door, nodding to Ellie and Liam as they shuffled by with their programs. Their timing was perfect. The opera was about to start.

Ellie was, in fact, so close to Liam that she could hear his relaxed, even breathing. Smell his cologne. His warm shoulder touched her bare skin. It was pure bliss and torture all at once. She could do nothing about the curious ache that grew in her stomach, radiating lower into her groin. She was captive. Silent. Left alone with her wandering thoughts.

What goes on in that head of his?
Maybe he is thinking of his dead wife.
So what if he is?
And you're thinking about him.
So what if I am? What would it feel like to straddle him, run my hands over his chest, around his neck, hold his face close to mine? Bury my tongue in his mouth and taste him slowly. Revel in the wet warmth of his mouth on my...

The thought made Ellie even more uncomfortable as she shifted in her seat, purposely moving closer to Liam as innocently as possible, searching for some little

E. J. Densmore

bit of satisfaction. Any relief from the tension that had mounted in her body.

Eventually the lights dimmed, elaborately costumed singers emerging from backstage. The singers' voices were heavenly echoes that enveloped them as Liam's rhythmic breathing lulled Ellie into an oddly peaceful half sleep, the physical tension finally subsiding.

Thunderous applause. Ellie snapped awake, her head still partially leaning on Liam's shoulder.

"Your wife is tired," one of the older gentlemen in their box commented as he rose to leave. "I usually snag the back seat myself so I can snooze!" he joked. His wife swatted him with her program.

"She *is* tired." Liam did not correct him. There was a tone of protection in his voice.

Ellie struggled awake. "I'm so sorry I fell asleep," she apologized, hoping she hadn't smeared lipstick on his shirt.

"It's been a long day," he said, defending her. "No need to apologize. Shall we get something to drink during intermission?"

"Sure," Ellie agreed. "Maybe I should drink some caffeine. I'm going to stop at the restroom first, though."

"I'll walk with you," Liam offered, of course the perfect gentleman.

Fine with me. You can escort me wherever you want!

Still a little foggy headed, Ellie entered the restroom and stopped immediately at the mirror. *Oh, thank God! Makeup still in place. No noticeable drool.* She smoothed her hair, touched up her lipstick, and took care of business as quickly as possible, knowing she left Liam waiting outside the door.

As she left the bathroom, she spotted him standing across the foyer, leaning against a pillar, relaxed and beautiful, eyeing her every step. It brought a genuine smile to her face as she lifted her hand slightly to signal she had seen him.

"Ellie!" a familiar voice called out to her from the left of Liam. But closer. She stopped where she stood, scanning a small crowd of passing people to locate the sound.

"Ellie?" a man stood in front of her. Someone possibly around her age with thinning blond hair and blue eyes peering back at her. Familiar blue eyes. A blond middle-aged woman in a plain burgundy dress and a string of pearls trailed behind him and then stopped at his side.

"How are you? What are you doing in Chicago?" The man reached out to pat Ellie's upper arm.

Dylan. Oh my God. Dylan! Ellie could barely recognize him; he had aged so badly. *Do I look like that? Obviously not. He could recognize you!*

"I...I'm good." She faked a smile, feeling at first embarrassed that she didn't recognize him, and then sick to her stomach that he was standing directly in front of her after all of these years. This wasn't the way she'd envisioned it. "I'm here to see the opera," Ellie stammered. *You're here to see the opera? No shit!*

"It's so good to run into you!" Dylan exclaimed stupidly, disregarding Ellie's idiotic response. "You look great!"

"Thanks." Ellie smiled feebly.

"My parents still sit on the board of directors at Civic. We're here all the time, but I've never seen you," Dylan explained.

"Oh, I live back in Wisconsin. I took my father's job at the university."

That sounded lame. "I took my father's job." Stupid.
Oh, who cares. He probably took his father's job too.

"This is my wife, Maddie." Dylan motioned to the woman at his side, who suddenly looked like all the color had drained from her face. She had the look of someone with money, perfectly bobbed blond hair and flawless makeup on a face that was probably once pretty, an impassive set to her mouth.

Maddie?

"Madison?" Ellie asked, just a bit too tinged with contempt.

"Hi, Ellie." She held out her hand tentatively.

Without thinking, Ellie spontaneously took Madison's hand, the meeting of their palms utterly repulsive. Suddenly a strong, protective arm was around Ellie, Liam's hand at her waist.

"Hello." Liam held out his other hand to Dylan, towering over him by at least four or five inches. After they shook, he then extended his hand to Madison, who looked up at him admiringly.

"Liam, this is Dylan and Madison. We're old friends." She couldn't help her sarcasm.

"Really?" Liam played along, but Ellie saw a flash of understanding in his eyes.

"Yes, we all used to live in the same brownstone. Dylan and Madison went to DePaul University."

"While Ellie was at the University of Chicago," Dylan offered, still looking amiable and clueless. Did he really believe she was happy to run into him? Jackass.

"This is Liam." Ellie leaned into Liam unconsciously, affectionately, and then without being able to stop herself, she said, "He's my husband."

"Oh." Dylan looked confused. "Nice to meet you."

"Likewise." Liam flashed a convincing smile. "Shall we head back to the box, love?" he asked Ellie.

"Sure." She smiled genuinely. She really did want to get away from them. She felt ashen and sick to her stomach.

"Good to meet you," Liam said dismissively and then led Ellie back toward the door to their box. The lights flashed, signaling the end of intermission. Ellie's palms shook. Liam opened the door quickly and ushered Ellie into the dark, tiny vestibule of their box.

"What's wrong?" he took both her wrists in his hands, steadying her. "You look as if you're holding back a scream."

"Stop," Ellie commanded.

"Holding Back a Scream." I know you know that I'm Avery Vaughn. OK. I know you know.

"Stop what?" Liam asked, feigning innocence.

"Stop taunting me," Ellie begged, angry tears threatening her eyes.

Liam's hands moved up to her shoulders, tightening. Then suddenly, he pulled her into his chest, his head bending to meet her mouth, where he forcefully pressed his lips against hers. She untensed, her entire body becoming limp, her mouth opening eagerly. His tongue met hers with insistence as she put both her palms against his chest, sinking into his forceful, sudden embrace. His lips were as soft and full as she'd imagined. He kissed her with a passionate urgency that was mirrored by the longing in the pit of her stomach as she lost all sense of time and place. He smelled so good. She reached up to touch his stubbled jaw, his hair. His hands moved down her back and pulled her in even closer, the kiss deepening with fierce, unchecked want.

Then just as suddenly, his hands released her, and he pulled hesitantly away, looking as though he, too, was surprised. A calmness returned to his face, a serene mask he was able to place on almost effortlessly.

Ellie stood trembling, a deep sigh raising and then lowering her chest as she caught her breath. *Oh my God. That was wrong. I want you. I want you more than I've ever wanted anything in my life, but that was wrong.*

"That was meant," Liam whispered heavily, answering her inner thoughts as if he could read her mind. "Don't overanalyze." Then taking her hand, he opened the inner door of the box vestibule and led her back to their seats.

Nine

October of Ellie Purnell's Thirtieth Year

I wait,
Holding the air inside my
Stressed lungs,
Wishing for "the dream" to die,
Washing out the hope
So that I can rest -
Shut my eyes.
Finally,
Be at peace,
Knowing that this is all there is,
This tepid existence,
Birthday parties, games,
Grocery lists and calendars.
I wait for my stupid heart
To sputter out its final futile pump -
To give in,
Give up,
Accept this fading into middle age,

Ambivalence,
(death)
Make it OK to simply tolerate the person who
Shares my bed,
Graying and bloating before my eyes,
Nothing here resembling love.
Resign.

—AVERY VAUGHN, "RESIGNATION"

"So what is it you would like, Ellie?" The therapist leaned in, clasping his hands in front of him gently in an attempt to be nonthreatening. Alec looked on passively, maybe even a bit bored.

What do I want? What do I want?

"I would just like for Alec to be able to have a few drinks and then stop. You know, like *most* people do," Ellie added for effect. "Be able to drink socially without getting wasted. I would like for him to go out and come home at a decent hour."

"So why can't he?" the therapist asked.

What do you mean why the fuck can't he?'

It was their fourth session of marriage counseling, and this guy was still asking the same stupid questions.

I have a question for you, sir. Why do I have to keep telling you the same thing over and over? It was bad enough that she had one stupid man who didn't listen to what she was saying. Now add this idiot to the list. And to top it off, she was actually paying this guy to be dense. Talk about adding insult to injury.

Maybe this is a ploy. Maybe he is setting up some epiphany for Alec.

Or maybe not.

"He can't because he's an alcoholic," Ellie stated matter-of-factly.

"Do you think you're an alcoholic?" the therapist asked Alec. Ellie cringed inwardly. *Do you really think he's going to say yes?*

"No," Alec answered immediately, avoiding eye contact with Ellie.

Oh my God, guy! Why do you think we're here? She glared at the doctor.

"So what do *you* think is the problem, then?" The therapist turned his body toward Alec.

"I don't really know," Alec admitted somewhat defensively. A long, deafening silence followed. Ellie crossed her arms angrily and shifted in her chair. It was taking all of her self-control not to lash out at them both by knocking everything off the large mahogany desk the therapist sat smugly behind.

I'll be damned if I'm going to look like the psycho here, the nagging wife. I am not going to fall into the role that Alec has set up for me.

She had to sit back and be patient. She knew that the only way to make things better was to "hear" Alec out in an environment that was nonthreatening. This seemed so fucking stupid, though. Yes, counseling was her idea, but she had to feign interest in his "feelings" in order to get him to listen to her at all. To make some changes.

Maybe it was a good question: What do you want?

What did she want? Maybe she just wanted to be happy again.

Again? When were you happy in the first place?

She just wanted to make this marriage work. She wanted her son to have two parents. Maybe she wanted another baby too, but she couldn't do that if she didn't have any help. One was hard enough. Could she really handle another colicky infant on her own? Not when she had a four-year-old to take care of. There was no way she could keep her sanity if she was working full time, fulfilling her obligation to publish, taking care of the house, and then caring for Jordan *and* an infant. Even with a housekeeper, a gardener, and her mother to help, it would be too much. After all, it would be Ellie who would be getting up in the middle of the night to nurse a crying baby. No one else could do that for her. Maybe she just wanted Alec to be present. To be sober. To talk with her. To give her moral support. To spend time with her and Jordan. Did she really care about the drinking? Maybe she wouldn't mind the drinking if he helped her out more. Picked up some of the slack.

Don't lie to yourself. You're lonely. The drinking takes him away as much as the traveling.

It did occur to Ellie that maybe she didn't really mind the drinking at all. If Alec were a more active participant in the running of the house, the caregiving, she might actually turn a blind eye to his overindulgence in alcohol. She let Alec build her a wine cellar in the basement of their house, after all. When he showed her the architect's plans, it crossed her mind only once that having that much alcohol in the house might appear an inadvertent nod of approval for his drinking habits. But then, it was such an extravagant addition to the house, really built especially for Ellie (Alec didn't drink much wine) that she couldn't refuse it. Maybe it was Alec's way of placating her. She wasn't sure.

"Can you tell him what you believe the problem is?" the therapist asked, addressing Ellie. Another long silence followed as Ellie contemplated exactly what to say. Hadn't she been telling him all along what the problem was? Hadn't she said a million times that she needed more help?

"I'm lonely," she almost whispered. She had blocked out the presence of the therapist, focusing directly on Alec, who sat in a separate chair at the other side of the office. It was a calculated move. Anger wasn't getting her anywhere. She decided to try vulnerable and desperate. Once the words left her mouth, however, she found she was not acting. The crack in her voice was authentic. Alec's face softened. It wasn't quite contrite or empathetic, but something lurked there. Something besides contempt and defensiveness.

"I feel like a single parent." The words flowed relentlessly like the blood of a head wound. "I work full time *and* I manage the house *and* the care of our son. When the nanny goes home, I am the only one taking care of Jordan. And you travel so much that when you get home, I want to spend time with you and talk to you. But you're so hungover or exhausted from drinking the night before that all you do is sleep. We never even talk. I'm just lonely."

Alec took a deep breath in and let it out slowly, pinching the bridge of his nose and massaging his eyes with one hand as if taking in what she said. "I'm sorry, Ellie," he mumbled from beneath his hand. It was a genuine apology. "I am doing the best I can. I swear to God. I thought building the house would make you happy."

"It *is* making me happy, Alec. I *love* the house. I love every detail you've designed especially for me. I just feel overwhelmed with everything I have to do on my own."

"I feel overwhelmed too," he admitted, setting his hands down on his knees and shaking his bowed head slowly. "I guess I thought that once the fencing business was successful, I'd be able to relax. But now it's like I have to maintain this level of success, this level of income. I don't know if I'll ever be able to rest. I feel like I'm on a treadmill sometimes, chasing this unattainable sense of security."

"So I'm hearing that you're both feeling stressed." The therapist utilized his active-listening skills. "What you need to consider, now that you're both talking to one another, is what your spouse can do to help you through your stress."

Ellie crafted her request carefully before she responded. "I would like Alec to come home from traveling feeling rested and willing to spend time with us. That also means putting me and Jordan before the needs of his mother." She knew the latter half of the request would be a bomb, so she braced herself.

To her surprise, Alec didn't so much as flinch. He just looked weary, suddenly a very worn thirty-one-year-old man-child.

"I would like her to trust me." Alec rested his elbows on his thighs and leaned forward, clasping his hands. His brown eyes bore into Ellie, but there was such a sweetness in them, such sincerity, that it stung her heart. "Let me be a man. I can handle my drinking, Ellie. Just trust me. Haven't I given you everything you want? Haven't I kept my other promises to you?" he pleaded.

Ellie sighed, nodding in agreement. "Yes, you have given Jordan and me everything we physically need. I just want more of you emotionally. I want to feel closer to you," Ellie lamented.

"My assignment for you this next week is to spend one night alone together if you can. Without your son.

Go out together. Leave the house and do something as simple as taking a walk together or going for a drive. Something that doesn't involve work, your child, or your house," the therapist commanded.

"That will be difficult," Alec admitted. "We are both traveling for work this coming weekend."

"Well, only you can decide how important this is to you," the therapist replied patronizingly. "Make time."

"He's kind of a dick, isn't he?" Alec laughed as they made their way to Alec's vintage Camaro. Ellie nearly choked with laughter.

"He really is," she agreed. "But I guess he has us talking, right? I guess that was the point of going to him."

"Do we really have to come back here?" Alec asked with disdain.

Ellie was hesitant to say no. It did seem to be helping, after all. She shrugged her shoulders noncommittally.

Alec walked to Ellie's side of the car, opening the door for her. Then he stopped suddenly, turning to his wife. "I love you so much," he swore, taking her face in his hands and kissing her gently on the lips. Ellie's hands hung at her sides initially, and then a sense of relief, a sense of hope even, inspired her arms to wrap around his neck and deepen the kiss. Maybe everything was going to be OK after all.

Maybe we are going to be OK.

"Ellie, if it really bothers you that much—if you really think it's such a problem—I won't drink so much," Alec promised. The way he phrased it made Ellie feel silly. Was she overreacting? Did Alec *really* have a drinking problem, or was Ellie just so scared that he would go down the same path as his mother?

"Thank you," Ellie sighed.

Maybe we are going to be OK.

"So where are you going again?" Maggie Lawson stood at the granite center island of Ellie and Alec's almost-finished dream home, looking out the back window at the contractors who were working feverishly to finish laying the brick patio and outdoor fireplace. It had been a warm October, but that didn't mean snow couldn't come at any time. The bricklayers were under contract to finish before winter. "This sure is a never-ending process," her mother observed absently as a warm, strong wind sent hundreds of fuchsia maple leaves spiraling wildly through the air.

"I'm going to Chicago," Ellie answered her impatiently. How many times had she told her mother where she was going? "I have a conference to attend. My boss, John Long, is giving a presentation at UIC. I'll be back Sunday afternoon at the latest."

"Grammie!" Jordan screeched joyfully from the balcony overlooking the great room.

"Slow down, Jordan!" Maggie Lawson commanded her grandson as he ran anxiously for the stairs. "How's that for a welcome?" She smiled proudly to Ellie.

"He loves his grandma, that's for sure," Ellie admitted, just a smidge resentfully.

Jordan flew down the stairs and ran into his grandmother's arms, squeezing his treasured dinosaur stuffed animal and his pajama pants in his chubby little hands. "Can I bring a movie to your house?" he asked his grandmother excitedly.

"Only if we can eat popcorn while we watch it." Maggie Lawson played along.

"Yes! Yes! I'm going to bring *The Mean Choo-Choo*!" He wiggled down and ran for the living room. As the doors to the entertainment center swung open with a crash, Ellie envisioned the awful mess Jordan would make rummaging through all the DVDs. Too late. She didn't have time to supervise. She needed to get on the road soon if she wanted to make it to Chicago before dark. She hated to admit it, but it had been a long time since she'd driven there (well, really, since she graduated from the University of Chicago), and she felt a bit nervous.

Is it really nerves? Or are you afraid of the memories?

Whatever. It was her first time away from Jordan too, and she was feeling tense.

"Are you nervous about leaving him?" Maggie asked her daughter, sensing something was eating at Ellie. Ellie's furrowed brow always gave her away.

"No, not at all, Mom. He's so excited to be having a sleepover with his Grammie and Papa."

To be honest, Ellie was sort of looking forward to some time alone, away from Wisconsin. She had every intention of disappearing to her hotel room after the lecture and submersing herself in a nice, hot bubble bath with a glass of wine and nothing else but the sound of complete, blissful silence. She would probably spend the next day attending lectures and finishing up a critical essay on Jane Austen's *Pride and Prejudice* that she hoped would be published soon. She was due to get something in print this school year, and God knows it was difficult to write with a rambunctious four-year-old around.

Ellie peered around the corner into the living room. Sure enough, DVDs were strewn all over the carpeting. "Jordan, go upstairs and get your overnight bag. It's on your bed," Ellie instructed her son gently. The tiny brown-haired cherub in corduroy overalls scrambled up from the floor and dutifully climbed back up the stairs to his room.

"Alec's away this weekend?" Maggie asked her daughter once Jordan was out of earshot. It was an innocent enough question, but the subtle timing was obviously calculated. Ellie searched her mother's face for an explanation, but as usual, it was stony.

"Yes, he's bidding for a huge contract to a possible client in Wyoming. Several cattle ranches, I think. I don't know for sure where he is. I can't keep track of *his* schedule too. He just tells me when he's going to be gone, and I manage."

"How's that going?" her mother asked cryptically.

"How's what going, Mom?" Ellie tried not to sound irritated, but it was difficult.

"How are you managing?" her mother clarified.

"How am I managing Alec not being here?" Ellie's squinched-up eyes and pursed lips betrayed her. She no longer looked ambivalent.

"Oh, Ellie, I'm just asking," Maggie explained with some annoyance.

"We're trying to work things out, Mom." Now Ellie glanced furtively up the stairs and lowered her voice. "Counseling has been OK. I feel like he's listening to me now at least."

"You know I'll do anything I can to help you," her mother offered genuinely.

"I know, Mom. You already do. You always have," Ellie replied. *Stop being so easy to anger. She really does just want to help.* "I just miss having a husband, and you can't be that to me," Ellie confided.

"And what exactly are you expecting of him?" Her mother sounded mildly exasperated. The sudden change of tone took Ellie by surprise.

"What do I expect?" Ellie couldn't check her frustration. Now she had to explain herself to her mother too? *Hell no!* "Mom! Maybe I expect him to be some sort of a husband to me when he's here. Maybe I expect him to be some sort of dad to Jordan."

"What is all this?" Her mother waved her hand over the house, motioning to the workers who were still laying bricks in the backyard.

"The house?" Ellie questioned.

"The house, the wine cellar, the bricked patio, the porch that wraps around your maple tree, your seventy-five-thousand-dollar car? Your four-car garage?" Maggie leaned against the kitchen counter, folding her arms in a challenge.

Ellie drew back, clenching her teeth. "Is all this supposed to make up for him being gone all the time?"

"Elizabeth Ann, why do you think he's gone all the time? So you can have all of this," her mother finished emphatically.

"Mom, I don't just mean physically gone. I mean mentally checked out. I mean not emotionally present or available." *I mean hungover.*

Did she dare say it? She felt like it was betrayal to admit Alec's drinking problem to other people, but maybe that was just enabling him to continue doing what he did without judgment. "He drinks a lot," Ellie blurted out and then felt slightly ashamed. Still against her better judgment, she continued, "He drinks alone. He drinks with his mother. He drinks when he's away."

Surprisingly Maggie's expression did not change. "So what, Ellie?" her mother replied flatly. "He drinks a lot. No kidding."

So she did know!

God, why can she always make me feel so ridiculous? Am I overreacting? Is it really not such a big deal?

"Does he cheat on you, Elizabeth?" her mother questioned.

"No." Ellie looked down at the floor.

"Is he abusive?"

"No," Ellie admitted. *Well, not exactly. Nothing I can't handle.*

"Does he love his son?"

"Yes, Mom, he loves his son," Ellie answered begrudgingly.

"Does he love *you?*" Maggie leaned forward to get her daughter to look up at her.

"Yes, Mom," Ellie sighed.

"Ellie." Maggie Lawson shook her head, stepping forward a bit for effect. "If you have all of those things, and this beautiful house to boot, and you *still* expect more, then you're expecting too much."

A minute or two passed as her mother's last words hung prophetically in the air. *You're expecting too much.*

"Am I, Mom?" Ellie asked sadly.

"He's just a man, Ellie. Not some romantic hero in one of your classic novels. He's a real-life flesh-and-blood person, and he has flaws. Just like all real men have flaws. Maybe he's doing the best he can."

My heart is hurting. I am just letting my heart be the guide, Mom. And it aches. Ellie opened her mouth to respond but fell silent.

"Elizabeth, marriage isn't easy. It's about stamina. It's about pushing through the tough times. It's about sticking it out for your children."

Is that what it was for you, Mom?

"Don't have such high expectations, Elizabeth. There's no such thing as the perfect man. Or the perfect marriage. You have a husband who works hard and who loves you. That's the best you can hope for."

Jordan's tiny half steps could be heard laboring down the stairs, his overnight bag thumping down the wooden stairs behind him.

"Ready to go, sweetheart?" Maggie Lawson addressed her grandson. Gathering the boy and his bag in her arms, she headed for the door. "He's in good hands, Ellie," she assured her daughter. "Enjoy some time alone," she advised, leaving Ellie shellshocked and mute at the kitchen sink.

"Pssst!" Someone whispered into Ellie's ear just as she was covertly sneaking a peek at a wall clock that hung to the right of the podium. John Long could talk for hours, endlessly. That droning monotone of a voice. After enjoying the blissful solitude of the hotel room Friday night, king-sized bed all to herself, no child to wake her with demands for food or cartoons, she had had to endure an entire morning of lectures. Now, a few hours past lunch, Ellie wondered how much more she could bear. Oh, God, the hands of the clock seemed forever stuck in the same place. Ellie's rear end was tingling. It had fallen asleep.

"Does this lecture make you want to scratch out your own eyes?" the mystery voice whispered, full of sardonic mirth. Ellie covered her mouth just in time to suppress a laugh. Turning slightly in her chair, she tilted her head to see who was talking to her. It was Professor Greer, that weird little elf of a woman, who sat directly in back of her. It's a wonder Ellie missed her with that crazy burgundy hair of hers, but there she was, leaning obviously forward in her chair, trying to get Ellie's attention as if they were two teenage girls passing notes.

"It's OK," Marta Greer joked. "Blink twice if you're still alive."

"Just barcly," Ellie whispered back, hoping the other people around them couldn't hear their conversation.

"Well, I'm sorry. I can't kill you and take you out of your misery. So don't even ask!" Marta laughed under her breath. "Meet me at the bathroom in five." Then she got up from her seat and slinked down the aisle toward the exit. Ellie tried to watch her go without moving her body completely around. With one eye on Marta and the other on John Long at the podium, Ellie realized that no one took notice of the clever escape.

You'll never be able to pull that off too, Ellie.

But, God! This is so boring.

How will anyone know what I'm doing? Everyone has to pee at some point!

Ellie continued to debate with herself, all the while watching the clock, which now seemed to move at double time while she was tortured by her indecision. Should she get up? Should she risk looking rude? Seven minutes had passed by.

No one will know what you're doing.

She stood up suddenly.

Don't look at anyone. Don't look. Just move!

Walking at the quickest pace she could without seeming conspicuous, she exited the lecture hall of the university and into the open relief of an empty hallway. Marta popped her head out of the bathroom doorway about fifty yards down the hall and then came gleefully skipping out, motioning to Ellie to hurry. Ellie quickened her pace, a girlish giddiness causing her heart to skip in her chest.

"I didn't think you'd come!" Marta grinned wickedly as she led Ellie out to the curb. "Let's get the hell out of here!" She started walking off the university grounds toward a busier street where she could hail a cab.

"Where are we going?" Ellie asked with surprise. Initially she thought maybe they were just escaping the lecture hall for a brief break. Obviously this Marta really meant to escape.

I hope this isn't going to get us into trouble! Would John Long be pissed that they walked out?

He probably doesn't even know. Unless one of the other brownnose professors rats us out.

Ellie was due to be tenured the following year, but this Marta Greer—she was an associate professor, new to the college, only teaching there for three months. She certainly had some spunk. Or some masochistic stupidity.

"Let's go drink!" Marta commanded more than suggested. Then she stopped suddenly. "You *do* drink?" she questioned, cocking her head.

Ellie looked at her watch. It said 2:35 p.m.

"It's five o'clock somewhere, right?" Marta drawled. It was the first time Ellie realized the curious half accent Marta Greer usually tried to suppress was really a full-blown, authentic southern accent. And a deep one at that.

"Sure." Ellie laughed.

"Yeah, I thought so." Marta smiled back. "I bet you don't get out much."

"Is it that obvious?" Ellie replied, suddenly feeling slightly embarrassed. Did this girl think she was lame?

She felt the need to explain herself, defend her pathetic lack of a social life.

"It's cool. I know you have a young son. I saw the picture on your desk," Marta offered. "I figured if I'm going to be staying in Wisconsin, I better make some new friends. So lucky you! I'm recruiting you to hang with me," she announced decisively. It was an odd, bizarrely forward statement that made Ellie feel like she'd known this girl all her life. Despite Marta's strangeness, Ellie instantly liked the woman. She had no pretention about her at all.

Marta seemed to know her way around the city. She ordered the cabbie to drive them toward Wrigleyville where they got out in front of a neighborhood tavern with a rainbow sticker in the window. Marta paid the man and shoved the rest of her money into her front pocket as Ellie followed mutely behind her. Then she entered the bar like she owned the place, sidling up to the counter on a high stool that kept her tiny legs dangling a foot from the floor. Leaning in on her elbows, she told the bartender, "Two SoCo shots! My friend and I are celebrating our escape!"

"Yeah?" the bartender looked disinterested as he went to work getting the bottle and lining up the tiny glasses.

"You don't mess around, huh?" Ellie asked, partly amused, partly intimidated. *I hope this girl doesn't think*

I can keep up with her drink for drink. I am woefully out of practice.

After a couple of afternoon shots, however, whatever worries Ellie had had were set to rest.

Was I rude to leave the lecture?

Don't care.

Can I keep up drink for drink with the little animal?

Don't care.

Should I check in on Jordan?

He's fine.

Is it too early to be this drunk? Ellie began laughing at the last thought.

No! Good for you! You deserve to be a little drunk.

"What's so funny?" Marta asked, lighting up a cigarette.

"I'm just happy to be drunk!" Ellie admitted.

"I thought you might be!" Marta seemed pleased with herself. "It's the quiet ones that are really the wild ones! It seems you and I will get along just fine."

"Yeah?" Ellie asked with a laugh.

"I figured a woman who looks as perfect as you might have some steam to blow off."

Ellie looked down at her fitted skirt and pointed leather pumps.

"Do I look like I'm trying too hard?" she asked Marta. The alcohol was making her unusually direct. She blanched at her words.

"Not at all." Marta laughed. "Take your hair down, though."

Ellie reached up and took out her clip, sending her wavy brown tresses tumbling over her shoulders. Then she removed her suit coat, revealing her bare arms in a tank camisole. It was liberating.

"Now I feel better!" Ellie leaned back in her chair.

"I'm taking you dancing," Marta announced to Ellie, as if she had no choice in the matter.

"Fun! Where?" Ellie slapped her knee excitedly.

"A friend of mine from Miami is going to be playing at Smartbar in a couple of hours. He's a really amazing DJ. Tonight is kind of a big night for me too. I'm going to ask my girlfriend to move up to Wisconsin with me," Marta explained somewhat seriously. Some of the levity had seemed to disappear from her expression. Ellie didn't know this girl well enough to read her, though.

"That might be a tough sell," Ellie blurted out. *Damn.* Without alcohol, she might have calculated a more diplomatic response.

"I know." Marta laughed unconvincingly and then took a long, serious drag of her cigarette as she stared at the back of the bar.

"I mean, I grew up there. I'm not putting it down, it's just the weather in Wisconsin is so cold. And, of course, the pace is…" Ellie tried backpedaling.

"A lot slower. I know," Marta lamented. "It's not Miami."

"No, it isn't," Ellie agreed softly.

"But *I'm* in Wisconsin now!" Marta exclaimed artificially, a forced smile giving her the look of a heartsick twelve year-old. Ellie didn't even know this other woman Marta spoke of, but she had a sneaking suspicion that things were not going to go as Marta hoped.

"Well, technically, you're in Chicago right now." Ellie tried to lighten the mood.

"Details!" Marta joked, the darkness not quite lifting from her face.

"And you seem to know it pretty well." Ellie tried for a new topic.

"I traveled a lot as a kid," Marta explained.

"To taverns?" Ellie kidded.

"Well, not exactly." Marta smiled. "Around taverns, near taverns. Taverns were full of possible victims! I was 'soul winning' with my parents."

"Soul what?" Ellie squinched up her face.

"Trying to save souls with my parents!" Marta explained, a wide, genuine grin spreading across her face as she waited for the irony to set in. Obviously this was a reaction she was used to. She seemed to be enjoying Ellie's visible battle with comprehension. Against her better manners (damn alcohol), Ellie began to laugh.

"You're lying!" Ellie accused.

"No, seriously, my father is a Baptist minister," Marta explained.

"No shit?" Ellie leaned in to search Marta's face for deception.

"No shit!" Marta laughed too, rubbing her tattooed forearm. "I'm the only daughter of a Baptist preacher and his *most* devoted wife."

"You were a problem child, I take it?" Ellie asked.

"What gives you that impression?" Marta feigned insult. "The Lord loves people like me. So much to fix, you know?" She took a long, bitter last drag of her cigarette and then forcefully snubbed it out in the ashtray. "You just have to accept the Lord as your savior and deny who you really are. I gave my parents a lot to pray about! And, oh, all the people I met when we traveled around to other churches! They all got to pray for me too!"

"So you've lived all over?"

"All over the United States! I've seen every single state in this fine nation of ours. My mother home-schooled me so we didn't have to stay in one place too long. They finally settled down in Tennessee when I was fifteen. *Daddy* has his own church in the hills, but I haven't seen my parents in a very long time. I left home when I was eighteen." Marta signaled the bartender.

"Just water for a while," Ellie begged. Marta nodded in assent.

"Yeah, imagine my mother's dismay when she realized that the daughter she raised to love reading didn't stop at the Brontë sisters and the New Testament! Ha!

Ha! I was also reading Gayle Jones and Don DeLillo and Chuck Palahniuk. Joke's on her!"

"From what I've heard, you're quite the Hawthorne scholar though," Ellie said, commending her.

"Why, of course, I am," Marta drawled purposely. "Who else could so relate to the plight of the Puritan psyche? I am quite the Bible scholar too, but that was not by choice. I always laugh when people try to out-scripture me in their critical writing. No such luck! This girl knows her verse!"

"So I've heard. Your reputation actually precedes you," Ellie said.

"Yeah, which reputation is that?" Marta laughed snidely.

"Your writing!" Ellie defended, not quite sure at first if Marta was kidding or truly offended. "The department was buzzing about your arrival. I guess a lot of people were surprised you'd accepted the position."

"What's so surprising?" Marta wondered modestly. "Your father made a name for the school years ago. And everyone knows you're there now. I jumped at the chance to be on staff with you. And besides, I need-ed a change of scenery. Someplace tamer and colder! Where maybe I could keep myself out of trouble."

"Well thank you for the compliment." Ellie held up her bottle of water and toasted her new friend. "Here's to living up to my father's legacy!" She took a long swig to conceal her wry smile.

~~~

Three hours and countless drinks later, they ate bad street-stand tacos in the back of a cab headed toward Smartbar.

"Thanks for saving me from John Long's lecture." Ellie held her hand over her mouth to keep the taco from falling out between giggles.

"No problem! The night's just begun," Marta assured her.

"I feel like I'm dressed wrong," Ellie lamented, suddenly feeling self-conscious about going into a club in her work clothes. The truth was, she hadn't really gone "out" anywhere since before Jordan was born. Anywhere without a child in toe, that is. She had been to plenty of zoos, children's museums, farmer's markets, shopping centers, outdoor fests with bounce houses, but she hadn't been to a club since before she met Alec. Ellie had, in essence, fallen into a vortex—sucked into every parents' bizarro world where each day's events revolve around snacks and nap time, diaper changes and runny noses, where dinner is no later than five, and all the streets roll up by nine o'clock—at which point she would drop into bed, exhausted. Being drunk in the back of a cab with a fistful of taco felt like an out-of-body experience.

"No one gives a shit what you're wearing!" Marta waved Ellie off. "Someone who looks like you could walk in wearing a burlap sack. Let's go!" Ellie offered to pay for the cab, but Marta refused her.

The little general led the way toward the front of the line of people waiting entrance to the club. *This isn't going to be good,* Ellie feared. People were already shooting dirty looks toward them as Marta prepared to cut. And then, a voice rang out, saving them from certain confrontation.

"Marta!" the sound came from the open door behind two hulking, black-clad bouncers. Marta darted in the direction of the voice, flying into the arms of quite possibly the most beautiful woman Ellie had ever laid eyes on. A tall, shapely, dark-skinned goddess embraced Marta, her long, French-manicured nails grabbing fistfuls of Marta's ratted, burgundy crop. As Marta held the woman's face tenderly, she strained on her toes to kiss her, the two momentarily lost in their passion, completely unaware of the street full of voyeuristic eyes. *Awkward.* Ellie stood behind Marta, dumbly waiting for an introduction.

Nothing like being the very weird third wheel.

"Oh my God, I've missed you, Paquita!" the beauty exclaimed to Marta once they stopped kissing. She stopped fussing over Marta for just a moment to eye Ellie suspiciously over Marta's shoulder.

"This is Ellie Purnell." Marta turned toward Ellie finally. "She's another professor at the college. She's the one I told you about."

Told her what? What would you have to say about me?

"Oh." The woman looked relieved. Then, to Ellie, she said, "Marta said the college must be a good place to teach if *you* were there, whatever that means."

Ellie laughed nervously against her will, her hand flying up to her mouth to stop the inappropriate reaction. *What a bitch!*

"I guess that's a compliment, right?" Ellie asked innocently.

"Of course," Marta said immediately and defensively, confirming Ellie's interpretation of the negative vibe. "This is obviously my girlfriend, Lilliana."

Ellie held out her hand to the woman who took it weakly, shaking only to placate Marta, who looked on apprehensively. Ellie felt a tug at her heart.

This isn't going to go well for you tonight, is it, little friend?

"Tony's going on in a half hour," Lilliana explained. "They're with me," she announced, pushing past the bouncers. Marta and Ellie followed her, all black leather pants and heavy silver jewelry, down the steps into a dark cellar of a club that immediately swallowed them whole. The darkness, the bass, the booming through their chest cavities. At once, they were absorbed into the walls, indistinguishable, just additional pulses of life adding to the collection of sound, breath, bodies. Ellie's head swam. She struggled to adjust to the strobing lights, looking down at Marta's feet in front of her to guide her through the confusion.

Adjust.

A weird feeling of familiarity assaulted Ellie as she remembered last being here with Dylan. A combination of disgust and wistfulness twisted her heart.

Bet you know the inside of the men's bathroom pretty well, don't you?

By the time Ellie regained her bearings, the three had woven their way toward the back of the club.

"Marta!" A younger Latin man with closely cropped black hair embraced Marta affectionately, flashing a dazzling, boyish grin with dimples that reminded Ellie of Alec.

I miss my husband.

The errant thought was a surprising comfort. She missed Alec! That was good. That meant there was hope.

"Tony, this is Ellie Purnell," Marta said, introducing him.

Ellie extended her hand, but the man immediately took Ellie's face in his thick, strong hands, kissing both cheeks. He was stunning. Really. And then another emotion suddenly surfaced. Arousal? Guilt. Ellie could feel her face and neck flush with shame.

Give me a break. He probably kisses everyone like that. You're so Victorian!

"So good to meet you, Ellie! You like to dance?" Tony asked Ellie emphatically, his accent thick and exotic sounding.

Geez, have another drink, Ellie!

"Yes!" Ellie smiled shyly. The truth was she couldn't remember the last time she had really danced, but the sound inside this basement bar was smooth and deep and could gradually drive a person into movement, even against her will. Into a hypnotic trance. And God knows Ellie was ready to be transported.

"I'll make it worth your while." Tony winked. He rubbed his hands together with excitement. "Wish me luck!"

Ellie patted his shoulder with encouragement as he left the small group of Marta's friends behind. Marta introduced the circle of people to Ellie, who only half listened to names. It was too loud to talk. And certainly too loud to make small talk with people she didn't even know.

Dance.

Ellie waved to Marta and disappeared into the crowd, absorbed like quicksand, instantly invisible.

Tony.

Ellie allowed herself to watch him from the floor. He couldn't see her from up there, right? His bobbing up and down as he mixed the music, the look of concentration that occasionally furrowed his brow, his fist in the air riling the crowd—his enthusiasm was endearing. He looked so carefree up there. What was it like to feel that happy? She admired him, making all of these people happy too. Making them dance. What power. What a wonderful power to have.

So she danced. For what must have been an hour, maybe more, she danced. Tony kept the crowd moving, surging, bouncing, slowing to a sensuous writhe, and then collectively crescendoing to full-out jumping, hands in the air, the entire mass moving as one. The sweat poured off Ellie, into her eyes, down her neck, between her breasts, soaking her silk camisole. She realized she was smiling. Crazily. Laughing and smiling so broadly her cheeks hurt. All the stress of marriage counseling, John Long, work, her mother-in-law, Jordan, Alec and his alcohol. Everything was gone.

Thank you, Tony! Thank you, thank you, thank you!

Sometime later, Ellie wove through the bodies on the dance floor toward a much-needed bottle of water. She was finally feeling less drunk. Not quite sober, but certainly much less drunk than she had been. Time to hydrate. As she approached the bar, someone slammed into her shoulder absently, accidentally, and then kept on going, nearly a blur before Ellie realized. *Marta!*

"Hey!" Ellie yelled out, but even as she opened her mouth, she knew it was futile. No way would Marta hear her. For a split second, Ellie felt confused. *She's running out.* That wasn't a leisurely departure. *Go after her!* Ellie's body lurched forward before her mind even had time to comprehend what was going on. She followed quickly after Marta who fled with conviction up the stairs, out into the cool autumn air, the ringing in Ellie's ears further confusing her senses.

"Marta." Ellie's own voice sounded distant.

No response.

Then to Ellie's horror, Marta darted into the street, the screech of tires piercing the air. The blare of a car horn. Marta flinched only momentarily and then stepped backward onto the curb, throwing her arm up to hail a cab. Ellie finally caught up to her.

"What the hell are you doing?" she demanded, grabbing Marta's arm. "You almost got hit by a car!"

Marta wrenched her arm free, defensively. "Too bad."

"Too bad? What do you mean too bad?" Ellie asked.

"Too bad I didn't get hit by a car." Marta laughed ironically and then broke into hysterical laughter. "Too bad. Too bad," she almost sang, signaling frantically for the next cab. She staggered away from Ellie, further down the sidewalk.

"Where are you going?" Ellie cried out, a sense of panic gripping her.

"Away from here." Marta coughed out the words. Her laughter had turned into sobs.

"Oh my God, are you crying?" Ellie realized. Marta turned her back to Ellie, covering her face with both hands. "Hey! Hey!" She tried to coax Marta's hands away. "It's OK. Tell me what's wrong." She tried again. The cab rolled up next to them. "Come on." Ellie put her arm around Marta and opened the cab door, ushering her in. "I'm just going to have him take us to my hotel. You can stay with me tonight," Ellie told her, but Marta didn't put up a fight; she said nothing as she stared quietly out the cab window, refusing to look in Ellie's direction.

By the time they reached the hotel, Marta had slumped over in the backseat of the cab, her eyes only partly shut. Ellie threw money at the cabbie, ran around the other side of the car, and yanked open the door. Marta nearly fell out into her arms.

Shit! What's wrong with her?

"Marta?" Ellie shook Marta's limp arm.

"Get your friend out!" the cabbie ordered.

Coming to, Marta coughed suddenly, spraying the open door with vomit.

"Get out!" the cabbie screamed.

"We're trying, asshole!" Ellie snapped back as she hoisted Marta from the backseat. "You have to stand, Marta. I can't carry you!"

"I know, I know," Marta mumbled, wiping her mouth with the back of her hand and forearm. "I'm sorry." She started to cry again.

"What happened?" Ellie asked gently once they were settled in the hotel room.

Marta was sitting on the end of the bed, her feet barely touching the floor. She looked like a defeated child, arms hanging limply by her sides, her makeup either kissed, cried, or puked off her face, her brightly tattooed arms making her cartoonish in multicolored grief.

"There's someone else," Marta whispered. Her face seemed to be changing color before Ellie's very eyes—pink and then flushed to ashen gray. Ellie instinctually grabbed the trash can, placing it strategically under Marta as she once again emptied her stomach of liquor and tacos. Minutes later she continued. "Lilliana won't move up here. She said she won't leave Miami. She won't leave Miami. She won't leave Miami," Marta repeated absently, hanging her head, woefully shaking it as if to free herself of the statement. "There must be someone else. She wouldn't tell me who, but I know there's someone else."

Ellie sat patiently on the bed next to Marta, resting her hand on Marta's shoulder, trying awkwardly to comfort this odd little girl of a woman who was completely beyond solace.

What should I say to her that won't sound trite?

She decided to say nothing at all. It was enough that she sat next to Marta on the bed. Surely Marta could feel her sympathy. After all, Ellie certainly knew what it felt like to have your heart ripped out.

"I have to…" Marta began when suddenly her head fell back against Ellie's hand. The whites of her eyes exposed, she licked her lips in what appeared to be an involuntary reflex and then snapped back up, looking completely coherent again. "I have to find out," she continued as if nothing happened.

Oh my God, what's wrong with her? Is she seizing? "Are you OK?" Ellie blurted.

"No, I'm not OK." Marta began sobbing again, her shoulders shaking uncontrollably. Her head fell back a second time, again causing her to lick and bite her top lip.

"What did you take?" Ellie demanded. "What else did you take at the club? Why is your head rolling back like that?" Marta didn't answer through her inconsolable crying. "Oh my God, talk to me!" Ellie begged.

"Just some G," Marta choked out between sobs.

"Some what? What is G?" Ellie asked, mortified.

"I'm fine. It's fine. I'm fine," Marta swore, her head lolling back again, the tick repeating more frequently now.

"You're not fine!" Ellie insisted. "You're not fucking fine. What does G do to you? Is this normal? Is your head rolling back a normal reaction?"

"I'm fine!" Marta cried and then instantaneously, eerily, stopped, grabbing Ellie's shoulders, her eyes deep black saucers searching Ellie's face. "Everything will be fine."

What should I do? Ellie felt panic rising in her.

"I'm fine. I swear to you, I'm fine," Marta slurred. "Bad reaction tonight." She laughed now. "You're good, aren't you?" she asked Ellie randomly, her eyes now focused on the ceiling. "You're good. You won't leave me."

"No, I won't leave you," Ellie answered, beginning to pace the room, warily watching Marta.

Should I give her some water? Food? Will she just throw up again? Don't let her lie down. Keep her upright.

"The black horse will come for you." Marta smiled, her eyes rolling back into her head as she slumped over onto the bed.

Oh my God! Stay with me! Ellie raced to the bed, hoisting Marta up by her armpits and dragging her toward the headboard. Marta's head straightened back up again.

"You're going to be OK," Marta reassured Ellie.

"I'm not worried about me," Ellie snapped with annoyance. "I'm worried about you!"

"You're going to be OK," Marta repeated. "This is supposed to…" she stopped suddenly as her body stiffened in Ellie's arms. It lasted only a few seconds and then her muscles relaxed. She regained control.

Oh my God! What should I do?

Marta sat upright, looking completely sober, her eyes wide and perfectly lucid as she firmly instructed Ellie, "Do *not* call an ambulance. I am fine. Sometimes this happens. Just a bad reaction tonight. You take me to a hospital, we're both losing our jobs."

Feeling terrified and livid, Ellie yelled at Marta, "Just sit up!"

Why? Why is this happening to me? How did I get stuck with this lunatic? What if she starts choking again or passes out?

Ellie scrambled to her purse, searching manically for her cell phone. Her hands fumbled to dial Becca.

Becca will know what to do. Becca will tell me what to do.

"Hello?" a tired voice asked from the other end of the receiver, followed by the loud beeping of Ellie's dying cell phone.

Oh my God, phone don't die on me!

"Becca!" Ellie implored almost hysterically. "Becca, it's Ellie! I'm with a friend who I think overdosed on something she calls G."

"What? Ellie, where are you?" Becca now sounded completely awake.

"I'm in Chicago at a conference. We went to a club. My friend's having some weird nervous-system reaction to what she took. I don't know if she's been seizing or what. She's thrown up a couple times."

"Is she conscious?" Becca asked calmly. "Can I talk to her?"

Ellie turned to look at Marta who sat on the end of the bed, again with her arms folded, looking irritated and completely coherent now.

"Can you talk?" Ellie asked Marta. Marta held out the palm of her hand with annoyance as Ellie gave over the phone.

"Hello." Marta's voice in the phone smacked of defiance. "Yes, I know what's going on. I feel OK now that I threw up." Silence. Marta sat and listened quietly. "OK. OK. Yes, I've taken this before. Well, not exactly. Yeah, I've seen people react like this. OK." She handed the phone back to Ellie.

"Hello?" Ellie searched into the phone, eyeing Marta doubtfully. Whatever weird reaction Marta had been having seemed to have ended temporarily.

"If she seizes again, you call an ambulance, Ellie, do you hear me?"

"Yes," Ellie answered her younger sister.

"You have to sit up with her, you know? Watch her," Becca instructed. "She needs you." The phone beeped and went dead. *Fuck!*

Marta had begun to cry again.

"Stop. You can't cry. It's going to make you seize again," Ellie begged. She sat down on the bed facing Marta, gently taking Marta's hands into hers. "You scared me half to death. How long do the effects of that last?" she asked hopefully.

"Maybe all night," Marta answered, sounding apologetic.

"Well, then, I guess it's going to be a long night," Ellie answered as she pulled back the covers, patting the pillows in invitation. "You have to sit up," she instructed Marta who settled back against the headboard. Ellie reached down to unlace Marta's worn Doc Martens—tiny little child's feet.

"She was the only person who ever really loved me," Marta whimpered barely audibly.

"Lilliana?" Ellie asked sympathetically.

"Yeah, she knew who I really am, and she still loved me," Marta answered, fat, heavy tears pooling in her eyes.

"I'm sure there's a lot to love," Ellie tried to console her.

"Don't be so sure," Marta answered dolefully. "I'm broken."

"We're all broken," Ellie admitted, her pity turning at once to such profound sadness she couldn't pinpoint its origin.

You spent three days on a floor one time. It's hard to watch someone else hurt like that.

Ellie settled in next to Marta on the bed, cradling Marta's head in the crook of her arms, the smaller woman leaning like a child against Ellie's chest. Ellie stroked Marta's hair, a mother's instinct, a natural attempt to soothe. Eventually Marta stopped crying, her breath becoming quiet and even.

Ellie's sticky lids struggled to open. Bright light streaming in through the open window, her eyes teared and burned, the familiar sensation of sleep deprivation. Her arm felt very heavy. *Marta!* Panic gripped Ellie as she realized they were both laying flat on their backs, surrounded by a sea of pillows.

"Marta?" Ellie shook her forcefully.

"What?" the sharp, sudden answer came back from underneath a mess of ratty burgundy hair. Ellie let out the deep breath she had been holding.

Oh, thank God you're OK!

Marta settled back down on the pillow, pinching the skin between her eyes in an attempt to stop the throbbing. No such luck.

"You're alive, that's what," Ellie answered with obvious disdain.

"I'm sorry," the voice whispered in an attempt to hide the certain onslaught of grief. "I didn't mean to show you my ass last night."

Ellie burst into laughter in spite of herself. "That's a colorful way of putting it!" she teased Marta who laughed a bit in return. "I forgive you, OK? Just don't ever do that to me again. Ever!"

"I won't," came the promise.

The truth was, Ellie felt sorry for her. She couldn't bear to listen to Marta demean herself anymore.

I will take the strange little imp for exactly who she is. No questions asked.

"I think I'll call you Id!" Ellie announced, poking Marta in the shoulder. "She who follows her base impulses against her better judgment."

Marta laughed weakly beneath the arm that sheltered her face. "I've never been known for my judgment," she admitted. "I guess you can call me whatever you want after sitting up with me all night."

"I guess you owe me," Ellie stated dryly.

"I guess I do," Marta easily admitted.

"You can start paying me back by never putting yourself down again in my presence," Ellie instructed sternly.

The poignant silence was audible. Marta could not respond. Ellie rested a hand on Marta's back, a gesture meant to comfort; her friend did not stir.

Scooting off the bed, she left Marta buried in pillows to go in search of her dead cell phone. *Damn!* The only charger she brought was in her car. Eleven o'clock, and she hadn't even checked in on Jordan since the afternoon before.

I am the worst mom ever, she thought, lamenting. Lifting the receiver on the hotel room phone, she hastily read the instructions for dialing out.

"Mom!" Ellie chirped unconvincingly into the telephone. Her head felt like it was about to implode.

"Ellie?" her mother sounded upset.

"What's wrong, Mom?"

"Are you still in Chicago? We've been trying to reach your cell phone. Are you OK?"

"Yeah, I'm fine. I talked to Becca last night. She knew I was OK," Ellie said, making an excuse.

"No, I mean this morning. We've been trying to call you since early this morning. Did you talk to Alec yet?"

"No, Mom. What's wrong?" Ellie asked with alarm, her heart now racing.

Nothing.

"Mom?"

"Alec's mom had an accident, Ellie. She hit her head. He found her this morning."

"Is she OK?"

"It appears she lost her balance and hit the corner of her kitchen table pretty hard. She's dead, Ellie. She bled out on her kitchen floor."

"Jesus, Mom," Ellie admonished her mother for such a blunt explanation. Maggie Lawson. Tell it like it is.

Ellie couldn't quite organize her thoughts, the flood of emotions. *Oh, no! Alec. Oh God! He's going to be devastated. He needs me!*

And you let him down.

I have to get home!

"Mom, where's Alec?" Ellie asked frantically.

"I imagine he's still at her house, Ellie. He found her this morning and called the paramedics, but she had been dead a couple of days. He called here asking if we'd talked to you because he couldn't get a hold of you. He said he kept trying to call your cell phone, but you weren't answering. I told him we'd keep Jordan while he made arrangements for her body to be picked up."

I'm three hours away.

"Mom, I'm leaving now. Try to find Alec and tell him I'll be there as soon as I can."

"Just be careful, Ellie. Don't go getting into an accident because you're trying to get home quicker," Maggie Lawson commanded her daughter. "And turn your phone on!"

"OK, Mom, bye." Ellie dropped the phone back into its cradle with her shaking hand, the pit of her gut once again queasy.

"What's wrong?" Marta asked, lifting her head weakly off the mattress.

"My mother-in-law is dead," Ellie said aloud, the words sounding so surreal she almost burst into laughter.

You're going right to hell!

I'm just nervous. Nerves make me laugh.

Maybe you're secretly happy.

Maybe I am.

"Should I say sorry?" Marta asked intuitively.

Ellie ignored the question.

"I have to go. My husband is probably beside himself with grief," she explained instead. "Stay here for as long as you want, Marta," she offered. Without lifting her buried head, Marta held up a thumb.

The three-hour drive back to Wisconsin was marked only by Ellie's internal debate—her conscience versus the overwhelming relief she felt.

Linda Purnell is dead! Then guilt. Then shame.

Relief!

Guilt. Shame.

Fear.

Alec would not answer his cell phone.

Ellie tried over and over once her phone was charged. Message after message she left. No answer. No call back.

Fear.

Is he OK? Did he freak out? Did he fall off the deep end?

No. He's pissed at you. That's why he's not answering his phone! You're in for it!

And the closer Ellie got to home, the more knotted her stomach became.

~

By the time she turned off the county road toward Linda Purnell's ranch, the wistful autumn sun was low in the sky, throwing long, sad shadows across the windshield of Ellie's Lexus. Linda's home still sat at the far end of the Purnell property, a fair distance from Ellie and Alec's estate home, hidden (thankfully) by the pine forest. Ellie would have to pass it on the way to her own driveway; if Alec's car was still there, she would be able to see him and stop.

Something about the drive in seemed different, though. Despite the sound of her own pulse drumming madly in her ears, the visible throbbing of her heart in her chest, there was another indistinct sound that grew louder as she approached home. Was it coming from outside? She hit the window button to lower the glass and slowed to listen. Heavy machinery. Construction? She drove further.

Then there in front of her—Linda Purnell's home. Half a home? Her eyes must be deceiving her. The structure was being bulldozed to the ground. Demolished before her very eyes. Three huge trucks worked to obliterate it, tearing into the roof and scooping back entire walls. Ellie screeched to a stop.

Oh my God, Alec! He's lost it. He's completely gone insane. Should I stop them? But even as she had the thought, she knew it was ridiculous. Too late. The house was almost leveled.

She hit the gas, tearing down the road and into the long gravel drive that led up to her house, hoping in vain that Alec might be there, but his car was nowhere in sight. Anxiously putting her car in park, Ellie rummaged madly through her purse.

Where did I put the damn phone? Then she spotted it on the floor. She would try just one more time. Dialing. *Answer, damn it!*

"Hello?" a voice asked loudly through deafening background noise.

"Alec?" Ellie implored. "Alec? Where are you?"

"Ellie?" the voice asked.

"Yes, it's Ellie!"

"Ellie, it's Joe Dobbs."

"Joe?" she didn't understand.

"Alec is up here at The Bear. I think maybe you'd better come pick him up."

Before Ellie could answer, she heard the sound of a struggle and a crash. Did the other phone fall on the floor? She waited.

"Don't," another voice finally said. Ellie's heart sank. It was Alec. "Don't come. Just leave me alone." He hung up.

Ellie sat for a moment staring at her front porch, the yellow and purple mums perfect in their ceramic planters, the happy wreath that mocked her from the front door. She had to go get him. She had no choice.

She made it to the town square in less than five minutes, pedal-to-floor as dusk moved in. Circling The Black Bear Pub several times, she finally chose a parking spot nearly a block away; if there was to be a scene, she didn't want to risk being spotted by anyone she knew, especially students. Alec made it somewhat of a risk to live and work in such a small town. People liked to talk. No doubt half the college would know about the bulldozers by tomorrow morning. By now, Ellie's stomach cramped violently with trepidation.

How should I approach him? How am I going to get him out of that bar?

She willed herself to get out of the car, catching a glimpse of her reflection in her window as she shut the door behind her. She looked haggard and shiny from the drive. First Marta and now this. Would this day never end?

Brushing away the stray hairs that had fallen from her ponytail, she set out for the bar. Then, as if her silent prayers had been answered, Alec stumbled out the front door of the tavern, down two cement steps to the walk, and wandered aimlessly toward his Camaro, keys jangling from his hand. Ellie was still half a block away. He didn't spot her.

"Alec," someone yelled. It was Joe Dobbs. He had followed Alec out. When Joe saw Ellie, he waved. She stopped, unsure. Should she yell back?

"I got this!" she answered Joe, dismissing him. He nodded in understanding and stepped back inside. Alec looked up. Too late. She had given herself away.

Wait. Wait to see what he's going to do.

His drawn, sad face was swollen from crying, visibly confused by the sight of Ellie, unexpected, standing in the middle of the street, an indistinct, faceless shape shrouded in the graying light.

Words tried to form on his lips, but he had no fight. His arms dropped to his side resignedly. Ellie ran to him, throwing her arms compassionately around his neck, cradling his face in her hands. But even still, he didn't respond. He stood motionless except for the rapidly beating heart Ellie felt against her cheek through his sweater as she embraced him. She reached down and gently removed the keys from his hand.

"Let's go home," she said coaxingly, leading him toward her car. He followed willingly.

They rode home without speaking—Alec staring numbly out the window, and Ellie too tentative to break the silence. But when they approached the remains of Linda Purnell's house, just a mess of scorched earth ringed with endless bulldozer tracks, Alec broke into a sob, the empty, soul-crushing bellow of a wounded animal, a sound that Ellie had never heard escape him before.

"Oh, God, Alec. I am so sorry." She reached over to touch his shoulder as she accelerated toward their house. She just needed to be out of the car. To hold him. Once in the driveway, she put the car into park, but Alec made no attempt to move.

Don't rush him. Let him have a moment and then get him into the house.

Ellie inched as near to Alec as she could in the front seat, taking his left hand in both of hers, kissing it. "I am so sorry, sweetheart," she whispered and then stroked the back of his head. His sobs mellowed to a quiet weep and then a sniffle. He pulled his hand back suddenly.

"Are you?" he murmured as if to himself.

Ellie recoiled instantly. She had heard him loud and clear.

Don't move. Wait to see if this passes. He's just emotional right now.

And drunk.

"Are you really sorry, Ellie?" he asked, an ominous undercurrent to his tone. He turned to look into her appalled face.

No ignoring it now! You have to answer. Choose your words carefully.

"Alec, it's been a long day for both of us. I have to pick up Jordan still. If you don't want to talk civilly right now, we can have this conversation tomorrow morning."

Oh, hell! Civilly? You know better than that! Brace yourself.

"Who said I didn't want to talk right now?" Alec's distraught expression morphed at lightning speed into a hot rage. "It's been a 'long day' for *you*, Ellie? That's interesting. I tried calling you at least ten times this morning. Where the *fuck* were you?" He waited for a response, his mouth curled into a snarl.

She hadn't planned on this. She hadn't concocted a story. Should she just tell him the truth?

No. That will make him even angrier.

You weren't doing anything wrong.

Yeah, but I wasn't there for him when he needed me. While he was finding his mother dead on the floor, I was out dancing.

"My phone went dead, Alec." She cringed at her insensitive choice of words. "I slept in. You know, I thought it was safe to sleep in since I didn't have Jordan. How could I have foreseen your mother's accident? I am so sorry I missed your calls. I'm so sorry, honey," she said, trying to apologize. It was an authentic apology. At that very moment, she couldn't have been any sorrier that things were unfolding the way they were.

"Fuck you, Ellie!" Alec yelled, punching the dashboard. Ellie slid across the seat, shoving open the door to escape. Alec followed her out, visibly wincing from the pain in his hand. She stood at the front door, fumbling with her keys. His hand shot up next to her head, boxing her in, as he propped himself against the wall of the house. He leaned into her face. "My mother died, alone, slow and horrible, on her kitchen floor. She laid there for days." His slurred voice was low and full of contempt. "Maybe if you had some sort of relationship with her, she wouldn't have been so isolated. Maybe she wouldn't have died the way she did," he accused.

"You're not even rational right now, Alec. How could I have saved her if I was in Chicago? How is your mother's death *my* fault?" Ellie defended herself.

You're just digging yourself in now.

I can't help it. I can't let him attack me.

"You hated her," Alec continued, unrelenting.

Don't take the bait. Don't take it!

Ellie finally located the house key. With a final fumble, she jolted the door open in an attempt to get protective space between her and Alec.

"What does that have to do with her death, Alec?" Ellie returned bravely, not denying his accusation as she consciously moved farther into the room away from him.

"She fell on Thursday, Ellie," he answered.

Don't say it. Don't say it.

She couldn't help herself. "So why didn't *you* check on her before *you* left, Alec? Why is it *my* fault?"

"Why? Why?" He swiped his arm out violently, sending the ceramic end table lamp careening across the room into the foyer wall, where it exploded onto the floor. "I didn't go there because we were at marriage counseling! I was with you, Ellie, remember? I was with *you!*"

Ellie stood dumbfounded for a moment.

So that's where he's going with this. What should I say to diffuse his anger? How can I turn this around?

Choose your words carefully. Don't incense him.

Or what? What's he going to do?

I don't know what he'll do. Do you want to find out?

I'm not going to cower in fear.

Well then have some compassion. Let him rant. His mother just died, for God's sake.

Ellie decided not to let her pride get the best of her; why fight back just for fighting's sake? He wasn't going to remember any of this, and he couldn't really mean what he was implying. *Could he?*

"Alec, please calm down. Please. Come upstairs and lay down with me." Ellie tried to appease him one last time.

"I'm not going anywhere with you, bitch," Alec swore, as he headed toward the liquor cabinet. "It's your fault my mother is dead. It's your fault she died alone on that kitchen floor, and I will *never* forgive you."

Ellie's face exploded into red-hot shame. His words felt like a physical blow. She stepped forward, her lips silently wording some futile plea. Then knowing better, she stopped herself.

Just go.

The sound of clanking bottles, the slam of a cabinet door. Ellie stealthily fled up the stairs into their bedroom, where she shut the door as gently as possible and turned the lock noiselessly.

Maybe you should hide in Jordan's room.

Out of sight, out of mind. If she wasn't down there to anger him, maybe he would forget about his resentment. She would wait. After all, he would pass out eventually, wear himself out, drink himself into oblivion.

Then she could leave to get Jordan without the risk of further confrontation.

She sat against the door, her legs drawn up to her chest, head resting on an angle against the wood. To her surprise, a sudden, steady stream of warm tears covered her cheeks.

This is your life. This is as good as it gets. Nothing is ever going to change.

There would be no second baby. No way could Ellie justify bringing another child into this mess. No way could she imagine taking care of a newborn with the threat of Alec's imminent binges always looming over the house. No. Her efforts would have to be focused on shielding Jordan from the truth. Protecting him from his father's behavior. Jordan would never have a sibling.

The deep, pitiful howls of Alec's grief echoed through the first floor and carried up the stairs to Ellie where she sat helpless behind the bedroom door. There was nothing she could do to help him.

Ten

I should have known
The tree you owned,
The tree you couldn't name——
The crown jewel of your land,
Its changing colors unacknowledged,
Its leaves,
Its smooth, pleading bark,
Its sullen sound in the wind,
Blowing helplessly there——
Begging for a look.
I should have known
It was just something you possessed,
As I allowed you to possess me,
Break me apart,
Underneath its lonely boughs,
The heavy sigh of branches.
Broken still.
Belonging now to you.

How could I not love that which you
Ignored?

—AVERY VAUGHN, "MAPLE"

A gray mist covered the rolling hills of Wisconsin countryside, leaving a shimmer over every leaf, every blade of grass. *Every "leaf" of grass,* Ellie thought as she easily jogged up the county road. Dawn was just preparing to burst forth, the robins blissfully heralding its arrival as the sky, a canvas of fluffy white lined by backlit rows of coral and slate, stretched brilliantly for as far as Ellie could see. As it turned out, the transition from running in solitude to running with a partner was much easier than she had anticipated. Being in Liam's presence at the rising of the sun each morning was something near transcendent. Forget the runner's high. She felt a curious calm simply being near him. It took only a few days for her to realize that the absence of crushing weight on her chest might actually be something similar to happiness. Maybe it *was* happiness? She wasn't sure. It had been a very long time since she'd felt that. It had been a very long time since she'd felt anything.

"You have been holding out on me!" Ellie accused Liam as she met him at the top of a hill, half a mile down from his house. He had jogged in place, waiting for her, watching as she made her final assent toward him.

"How do you mean?" He smiled radiantly, the light-brown stubble on his face smattered with auburn flecks.

"You are a practiced runner, Dr. Curran," Ellie said, chiding him.

"What can a man do without mountains to climb, Professor?" he asked as he joined Ellie, matching her pace. "I've not run any marathons, but I do train, Elizabeth. I just didn't want to brag. Besides I doubt I could outrun someone who runs for her life."

Ellie didn't respond. *Interesting choice of words, Liam.* He was right, of course. She did run for her life, and he knew it.

In just the short two weeks since they'd returned from Chicago, the two had fallen into a comfortable pattern. Every morning, they would meet to run. Some days, especially on weekends when they didn't have to rush to work, those runs culminated in long talks as they walked another couple of miles together to "cool down."

Although, really, there was no cooling down.

And because of this, Ellie kept her conscience clear by avoiding his house. *Too much temptation.* When Liam still slyly challenged Ellie about writing poetry, she continued to play coy. There was an unspoken understanding that Liam knew her pseudonym, knew that she was

Avery Vaughn. If he read her poetry as confessional facts and not fabricated fictions, then he must already have pieced together her personal history, but Ellie still played innocent. This way, she could avoid talking about anything unpleasant and just be present with Liam in the now.

Isn't that his philosophy, after all?

And there was no talk of the kiss, although the memory of it, the tension it created between them, hung in the air like a sweet, stifling humidity.

Ellie turned the volume on her music off so she could listen only to Liam's breath, the sound of their feet falling into perfect sync. Why had she thought this wouldn't work? Running together. Running next to Liam every morning felt like the most natural thing in the world. As if they'd been doing this together for centuries.

She led them on an alternate route past town in order to avoid jogging near campus, to avoid being seen. *With Liam.* Really she avoided routing them through the town square or toward the campus due partly to a creeping guilt that lurked in her subconscious. Guilt for the feelings she was starting to have.

And what feelings are those, Ellie?

I don't know, OK? I don't know.

The other reason she avoided town was her selfishness. For an hour each morning, she could keep Liam all to herself. She didn't want to risk seeing someone they knew, not necessarily because a harmless run might look questionable but because she wanted to bask in his undivided attention.

"What are you thinking?" Liam smiled warmly.

Should I admit I was thinking about him? Who am I kidding? He already knows. That's why he asked. He's toying with me.

"I wasn't really thinking anything." Ellie partially told the truth. She was just blissfully lost in the moment, aware only of the lightness she felt in his presence. Even the silence between them was comfortable.

"Very good," Liam said. "You're learning."

"Learning to be present in the moment, huh?" Ellie raised an eyebrow.

"Sure," Liam answered, "but I suspect you've mastered that already by running. This is, after all, your meditation, is it not?"

"It is," Ellie agreed. They ran a bit further in silence. "So what is it I'm learning?"

"Whatever you need to learn," Liam replied ambiguously.

Ellie laughed. "Of course that's what you'd say." She shook her head. "I am going to be forty in a few months, Dr. Curran. I don't suspect you can teach this old girl many new tricks."

"Nonsense. We all have lifetimes to learn. Your soul could be a mere baby," Liam answered seriously.

"You seem very sure of that." Ellie glanced over at his earnest face.

"At this moment, I've never been so sure of anything in all my life," Liam replied solemnly. Then with a self-amused chuckle, he finished by saying, "And in *this* lifetime, Elizabeth, I could teach you a lot. Trust me."

I bet you could teach me something.

"Is that a promise, Liam? Are you going to school me at our next debate?" Ellie challenged.

"Perhaps." He smiled, again giving nothing away. Then unexpectedly, he added, "I will school you wherever you'd like. Just say the word."

Ellie's stomach dropped.

I'd let you school me too.

It took every ounce of self-control not to push him off the road and into the trees where she could frantically pull off his sweaty shirt. God, she would bury her face in his chest, lost in the scent of him, straddling him as she ran her hands down the muscles of his torso, the hard lines leading diagonally to his groin.

Not that she'd dreamt about this.

Or even given it much thought—every single waking hour since Chicago.

This is why you're guilty.

Ellie couldn't utter an actual reply over the screaming of her body. A look of complacency spread across Liam's face in response to Ellie's flustered silence.

They jogged on, Ellie unconsciously setting a faster pace, perhaps trying to impress Liam, but he kept up, his legs much longer than hers. Everything he did seemed graceful and effortless. He was perfect, almost unearthly. If she reached out to touch him, maybe he would disappear like pixie dust, bursting suddenly, a million bits of shimmering light into nothingness, a figment of her imagination.

Before she knew it, Liam was leading, and she following. He wound them around the back side of campus and back up the road, right toward Joe Dobb's mother's house. And then there it was—the gravel road leading down to a partially obscured cottage ringed by hickories, the flower garden following the adjoining flagstone path to the front door still meticulously kept. Liam had obviously spent much time tending to Mrs. Dobb's property. No wonder Joe was so happy to have him as a tenant.

Ellie hesitated just long enough to break stride with him. He understood her hesitation. He knew. He always seemed to know.

"Just let me make you breakfast," he offered almost shyly.

"Sure," Ellie agreed, against her better judgment. She couldn't help herself. She was curious. "I can't get too full though, if I have to run back."

"I'll drop you home," Liam suggested.

I don't think that's a good idea.

"It's only a mile," Ellie answered quickly. "I can just walk it."

Liam shrugged. Surely he understood her dilemma.

Yet he purposely put you in this position.

There are any number of positions he could put me into!

Liam opened the door to reveal a quaint country home with dark walnut floors bathed in early-morning sun. As Ellie entered, Liam's scent assailed her. The intoxicating soapy smell of him permeated the entire home. Unconsciously she stopped to breathe it in deeply. Liam pretended not to notice.

Stop swooning, fool. Pull it together!

A small throw blanket hung over the sofa, an old cup of tea on the side table, a stack of books littering the coffee table, his open laptop, an acoustic guitar laying across a chair and its ottoman. The house looked lived in, loved. There was an air of calm about it. Ellie stepped further inside, looking around, and that's when she noticed. The books on the coffee table were ones she'd written. She stepped over and picked one up.

"Should I autograph this for you?" she teased. It was a thin book of critical essays, her first book to be published.

"Would you?" Liam laughed. "Please make it out to Liam, your biggest fan!"

"You are my *only* fan, Dr. Curran!" Ellie laughed. "I think only two hundred of these books went into print. This is practically a collector's item."

"Just think how valuable it will be when you sign it 'my love eternal, Elizabeth,'" Liam said teasingly, from the kitchen. He had begun digging out a frying pan.

"Toss me a pen!" Ellie instructed. "Should I be flattered or scared? Anyone who's read this many of my essays borders on obsessive!"

"I can think of worse things to be obsessed with, Elizabeth. I'll give you a pen, but don't defile my books!" Liam warned playfully. "And don't sign anything you don't mean! Once it's in writing, it must be so."

Ellie took a pen from Liam's hand and set to work on the front inside cover of the book:

> *My dearest Liam,*
>   *Everything is as it should be.*
> *Yours forever,*
> *Elizabeth*

She set the book back down on the table with authority.

"There!" she said with satisfaction. Liam eyed her warily from the kitchen and then set back to work cracking eggs.

"Can I help?" Ellie asked looking up at the clock. She would have about ten minutes to eat if she was to make it back home in time to shower and get to work by nine. It was already going on 7:00 a.m.

"Absolutely not," Liam refused. "Come sit by me while I cook."

Ellie obeyed by taking a stool at the breakfast bar overlooking the galley kitchen. "You enjoy cooking?" she asked.

"I enjoy cooking for other people. It isn't so interesting cooking for oneself, although I certainly like to eat! For me, most of the joy of cooking comes from experimenting with food that I've grown or caught."

"Who taught you to cook?" Ellie asked absently, trying to prevent herself from openly staring at Liam's every move, gaping at him every time he turned to get something from the refrigerator.

"My parents are both decent cooks, although really we had a housekeeper most of my life who did the majority of the cooking," Liam explained. "Katherine was a great cook. She traveled all over the world as a kid and learned most of her skills abroad. She taught me a lot about cooking."

The mention of his dead wife was sobering. Ellie feigned a smile, but she had some strange, unexpected emotion overwhelm her.

Jealousy?

Oh, please. She's dead, and you're married. What's to be jealous about?

And yet, there was no denying that bittersweet tug at her heart. Mention of Katherine made it difficult to pretend that only this moment existed.

"I see you have a guitar." Ellie changed the subject by pointing to the other side of the room.

E. J. Densmore

"Yes, I brought that with me. It relaxes me to play at night sometimes."

"What do you play?" Ellie wondered.

"A bit of everything, I suppose," Liam answered. "I grew up on American punk rock. British music bored me. Obviously I play a lot of classical, things I learned at university. Irish folk songs my dad used to sing. Some indie rock, contemporary stuff."

"It seems your musical tastes are just as eclectic as mine, then, Dr. Curran."

"I don't know about that!" He laughed.

"I'm surprised you need to play guitar to relax. Don't my essays put you to sleep?" Ellie teased.

"On the contrary, Elizabeth. I find your mind fascinating." He smiled, looking up from his task, his long, muscled forearm flexed as he scrambled the eggs. "Your writing is full of fire. Always fiercely on the side of the heroine. A champion of the misunderstood, downtrodden female protagonist. I wonder if there is a male character in all of literature who might escape your brutal dissection."

"Do any deserve to escape it?" Ellie played along.

"I'm sure I could think of some," Liam answered. "There must be at least one male character with whom the contentious Dr. Lawson can sympathize."

"Purnell." Ellie corrected him instinctively.

"Ah, yes," Liam scoffed without looking up. The sharp crack of cold eggs hit the blistering skillet, splitting the awkward air.

What did that mean?

The steady sizzle temporarily filled the space as Liam finished setting out fruit and juice so they could eat. Ellie eyed the clock wistfully. She wanted desperately to stay here with him. If only she could stop time.

~

"You look happy."

The voice startled Ellie as she wandered dreamily through the front door of her home, soaked through from her return run. It was Alec, leaning against the kitchen counter, cradling a massive thermos of coffee as he surveyed the backyard.

"You're up early," Ellie replied, startled. Surely she had started to blush.

"I have to pick up investors from the airport," Alec reminded Ellie with some exasperation. "Remember? Dinner? I sort of need you to be charming. Help me schmooze these guys."

"Oh! I completely forgot," Ellie admitted.

Too busy thinking about other things.

"I was thinking that maybe on Friday night we could have a cocktail party," Alec suggested.

"God, Alec, that's only two days away." Ellie felt all the calm she'd worked so hard to achieve transform suddenly into a stress line between her eyes.

"I'll take care of everything," Alec offered. "We'll just cater. I'll call the cleaning lady and have her come tomorrow. Why don't you invite John Long and Marta and your parents? Becca too. What about that British professor and his students? The more people, the better."

"That's an odd mix, don't you think?" Ellie wondered doubtfully, her stomach twisting suddenly into little knots. Liam and Alec were compartmentalized parts of her life. The idea of introducing the two left her feeling somewhat nauseous.

"It could be interesting, I think," Alec answered. "Maybe odd is good. These investors are going to be in town until Saturday, and I want to make a good impression. Our home is certainly a symbol of the business's success, and it might be a good distraction to have some different people here for them to talk with. God knows it would be a help to me. I can only entertain people myself for so long."

"I didn't think you found the English department very interesting," Ellie said, somewhat defensively.

"You know what I mean, Elle." Alec turned dismissively, filling his thermos up again and screwing the cap back on.

"Sure, that's fine." Ellie acquiesced. How could she say no?

A very short hour later, hair still slightly damp, she dashed up the stairs of the liberal-arts building toward her office.

Shit. Shit. Shit. I'm going to be late.

"Ellie!" Long's voice caught her by surprise as she was reaching for her door handle. He had popped his head out of his office hastily. "Could we possibly meet in a half hour? Right now I have a pressing issue I need to attend to."

"Absolutely, John," Ellie answered, hoping she didn't sound too relieved. She and Liam were scheduled to meet with him in, oh (she glanced at her watch), three minutes.

We can absolutely postpone the meeting even though I'm sure your "pressing issue" is not very pressing.

Long's head made a reappearance. "Could you just walk down to Dr. Curran's office to let him know?"

"Sure, John," Ellie agreed, tossing her bags recklessly onto her desk and heading back down the direction she had just come. The morning had started out so lovely: sunrise and Liam, breakfast. But now it was quickly spiraling downhill. She felt her face starting to pinch up. Tension. Not just from running late, but from this mounting anxiety over inviting Liam and John Long to her house on Friday.

Will Alec behave himself?

But as soon as the thought entered Ellie's mind, it was dismissed. Alec would not act a fool in front of potential investors, so inviting people to their home was probably pretty safe.

You think, huh? Safe for whom?

Well, safe in the respect that Alec wasn't likely to get wasted and piss in the flowerbeds. It was amazing to Ellie how much self-control he could exert when it came to money, when it came to making a favorable impression on people who might possibly invest.

Let's face it, you're nervous to have Alec and Liam together, as if they can see into your soul, know what you're thinking.

Well, the one certainly can.

And there it was: The one certainly can.

She wasn't afraid of Alec meeting Liam, of Alec being suspicious of their friendship. She was afraid of what Liam might think. She didn't want to be seen in the role of Alec's wife. She wanted just to be her, Elizabeth, like she was able to do in Chicago, like she was able to do at work, a world apart from Alec and home. That way she could wear her mask still, perpetuate the persona—the perfect, unflappable, fun, together Elizabeth. Not the sullen, resigned Ellie, wife of an alcoholic.

Don't be stupid. Liam already sees beyond that.

Does he?

Feeling a sense of trepidation, Ellie wandered down to Liam's temporary office. His laptop sat open on his desk, but he was nowhere to be found.

"Hey! Have you seen Liam?" Ellie asked Marta, who came up the stairs eating a bagel, late as usual, her leather satchel crammed full of crumpled papers.

"He's probably setting up for me. Go look in the lecture hall," Marta answered with her mouth half full.

Ellie's pace slowed as she went back down the stairs. Every step closer she got to Liam was a step closer to asking him to this stupid party on Friday. Then right before she reached the door of the lecture hall—laughter. A woman's familiar laughter. Ellie stopped instinctively.

Listen.

It was Megan. Ellie's heart dropped. Against her will, her feet propelled her two steps further, hand on the door. She stopped.

Through the narrow rectangular window of the lecture-hall doors, she could see Megan's figure, tall and impossibly lean, bent over Liam at the front table, her long, blond hair cascading down across her shoulder, obscuring her face. Liam looked up at her (probably right at breast level) with intense interest, his head then cocked to the side as if in thought. He stood then, patting Megan's shoulder, the way he did Ellie's sometimes, the friendly but oddly sensuous gesture that made Ellie weak in the knees. Megan's voice was barely audible and then he laughed, as if on cue, easily and naturally. The sound crushed Ellie.

Are they flirting?

Oh my God, what is wrong with you? What right do you have to react this way?

But the internal scolding made no difference; a storm of indecipherable emotions swirled within her as she pushed open the door just slightly too abruptly.

Suave entrance.

Neither Liam nor Megan looked surprised to see Ellie, whose face was as placid and fixed as ever. *Professional faker.*

"Good morning," Ellie chirped, sauntering casually over to the table where Liam sat and Megan hovered shamelessly.

"Hey!" Megan answered, still looking star struck.

Young fool. You don't hold your cards very close to your chest, do you? Why don't you just give him a lock of your hair? Your panties?

Ellie turned to Liam. "John doesn't need us in his office for another half an hour. He wanted me to let you know."

"Well, good," Liam answered and then addressed Megan. "That gives me some time to look this over." He held up a stapled manuscript with Megan's name on it. She looked embarrassed.

"I thought it would be beneficial to have another set of eyes edit my work," Megan said, apologizing hastily for the slight; it was customary for Ellie to critique Megan's writing, especially things she would submit for publication.

"Oh, that's OK!" Ellie waved dismissively. "It *is* good to have someone else read your work if they're willing. My father was always a second set of eyes on my work. Even the infamous *Frankenstein* contradictions." Ellie smiled snidely at Liam.

"And yet you published both," Liam shot back without missing a beat, rather meanly.

"I'm stubborn," Ellie replied, still smiling.

Stifling a small snort of agreement, Liam looked back down at the papers littering the table in front of him.

"Well, I'm going to set up for your ten o'clock, then, Ellie." Megan dismissed herself, sensing the awkwardness. "Thank you, Dr. Curran," she said with one long, last eyelash-batting look in Liam's direction as she headed for the door.

"Oh, Megan." Ellie couldn't resist. "Did you finish the research for next week's PowerPoints?" (It was so Dr. Messing of her.)

"I'll get that done too," Megan answered quickly, and she was gone.

Good. You do that. Ellie had to work very hard to suppress the Cheshire-cat grin that threatened to burst onto her face.

"Pretty tough on the help, aren't you?" Liam raised an eyebrow.

"I could be much tougher, and you know it," Ellie answered defensively. "You wouldn't believe the things

I had to do during my fellowship at the University of Chicago. And this isn't exactly the University of Chicago."

"I suppose it isn't, but it's a prestigious enough program to have you as a professor."

"Yes, as fate would have it," Ellie answered bitterly. *You're not going there. Not this morning.*

"Ah, yes. Tell me about fate." Liam said.

"What would you like to know about fate?" Ellie cocked her head to the side with a smirk. *I'll take your challenge.*

Something strange compelled her. Anger? Jealousy? The need to prove his expectations wrong? He expected her to shy away, ignore the question, pretend as if she hadn't seen Megan—hadn't been affected by it. But she wasn't going to back down this time. Circling behind him, she leaned against his back, so close her chest almost brushed against his shoulder as she reached for Megan's paper.

"No," Liam admonished her, his powerful hand landing on top of hers. "You're not looking at this until you answer my question."

Ellie leaned in, pressing her breasts against his hard back, her lips brushing his ear as she whispered, "I don't know what you mean, Professor. I just want to see the paper."

Liam's hand tightened slowly around hers, his breathing almost stopping.

We can stay like this forever, Liam. We don't have to move.

Suddenly he took his hand up, and Ellie snatched the paper triumphantly.

"I don't really want this," she said, flinging it back onto the tabletop. "I just wanted to call your bluff," she declared smugly.

That's what you get for flirting with that amateur.

Liam looked breathless and spent. For a moment, he shut his eyes as if to regain composure.

"Very well," he said quietly.

Ellie thought she had won when suddenly he shot up from the chair, looming over her—half in humor, half in exasperation—his broad shoulders blocking her line of sight, a beautiful wall refusing her escape.

"Tell me about fate, Elizabeth," he demanded, his voice low and serious. Ellie's smile started to fade.

Fine.

"I got pregnant, Dr. Curran. As fate would have it, I ended up here with my father's job," Ellie blurted out without breaking Liam's intense gaze. Surprisingly she felt relieved, not ashamed, to articulate the truth.

"And as fate would have it, I found you here. So as I've said before, everything is as it should be," Liam answered without smiling. "I have no interest in that girl," he added with annoyed finality and sat back down at the table.

Damn it. He knew.

Ellie turned toward the door.

"I'll see you in Long's office," Liam called after her.

"Yes," Ellie said, without turning around.

"So it really is Dr. Curran's choice of debate topic this time." John Long sat back in his swivel chair, rocking a bit as he wrapped his sausage-like fingers into folded palms over his rotund belly. "Have you had any thoughts on the matter, Professor?"

"American literature, then," Liam suggested. Ellie sat back quietly, watching the two. A weird, peaceful resignation had overcome her; she wasn't going to argue. It was as if finally being honest with Liam had freed her. Even just the tiniest bit. Going into this meeting felt much less tense. Somehow she sensed that Liam would choose a subject suited to her. She trusted him.

Don't be a fool.

I can't help myself. I can't help the way I feel.

Don't agree to being locked in a box.

I'm not that stupid anymore. I'm not twenty-four, for God's sake.

You're acting like it.

"Ellie, any novels in particular that you'd like to discuss at the debate?" Long asked.

"I trust Dr. Curran to choose." The words left her mouth without check.

Why did you say "trust"?

Liam looked pleased. "Why not *The Scarlet Letter*?" he suggested.

Ellie's eyes shot up from her legal pad. Was he taunting her? Their eyes locked across the table, but there was no mockery or mirth in his expression. He was serious.

How fitting. The Scarlet Letter.

"I suppose we'll have to meet about research." She just couldn't resist. The corner of her mouth threatened to curl into an ironic smirk. Liam's face gave nothing away as his foot nudged her under the table.

"Extensively," he agreed without looking away.

"Have you done much research on *The Scarlet Letter*, Dr. Curran?" John Long inquired.

"I have," Liam answered. "As a matter of fact, I am doing research currently. Things I'm sure Dr. Purnell would be very interested to know." He touched his upper lip, tracing the line of his stubble, in an attempt to suppress a smile. "I'm aware Elizabeth likes arguing for the misunderstood female protagonists. Hester Prynne is never tiring to discuss. I should think you'd defend her adamantly," he said, addressing Ellie.

"Absolutely." Ellie sucked in her breath as Liam ran his foot up her bare calf to her knee.

"Excellent," John Long exclaimed. "Let's plan on the next debate in two weeks, then. That gives me enough time to send out invitations and make arrangements with the university."

"Can we have it outdoors this time, John?" Ellie suggested. Her voice was breathy, heavy from distraction. Liam let down his foot, freeing her from the tension.

"I think that is a grand idea!" John Long proclaimed. She smiled widely. Why did Marta hate him so? He had to be the most agreeable person on earth. Maybe he, too, was so smitten with Liam that any suggestion made at that moment would be welcomed with unchecked enthusiasm.

Liam and Ellie got up from their chairs to leave when it suddenly struck her.

Don't forget to ask them to the party.
Shit!

Ellie turned back, purposely looking only at John Long when she blurted, "Alec and I are having a cocktail party at our house Friday night. Would you both like to come?" She looked up at Liam, his face full of amused surprise.

"I will definitely come," Liam answered directly. "I wouldn't miss it for the world."

Ellie stood tensely at the kitchen island as she struggled with a very expensive bottle of Chenin Blanc and a very stubborn corkscrew. Surely there had to be some hired help at their party who could actually help. (She hated to be that way, but why was she opening her own bottle of wine? Hadn't they hired people to do that for them? Wasn't that the point?) All the servers seemed busy elsewhere at the moment, and a glass of wine (to take off the edge) could not be delayed.

Emergency!

People would be arriving within the half hour, and Ellie felt like she'd been running a marathon since the morning. Three solid hours locked in her office, pouring over every book of Liam's she could get her hands on in preparation for the next debate, had sapped every bit of her energy for the day. Not that spending time with Liam's writing was a chore, but she was emotionally and intellectually spent. His books were intense reading that required her full concentration as she jotted notes in the margins, constantly distracted by thoughts of the author himself. Instead of being able to form any intelligible arguments against what he had written, she found herself daydreaming about the author. Where was he when he wrote this essay? What had he been wearing? (She liked to imagine him shirtless in his pajama pants, typing on his laptop while sitting in bed.) Was he alone when he wrote? Did Katherine read what he published? (Fantasy halted.)

It was exhausting. Liam's brilliance. No wonder he had so many admirers. It was difficult to comprehend how someone so beautiful could be so intelligent. Ellie felt she was in over her head. Not just in the debate. Just in over her head in general. She could think of little else but Liam, resisting the urge to stalk him in his office, follow him around the liberal-arts building all day, ditch her own lectures to sneak into the back row of his, anything to give her an excuse to bask in the sound of his voice, that reserved British accent that at once could be so full of humor and then serious and commanding. She wished she could quiet her mind, somehow get some rest from the thought of him.

Finally! With one last forceful tug, the cork popped ceremoniously from the bottle's neck. She sighed deeply, pouring herself a glass and then leaned against the counter to survey the scene as she took a long, healthy gulp. The yard looked lovely, bathed in the soft, white light of hundreds of tiny bulbs that had been strung through the trees. *Nice touch.* From their speakers, a woman's mellow voice, just audible above smooth, jazzy clarinets, floated through the yard and patio. Alec could definitely find the right help. Good lighting. Good music. *I hope the food is as good.* Wine was not an issue. They certainly had enough wine in the cellar to throw a successful party.

"That's a nice dress. Have I seen that one before?" Alec commented as he entered the kitchen from the back patio. He had been giving the servers and bartenders instructions. As promised, he had taken care of everything for the party, and he expected the same sort of excellence from these "employees" as he did from his own workers. Ellie didn't dare tell him she had had to open her own wine bottle even though she saw him eyeing the evidence when he came in.

"No, it's new," Ellie said. "I bought it in Chicago." She was wearing the dress she had bought for the opera, paired with flat sandals to make it look more casual.

Of all the things in your closet, you chose this.

She smiled to herself. *The dress makes me feel sexy and confident, and with the shit show that might possibly ensue, I need all the confidence I can get!*

By half past nine, the party was in full swing. Three businessmen from Texas and one of their wives had been the first to arrive. Alec gave them the grand tour of the house, the garages equipped with all of his classic cars, the gardens, the wine cellar, the expansive home theater that only Jordan used. Eventually they all ended up outside by the stone fireplace, drinking some expensive scotch Alec had bought specifically for one of them. *Again, nice attention to detail.* Alec had done his research; he knew his audience, and he aimed to please. Waiters brought around little trays of hors d'oeuvres. Ellie was only stuck playing the role of charming wife until everyone from the university, including John Long and his equally awkward wife, had arrived. Then she mingled with her own guests.

The group of twelve or so graduate students who came to the party initially acted tentative and shy, but they found a comfortable spot outdoors in the muted light of the lanterns where alcohol, the great equalizer, dispelled any reticence. It was only a short while before the investors and the students were talking art, travel, and literature.

Please, God, no politics. They're from Texas.

At some point, John and Maggie Lawson snuck in, finding their way into the conversation. Ellie's mother, meeting the guests from Texas, had sniffed out the other horse people, and, like Alec, was busy striking deals. Surely these people could use a new horse! Marta ambled in at some point, conspicuously relaxed, finding herself a glass of red wine and a comfortable spot between the students.

Well, conspicuously relaxed, to you, Ellie. Don't be jealous! You wish you could feel that relaxed. But no, she had to be the gracious hostess. Attending parties was way more fun than hosting them. Ellie nodded across the patio to Marta where some of the university group sat on the benches under the fabled maple tree that grew up through the patio. Marta lifted her glass, a knowing grin spreading slowly across her face. It was the "I know you're in misery, but I'll toast to you anyway" grin. Much better times were had at The Bear, singing karaoke, where Joe Dobbs was the one running around doing the serving.

Somewhere inside the house, Ellie had heard Becca's laughter. But no Liam yet. Forcing herself to grab a napkin of food, Ellie scurried into a dark entryway where she could eat quietly, obscured from the party, just a quiet moment to herself to breathe. From where she stood hidden, she could assess the party; everyone seemed to be having a good time. Everyone was eating. Everyone was drinking. There was a lot of animated conversation. She breathed a sigh of relief and sipped only her second glass of wine. *Sadly the hostess never gets to eat or drink. Too busy talking.*

Then he appeared. Liam. He seemed to float in from nowhere, so tall, his head almost brushed a string of lights above him, setting him aglow. Suddenly he was by Alec's side, extending his hand. All heads turned to watch. How could they not? Becca followed close behind Liam. They must have met in the kitchen before coming out. Certainly that had been the sound of her laughter. Liam seemed to elicit that response. Now Alec was smiling and nodding his head, patting Liam on the shoulder and laughing. Ellie felt her stomach tumble.

A little weird, huh?

It's the surreal experience of watching fantasy meet reality.

The reality is that I am standing in the doorway, watching this party unfold instead of participating in it. Ellie would rather have retreated into the garden alone. *Well, not completely alone.* At least away from the empty, polite small talk that took so much effort. It was more comfortable to be an outside observer than a participant.

"Hiding?"

The putrid smell of Scotch assailed Ellie. She turned toward it suddenly, though her reaction was to turn away. One of the Texans stood so close to her, she had to pull back her head to focus on his face. He was obviously drunk.

Really? Can I just catch a break from this bullshit?

"You scared me!" she exclaimed as sweetly as she could. (You scared little, innocent me, you big, silly man! Oh, stop, sir! You're too wily, and I'm too cute. Now give me your money.)

"I'm sorry, ma'am," he drawled with a laugh and then wrapped his thick arm around Ellie's small waist. His sweaty paw came to rest on her rib cage just under her breast, a very calculated move. Clever for a drunk. She stopped breathing for a moment.

How are you going to gracefully get out of this one? Pull away without obvious repulsion. Bruised egos don't bode well with arrogant men.

"You're having a good time, I see." She couldn't contain her sarcasm. (Lifelong self-defense mechanism.) "Did my mother try to sell you a horse?"

"Yes." He laughed vigorously, the reek of liquor creating a cloud of noxious fume like a cloud around him. "And your husband is trying to sell us his business. You're the one who should be doin' the sellin' though, honey. Look at you!" He squeezed Ellie into his side. "I bet you could sell an igloo to an Eskimo! Just show up in that dress."

Ellie smiled feebly, shaking her head. "You're too kind. Really," she responded unconvincingly as her eyes searched the room for some means of elegant escape.

"Yeah, what I want to know is whether you're part of this deal," the Texan wondered out loud, with a slur. "Do we get to talk through you or do we have to communicate with that bore of a husband you have?" he teased maliciously.

"Oh, I'm just an English professor. I don't make the money. I spend it. Isn't that what women are supposed to do?" Ellie would have laughed at her own ironic joke if she hadn't been so overcome by the acrid fumes oozing out of this man. His grip simply would not loosen.

"That's what my first, second, and third wives would say!" he guffawed, almost doubling over from his own humor. Ellie tried wriggling out of his grasp but to no avail. His hand now traveled up and down her side to her hip bone and back up again. To her relief, the patio door slid open and Alec entered, catching Ellie's frantic, wide-eyed plea.

Help! Rescue me!

He looked at her absently, almost amused.

Oh my God, does he think I'm joking? Then behind Alec followed John Long and Liam, most likely following on a tour of the house. Alec was playing the host, not the hero, and apparently, he would not be deterred from his mission.

Damn him. Why does he have to be so dense sometimes?

As Ellie watched desperately, Liam slid the door shut, catching a glimpse of Ellie in his peripheral vision. A manufactured smile grew wide across his face as he walked forward toward Ellie and the Texan, his hand outstretched, eyes only on the man.

"I don't believe we've met." Liam's voice was loud and clipped, his accent so Irish it caught Ellie by surprise. "I'm Liam Curran, a colleague of Dr. Purnell's."

"Good to meet you," the groper replied with annoyed surprise, forced to release his hand from Ellie's waist in order to shake.

"Dr. Purnell, huh?" the man, turning back to Ellie, scoffed unintentionally.

"Your sister has been asking after you." Liam raised his eyebrows, giving Ellie an excuse for exit. "I believe she's on the patio waiting to speak with you. Mr.?" He turned to the man.

"Andrew Mitner," the man replied.

"Mr. Mitner, shall we find Mr. Purnell? He'd like to give us a tour of the house."

"I've already seen it," the man answered begrudgingly.

When Andrew Mitner saw that Liam would not be dissuaded, he let out an exaggerated sigh.

"After you." Liam held out his palm, signaling the hall ahead. Alec could be heard talking to John Long in the kitchen, presumably waiting for Liam to return. Taking her cue, Ellie scampered toward the patio door, not turning to look back until she reached it. As she grasped the door handle, she locked eyes with Liam, who still stood in the shadow of the hall, arms folded, watching her to ensure a safe exit. Tension stiffened his posture.

"Thank you," Ellie mouthed, resisting the urge to run back to him. His facial expression remained unchanged, dark and unreadable.

Liam had used a believable enough lie in Becca. As Ellie walked out, there Becca sat on the patio beneath the maple, sandwiched closely between Marta and the base of the tree. The two appeared lost in serious conversation.

"My two favorite people!" Ellie cried with a sense of relief.

"Hey." Becca stood to embrace her older sister warmly. "You've been so busy tonight I haven't been able to corner you. Nice party!"

"Alec really planned everything. I'm just trying to be gracious and getting groped in the process." Ellie laughed.

"Oh my God! What happened? Who?" Becca held out her wine. "Here, take this!" She was still wearing her scrubs, with her straight, sandy bob tucked neatly behind her ears. Ellie swiped it from her, glancing over her shoulder to see if anyone was watching and then downed it.

"How's that for ladylike?" Ellie laughed. "One of those awful men from Texas decided to sneak up on me and cop a feel," she whispered, looking over her shoulder again. "I see you got dressed up, Becca!"

"It's just your house. I figured I'd come as the real deal! I don't have any blood on me, do I? No horseshit on my shoes?" Becca laughed loudly.

"God, Becca, you sound more and more like Mom every day!"

Marta laughed uneasily, knowing this was probably not a compliment. Becca pushed Marta's shoulder reassuringly.

"It's OK, Marta. Ellie needs to release some of her pent-up anger occasionally by making Maggie Lawson digs, which always have something to do with horseshit!"

"Are you saying I should be more original?" Ellie asked.

"Nah, I love it!" Becca smiled a wide, sweet grin that made her appear much younger than she was. "How'd you get away from the creepy groper? What'd he do?"

"I'm standing in the dark entry of the mud room, trying to scarf down a bit of food, and he all sidles up to me like, 'Hey, are you part of the business deal?'"

Marta and Becca laughed simultaneously, looking eerily similar, two halves of one whole. It had never occurred to Ellie until that moment how similar they could be.

"How did you get out of that?" Marta asked, leaning back comfortably against the tree.

"Liam," Ellie said quickly, working very hard at non-chalance. Both Becca and Marta began to laugh again. "You two seem like you're conspiring." Ellie wagged a finger at them. "No fair. I want to know what you both think is so funny!"

"We were just dissecting your eclectic guest list," Becca answered with mock innocence. She nodded inconspicuously across the patio. "Mom's working the Texans. Dad's working the graduate students. Look at him. He's in his glory with an audience of admirers. I don't know why he ever agreed to retire."

I do. Coerced by Mom in order to open a spot for me.

"Megan trying to work Liam." Marta snickered.

"She's here?" Ellie asked. "I haven't seen her yet."

"I think she went into the house," Marta answered.

A hot wave of resentment swept over Ellie. Becca watched her sister with curiosity.

"This Dr. Curran's pretty charming, huh?" Becca asked with some amusement.

"Easy on the eyes too," Marta answered. "Ellie will deny it to her grave, but I know she doesn't mind his attention."

"Shhh!" Ellie admonished them both for their teasing and then leaned in, asking Becca quietly, "Have you met him?"

"Yeah, in the kitchen on the way in. He knew who I was right away and introduced himself," Becca answered.

"Well, your scrubs probably gave you away. He knows I have a sister who's a veterinarian."

"How does he know about your family? Have you two have become friends?" Becca questioned with a wink.

"We've been running together…" Ellie put her finger up to her mouth in a symbolic stay-quiet gesture.

"Oh." Becca was genuinely surprised. Ellie could almost see the wheels in Becca's head turning as she processed the admission. Becca looked to Marta for clarification but was only met by Marta's smirk as she looked down at the patio shaking her head. For a moment, Ellie feared Marta might give away the secret of their Chicago trip.

"I think she has a terrible crush." Marta almost giggled. Becca began laughing too.

What is up with the two of them? They're both acting like they're high. Marta maybe. But Becca? No way.

"How much have you had to drink?" Ellie accused Becca.

"Nothing, Mother! You drank it, remember? Be a hostess and grab me another glass," Becca joked.

By this time, Alec was leading Liam, John Long, and the now infamous Mr. Andrew Mitner of Texas back onto the patio. Liam took a comfortable seat by the fireplace and was immediately surrounded by Jim Lawson, Megan, and four other graduate students, presumably geared up to talk literature. Ellie hadn't seen her father this animated in a very long time.

"Ellie!" Alec summoned her over. The investors were leaving.

Thank God.

Even as Ellie shook hands, endured one more good-bye grab, and tolerated a round of cheek kisses, she was aware that Liam watched her. One ear on his present conversation, and two eyes on Ellie. She glanced over. Yes. His gaze followed her around the patio. He watched her every move, not even trying to be covert about it. He patted the seat next to him. Her heart leapt into her throat.

Can you sit next to him without being so obvious?

Obvious about what? He's a guest at my house. I haven't even said hello to him yet. Besides my father is over there. My students. This couldn't be any safer.

Ellie said her final good-byes to the investors (don't let the door hit you in the ass on the way out) and then made her way toward the empty seat. Alec turned to a large group of his top management who had been invited over, people who were employees but also friends. They had claimed the stools around the outdoor bar and were getting louder by the moment. Now that the investors were gone, the pressure was off. They toasted one another loudly, congratulations all around for what they presumed was a done deal (*See what you could*

have screwed up if you'd put Andrew Mitner in his place?).
Alec had no reason not to let loose.

Great. Please, God, please, please let Alec behave.

"My wine?" Becca asked and shrugged as she watched Ellie retreat.

Ellie pointed to the waiter and shrugged back. Becca nodded in understanding and then waved Ellie off. No sooner had Ellie hesitated that Megan slid into the empty seat next to Liam. If he was surprised or dismayed by Megan's appearance, he did an award-winning job of concealing it.

Maybe he's as good an actor as you are.

"Hi." Ellie forced herself to smile as she approached the group. Between her apprehension about Alec losing control and her annoyance at Megan sidling in, she felt sure her face was pinched into a sour knot.

"There she is!" her father exclaimed, leaning in to kiss her.

"Hi, Daddy. Hi, Megan. You're having a good time?"

"Yes, thank you for inviting me, "Megan answered. "Your house is…well, it's amazing. Really."

"Thanks, Megan," Ellie replied. *Blah. Blah. Blah.*

"Come sit," Liam instructed. It was surprisingly firm, an order, not a request. "You've been running around all evening," he said, softening. "A truly charming hostess. I think you've earned the right to relax a bit, wouldn't you all agree?" he asked the group. They all murmured in agreement.

"I can't!" Ellie refused. "I promised Becca more wine."

"Here! I brought you one instead." Becca appeared at Ellie's side, holding a new glass out to her.

"You're wonderful!" Ellie exclaimed. *Becca, my savior.*

"Both my girls!" their father exclaimed genuinely.

"You're a lucky man!" Liam commented.

"That I am," Jim Lawson said, kissing Becca on the top of her head. "Do you have children, Dr. Curran?"

"No, sir." Liam shifted uncomfortably in his chair. "My wife traveled quite a bit for work. I suppose it wasn't meant to be."

"What does your wife do?" Ellie's father asked.

"She was an opera singer," Liam answered briefly. Ellie watched him manage his emotions carefully. Megan looked on tentatively also. Surely she knew his wife had died—after all, she, too, could do her research well. The university group collectively held their breath as they waited for the conversation to turn. "Katherine Curran," Liam finally offered.

"Oh, yes." Jim Lawson's brow furrowed pensively when suddenly the light of realization appeared on his face. "She is…was a wonderful performer. I saw her once in London." He paused, taking a sip of his wine. "I'm sorry."

Liam nodded.

"You're from North Yorkshire, Professor?" Jim Lawson changed direction.

"I am, sir. Ingleton. I grew up virtually at the foot of Ingleborough."

"Lovely, haunted area," Jim mused. "We visited there once, remember, girls?"

Maggie had, by this time, wandered into the group. Alec and his friends were trading stories loudly behind them. Everyone, including Ellie, had had their fair share of the wine cellar's offerings.

"You're thinking of Devonshire, Daddy," Ellie said, correcting him. "And Dartmoor National Park certainly does live up to its fabled reputation. It sounds beautiful where you're from, though, Dr. Curran," Ellie offered, almost comically polite. Liam looked amused.

"It is, Dr. Purnell, quite lovely," he answered politely.

"I'm not thinking of Devonshire," Jim insisted. "I've hiked the Three Peaks in Yorkshire. It's quite a beautiful, romantic place. The downs. The caves." He seemed aggravated and then turning to his wife, he added, "Don't you remember the day we found the waterfalls? It was breathtaking. We stopped there to eat lunch and then it started to rain. We stayed in that tiny bed and breakfast. Don't you remember?"

Smiling wryly, Maggie placed her arm through her husband's and said, "That wasn't me, James."

"You must be thinking of our trip to Devon, Daddy." Ellie scrambled. "We should try to find pictures to show Dr. Curran."

"That's a wonderful idea, Ellie," Maggie said patronizingly.

"Dr. Lawson," Marta stepped in cleverly. "Have you met, Megan, Ellie's graduate assistant?"

"I haven't been formally introduced, no," Jim Lawson replied, slightly confused by the sudden turn of conversation.

"She wrote her master's thesis on your poetry! I'm sure she has much to ask you but is too shy," Marta said manipulatively. "Megan, Dr. Lawson."

Megan got up to shake Jim Lawson's hand, conveniently freeing the seat next to Liam. He stood for a moment until Ellie inconspicuously maneuvered her way toward the seat and then they both sat back down again, as close as humanly possible—Ellie's knee brushing his slightly as he set his hand on her far shoulder for a moment, that "friendly" gesture that made her feel weak.

"Your hair." She reached up to a tiny flip that had grown from the waves near Liam's ear. "It's getting long." She smiled. A wide grin spread across Liam's face as Ellie suddenly realized...

She pulled her hand down instantly.

What is wrong with you, reaching for him like that?

No one seemed to notice. Megan and her father were instantly lost in conversation, and the other graduate students were listening intently. It wasn't every day that they were in the presence of a poetic genius.

At that moment, Liam and Ellie were all alone in the midst of everything.

"You got here pretty late," Ellie noted absently.

"It seems I got here at just the right time," Liam said. "One minute later, and who knows what that awful man would have done."

"Don't be silly," Ellie brushed him off. "I can handle a ridiculous pig like that. The only reason I didn't shove him into a wall was because I didn't want to jeopardize a deal by embarrassing him."

Liam didn't respond, his silence implying disapproval. Ellie suddenly felt the urge to defend herself (*I'm not a whore for money, if that's what you think.*).

"Regardless, I'm sorry I wasn't here sooner," Liam finally continued. "I napped after work. I suppose I needed proper rest in order to attend such a party!" he teased.

"I'm the one who needed a nap!" Ellie admitted. "I spent all afternoon searching your books for essays on *The Scarlet Letter* or Hawthorne, anything I could find."

"Some intense reading, huh? I'm glad to hear you're finally doing some research, Elizabeth! You won't find anything published on Hawthorne, though. I was telling Long the truth when I said I was doing research right now. Having a discussion with you about *The Scarlet Letter* will be most beneficial," Liam explained matter-of-factly.

Smirking, Ellie narrowed her eyes. Was he serious?

For a very long time, they sat content next to one another, listening quietly to all the conversations happening around them simultaneously. Their shoulders now touched. Their forearms touched, his soft, auburn hair tickling her elbow. Ellie breathed in as deeply as she could, the smell of Liam's soap and cologne, the fabric softener in his clothing. She was lost in him. Completely lost as if everything else—everyone else—had been stilled. The world in pause around them.

He leaned back a bit in his chair, swirling the pinot noir in his glass, looking up toward the tree.

"This is a very nice home," he remarked absently. "It suits you. Especially the tree." He stood deliberately, looking up into the branches, lost in contemplation. "These leaves turn a bright reddish hue in autumn, yes?"

Ellie nodded.

"Beautiful," he thought aloud. "You had the patio built around the tree?"

"I did," Ellie admitted.

Liam smiled. "It reminds me of *The Odyssey*."

"That's what Ellie always says," Alec announced loudly from his seat at the bar. He had obviously been listening to their conversation. A few guests nearest Alec stopped to listen with some curiosity. "She begged me not to let anyone cut down that stupid tree so we just built the patio around it." Alec paused, and then, as if he couldn't help himself, added with a smirk, "Of course, you know why she loves this tree, don't you?"

Ellie shot Alec a look that could have knocked him face first into the ground. There was no time to be subtle. *Oh, God, please don't let him elaborate. No one needs to know that this is the first place we had sex.*

"I imagine it reminded her of Penelope and Odysseus's bed. Isn't that what you mean?" Liam feigned helpfulness, but Ellie knew better.

"I have no idea what she meant." Alec snorted. "All I know is that the architect had to change the plans in order to accommodate this tree."

"Well, certainly you've read *The Odyssey* or at the very least her essay about Penelope? You know, Odysseus's wife? It's the essay that's all about their marriage bed, which was built out of an olive tree that grew through their house."

"No, I've never read that essay," Alec admitted, the jovial tone gradually leaving his voice.

"Oh, it's brilliant. Your wife is a very talented writer," Liam continued relentlessly.

"She is," Jim Lawson, distracted from his own conversation, piped in cluelessly.

"I'll take your word for it, Liam." Alec dismissed him, but Liam wasn't giving up so easily.

"I would say her essays on *Pride and Prejudice* are some of my favorites, but the essay on Penelope really captures her true voice. You should read them sometime, Alec. The book was published some ten years ago, yes?" Liam turned to Ellie, his eyes full of some emotion she couldn't identify. Contempt?

"Yes," Ellie answered immediately, as if Liam's voice commanded her like a marionette.

You will pay for that, Ellie.

But Alec only chuckled, not seeming offended in the least, emptying his wine glass in one last huge gulp. Setting it on the bar, he answered, "I'll leave the reading to all of you, Liam. While you're discussing books, I have a company to run." He turned back around to face his friends at the bar.

No one in the university group moved as Liam leaned back in his chair, folding his arms casually, a sardonic smile appearing on his face. He had elicited the response he desired, as usual.

"Ma'am, if you would like us to serve more wine, we're getting low." A waiter appeared at Ellie's side.

"I'll bring up some more bottles," she answered with a relieved sigh, almost darting from her seat to put some distance between herself and the discomfort of the scene.

Her face smarted as she wandered down the cellar stairs.

What just happened? Should she laugh or cry? *What the hell was that about?*

The cool, dank air enveloped Ellie as she absently ran her fingers over the bottles, leaving faint lines in the dusty glass. She stood for a moment in the darkness, her hand resting on the shelf as she tried to remember what exactly she had come here for. *Peace.*

"Let me help you." It was Liam's voice coming from the bottom of the stairs in the darkness. He flicked on the lights. "Are you hiding down here in the dark?"

"No," Ellie answered.

"No, I can't help you; or no, you're not hiding?" Liam's voice got closer.

"Why do you always sound as if you're laughing at me?" Ellie asked with frustration.

"I'm not laughing at you to be mean spirited." Liam came around the corner to stand in front of her.

She dropped her hand from the shelf so that both arms hung at her side momentarily, a gesture of surrender.

"You just take everything so very seriously, I can't help but find amusement in it," he explained.

The impish look on his face was almost too much to bear. Ellie felt the urge to either slap him or take his ridiculing face into her hands and kiss him. Instead she stepped in toward him, placing her hands on his hard chest, looking up into his eyes. Immediately the mirth drained from his face. The proximity was too much for them both. Liam took a deep, ragged breath in.

"I want to touch you." Ellie breathed against his chest, burying her face in the hollow of his pectorals, directly at his heart. It was racing in his chest.

"Then touch me," he whispered into her hair. She looked up to search his face, now full of longing. Gently taking her small hands into his, he brought one of her hands up to his mouth to kiss her open palm. The other hand he guided down the lines of his taught stomach, resting just at the low waist of his jeans. She leaned her head into his chest again, overcome by desire.

How far are you willing to go?

Then he slipped her hands beneath his shirt, the exquisite sensation of flesh on flesh, his soft, downy hair through her fingertips, the smell of him overwhelming her.

The lights flickered.

Women's laughter.

"Come on!" a familiar voice giggled.

"Leave the lights off," instructed another familiar voice.

Ellie and Liam sprang away from one another to face the sound of feet trampling loudly down the cellar steps.

More giggling, when around the corner came Becca, dragging Marta behind her by the hand. Both women had the air of children escaping punishment, sneaking down the stairs so that no one would see.

Ellie and Liam had barely enough time to separate before coming face to face with the two —eight startled, confused, suspecting eyes staring back at one another.

"Hey!" Ellie tried for casualness.

"Hi," Becca answered with surprise, dropping Marta's hand. "We thought we'd help you bring up more wine." It was an obvious lie.

"OK," Ellie answered awkwardly. "If we each bring two bottles up, that should hold us over for a while." Her shaking hand tried to shimmy a bottle from its bed. Liam stood in back of Ellie, conspicuously quiet.

"Let me get that for you," Liam offered, steadying Ellie's wrist. He had regained composure, easily sliding the bottles out of their slots and handing them to Marta and Becca. The women cradled their bottles gingerly in their arms, all strangely silent and then trudged back up the stairs, defeated, as Liam followed closely behind.

Eleven

April of Ellie Purnell's Thirty-third Year

Farewell, thou child of my right hand, and joy;
My sin was too much hope of thee, lov'd boy.
Seven years thou wert lent to me, and I thee pay,
Exacted by thy fate, on the just day.
Oh, could I lose all father now! For why
Will man lament the state he should envy?
To have so soon 'scaped world's and flesh's rage,
And if no other misery, yet age! [...]

—BEN JONSON, "ON MY FIRST SON"

"You don't really have to go, do you?" Alec asked with an impish grin. He reached out for Ellie with greasy hands as she backed away.

"Don't touch me!" she squealed in protest, backing out of the garage. Alec held his hands up in the air, surrendering.

"Come back here, and I won't chase you! I promise I won't touch you with my dirty hands. Just come back." He laughed.

"OK," Ellie conceded, moving slowly back toward him, eyes wide with anticipation. She stopped directly in front of him, just daring him playfully. He stepped in to kiss her. First just a chaste peck on the lips. Then he moved into her more forcefully, opening his mouth to slowly take her tongue. She was suddenly no longer in a hurry to leave, bags dropping to the floor of their garage as she took his face into her hands.

"You can't touch me!" she whispered as she pulled her mouth away temporarily.

"I'll wash my hands," he promised. "Just stay here. You don't really have to go into work today."

Ellie kissed him again. "I do," she finally said with a sigh. "I can't get anything done here. I have to get this essay finished before next Friday. I promised Long a submission for the literary review, and I don't have any idea what I'm even going to write about."

Alec looked unsympathetic. "You know, I could relieve you of all that pressure, Ellie!"

"I bet you could, Alec," she teased.

He laughed, "I didn't mean *that*! Of course, if you'd like me to relieve your stress right here on the hood of the car, I will!"

Ellie glanced tentatively over at the front door of the house. Jordan was sleeping on the front-room sofa just inside the door. The offer was tempting, but she really didn't have the time. Staying home, even just one minute longer, to have afternoon sex in the garage would be just another way to avoid getting started on this paper.

"I really *do* have to go," Ellie pleaded.

"Why don't you just quit your job, Ellie? I would love for you to be home. So would Jordan." Alec was serious now.

Here we go again.

"Jordan is going to be seven tomorrow, Alec." Ellie rolled her eyes, snatching her fallen bag from the floor of the garage. "Why would I stay home if he's in school all day?" She knew what was going to come next.

"That's why we should have another baby, Ellie. I think we should go ahead and see a fertility specialist. Find out why you haven't been able to get pregnant. I mean, even if it's me, I'll do what I have to do." His eyes looked so earnest that Ellie almost felt guilty.

I haven't "been able to get pregnant" for the past three years because I've been taking birth control. Every single morning, without fail, she secretly pushed that tiny pink pill through the back of its tinfoil shelter and swallowed it gratefully. It was what allowed her to keep teaching, keep writing (keep breathing).

"I know, Alec. I know you would." She would leave it at that. Maybe it could hold him off until their next counseling session.

The truth was she didn't ever want to have another baby. Not because she didn't want Jordan to have a sibling. She just couldn't risk the possibility that things would go back to the way they were. In the beginning. When Jordan was an infant, a toddler. Who never slept. Who cried constantly. Back when Alec drank constantly and didn't do a goddamned thing to help. When Ellie was completely and utterly alone.

No thanks.

Life right now was at least tolerable (if not good). OK, good. It was the best it had been in a while. Alec actually helped with Jordan now, occasionally picked him up from school, took him to all his soccer practices and games, gave him a bath every once in a while, or prepared the occasional box of macaroni and cheese. He hadn't stopped drinking completely, but at least he tried to hide it. They had even stopped fighting about Alec's mother for now. Three years in the grave, and maybe Linda Purnell was finally dead! (Probably not, but one could hope.)

Ellie leaned in to kiss Alec quickly one last time. He looked disappointed.

"Fine, go." He pouted.

"I'll be back in a few hours," she promised. "Jordan's lying down on the sofa. He's been complaining about a stomachache all day. It figures. The day before his birthday party."

"Yeah, he's been pretty crabby lately," Alec noted, returning to his work underneath the hood of the Camaro.

"Maybe give him a little dry toast and some applesauce if he feels up to it. He was drifting off when I came out here," she instructed. "Call me if you need me. I'll be in my office."

She exited quickly toward her car before Alec could use any more coercion tactics. He meant well, she supposed, but all she felt suddenly was annoyance. He had no idea (respect for?) what she did for a living. Yes, teaching English at the university, he got that, but writing about literature—critical writing—seemed almost frivolous to him; he had never said as much, but it was in his attitude, his tone, as if submersing oneself in the world of theory, philosophy, thought, was a monumental waste of time. Even after Ellie's first book of essays was received with glowing accolades from her peers, even after its publication, Alec still didn't seem convinced that her life's work had any real merit. To him, she was his wife and the mother of his son. Wasn't that enough?

They talked about it in therapy once. Only once. Alec's disinterest in her writing. He had sat back passively, almost amused, and listened to her as she clumsily sputtered out her honest feelings painfully, like pulling back a thickened scab.

Imagine if he knew about the poetry.

No. She was right to keep that a secret, to keep writing as Avery Vaughn. Why open herself up to certain derision and criticism? Alec dealt in all matters practical. To him, there was no reason to float about in the world of ideas, and talking about it with a therapist wasn't going to change his mind.

All of that made little matter. Ellie was too busy with teaching her classes, writing deadlines, managing a household, and taking care of Jordan to be preoccupied with garnering the respect and understanding of her husband. Life was just too busy. Some weeks, especially when Alec traveled and Jordan had multiple games, they barely saw one another at all. It was enough that everything seemed to be running smoothly in their everyday lives—even if just superficially. Who had time to be unhappy? Unhappiness was an indulgence.

Despite her best efforts, after locking herself in the solitude of her university office, Ellie was no closer to having an original thesis for her essay than she was when she left home. The easiest route would be to write about what she was currently teaching: Renaissance poetry. *A comparison of Shakespeare and Ben Jonson?* Boring. Unoriginal (uninspired). That wasn't going to cut it.

She actually tried practicing yoga at one point in the afternoon, bending gracefully into a swan dive, hoping that the blood rushing to her head would stimulate some creativity. No luck. She was too preoccupied with the details of Jordan's birthday party the next day. Maybe she would just call it quits and hope that an idea would come to her naturally, maybe as she was showering (where she had all her brilliant ideas) or when she was hanging streamers or Swiffering the floor. She had to come up with something. Long would be hounding her on Monday morning for sure.

At the end of three hours of aimlessly poring over papers, sifting through notes, and straightening her desk in a vain attempt to inspire herself, she decided just to head home. The idea would come. Obviously she couldn't force it. Pulling into the long gravel drive, she was surprised to see Alec still outside working on the car. The bright, spring-afternoon sunshine filtered spottily across the driveway through the high, upward-reaching branches of the black locust trees that had just begun to bloom. Ellie slowed the car, lowering the window. Something wasn't right.

"Where's Jordan?" she asked with concern, a sense of foreboding looming heavily over her.

"He's still sleeping." Alec shrugged. "I checked on him a couple of times this afternoon. I was just in there twenty minutes ago."

395

"Does he have a fever?" Ellie hastily threw the car into park, leaving her bags on the front seat as she flung open the door. Seeing her alarm, he came out from behind the hood, rapidly wiping his hands on a rag.

"He wasn't hot, Elle. I mean…I don't think he was hot."

"He didn't want to eat or drink anything all day?" Ellie called out in the direction of the garage as she hurried toward the front door.

"I don't know," Alec answered as he followed, concern now furrowing his brow. "I didn't wake him."

"Jordan," she called as she came flying through the front door of the house. She was at the sofa in two strides, on her knees at Jordan's side. "Jordan!" her hand was on his arm, his head.

He wasn't hot at all. In fact, he was almost cold. Clammy and…damp? The bottom of shirt, his pants. Had he wet himself? He smelled of urine. "Jordan!" Ellie grabbed his small, still face in her hands. "Jordan!" He didn't respond.

"Oh my God, Alec! Call nine one one! Something is wrong. He's not waking up!"

Alec nearly tripped, backing over the end table, shocked into action by his wife's hysteria.

Should I lift him?

Too late. Her instincts moved her body, free of judgment. Jordan's limp torso was already in her arms, limbs dangling obscenely to the side. She cradled his head to her chest, kissing the top of his head as if this alone, this magic mother's touch, would make everything OK, just like every booboo he'd ever gotten—cut, scrape, belly ache. Even though her throat constricted, she willed herself not to cry.

Keep it together. Keep it together. He's going to be fine. He's going to be fine. He's going to be fine.

"Is he breathing?" Alec yelled from the kitchen. "They want to know if he's breathing." He ran back into the living room, looming over Ellie as she clenched the contorted body of her almost-seven-year-old baby boy.

Breathing? She hadn't even thought to check. Holding his little mouth mere centimeters from her face, she tried to assess his respiration over her own rapid breathing. There was air. His chest moved shallowly, but there was air.

"Yes, he's breathing. Very lightly."

Alec relayed the information to the EMS operator. "No, he has no special medical history," Ellie heard Alec answer as he paced nervously back and forth through the great room, around the kitchen island, back toward Ellie and her precious son on the front-room floor.

"Tell her he's been complaining of stomachaches. He's been really tired and crabby. Maybe he has a virus or something. But no fever. He never had a fever," Ellie was rambling frantically at Alec now, her voice rising with every word. His eyes were wide and crazy as he clenched the telephone with whitened knuckles.

"How long was he sleeping, Ellie?" Alec demanded.

"What do you mean?" she couldn't make sense of what he was asking. *I was gone all day. I don't know how long he was sleeping.*

"When did he fall asleep?" Alec raised his voice to get through to her.

"I don't remember," she yelled back. "I don't remember exactly." Unconsciously she started rocking Jordan, soothing him, soothing herself. "He came down here around one o'clock. He said he was thirsty again, so I brought him another juice box and had him lie down. Maybe it was one thirty." She tried to do the math in her head, but she couldn't add the hours. She couldn't think straight. Was it five o'clock? Five-thirty now? How many hours had he slept (been unconscious)?

"Thirsty?" she heard Alec ask. He sounded as if he were in a tunnel now.

Don't you dare pass out, Ellie. Keep it together.

"He was thirsty, Ellie?" Alec asked her with confusion as he repeated the question that had obviously come from the other end of the telephone.

"Yes, he'd been thirsty!" Ellie managed to get out. "Today all he did was drink one juice box after another. And then he wanted water."

Stop fucking asking questions and get someone here! Just get here! Oh my God, just get here! Just get here.

"Yes, he's seven," Alec barked into the telephone. "No. No medical history."

Far off, hollow sirens echoed in the distance and then grew closer, until they were screaming down the driveway accompanied by the angry crunch of flying gravel. Alec tore open the door to let in two eerily calm paramedics. Before Ellie could even protest, they took the boy from her arms, lying him down gently on the floor, confirming his respiration, checking his pulse.

Keep it together. Stay rational.

"Ma'am, does your son have diabetes?" one of the men asked as they began loading Jordan onto the stretcher. The other man skillfully harnessed Jordan down, so quickly that Ellie barely had time to process what had been asked.

"No. Not that I know of," Ellie stammered. "No one in my family has diabetes." She automatically followed these strangers as they carried her sweet, helpless son out the front door.

"Get in," the other paramedic ordered her as they loaded Jordan into the back of the opened ambulance. The first paramedic slammed the doors shut and slid calmly into the driver's seat as he called to Alec, saying, "Meet us at the hospital," the shrill sirens signaling their departure.

Ellie, crammed into the corner, sat in saucer-eyed shock.

"What is his name?" the paramedic asked.

"Jordan," Ellie answered. *Do not cry.*

"Talk to Jordan, ma'am. He can probably hear you. Tell him everything is going to be OK."

Ellie leaned in awkwardly, as if she needed this young man's permission to speak to her son, as if she had relinquished all her rights as a parent when she stepped into the back of the ambulance. The paramedic was now the one in charge. She could no longer make things right with her magical parent powers. She had lost control.

No. You are not going to lose control! You are going to keep it together. Her heart was racing so quickly she saw shooting stars in her peripheral vision.

"Jordan, Mommy is here with you. You're going to be OK." She set her hand on his arm unconvincingly as the man hovered over Jordan, completing more assessments. Ellie had no idea what was going on.

"Your son's blood sugar is critically low, ma'am. I'm going to give him glucagon," he said as he reached for a small box above him. Deftly removing what appeared to be a syringe, he popped off its protective lid and jammed the exposed tip into Jordan's thigh.

Nothing. No movement.

Ellie searched the man's face for a reaction. He was stoic, undeterred. Maybe she was expecting the shot to work like adrenaline to the heart, Jordan sitting up suddenly, eyes wide and alert.

"What's supposed to happen? He's not waking up! He's not waking up!" Her voice—frenzied, primal—sounded foreign to her. *Keep it together.*

"It can take up to fifteen minutes. He might need another shot when we get to the hospital. Just keep talking to him. As calmly as you can," the man suggested as inoffensively as possible.

Just save my baby. Please. Just help him.

"Jordan, Mommy is with you. Jordan, Mommy loves you. Wake up, sweetheart." Ellie stroked his arm.

Jordan's stretcher was whisked away at the hospital, behind the swinging doors of the emergency room as Ellie stood helplessly alone in the stark, white hall. Fluorescent lights searing her burning eyes, she leaned against the wall, a wave of despair and nausea threatening to knock her to her knees. Alec flew through the emergency-room entrance, and then spotting Ellie, stopped. He finally hastened toward her from the far end of the hallway. The closer he came, the closer she grew to unloading her pent-up emotions. When he finally reached her, she leaned into his chest, her heart sinking, expecting his arms to shield her. But instead, he hesitated. No embrace. Just a clumsy squeeze of the shoulders as he pushed her gently away.

"He's going to be fine, Ellie," Alec insisted. "We can't get upset. Let's not get upset here. He's going to be fine." He sounded as if he was trying to convince himself.

"What do you mean don't get upset? How can I not be upset?" She pounded her fists on his chest.

He grabbed her wrists immediately, staring into her eyes, stone faced. "He is going to be fine, Ellie."

"Why didn't you wake him?" she began to sob. "Why didn't you think to wake him, Alec? Why did you let him sleep all day? Why?" She stumbled toward the mercifully empty waiting room.

Alec hurried to her side, grabbing her elbow. "Why didn't you know he was sick, Ellie?" he hissed in her ear. "You're his mother. Why did *you* let him sleep? Why did you have to go to work when you knew he wasn't feeling well?"

She snatched her arm away from him resentfully.

Why did *you have to go into work when you knew he wasn't feeling well?* Finding her way through bleary eyes to the corner of the waiting room, she sunk down into a chair, weeping quietly into her hands.

Just one more minute of this. Then pull it back together again. If you don't…if you can't…

What dark place would she retreat to if she couldn't get her emotions under control? Panic from such a possibility then sent her heart racing. For a moment, she felt as if she might lose touch with reality.

Stop it.

Alec finally sat down next to her. "I'm sorry I said those things, Ellie," he confessed shamefully.

She waved her hand at him. It didn't matter. He was right. She never should have left Jordan. What sort of a mother was she?

I will never leave him again. Dear God, just let him be OK. I will never leave him again. I promise. I will never ask another thing for myself for as long as I live. Just let him be OK.

"Did you bring your cell phone?" she asked Alec once she realized she had no purse. He nodded. "Can I call my parents to let them know we're here?"

He handed her the phone and then sat straight up in the chair, arms folded, eyes fixed firmly on the emergency-room doors, expressionless.

No sooner had Ellie finished talking to her mother that a young resident, a woman not much past twenty-six, came through the swinging doors. "Mr. and Mrs. Purnell?" she asked.

"Yes," Ellie answered as she and Alec both stood.

"I'm Dr. Patel." She smiled. "Jordan is awake."

A relieved whimper escaped Ellie as she reached up to cover her mouth.

"Can we see him?" Alec asked quietly.

"For a moment," the doctor answered. "We are moving him to the ICU until we can get him stabilized. From what the paramedics told me, your son seems to have been in a diabetic coma. He's responding to the glucagon, but we need to get his blood sugar levels regulated."

"How do you do that?" Alec blurted out.

"Well, that can be a tricky process," the doctor responded patiently. "It can be a waiting game. In a patient who has been newly diagnosed with diabetes, it's not unusual for blood sugar levels to fluctuate wildly." Noting Alec and Ellie's blank faces, she assured, "We will have a nurse explain the disease when we have a definite diagnosis. I don't want to jump to conclusions just yet."

"Is he lucid?" Ellie wondered.

"I didn't have a conversation with him," the doctor explained. "I just came out here as soon as we were sure he'd come out of the coma." She paused before adding, "We have a lot of tests we still need to run, Mrs. Purnell. We need to assess any damage to Jordan's organs."

"What do you mean? Alec asked, his voice hoarse.

"Organs such as the brain and kidneys can be damaged during an episode like the one Jordan just experienced. In addition to getting his blood sugar managed, we need to assess any long-term damage that may have occurred."

"Brain damage?" Ellie whispered.

"Let's try not to jump to any conclusions, yet," the doctor suggested hopefully.

Ellie felt as if she was going to vomit, a stale sick taste traveling up from her stomach to settle in her mouth. As the doctor turned to lead them into Jordan's room, Ellie's feet were cinder blocks, weighing her down with fear and guilt.

Why couldn't you just stay home today? Why did you leave him?

By the time they reached the ICU, Jordan was already hooked up to a myriad of machines, IVs run, rhythmic beeping breaking the silence of the room. Alec stopped suddenly at the end of the bed, as if staying there would prevent the nightmare from being reality.

"Jordan, Mommy's here, honey," Ellie almost sang to him as she bent to kiss his face.

He turned slightly to look up at her, eyes glassy and unfocused, "My juice box. Where's…my juice box?"

"It's OK, sweetheart, just rest. I'll see if I can find it for you," Ellie said soothingly. She didn't try to wipe away the tears that ran freely now from the corners of her eyes; it wouldn't upset Jordan, who was still not coherent. He couldn't recognize that his mother was crying over him; he could barely recognize his mother at all.

Alec buried his face in both his hands. "I'm sorry," he mumbled. "I'm so sorry." Ellie looked up at him absently, too consumed with her concern for Jordan to think about offering comfort to her husband. By the time her confused mind suggested she should reach out to him, hold him, reassure him with a touch, it was too late. He had turned suddenly and disappeared through the door, leaving Ellie to stand vigil alone.

Doctors, nurses, people in and out. Ellie retreated to the corner chair in a fog, her stomach and jaw clenched with anxiety.

"Farewell, thou child of my right hand, and joy; My sin was too much hope of thee, lov'd boy."

You stop thinking that right now. He's going to be fine.

And what if he isn't fine? What if he's brain damaged? What if he's never the same again? It will be my fault. Look at him lying there! If I weren't so preoccupied with finishing (starting) this essay for the review, I would have been home with him today. I could have been home with him every day. Every day of these seven years, I could have been home with him. Every single breath he took, laugh he laughed, picture he colored, word he uttered—I could have been there to witness. But I wasn't. I was working. I can never get back everything that I missed. And what if this is it? What if this is all the time I have with him?

The intensity of her regret rendered her immobile. She remained a fixture in the corner chair, blankly observing the activity in the room, every nerve in her body aching with contrition. There was no getting back all those moments, and now here they were, in the ICU. Just her and Jordan. Like the desperate early days in the pole barn. Full circle. Just Jordan and his helpless, ineffective mother.

"Seven years thou wert lent to me."

Stop it. He's not going to die.

And what if he does?

But she couldn't allow herself to go there. Even her subconscious was smart enough to banish that ultimate fear from her stream of thought. No. She would not think about that directly. She couldn't.

"Ellie." Her father's voice filled the small room.

She flew into his arms, convulsive sobs jarring her entire body as her mother set a hand on Ellie's shoulder.

"What happened?" her mother asked gently, wandering over to lovingly assess her grandson. "How is my beautiful boy?" Maggie Lawson asked him, the rare tone of tenderness reserved only for her grandson, making Ellie sob even harder.

"He slipped into a diabetic coma, we think," Ellie managed to choke out. "I was so stupid. I should have known the signs. I was so stupid."

"Stop saying that, Elizabeth," her father commanded the top of her head as he held her more tightly. "How were you supposed to know the signs? No one in our family is diabetic. How would you know to suspect such a thing?"

"I left him with Alec so I could go into work when I should have stayed at home with him," Ellie lamented.

"Where *is* Alec?" her mother wondered suddenly.

"I don't know. Maybe in the waiting area?" Ellie answered, pulling away from her father's chest as she began to compose herself. "He was really upset."

"So are you," her father noted.

"I'll go find him," Maggie Lawson offered. She tenderly ran her hand over Jordan's head and then hesitantly left the room.

"I don't want to hear you blaming yourself for any of this. Do you understand me?" Jim Lawson instructed his daughter sternly, his usually passive, amiable face now serious and dark.

Ellie shook her head, tears threatening again.

"I'm serious, Elizabeth Ann. You need to focus on Jordan getting well, not on what could have or should have been. That will drive you mad. Trust me." He led his daughter back to her seat and, leaning against the wall, assumed a protective stance where they both fell into a long, tense silence.

Finally Maggie Lawson reemerged. "He's too upset to come in," she explained. "He's staying in the waiting area for now."

Ellie's father acknowledged this with a grunt as he folded his arms.

Jordan stirred again in his bed.

"Hi, sweet boy." Maggie Lawson coaxed her grandson awake.

He looked out into nothingness. "The horse!" he jabbered excitedly. "The black one."

"Yes, baby?" his grandmother answered. "He's asking about Whisper, Ellie!"

"Mom, he doesn't know what he's saying. He's just babbling. He doesn't know it's you."

"It's OK." Jordan's voice was insistent. His head fell back against the pillow. "The horse is OK."

"Yes, everything is OK," Maggie Lawson assured him.

"Mommy, the horse," Jordan repeated with agitation.

Ellie rose from the chair. "OK, sweetheart. I hear you. Yes, it's OK." She placed her hands on his arms until he settled back down again. "Just rest, Jordan. Just rest."

Though the hospital would have allowed Jim and Maggie Lawson to stay in the ICU for as long as they wanted, Ellie insisted her parents go home around 11:00 p.m. There was nothing to be done at the hospital except wait as Jordan continued to rest and the hospital staff continued to try and regulate his blood sugar. The Lawsons could just as easily wait for news at home, in their own beds. No tests would be run until the morning.

Sleep was a fine idea, but Ellie wasn't going to be sleeping tonight. Not here. Not anywhere. She would be awake, watching her son breath. All night long. Wild horses couldn't drag her away (not even Whisper).

"Do you want me to send Alec back in when we leave?" her mother asked.

"Sure," Ellie replied, although, at this point, it didn't really matter. Alec wasn't going to be a comfort to her, and she simply didn't have the energy in her to console him either. She could only think of Jordan. She could only be a mother right now, not a wife; she could only take care of her son.

Her parents kissed Ellie's cheek and went off.

After several minutes, still no Alec. Ellie ventured out of the ICU, down the hall toward the emergency-room waiting area and out into a wide-open space full of unfamiliar faces. Alec was nowhere to be found. *Did he just leave?*

She considered calling her mother's cell phone to see if her parents had, in fact, talked to him before they left, but why bother? She would just call Alec herself. She found a house phone in the ICU lounge and dialed Alec.

His phone rang and rang and rang and then went to voice mail.

"Just looking for you. Call room one twenty-five," she left as a message. She returned to her chair in the corner of the ICU room. Someone had left her a blanket. Covering herself awkwardly, she settled in for the night.

Ellie's head snapped up suddenly, a heavy, sick feeling of fatigue partially gluing shut her swollen eyes. Her entire mouth felt like paste as she licked her cracked lips. Had she actually fallen asleep sitting up? Glancing up at the wall clock, she saw the time was 2:00 a.m. No blinking messages on the hospital phone. Rubbing her eyes, she walked over toward Jordan to make sure he was still breathing, the neurotic obsession of every mother. Satisfied, she walked down the hall again, a restless specter roaming the halls. Finding the house phone once more, she redialed Alec's cell.

"Hello?" he surprised Ellie by answering on the first ring.

"Where are you?" she asked with confusion.

"I'm at home," Alec readily admitted.

"What…what do you mean you're at home?" Ellie stammered. What was he saying? A myriad of emotions competed for dominance. "Why didn't you tell me you were going?"

"You had your parents there," Alec explained. "I didn't think I'd be missed."

What?

"What are you talking about?" Ellie asked; anger was winning out over confusion.

"I mean, you had people in there with you. I didn't think it would matter if I left."

"Matter to whom?" Ellie insisted.

"To you," Alec answered.

"What about your son?" Ellie wondered snidely. "Would it matter to him?"

"Is he awake?" Alec slurred.

Oh my God, he's fucking drunk! I cannot believe it. He left here to drink! He fucking left here to drink!

"Are you drunk?" she asked, already knowing the answer. White-hot rage suddenly blinded her. Had Alec been in front of her, she would have channeled the wiry ball of emotion—the guilt, fear, sadness, anger, and now contempt—that had churned inside her all day into claws, shredding off the skin of his face. Something deep within prevented her from her next instinct—to slam down the receiver and tear the phone completely out of the wall, screaming all the while.

"No, Ellie, I'm not drunk," he lied. "I'm just upset."

"You're a liar, Alec. I can hear it in your voice. Great coping tactics. I'm sure your son would be proud. And no, Jordan isn't awake. What difference does that make?" she controlled her voice as best she could. "What difference did it make that my parents were here? Don't you want to be here for your son?" *(Don't you want to be here for me?)* But even as she asked all of these logical questions, she knew whatever answer Alec gave made no difference. She was talking to a drunk. In his state, he could rationalize whatever it was he did. He would believe his own bullshit, and they would go around and around in verbal circles.

Instead of waiting for an answer, she swore, "I will *never* forgive you for this, Alec. Do you understand me? You disgust me." Then she jammed the receiver into its cradle. *I hate you, Alec Purnell. I fucking hate you. You are weak! You are weak.*

Now she was wide awake, charged by disdain. How could Alec be so selfish? How could he possibly be so selfish? She returned to her watch in the far corner of the hospital room, her anger mellowing into self-pity. *I cannot believe he just left us here. He just left!*

He will never emotionally support you, Ellie. You are all alone. You have to be the strong one.

The fact was that Alec was her son's father. That would never change. She and Alec were inextricably bound for all of eternity. There was no getting away from him now. And there was no changing him. She had tried that. God knows, she had tried to get him to change in therapy. For years, she had tried to get him to change.

I guess Alec's drinking is your cross to bear, just like Jordan's diabetes.

So then, suck it up, Ellie. This is your life. This is the hand you were dealt. If you go screaming for the hills now, who is going to protect Jordan? Who is going to shield him from Alec's behavior?

In solitary despair, Ellie closed her eyes, trying to relax her grimaced face as she massaged her sinuses. *Breathe in. Breathe out. Everything is going to be OK. Jordan*

even said so himself. Tomorrow morning, Alec will show up
sober, and the darkness of tonight will all be behind us.

"Farewell, thou child of my right hand, and joy; My sin
was too much hope of thee, lov'd boy."

The lines of Ben Jonson's poem persistently invaded Ellie's train of thought again. As much as she tried to prevent the lines of his elegy to his dead son from invading her headspace, she could not. They hung on stubbornly like song lyrics, replaying in her mind over and over, the soundtrack to today's hell.

"Too much hope of thee" sure sounded like a lot of guilt to Ellie. Certainly she could relate to that; this father blaming himself for loving his son too much, placing too much hope in the child's future. Somehow believing superstitiously that overloving could lead to his child's death. Could a person ever love his child too much? Could any amount of love for one's child ever be considered a "sin"? No. That sounded like a whole lot of guilt.

Farewell, my dear Jordan. I'm sorry your father is a drunk.

My sin was too much hope in him. I was damaged and
lonely, and he knocked

Me up.

And now you have to suffer for it.

Maybe Ben Jonson, deep down, felt guilty about the circumstances of his child's life too. Hell, maybe that's what all elegies were. Just admissions of guilt and failure, as in "Look at your shitty life that I could do nothing to save. I am useless and godless. If I were sure there is a God, I wouldn't be lamenting your death and regretting the limited, imperfect events of your life."

How's that for a controversial idea? Literature professors everywhere would be up in arms!

As Ellie sat numbly in the corner chair, watching Jordan's tranquil face, she felt sure she had stumbled across a unique theory. There was no possible way sleep would revisit her that night, she knew. May as well try to write. She went in search of paper and pen, making mental comparisons between Jonson's elegy and others she knew by memory, ones written by Theodore Roethke and Edna St. Vincent Millay. Ones written by Walt Whitman. She would reference them all. She might as well try to focus her wild emotions into something constructive while she sat awake waiting for Jordan to heal.

When early-morning light finally entered through the institutional panes, Ellie had scratched out twelve pages. It had been both the easiest and most difficult essay she had ever written, and undoubtedly, the most inspired and personal. It felt less like an essay, and more like an admission, a cry for help, a plea:

I have done my child wrong. I have failed him. I brought him into this world, but I cannot guarantee his happiness or his safety. I cannot trust his father not to damage him. Please,

God, if you do exist—if you are listening—save my little boy.
I promise I will never ask for anything again for as long as
I live. I will accept this life as my fate, without complaint. In
complete resignation, for Jordan's sake.

Jordan stirred in bed, causing Ellie to rise to her feet anxiously. She stood at his waist so he could see her if he awoke. His eyes fluttered open slowly. They appeared normal, focused.

"Where's Daddy?" Jordan asked immediately. The question sent a fresh wave of contempt over her. Alec didn't deserve this child's unconditional love, and yet here it was. Ellie hesitated as she chose her response carefully.

"He'll be back soon," she answered ambiguously. If he wasn't, he could answer for himself. "How are you feeling today, sweetheart?" She reached out to brush the hair from his forehead.

"I'm hungry!" Jordan complained. "Can I have something to eat?"

"I might have something in my purse." Ellie paused, remembering she had no purse with her. *And anyhow, you can't just give him any snack now. He's diabetic.* The realization was sobering. "Let's get a nurse to bring you something," she suggested. She stuck her head around the corner to summon a nurse and then stood back at the side of Jordan's bed. By this time, he had sat up and looked every bit himself except for the ashen hue of his skin.

"What happened, Mommy?" he asked sweetly.

"We aren't exactly sure yet, Jordan," Ellie answered, choking back tears. "The doctor is going to do some more tests today, and then we can let you know for sure. I'm glad you're hungry! Grammie and Grandpa were here yesterday and were really worried about you. I should call them and let them know you're awake."

Without taking her eyes from Jordan, she called her parents to share the news of Jordan's waking. She hesitated a moment. *Should I call Alec?* She placed the receiver back in its cradle.

The Lawsons returned within an hour, right in the middle of the largest breakfast Ellie had ever seen Jordan consume: eggs, toast, fruit, and sausage.

"Jordan!" Maggie Lawson's voice cracked with emotion as she saw her grandson. "Happy Birthday, beautiful!" She carried with her two huge balloons and a small present. Jordan ripped it open eagerly and then squealed with joy: a handheld game system!

"Thank you, Grammie! This is exactly the one I wanted!"

Too bad he'd be using it at the hospital instead of enjoying it at his birthday party at home.

The nurse hovered protectively over Jordan once he finished so that she could measure his blood sugar and give him insulin. "We are going to test his kidney function and perform an EEG this morning also. You can come with us, Mom," the nurse informed Ellie. "We'll be moving Jordan to a regular room on the pediatric floor today, so if his grandparents want to wait there, they can."

(No one asked, "Where's his father?")

She spent several hours with gritted teeth and a locked jaw as Jordan happily chatted up the entire hospital staff. (*"I feel fine today, Mommy. Why can't we go home and have my birthday party?"*)

Jordan, if these tests come back fine, we will have a party like you've never seen before! Oh, to be a child—blissfully unaware. Ellie would willingly take the burden of worry from him, though. Just seeing him laugh, hearing him talk easily and naturally, eased Ellie's apprehension a bit. ("*Mom, it's OK.*")

By early afternoon, Jordan was ready to be wheeled back down to his new room—a home he would keep for the next four days until the doctors finally got his blood sugar and insulin doses regulated. Ellie walked haggardly behind the bed as the orderly rolled it into Jordan's room in the pediatric ward.

"Daddy!" Ellie heard Jordan exclaim before she could follow through the door. As she entered, she was greeted by the sight of Alec embracing his son, her parents waiting patiently in the chairs next to the window.

"Happy birthday, Jordan." Alec kissed his son repeatedly as he wiped his eyes with the back of one hand. "I was worried about you, buddy."

"I was worried about you too, Daddy," Jordan replied brightly.

Everyone laughed but Ellie.

"I have good news," Ellie announced without flourish. "The initial tests have all come back good."

"Oh, thank God," her mother cried.

"That's wonderful news, Ellie." Jim Lawson stood to hug his exhausted daughter who stood limply in his arms. As he moved aside, Alec approached from the far side of Jordan's bed.

"I knew everything would be all right," Alec insisted. He placed his hand tenderly on the small of Ellie's back, only to find it permanently stiffened.

Twelve

Lithium eyes,
Glazed and blind,
Wide,
Worn,
Wringing hands
Sworn to grasping at illusions,
Air,
The dream so dear,
The fantasy you prolong,
The hope that floats
Like a black balloon
In the fluffy white of a
Magritte sky
Is all just vapor,
Tiny, toxic particles
That choke you while
You sleep.
He is a falling star,
So far beyond your reach,
The tragedy is comic

As you hold your palms out,
Fingers splayed in giddy
Anticipation,
Hair wild,
Stuck to your sweaty head.
He falls to earth,
Disappearing into nothingness.

You are the worst of fools
To believe.

—Avery Vaughn, "Worst of Fools"

The Saturday morning after Alec's cocktail party, Ellie set out on her run, but when she reached the top of the hill, Liam was nowhere to be found. She felt a surprisingly sharp dagger of disappointment. *Maybe he was just too tired this morning.* Maybe that's why he didn't make it out. The party hadn't wound down until nearly two in the morning. Not everyone could sleep for four hours and get up and run. Ellie was cursed with insomnia. Running was her only choice.

By Sunday morning, when he hadn't returned her text (Hey! Missed you this morning) and was still nowhere to be found, a crushing depression took hold of Ellie. It lasted exactly one hour, the duration of her lonely Sunday morning run, as she debated whether or not she should show up at his cottage (banging frantically at the door). Then her pride got the better of her.

Stop thinking like some desperate teenager. Get a hold of yourself and have some dignity. You will not *go to his home. You will* not *text him a second time. You will pull it together. He's probably just busy.*

Yeah, like busy with Megan.

She couldn't argue with herself. Maybe he *was* with Megan. Oh, God. Maybe he was.

When despair threatened, she strangled it with anger, the best defense she knew.

By the time she arrived at work on Monday morning, wearing the most expensive shoes she owned, finding comfort in her tailored dress, hair, and make-up flawless to hide her bruised ego, she had decided not to talk to him. She would not so much as look in his direction.

"Look at you!" Marta stuck her head into Ellie's office after the last class of the day. "What's wrong?"

"Nothing, Id," Ellie snapped.

Marta laughed. "That was convincing, Ellie. What's up? You look like you're going to prom." She hesitated at the door. It was apparent Ellie wasn't in the chatting mood. Certainly not in the mood to be teased. Marta didn't dare step a foot farther into the office.

Ellie looked down at her dress, suddenly self-conscious. It was beige linen, hardly flashy. Marta was just being an asshole.

"Oh, by the way, Liam's been looking for you." Marta grinned before disappearing back down the hall.

Ellie panicked. She wasn't ready to see him. She felt foolish for the way she had acted on Friday night in the wine cellar. It was obvious he didn't feel the same about her as she did about him.

Even though he said, "Touch me, then..." and grabbed your hands?

Then why did he fall off the face of the earth for two days?

If he caught her here in her office right now, what would she say to him? She had no right to be angry, and yet she was. It was totally juvenile, she knew, but she couldn't help it. *Run.* She snuck down the back staircase to hide in the far lecture hall, hoping against hope that Megan had already cleared everything out for the day.

Well, not "hide" really. Just avoid.

That way, maybe she could have just a little bit more time, just one more day, to get over her hurt feelings and embarrassment. Then she could act civil.

When she got to the lecture hall, the lights were off. Thank God. No lingering students. No Megan. Ellie entered the merciful twilight of the lecture hall and sat, slumped forward, emotionally drained, in the front row facing the podium. She closed her eyes, reaching up to massage the back of her neck when she heard the lecture-hall doors click open.

"I haven't seen you all day!" Liam exclaimed brightly. "What are you doing sitting in the dark?" He stopped halfway between Ellie and the door, cocking his head quizzically.

So that's the way you're going to play it, Liam?

"Oh, I just have a headache," Ellie lied. *More like a heartache.* "I misplaced a folder of notes"—another lie—"and I came back here to see if I left it."

"Can I help you find it?" Liam asked, looking around.

"No, it's OK," Ellie dismissed him. She watched him search the room, resenting his long limbs, both graceful and masculine, full of that same infuriating air of self-confidence and nonchalance he always had. And then her big, stupid mouth opened against her will. "Why didn't you run this weekend?"

Liam immediately stopped what he was doing. He began to speak then stopped as if he wanted to choose his words more carefully. The pause was excruciating. "I didn't feel well Saturday morning and slept straight through until nearly ten o'clock, Elizabeth. When I didn't hear from you Saturday, I thought perhaps you…"

Ellie looked at him doubtfully.

"You thought I what?" Ellie asked just a bit too hotly.

Liam looked surprised at her reaction. "I thought perhaps you had second thoughts about what happened

Friday night. I thought I had better let you alone. Give you some space."

"I texted you Saturday, Liam."

"I wish I had gotten it, Ellie. If I had, it would have saved me the agony of worry all weekend."

"Worry?" Ellie sounded snide.

Liam still looked perplexed, but slowly his expression turned to frustration. Ellie felt the slightest bit satisfied to be getting a reaction out of him finally. A reaction other than amusement.

"Yes, worry, Elizabeth. Worried about your well-being. Your husband had had quite a bit to drink that night."

The words hit Ellie like the crack of a whip, hot shame rendering her mute.

No way am I going there with you, Liam.

"What? Now you have nothing to say?" Liam challenged her. "Are you going to deny it? Defend him? Your prince of a husband who would sell you out to his business associates!"

Still Ellie said nothing, her face pinched in defiance.

"What was it he said?" Liam changed his voice to the best American accent he could imitate, "I have a business to run; you can read my wife's useless essays yourself."

Ellie held her breath proudly, pulling herself up out of the chair to face him. Liam stepped in toward her, making an obvious attempt to control his emotions, what had now grown into anger.

"I had very good reason to worry about Alec Purnell after I had provoked him. Maybe I even felt guilty about leaving you to a possible reprisal, but damn it, Elizabeth, stop playing games with me."

"What do you mean?" Ellie broke her silence finally with indignation.

"Don't you dare act coy! You know damn well what I mean. Stop hiding! Stop pulling me closer and then running from me. There is nothing left to hide! I already know you, *Avery*. I already know everything," he insisted through clenched teeth.

Before Liam could grab her arm to stop her, Ellie rushed toward the lecture-hall doors as fast as her platform heels would allow.

Don't go back to your office. He'll follow you there.

She swung open the outside doors, entering the relative safety of the university quad. Outside sat a dozen or so people. She was protected from a scene although she doubted the great Dr. Curran was capable of something so undignified. If he were following her (she didn't dare turn to look), he wouldn't press her any further in the presence of onlookers. He was, after all, a gentleman.

So where are you going to go, Ellie?

And before she knew it, she was feet away from the university library's front steps. She took them two at a time until she found herself going through the front doors and into the still, quiet confines of the stacks, past the disinterested student workers behind the circulation desk, earphones jammed into their ears. She would descend into the abyss of the library, down three flights into the confines of her writing cave, to hide.

I'll show you Avery Vaughn.

The farther down Ellie went, the quieter it became—cool and dank, the comforting smell of a million browning pages. As her pace slowed, she breathed it all in slowly and then exhaled. Now she was safe from confrontation, down here in the library dungeon, where she didn't have to answer to anyone, where she didn't have to pretend she was the perfect Dr. Purnell. It was the only place she could be truly honest, even if it was just on paper.

When she reached the farthest end of the library basement, the tiny room adjacent to the boiler room, she ran her hands along the shelf, searching for the worn leather notebook "Avery" kept hidden there. Maybe she would just scribble out a short rant to collect herself and then head back up to the surface again. Something like "Fuck you, Alec, for stealing my youth, for drinking yourself into stinking oblivion" or "Fuck you, Liam, for being so glib. If you really knew me so well, *you* would be the one running." It didn't have to be artful—what she wrote. Just something quick and angry that would still her racing heart.

No sooner was her hand on the book that she detected movement in her peripheral vision. Startled, she stumbled back, bumping into the small corner table, slightly rattling the chairs.

It was Liam.

"Oh my God." She grabbed her heart. "You scared me." Suddenly she felt silly and childish.

"I said to stop running." Liam, flushed and angry, rounded the side of the ceiling-high bookcase. "And yet, here you are, literally underground." He put his hand up to his face as if surprised to find sweat there. Dismayed, he whipped off his suit jacket, flinging it onto the chair. "What are you so afraid of?"

"What answer are you looking for, Liam?" Ellie inquired with frustration. "What do you want me to say?"

"I just want you to stop being afraid to be who you really are, Elizabeth. To speak freely. To be honest. To trust me. My God, to let me get close to you." He stepped toward her, his face now softening with his plea.

"I don't know how," Ellie shouted defiantly, stepping in so close their torsos almost touched.

Liam grabbed her by the shoulders before she could flee again, pulling her into him so tightly it almost knocked the wind out of her. Then suddenly, his lips were on hers, his tongue invading her mouth, kissing her passionately, frantically. Ellie couldn't fight it. Didn't want to fight it. He overpowered her, firmly grasping her hair at the nape of her neck with one hand as he wrapped his tensed arm around her waist, holding her in place. She answered by pushing her body into his, reaching up to his face, his hair, pulling his head into hers.

And then Ellie was a frenzy of hands, madly groping at buttons on Liam's shirt as his knee parted her legs, knocking her to the table. Her head tilted back, neck exposed, hair trailing down her back, his mouth leaving hers to travel the length of her neck, her ear, devouring her. He reached between her legs, fingers swiftly under her panties and then suddenly inside her. Ellie cried out.

"Not here," she breathed heavily. "Not here."

"Yes, here!" Liam demanded.

She didn't want to stop him. His fingers left her quickly as he undid his belt, his zipper, freeing himself. And then, from the end of the table, he leaned over her, entering her deeply in one powerful thrust. Ellie gasped at his size, filling her completely. For a moment, neither moved, as if the feeling were too exquisite to bear, and then Ellie's body reacted by meeting Liam's passion with legs that parted wider, and hips that raised to meet his thrusts.

The chairs toppled over. The table hit the wall. Ellie clawed at Liam's shirt, trying desperately to get at his bare skin, the heavenly smell of him. She needed to be completely submersed. He pulled almost all the way out and then slammed into her again with a moan. Over and over and over. Hammering out his frustration.

God, don't stop. Don't ever stop.

Ellie's head fell to the side, mouth open in ecstasy, as Liam pinned both her wrists to the table above her, face buried in the hollow of her neck. He moved slower now, able to control his passion, licking, kissing her neck, her chin, back up to her mouth again.

"This is how." He moaned. Ellie dug her nails into the small of his back, rock hard beneath his dampened shirt. The sound of his voice brought her to climax, back arching up from the table, legs quivering. She sucked in the air to prevent yelling out. It undid him. He thrust into her again, pulled out and then in one last time, shuddering on top of her as he finished.

She wrapped herself around him for a moment, legs at his waist, arms enveloping his head as he rested awkwardly on her chest where her dress had gathered obscenely. She could feel him start to move out of her and felt overcome with emotion.

Don't leave me.

How can you think that? What have you done?

Shut up! Just shut up! I don't want to cry.

Liam pulled out, reaching down hastily for his jeans, buttons ripped from his white oxford. Hair disheveled, glistening with sweat—he was beautiful. The sight of him tore at Ellie's heart. His face no longer contorted in anger or flushed with desire, he looked like a child, full of contrition.

What could she say now? What words were there? How should she act?

Sliding her dress back over her hips, she stood up and smoothed her hair awkwardly.

"Maybe I should be alone," she whispered.

You don't mean that.

Liam nodded in understanding and grabbed his coat from the fallen chair. With one long, sullen look toward Ellie, he turned the corner of the bookcase and was gone.

Dazed, Ellie sat for a long moment, straining to hear his footsteps on the worn carpeting of the library as he retreated, trying to hold onto something of his. But the only sound her ear could catch was the labored rattling of the ancient cooling system. Why did she keep sending him away?

You're married, fool. That's why. You think he's any different than any other man you've ever met? You just let him fuck you on the table in the library basement. Easy American!

Ellie looked around the tiny space absently, the table pushed up against the wall now. The chairs still on their sides. Full of shame, she straightened the space as noiselessly as she could. Then reaching deeply into the bookcase again, she located Avery's book. That's when the tears came like torrents, uncontrollable streams of…guilt?

No. She wasn't guilty. And maybe that's why she cried. She didn't feel guilty at all. Maybe she just realized how very lonely she had been.

And it's what you wanted. Do you cry now because you fear that fuck on the table is it?

What happened was almost certainly a temporary fix to loneliness. And a five- minute fix at that. She allowed herself to sob quietly into her hands. Even the badgering voice of her conscience left her alone while she emptied her chest of the suffocating weight that had been stored there. When she was still again, the tears having all escaped, she opened the book and scribbled a couple of lines:

> *What if you are more than just this?*
> *What if I could believe in you? If I could trust you not*
> *to destroy me?*
> *What if this is meant?*
> *What if all of this is meant?*

Once she was sure her face was no longer puffy from crying, she ventured out of her hiding place, back through the university stacks and up the three flights to the surface. This time, she felt like all eyes were on her, but nothing in her face or dress gave her away. It wasn't strange for an English professor to be walking through the library. There was nothing unusual in that. No one was paying attention except maybe for the security cameras that would have documented her arrival and departure, Liam's mad dash after her and his certain remorseful retreat. The thought instantly stung her.

Go to him!

But she didn't dare. No. She would go back to her office and gather her belongings. Then she would go home and put her hands in the earth, pull weeds. Sit in the middle of the flowers and finish the gardener's work. Maybe drag out the hose and water the plants aimlessly. Or maybe she would just make dinner or clean or do a load of laundry. Something normal. Something a mother and wife would do on a Monday night.

Or maybe you should lock yourself into a room for a couple of days, just like Daddy used to.

Oh my God, I'm just like him, aren't I?

But she immediately pushed the thought from her mind before it set up shop and drove her even farther into despair. If only there was someone she could tell her secret to. What difference would it make if she had though? What would she even say?

"I slept with Liam." That would be too mild, wouldn't it? "Sleep" was such a misuse of terms. OK, try again.

"I let the illustrious Dr. Curran fuck me on the table in the library in the middle of the afternoon." That would be closer to the truth.

What about, "I have been flirting shamelessly with Liam Curran for three weeks now, and after allowing him to stay in my hotel room in Chicago, kissing him at the opera, and fondling him in the wine cellar of my home while my entire family was upstairs, we finally attacked one another (yes, I was as much to blame) in the library basement"?

Sounds like guilt to me.

It's more complicated than simple guilt, and you know it.

Ellie's stomach felt queasy as she skulked back into her office, hoping desperately that no one would be waiting around to talk to her. Fortunately the English department was silent. At least she would have an evening to sort through her complicated feelings and design a mask to present, to practice nonchalance, disconnection, before she had to face Liam and all her colleagues the next day.

That should be no problem at all. Shutting people out is what you do best.

When Ellie arrived home, the hood of Alec's 1980 Corvette was propped up, father and son leaning inside of it, hands full of grease.

"Hi," Ellie said with artificial lightness as she walked up.

"Hey, Mom." Jordan looked up from his work, brown eyes shining with excitement, the smile on his face summoning his one dimple. God, he looked so much like his father. "Dad's showing me how to fix the engine." He stopped what he was doing, blackened hands held up in the air, a surrender of sorts, and walked over to his mother to kiss her lightly on the cheek.

"Hey," Alec, looking terribly happy also, greeted Ellie as she entered the garage. "My lunch meeting got canceled so I came home early today." He seemed so relaxed that Ellie wondered if he'd started drinking already. It was a little early in the day (even for him). Maybe he was just happy doing what he loved most of all: being with his son and working on cars.

Don't be ridiculous. What he loves most is his liquor.

"I'm glad you guys are having fun! I'm going to go change," Ellie informed them. "Make sure you clean your hands really well before touching anything in the house."

"We know, General," Alec answered. Jordan laughed in good nature. "Did you have a presentation today?" Alec called after her. "You're so dressed up."

Ellie shook her head without turning around.

"Hey! Good news!" Alec called after her. "Andrew Mitner called this morning. He's willing to invest in the expansion. He said he'd do it only because he likes you!"

Ellie cringed inwardly. *I wonder if that will cost me in flesh.*

As she climbed the stairs to their bedroom, the image of Alec and Jordan working under the hood of the car brought on a fresh wave of guilt.

Fine. So it is guilt. I admit it.

But not because she felt like she had broken her marriage contract. That "promise" meant nothing anymore. Alec broke that deal long ago when he refused to stop drinking. All those useless years in marriage counseling. Every time he reached for another Jack and Coke, he pissed on that promise. The guilt came from betraying the promise she made to stay in this marriage for her son. The deal she made to sell her soul.

Well, hell, it wasn't much of a deal really. She had already sold her soul when she unwittingly said "I do." And now this lie that she perpetuated, this "happy" marriage she faked for her son's sake, was even more of an act. At this point, which was worse—pretending to love Alec for Jordan's sake and sleeping around with other men or telling Jordan the truth ("Your father is an alcoholic, and I haven't loved him for a very long time")?

Ellie sat down heavily on the side of the tub, pulling her swollen feet out of her torturous shoes. As she stood to unzip the side of her dress, that's when she noticed the bruises on her wrists. *Oh, fuck!* She stepped out of the dress hastily, turning her backside toward the mirror so that she could inspect herself. Nothing there—but on the inside of her thighs…She laughed in spite of herself. A crazy, hysterical laugh.

Good luck explaining those.

What would Alec do? Go kill the man who did this to her? Doubtful. That would require him to be sober enough to find Liam. Who knows? Maybe Alec wouldn't care at all. They had developed such a comfortable routine of denial and avoidance that Ellie doubted Alec would even care what she did as long as it didn't affect his routine. As long as she turned a blind eye to his drinking, he let her go anywhere, do anything, spend any amount of money, no questions asked. Everything in the Purnell household ran smoothly. The only person who would really care was Jordan. And with his health, Ellie couldn't risk such an upheaval.

Jordan's so much better now, though.

She dismissed this final thought. It wasn't as comforting as her subconscious had hoped. Becoming a mother was a life sentence of worry and guilt, especially when you had a sick child. Somehow seeing Jordan contentedly working in the garage with his father had helped put everything into perspective. This was her life, like it or not. Liam was an indulgence. And maybe these bruises were the mark of shame she would bear just long enough to remind her of how selfish she had been.

She stepped into the shower, letting the almost scalding-hot water hit her in the face as she leaned against the wall, arms outstretched, palms against the tile. Instead of relief though, a cleansing, she felt a deep and inexorable sadness invade her. She was washing off

Liam. Any traces of him on her skin, in her hair, between her legs. Suddenly she didn't want to scrub anything clean. She didn't want to wash him away.

Her phone beeped inside her purse on the bathroom vanity. A text.

She couldn't get out of the shower fast enough, hurrying to wash herself now so she could check her phone. Grabbing a towel from the rack, wet hair stuck to her neck and back, she dried hastily and began rummaging through her purse for the elusive cell phone. Standing naked in the bathroom, one hand holding the towel, one scrolling the phone, she found what she had expected (hoped for). A text from Liam:

I'm sorry. That was not what I intended.

"I'm sorry. That was not what I intended"? What does that mean?

Ellie sat down morosely on the lid of the toilet, cradling the phone in her open palm as she stared at the screen, still contemplating its meaning.

"I'm sorry. That was not what I intended."

Should she text back? God, what would she write?

"I'm not sorry."

No, that would sound slutty. On some level, it might sound encouraging too. And really, she wasn't trying to encourage any more infidelity.

Should she text back saying, "What are you sorry about?" or "Why are you sorry?"

No. That sounded pathetic, searching.

What about "What did you intend, Liam"?

Did he intend to follow her to the library just to argue with her more? Did he want her to piece together the story of her poetry for him, admit she no longer loved her husband? What, ultimately, were his intentions?

Maybe she should just ignore the text all together. After all, what was there to say? The truth? What was the truth?

Liam, I am ashamed to say that I do not regret what happened. In your presence, I am whole.

She could never write that. The truth was that Liam was not hers to keep. He was a fantasy, not her reality. And she had a son who needed her. And besides, what did she really know about Liam except for what she chose to believe? What did she know besides what turned up on her Google searches, what limited interviews showed up on YouTube, and the philosophy he presented through his writing?

But, as you well know, a person's writing speaks volumes about them.

And so what? It didn't make Ellie capable of reading his mind or knowing his intentions.

So why don't you just ask him his intentions, then?

That's a lovely sentiment. Surely he would be honest as all men in my life have been.

Then how can you "feel whole"?

(Liam's voice: "Stop overthinking. Everything is as it should be.")

Ellie sat for a very long time, rivulets of water running down her back toward tiny pools on the bathroom floor.

Everything is as it should be. Everything is as it should be.

She tapped onto the screen of her phone.

To: Liam

Everything is as it should be.

She hit send. It was done.

Texting that mantra almost felt like a desperate plea, as if launching it out into the universe, this idea of perfect order, made it so. It not only exonerated her from any guilt or wrongdoing but also allowed her to take the first deep breath she had since she watched Liam depart around the side of the library bookcase. She realized she had been taking very short breaths, only marginally staving off a full-blown panic attack.

Taking the phone with her into the bedroom, she dressed in a tank top and yoga pants and then curled into the fetal position on her bed, facing the wall. She waited for another beep, another text. Nothing.

"There's no seat here at the table for you." *Maggie Lawson turned to look angrily at her daughter. She placed her hands protectively on top of a deck of cards. Around a dimly lit poker table sat a twenty five-year-old Dylan, Liam, and a younger, dimpled Alec, each holding five cards close to their chests. Ellie could not see herself but sensed she was a child, pigtails still, just big enough to see the chips scattered across the tabletop.*

"Come with me," *Jim Lawson instructed, taking Ellie's hand. He was much younger too, maybe only thirty-five, hair still black. Ellie followed her father hesitantly, glancing back over her shoulder to see everyone but Liam focused on his game. Liam's eyes watched her intently as she moved farther away from him across the room.*

Then Jim Lawson and his daughter were entering through the front door of Ellie's childhood home as it had appeared in the '80s—dark paneling, orange flowered sofa—when suddenly, the room was filled with naked women. A hundred naked women, surrounding them, grabbing Ellie's arms, forcefully pushing her toward some indecipherable sound. A baby crying? The sound grew louder and more insistent. Was it an injured animal?

They stopped. There on the floor, rolled into a ball lied Jordan, his fourteen-year-old body contorted in a position of agony. His mouth opened to release the wails of a newborn, the screeching misery of an injured cat.

How can I help him? I'm too small, *Ellie thought as she reached out for Jordan, trying to comfort him.*

The room transformed into a bright summer day, Jordan no longer at her feet. He had morphed into the most beautiful, shiny black horse Ellie had ever seen. It's breathing labored, one pleading brown eye, it looked up at her from the bed of a shallow stream where it lied helplessly on its side. (The river behind their ranch?) She didn't know for sure. It felt like their river, their ranch, only different. The freezing water washed over Ellie's feet. Suddenly Jordan appeared at Ellie's side. Confused, she looked back down at the horse and then back up to Jordan.

"Help it," Jordan instructed his mother.

"I don't know how," an adult Ellie cried out urgently.

"Mom, it's OK." Jordan shook his head patiently, leaning down to touch the horse's face. On contact, the horse lifted its head, struggling awkwardly to get onto all fours. Then just as suddenly, the animal stood, shook its head, and disappeared at a gallop into the pine forest.

"See!" Jordan smiled benignly, "This is what was meant."

Ellie's eyes snapped open with a start, the confusion of the dream still real and fresh. The moon shining through the tall, exposed windows of their bedroom told her it was still the middle of the night. Exhausted by the bizarre dreams that had plagued her since she had fallen fitfully asleep after her shower, she rolled onto her side, facing away from Alec. A stream of tears, free of sound, ran from the corners of her eyes, over the bridge of her nose, down toward the mattress.

I wonder where Liam is right now. Is he sleeping? Dreaming? Thinking of me?

The thought was too poignant to contemplate. Ellie willed herself to think of anything else. The next day's lesson. Poetry. Song lyrics. An empty box. But the images of her last dream hung on her heavily. Liam's protective eyes watching her from the poker table. The sick, black horse. The river. Jordan telling her it was OK. Such a deep melancholy had settled into her bones, she was paralyzed, prevented from even wiping her face dry.

She closed her eyes and then opened them again. The moon had traveled farther across the night sky. Her eyes drifted shut and bolted open again as gray, early dawn now infiltrated the room. She felt physically ill from lack of sleep. Today she would not run.

~

As she parked her car in the university parking lot, Ellie caught a glimpse of herself in the rearview window. There wasn't enough makeup on earth to cover the dark bags that had exploded under her eyes overnight. It was almost embarrassing. Could she get away with wearing sunglasses all day? Maybe have class outdoors? *Actually that's not such a bad idea.* It would give her an excuse to be out of the building, under one of the massive cottonwood trees near the quad, someplace peaceful where maybe she wouldn't feel so trapped.

When Ellie suggested it to the class, Megan groaned.

"It's so hot outside," Megan complained under her breath to Ellie. It was apparently Megan's turn to dress up. She wore a flattering white, fitted sundress with a three-quarter-sleeve cardigan, her beautiful, golden hair in soft curls flowing down her back.

Ellie looked at her absently. "I can teach today, if you want," she offered graciously, excusing Megan from her duties. "You look so cute in what you're wearing. I don't want you to get grass stains! Are you going out after work?"

"I have a meeting with Dr. Curran about my essay," Megan chirped happily. "Thank you so much! I really could use some time to make the changes he suggested before meeting with him again. I've been so busy editing *your* work that I haven't had a chance to get to mine."

"Well, I'm glad to help." Ellie never told a bigger lie in all her life (*Meeting with him* again *?*). She felt as if her last meal was fighting her stomach in an effort to exit through her mouth. *Last meal?* Exactly when had that been? Yesterday's lunch? Did she even drink anything this morning? She couldn't remember. "Where's your meeting?" Ellie forced herself to ask.

"Probably the library. Maybe The Bear. He said to stop by his office after class and we'd decide," Megan answered.

"OK, good luck," Ellie mumbled as she searched her purse for her sunglasses, slamming them onto her face before her bleary eyes would give away her dejection. She announced loudly over the talking of the class, "Let's head outdoors!"

Ellie couldn't get out of the building and away from Megan fast enough. Salty, choked-back tears ran down the back of her throat as she led the students toward a shaded patch of grass. The idea of Megan and Liam sitting quietly in the library, poring over Megan's work, hands accidentally (or purposely) brushing. Or worse, the idea of Liam and Megan drinking at The Bear, laughing, telling stories was maddening. Ellie needed to banish the thought if she was to survive a three-hour class. (Hell, survive at all.)

Megan was wrong about it being too hot. It was a perfect Wisconsin summer afternoon. Seventy-five degrees, low humidity, a breeze just strong enough to send the cottonwood leaves tingling like little bells on the their stalks above Ellie's head all afternoon. Two cardinals, in harmony, called to one another from nearby trees. It was a wonderful distraction. Ellie sat cross-legged, bare feet in the grass, hair blowing behind her, sunglasses shielding her emotions, submersed in the poetry of Gerard Manley Hopkins. ("Glory be to God for Dappled Things") Perfect! Glory be to God for this beautiful afternoon and something to think about other than Liam.

She let the class go twenty minutes early but remained in the grass for some time afterward, undecided what to do next. She was so exhausted that she could barely think rationally.

Twenty-four hours ago, you were in the library with Liam.

She hated to admit it, but she wished their tryst hadn't been so fast. Why, in the moment, couldn't she have slowed things down, held him to her, refused to let him go? Why did she tell him to leave her alone afterward? Why?

So go to him now! Find him.

She found herself getting up, shoes in hand, heading back toward the liberal-arts building, her hair windblown, sundress wrinkled from sitting in the grass all afternoon. She looked wonderfully childlike—lost, charmingly vulnerable.

There was no stopping her trajectory, straight for Liam's office, like a moth to light (or a dumb insect to a bug zapper, where certain annihilation awaited). Her pulse quickened as she neared his door, which was cracked just slightly. She stopped. Late-afternoon sun saturated the tiny room, blinding, explosive light that sent bits of dust floating through space like confetti. Liam sat with his back to the door, eyes shut. Was he meditating? Ellie could barely breathe as she stood in the hall watching him through the crack in the door. He was the most flawless thing she had ever laid eyes upon. If only she could reach out to him, take him into her arms, absorb his energy.

There was no way she could disturb something so perfect. She turned to escape quietly down the hall.

"Elizabeth," Liam called quietly to her, eyes still shut. She halted, slightly embarrassed that she had been caught. "Come in," he instructed.

"Hi," Ellie uttered nearly inaudibly. She entered the room slowly, standing directly in front of his desk.

"Hi." He smiled mildly. His eyes in the afternoon sun were a brilliant, impassive green. "I watched you in the quad today," he mentioned almost casually. "That was a good idea to have your class outside. I fear you'll have an advantage in our next debate if we hold it outdoors. You seemed quite at ease."

Ellie smiled back. "You already knew that about me."

"That I did," he admitted. He folded his hands in front of him as if he were receiving a student, shoulders back, sitting straight up in his chair, a closed, formal appearance. Ellie expected him to say, "And what can I do for you today?" Her throat felt like it was constricting when it occurred to her that she was still wearing her sunglasses. She reached up to remove them. When she made direct eye contact with Liam, there may have been a millisecond of emotion, but then it was gone as quickly as it had appeared. Had he noticed the bruises on her wrists?

"I just...I thought I would check on you," Ellie stammered. She felt faint.

"Thank you," he said without smiling this time. "I'm fine. I've been very busy with meetings all afternoon."

For a very long, awkward moment, they stood looking at one another and then Liam rose from his desk, towering over Ellie in her flats. "And actually, I have another in a few minutes," he continued dismissively.

"OK," Ellie managed to choke out in shock. *So this is the way it's going to be?* She felt as if she'd been hit in the face with brick. Turning to leave, she consciously controlled her pace (*walk slower*). Her instinct was to tear out of the office, the building, the state, run as far and as fast as her feet would propel her.

"We can talk tomorrow?" Liam asked politely.

"Sure," Ellie whispered without turning around to look at him.

Driving home from work, she found her car turning south toward her parents' house. She knew Alec had taken Jordan to soccer practice; there was no need for her to be home. The garden could wait. The house cleaning could wait. The first stack of summer essays could wait. All of it would wait for her. Maybe she would go to her parents' house and take out one of the horses. Her mother would probably have a heart attack if she saw Ellie saddling up to ride; it happened so infrequently.

As she pulled carefully into the long gravel drive lined by oaks, she was surprised to see people riding in the outdoor arena. Pulling closer, she realized, with even greater surprise, that one of the people riding was Marta. Ellie stopped her car for a moment to gape, open mouthed, out the side window. Marta riding a horse? Surely she had crossed over into bizarro world, been sucked into some alternate universe. Or maybe this was just another weird dream sequence. The laughing instructor, all mirth and gentle patience, was, of course, Becca.

Ellie parked her car by the far stable and headed over toward the fence, one of Alec's original creations. (The fateful fence that began it all.) She stood with her arms and elbows resting on the top rail, face peering into the arena quietly so as not to disturb the two. Though they had seen her, they were too occupied to chat just yet. Marta wasn't exactly a natural. Becca waved to Ellie, and she nodded in return.

How weird that Marta never told me she wanted to learn to ride. Weird, too, that she didn't tell me she was coming here today.

You've been pretty self-absorbed lately.

Ellie had no response for her subconscious now. She couldn't even begin to address the "shitty friend" accusations that might start rolling around in her head.

She and Marta had always had an unspoken rule: neither of them would demand too much from one another. That was the way their friendship worked. Maybe in a friend, Marta really *did* need more, though. And God knows, Becca would be an infinitely more attentive friend than Ellie. Becca, the Zen master.

Stop making yourself feel worse.

Too late. Ellie felt crestfallen, as if the entire world had rejected her. Maybe she would slither back to her car and return home to her bed, pulling the covers over her head. Forget riding.

Instead she stood transfixed at the fence, dust kicking up into her already wild hair. The horse Marta "rode" was Whisper, once young and unruly, now broken and submissive in her adulthood. Usually the most even tempered in the stable, she was having a good, wild time at Marta's expense, breaking into a run, bucking. Certainly the horse could sense its rider's apprehension and lack of skill; Marta unquestionably wore proof on her pale face. Whisper was misbehaving simply because she could. Horses, like children, knew when they had the upper hand and would test their limits to see what they could get away with.

Why is she putting herself through this misery? She hates animals.

Becca rode in close on her horse, scolding Whisper sternly. Once Whisper settled, realizing there was, in fact, a boss in the ring, Becca grabbed the reigns of the horse and led both back toward the fence. Dismounting first, Becca let her horse run free in the arena as she secured Whisper to the fence. Then she reached up protectively to help a visibly shaken Marta down from the saddle. Ellie had to stifle a laugh.

You're not in Miami anymore!

She was about to yell something snarky, give her friend just a little bit of shit, when Becca took Marta into her arms compassionately, her soothing hand resting at the back of Marta's head, smoothing her hair. Ellie blinked in sudden understanding.

Oh my God. That is why. That is why Marta is putting herself through this misery.

How could you be so dense? Your sister is thirty-seven years old, never married, never had a serious boyfriend.

Becca's always been brilliant, preoccupied, busy with school, busy with her animals. But...

"To what do we owe the honor, Dr. Purnell?" Maggie Lawson strode up next to her eldest daughter, finding a place at the fence.

Startled, Ellie had no immediate response. She searched her mother's face momentarily for any sign of realization. If her mother knew about Marta and Becca, she wasn't letting on.

"I thought maybe I would ride," Ellie announced with a sideways glance.

"Really?" her mother looked at her suspiciously. "What's wrong? Are you and Alec fighting again?"

"No, Mom." Ellie felt suddenly annoyed, a reaction her mother could always illicit. "I do feel like I have some steam to blow off, though. I thought maybe it would do me good to take one of the horses out on the forest trail."

"Well you can't ride in that." Maggie Lawson pointed to Ellie's sundress. "Why don't you just come up to the house? I'll make you girls dinner."

"I don't want to eat, Mom," Ellie insisted.

"You want to be alone," her mother conjectured. "I got it, Elle. What's new? I'll make you something anyhow. If you really want to ride, I'm sure there are clothes in the house for you. Boots are in the mudroom. You can eat when you're done."

"Hey!" Becca called out happily as she and Marta came within earshot. "What are you doing out here?"

"I might ask you the same thing," Ellie couldn't help herself from saying.

"Teaching Marta to ride," Becca stated unabashed, not taking the obvious bait.

"You've got your work cut out for you!" Ellie teased. Marta pooched out her bottom lip in mock insult.

"Oh, she didn't do so badly. Whisper was being naughty today and really gave Marta a scare," Becca defended. She patted Marta's shoulder. "Next time will be better, I promise."

"I think Marta would like to help birth the foals too," Ellie offered. Marta mouthed "Fuck you" to Ellie while Maggie Lawson wasn't looking. Ellie laughed for the first time in days.

"Are you girls hungry?" Maggie asked.

"Starving. What are you cooking?" Marta replied.

"How about barbequed pork chops? Becca tells me you're a Southern girl. I figured you wouldn't mind barbeque."

"Becca tells me you're a Southern girl?" She's been talking to Mom about Marta? Ellie had to consciously keep from letting her mouth hang open. Maybe she wouldn't ride, after all. Having dinner with them seemed too good to miss even though she felt oddly like the third wheel, a designation she never anticipated in the presence of Becca and Marta, the two people closest to her.

"Pork chops sound amazing, Mrs. Lawson," Marta answered. Was there a drawl back in her voice?

Ellie burst out again, covering her mouth suddenly. Marta with manners? Maggie Lawson shot her a harsh look.

"You're in a unique mood today, Elizabeth Ann," her mother admonished.

"This is a nice surprise to see you out on a Tuesday afternoon though," Becca said, redirecting the conversation as they headed toward the house.

"Yeah, I thought I might ride," Ellie admitted. Her sister eyed her with concern. God, was Ellie that transparent? Everyone knew she only rode when she was upset? "I thought maybe I'd visit with Daddy for a while, but now that you guys are here…"

"Good thing," Maggie Lawson said, chiming in. "Your father is out antiquing again. I swear if he brings back anymore garbage from these estate sales, I'm going to go crazy!"

"He needs a different hobby," Becca laughed. "Something constructive. I keep trying to get him to ride again."

"Where were *you* all day?" Marta asked Ellie.

"I had class outdoors," Ellie answered. "Can't you tell?"

"I guess you look a little windblown," Marta conceded. "But I thought maybe you just drove here with the windows down!"

"No." Ellie laughed. "It was beautiful weather. I couldn't stand to be indoors today."

Again Becca appraised her older sister. Ellie could feel Becca's eyes searching the side of her face. She didn't dare look at Becca directly lest her little sister would reach into her brain and pull out the very truth in a mere moment. No, there were other people there with secrets apparently. Ellie was suddenly more concerned with getting to the bottom of those.

"Wasn't Megan doing most of the teaching today?" Marta wondered as they entered through the back mudroom where they began stepping out of their boots.

"I let her work on corrections to the essay she's trying to get published," Ellie answered as casually as she could. "She had a meeting lined up with Dr. Curran this afternoon. She was supposed to meet with him after class." *(At the bar. Or maybe in the library, where he fucked me yesterday.)* She had to keep herself from laughing again. Her melancholy had turned to hysteria, it seemed. She was so fatigued, her emotions were literally upside down.

"You mean Liam?" Becca asked suspiciously.

"Yes," Ellie answered, a strained muscle in her cheek twitching involuntarily.

"I don't think so," Marta said, piping in. "He wasn't feeling well today. He left right after classes were over."

"I saw him in his office," Ellie argued. "And he told me he had a meeting to get to." *Yeah, a meeting at his house. Possibly in his bedroom.*

"Oh, so he *did* find you. He kept asking me all morning if I'd seen you," Marta explained.

"He didn't find me." Ellie sounded just a bit too bitter. "I found *him.* In his office."

"Were you looking for him?" Becca asked with pretend innocence.

Ellie craned her neck to see if their mother had overheard the question, but Maggie Lawson was already busy in the kitchen, pulling thawed meat from the refrigerator. Ellie didn't answer, but her silence confirmed Becca's suspicions. The younger sister finished unlacing her boots and set them under the bench.

"When were you two going to tell me?" Ellie asked suddenly, blocking the entryway to the kitchen.

"About riding?" Becca asked.

"I've been coming here for a few months now," Marta admitted. Ellie was almost knocked over by shock.

"Really?" she asked in disbelief. "Well, why…I don't understand why you wouldn't say anything. I mean…"

Becca and Marta stood next to one another, almost protectively, a united front against whatever unstable reaction they had expected from Ellie. Ellie felt tears well up in her eyes again.

"Do you think so little of me that you thought I wouldn't be happy for you?" Ellie managed to get out a choked whisper.

"Oh my God, honey, no!" Becca stepped in toward her sister, wiping her tears. "We just thought we'd wait. Maybe you would think it was too weird."

"Do Mom and Dad know?" Ellie asked suddenly.

"Well, they were with me the night I ran into Marta at The Bear about six months ago. We hung out that night, and the next."

"And the next!" Marta added with a smile.

"So this has been going on for six months?" Ellie asked incredulously, directing her question to Marta.

"She knows about Lilliana in Chicago, if that's what you're asking, Ellie," Marta explained crossing her arms. "We decided Friday at your party to be exclusive. There aren't any secrets here."

"Just a lot of surprises, I guess," Ellie quipped. "Or, I guess, just surprises for me." She felt like she was seeing her sister for the first time, looking at a complete stranger. Who was this person? "Why didn't you ever tell me you were gay, Becca?"

"Ellie, you never cared to know." Becca shook her head with dismay.

It was saddest thing Ellie had ever heard.

"Well, I am happy for you both," she admitted sincerely. "I am just...I am sorry that you both felt you couldn't tell me until now." Once the words left her mouth, she felt another rush of emotion. Embarrassment? Shame? Self-pity? How could the two people in the world who she trusted most not trust her?

"I think I'm going to skip dinner," Ellie said, pushing toward the back door. Becca ran after her.

"Don't be like that, Ellie," she pleaded. "If you're really happy for us, then be happy. Stop making everything about you."

"I'm not making this about me, Becca. I'm just trying to understand how a person, you, my little sister, my closest friend, the person I trust most in the world, thinks so little of me that she can't even tell me she's a lesbian. All these years. You can't even tell me you're dating my best friend."

"I love her," Becca corrected her.

"Even worse. You're in love with someone, and you can't even share that information with me!"

"Are you fucking kidding me?" Becca questioned, suddenly furious. Ellie's eyes grew as wide with surprise at Becca's uncharacteristic outburst.

"Ellie, you are the *queen* of secrets. You are the most closed-off person I've ever known. How dare you have *your* feelings hurt that I didn't confide in you when you have *never* confided in me? I've spent my entire life tiptoeing around your feelings because you've been so goddamned sensitive. You wear your heart on your sleeve for everyone to see, but then you refuse to talk about it. Ever since we were kids. You would get upset about Mom and Daddy, but you would never talk about it. Dylan, that piece of shit. I hated him. Everybody knew he was cheating on you, but never a word about it from you! And what about Alec and his drinking?"

Ellie folded her arms across her chest, watching her sister's rant with a mix of horror and indignation.

"You think I don't know what's going on?" Becca continued, working herself into rage that had been building for thirty-seven years. "I *always* know what's going on, Ellie. I know you! I have sat by and watched you hurting and been powerless to do anything about it because you won't confide in me." She stopped to catch her breath and then let out a low, ironic chuckle. "And now you're insulted and hurt because I'm in love, and I didn't tell you?" She shook her head as she walked away. "Funny, I could accuse you of the same exact thing."

Ellie stood paralyzed in the gravel drive, oak branches swaying overhead, dusk stealthily moving in. Becca strode heavily back to the house and then turned suddenly.

"Liam and Marta are having a cookout for their students Friday night at Liam's house. Stop acting like a damn fool and go to him. Before it's too late," she ordered finally, the screen slamming behind her.

Thirteen

Ellie stood in the middle of the driveway, Friday's late-afternoon sun beating down on her as she idly watched Alec load a suitcase into the hatch of their SUV.

"You sure you don't want me to drive out tomorrow?" she directed the question to Alec as much as Jordan.

"It's a long drive out to Iowa, Ellie. Don't bother. There are supposed to be bad storms tomorrow. You should probably take in the patio umbrella and the chair cushions tonight. Make sure all the cars are in the garage."

Ellie brushed the hair off her forehead, folding her arms across her chest. "OK," she answered, trying her best to make a mental note of the instructions. Her brain felt foggy from not sleeping well all week. It was hard to believe that the party they had had with the investors was just last Friday. And her experience with Liam (a familiar pain stabbed at her chest) was just four days ago, an eternity. He had not so much as looked at her all week. Ellie hadn't slept, hadn't run, and really hadn't eaten since then. It was as if she existed now in a weird parallel world, a hallucination of sorts, where everything was the same, just slightly different, darker.

If only she could get some sleep.

"Good luck at your tournament, then," she offered with forced enthusiasm. She embraced Jordan, who was now as tall as she was.

"Thanks, Mom. I'll text you our scores," he promised.

"Be careful," Ellie instructed Alec as he slipped into the driver's seat and started the car. "Double-check his numbers after he plays. Keep extra juice with you."

"I will," he called out as he waved an arm out the window without turning around. Ellie remained in the driveway as the car slowly pulled away, rounded the corner onto the county road, and was gone.

For a moment, she stood motionless, unsure what to do next. Her brain couldn't order any coherent thoughts as she mindlessly tuned into the happy chattering of a flock of finches overhead. Maybe she would just lie down in the gravel and go to sleep.

Good luck with that. You may never sleep again!

Instead she ambled tiredly to the back patio and secured the furniture against the predicted storms like Alec had suggested.

Maybe you should show up at Mrs. Dobb's cottage for Liam and Marta's barbeque.

Or maybe not. How would she be received at such a party? No one in the English department had so much as crept near her office in four days, allowing Ellie a wide berth to melt down, rip out her hair, swear, retreat into a corner, rock in the fetal position—do whatever it was they had expected she would do privately, to manage her poorly disguised foul mood.

Fools. They didn't really know her at all. The sour look she wore on her face was as bad as it ever got. She was the master of self-control. What did Marta think would happen now that Ellie knew about her and Becca? Pout? Cry again? (Not likely.) Stomp her feet? And yet, Marta had avoided Ellie like the plague.

And Liam? Well, he was "busy." He said so himself. Busy with very important meetings apparently. It wasn't like he had given Ellie a personal invitation to show up at his house. (No, he only fucks you on library tables. Beyond that, let's keep things professional, shall we?)

And Megan, God love her, could sense when a little bit of ass needed to be kissed. She had waited on Ellie hand and foot all week, trying to brighten Ellie's mood (Megan would do just fine in the world)—but Ellie doubted the scholarly beauty queen wanted to toss a few back with her slave-driving advisor on a Friday night.

And Becca? Well, who knew? Who fucking knew what she would be like if she was there? *Mini Maggie perhaps?* Ellie laughed out loud in spite of herself as she carried the patio umbrella into the garage. Never had she thought her mild-mannered sister resembled their mother in any way, but now—after Becca's wild-eyed tongue-lashing in the Lawson driveway…Now the comparison had crossed Ellie's mind several times. Could Ellie risk another Maggie-Lawson-style smackdown tonight? She didn't really have the energy for it. God knows, she wouldn't go looking for a confrontation, but as it was, people lately seemed to be calling her out against her will. *("Stop acting like a damn fool and go to him. Before it's too late.")*

Maybe she would just show up at the barbeque, test the waters. Have a couple of drinks. Observe.

Ellie closed the garage door and returned to the house, climbing the stairs to her bedroom. Yes, she would go to the party, and she would look good doing it. But considering she looked like a sleepless hag at present, that was going to take some serious work. What was the rush anyhow? She would take her time getting ready and then slip into the party once it was well underway. That way she could avoid drawing too much attention to herself, at least partially obscured by the darkness of nightfall.

Presumably everyone would be at least a few drinks in—also a cushion for softening the blow (or perhaps not, as Ellie knew intimately from experience). Alcohol had a mellowing effect on *most* people, and that was the chance she was willing to take. It was a fairly low risk though, and she always had her two feet to trust. She knew how quickly she could run if she had to.

By the time nine o'clock rolled around, she was still dawdling at her house. Not a single text on her cell phone. No missed calls. *Maybe you shouldn't go.* The doubt was enough to slow her down as she reapplied her lipstick, smoothed a piece of frizzy hair.

Stop procrastinating and just go if you're going to go, already.

She slammed the last of the espresso she had brewed for herself as she stopped to look at her reflection in the full-length mirror—jean capris and a fitted, sleeveless top, appropriate for a barbeque, but very flattering. The caffeine was finally doing the trick. She actually felt awake enough to dance. She smiled to herself, doubtful any dancing would be going on. Sparring, possibly. But dancing? Probably not.

To her annoyance, when she arrived at Liam's, there were so many cars lining Mrs. Dobbs's driveway that Ellie had to park nearly on the grass all the way at the end under a pine tree.

Drunken coeds had better not hit my car (my consolation prize for putting up with Alec's bullshit).

Apparently a party thrown by Marta and Liam could really draw a crowd. Ellie didn't realize there were that many students around during the summer session! A resentful pang twisted her heart.

Yes, all these people were probably told to come, and you were given just the casual invitation from your angry sister.

Ellie stopped suddenly. What if Becca wasn't even here? How foolish would Ellie look showing up then? She searched in the darkness for Becca's red jeep. Spotting it near the front of the house, she moved forward again hesitantly.

Smoke rose from the backyard, filling the air with the familiar summer smell of a bonfire as Ellie drew closer to the house. She decided to sneak around back instead of entering conspicuously through the front door. More than likely, most people were outside anyhow, enjoying the cool, crisp night air that had snuck in from the surrounding pine forest. The sky was surprisingly clear, a black canopy with brilliant silver starbursts scattered heavily. There certainly was no sign of a storm tonight.

As she neared the back of the house, she heard a guitar and several voices singing, but still, the party sounded surprisingly quiet for the number of cars that were parked out front. There was some giggling, some soft voices engaged in private conversation, but mostly just the sound of two or three men singing. British accents. And one very Irish-sounding voice, the loudest, singing…"Oh Danny Boy"? She almost began to laugh at how sentimental, how absurd for a barbeque, a bonfire…but the voices were so lovely. It wasn't meant to be a joke. She emerged from the darkness to see twenty or so people gathered around a fire, standing, sitting on lawn chairs, crowded onto horizontal logs, all focused intently on two of the students from England and the ever-fascinating Dr. Curran, who was effortlessly playing the guitar, perched high on an upturned log overlooking the group. It was his voice she had heard. His broad, lilting Irish accent as he closed his eyes, singing unabashed.

Ellie tilted her head quizzically. *Is he drunk?*

"Dr. Elizabeth Purnell!" Liam announced suddenly, halting the singing. He had spotted her. Every single head whipped around to look in Ellie's direction. Her face, neck, and chest burned crimson as she froze where she stood. "I didn't think you'd make it this evening!" he added with what seemed to be an amiable laugh. He *was* drunk. Ellie forced a smile as she scanned the crowd, locking eyes with Marta, who looked at her with amusement. The crowd looked on expectantly.

"I'd have come sooner if I knew there was going to be entertainment, Dr. Curran...although 'Danny Boy' is a little maudlin for a barbeque, don't you think?" she answered quickly.

"It was a request, Dr. Purnell. We are taking requests," Liam insisted.

"You and the guitar?" Ellie teased.

"Yes, the guitar and me." Liam grinned. By the light of the fire, his eyes were emerald green and full of mischief. Ellie moved closer. "I believe I promised you a song, yes?" he asked, turning the guitar upright. He began to expertly pluck out a tune as if he were playing the bass violin.

Ellie watched him with undisguised admiration. Awe, even. And what did she care who knew? They all looked at him the same way. In his presence, she immediately forgot her anger. Tilting her head toward the sound, as if there were no one else in the world but the two of them, she was lost in his strange, improvised rendition of some classical song turned beatnik jazz. She knew what he was playing long before she dared to answer; it was just too beautiful to end.

"Mozart's twenty-ninth, Dr. Curran?" she asked.

"You're very good, Dr. Purnell." He stopped suddenly, smiling again. "I know you love music. Shall we see if she can name some other songs?" he asked the group. He was answered with a chorus of enthusiastic, drunken yeses. Ellie glanced tentatively over in Marta and Becca's direction. They sat on a far bench, arms entwined, still looking deeply amused and very unwilling to help her out of a jam.

"So now *I'm* the entertainment?" Ellie joked, but inside, she felt uncomfortable. It suddenly felt more like a challenge than harmless public flirting.

Fine. I'll play your game, Liam. I'm the sober one, remember? "OK, Dr. Curran, play on."

"I'm going to make this difficult for you," he promised mischievously.

"I doubt it, Dr. Curran."

"Oh, she is a smack talker also," he told the group, his accent still sounding very Irish. "You know I love a challenge, Dr. Purnell!"

"I do know that," Ellie admitted, folding her arms. "Bring it." The crowd laughed.

Liam set the guitar sideways on his knee again, his long, sinewy forearm wrapped casually around it while the other tense hand sensually gripped the neck, strong fingers forcing the strings into submission. Intense concentration stilled his face as he began to play. After a few cords, the lyrics popped into Ellie's head like an ancient jingle, locked in an adolescent vault. It was the pop-punk version of a '90s love song, full of teenage angst.

"So sentimental tonight, aren't you, Dr. Curran?" Ellie teased as she moved closer. The group of young students looked confused. They couldn't possibly know a song so obscure. "The Descendants," Ellie concluded.

Liam stopped playing, feigning disappointment. "Oh, you *are* good, Dr. Purnell. Perhaps I have underestimated my opponent, everyone." The group cheered him on.

"You can stump her," one of the former singers said encouragingly.

"He forgets I know his musical influences," Ellie played to the group. "American punk rock! Very pre-dictable. Entertaining, but predictable, Dr. Curran."

Liam pretended to pout. "Very well. Let's try something terribly British. Earlier."

"You're going to put the young ones to sleep with music so old!" Ellie joked.

"They've had their requests already!" Liam insisted. "It's good to school them in a bit of musical history!" He laughed at his sarcasm. "You know, give them a little appreciation of musical origins—the great era of the eighties and nineties! Bruno Mars and Mumford and Sons are not the first musicians to have ever played. And that electronically made rubbish you call music…"

"Now, now!" Marta scolded.

Ellie laughed. "Yes, the elders of this gathering will now begin to reminisce. We'll culminate this musical performance with stories of how we once wrote our essays by hand with paper and pen and sat in the library to do research with actual books. A lamentation of life before the Internet, if you will!"

The crowd roared.

"It's true!" Liam agreed emphatically. "Can you imagine having to do research in such an archaic way?" he asked the group of students. Then he stopped, wagging a finger at Ellie. "I see you're quite wily, aren't you, Dr. Purnell? You're distracting me!" He began to play again. Ellie allowed him several measures even though the song was obvious immediately.

"Dr. Curran, you're toying with me now!" Ellie accused with a smile as he continued to play. "This is no challenge at all!"

"Morrissey!" Becca yelled out.

"The Smiths," Ellie corrected.

"Same difference." Becca laughed.

"You're correct, of course, Dr. Purnell," Liam said, congratulating her. Ellie curtsied as the group applauded and whistled.

"Sing it!" someone yelled.

"Perhaps in a bit," Liam suggested. "I have another for you." He looked directly at Ellie, his expression suddenly less jovial.

"OK," she agreed, folding her arms and tilting her chin up in challenge.

"I'll oblige you, Dr. Purnell, and play one they might know too. You can't help her out, though!" he warned the group. "This is a true test…"

Liam expertly launched into a vaguely familiar baseline, cleverly tapping the side of the guitar to mimic the drumbeat between phrases. The students began to squirm in their seats. It was killing them not to blurt it out.

OK. It's something contemporary.

She knew the melody but couldn't quite place the song. Then he launched into the melody, strumming the seemingly upbeat notes effortlessly. Suddenly the lyrics came to her.

"Vampire Weekend," Ellie declared without triumph. There was a theme emerging. He had chosen each song carefully.

I get it, Liam. Stop taunting me.

"I am thoroughly impressed, Dr. Purnell," Liam admitted. "I thought for sure I could stump you with that one."

Ellie forced a smile. "Odd choice of songs, Dr. Curran. Songs about love and faith. Or really, lack of faith."

"Aren't they one in the same, Dr. Purnell—love and faith?" he countered.

"Perhaps," she conceded.

"And besides, who better to understand lack of faith?"

Ellie's face stung with his barb, but she managed to retort, "Dr. Curran, the crowd is probably growing bored. I bet they'd rather hear you sing again, and I believe I've beaten you fair and square! Haven't I earned myself a drink at least?" Ellie played to the crowd. Several people yelled in agreement.

"One more! Just one more!" Liam insisted. "Someone, fetch my lady a drink," he commanded playfully. One of the former singers jumped up to find Ellie a cup. "One more song. I know you will know this one too, but I'd like to play it for you anyhow. I fancy this a theme song of sorts."

Ellie clasped her hands in resignation as he bent his head over the guitar again, playing slowly at first and then finding his rhythm as he lost himself in the melody. It sounded strange to Ellie on a guitar, almost a satirical folk version of the song, but there was no mistaking it. The lyrics came to her like a whip in the face. It was a morose song by Depeche Mode, one she had grown up with, one of her favorites…a song about being properly understood.

"I don't know this song," Ellie lied sweetly. Some in the crowd booed in jest while others yelled out encouragement.

Liam looked up from his guitar but continued to play. "I don't believe you," he goaded. "You have to know this song. I believe it was written specifically for you." He slowed down the tempo as his eyes seared into Ellie's face, searching for a change in her expression. He knew.

"I'm sorry, Dr. Curran. I don't know this song. I guess you win!" Ellie conceded with a bow. Liam's eyes, still focused on her face, narrowed as he stopped playing. The crowd exploded into applause as the student returned with a plastic cup of something that resembled beer. He was just in time to save Ellie from any more public contest. Taking the glass from the young man with a grimace, she nodded a thank you. Even with her nerves frayed, she still wasn't desperate enough to drink whatever was in that cup. She turned toward the back door of the house in search of a moment of peace.

Liam followed fast behind her.

"Dr. Curran." She stopped suddenly at the door and spun around to face him.

"You *do* know that song!" he whispered in frustrated indignation.

A wide, deviate smile spread across Ellie's face. She had made him angry.

"Yes, I do," she said very slowly, "but I'm not playing games with you anymore."

"Nor am I," he answered, grabbing her arm and pulling her into the house toward privacy. No sooner had the wooden screen banged shut against the frame, he had her up against the wall, his strong hands in her hair, grasping the sides of her head as his mouth took hers forcefully, his tongue demanding a response. She was his, pressing into his tensed torso, feeling his arousal hard against her abdomen. Her answer came as frantic hands inside his shirt, up his muscled abdomen and then around the low arch of his back. He deepened the kiss, running his hands down her neck, her shoulders, tracing the outline of her arms, until he had taken her hands in his, stopping her exploration. Then, abruptly, he stopped kissing her.

"No," he said firmly. Ellie let her head fall back against the wall with a sigh of frustration. "I shouldn't have...we can't keep doing this."

Ellie was perplexed. *Do you want me or not?* "Then stop baiting me," she demanded with irritation, her want for him so deep she throbbed in agony.

"Then you should stop also," he answered, still holding her hands firmly in his. "Everything is as it should be?" he questioned her cryptic text.

Hopeful, she stood on her toes to kiss his chin. "Sure, Liam. Isn't that what you believe?"

"Is it what *you* believe, Elizabeth?"

"It depends on what you're 'sorry' for," she said, quoting his text response.

"I am sorry for this," he answered seriously, holding up the fading marks on her wrists. "This was not what I intended," he admitted with contrition, bringing the inside of each wrist to his mouth to kiss them tenderly. "I suppose I am struggling within my earthly limitations, but to take that which was not given to me freely…" He sighed shamefully, slowly closing his eyes.

"That's what you've been silent over?" Ellie gasped in amazement, realizing that shame was what had kept him away from her all week. "You think you took what wasn't given freely? I was a willing participant."

"Not in the way that you should have been. It was wrong," he lamented.

She freed her right hand to touch his bent face.

"Take me then. I give you permission," she commanded him in a passionate whisper.

"I can't, Elizabeth. If I do, I won't give you back." He gripped the hand that she had rested on his face, kissing the open palm. "You don't yet mean what you say."

Ellie looked up at him quizzically.

What else can I do?

She *had* meant what she said. There was nothing that she wanted more than to give herself to him. Completely. *Take me.*

"Then what is it you intend?" she asked finally, a note of desperation in her voice.

"You aren't ready to know my intentions," Liam answered with finality, though his face looked conflicted.

"Dr. Curran!" Megan came forcefully through the back door, followed by three or four others as Liam carefully dropped Ellie's hands and stepped away.

"We want more music!" she implored coquettishly.

"Fair enough," Liam said, acquiescing. "Will you come back out?" he directed his question to Ellie. She just nodded her head solemnly, unsure whether or not she could endure the torture of watching Liam all evening without the ability to touch him. Stupid Megan. Of course she had to be the one to steal him away. If only Ellie could have had just a couple more minutes alone with him.

Then what? Plead with him? For what? What do you expect will happen? Where do you think this is going?

She had no answer.

As she remained planted in her spot against the hallway wall, Liam followed the group of students back out the door, one last, lingering look in Ellie's direction. Then they were gone. She finally let out the breath she had been holding as a familiar sadness set in again. She couldn't bring herself to go out there just yet. It was too much effort to pretend. (Or to be known under Becca and Marta's watchful, expectant eyes.) Instead she wandered aimlessly into the kitchen, surveying the leftovers from their feast, a potluck of early nineteenth-century American dishes the students had contributed, meant to compliment the whole chickens Liam had grilled. They were reinventing the meals of Emerson and Thoreau, Poe and Hawthorne, as a celebration of their first four weeks of American literature class. Clever idea. And cool. No wonder people adored Liam. He was fun.

And dazzling, and confrontational and talented and witty. Beautiful. Infuriating. Baffling. (Hot.) Secretive?

Ellie's stomach lurched at the smell of the food, a collection of random spices churning the kitchen air. Turning away, she spotted a bottle of white wine tucked into the corner of the counter near the side of the refrigerator. It was still cold when she picked it up. Sauvignon blanc. She smiled. *So he did expect me to come.* Once she opened the bottle, she swigged directly from it, a sense of salacious self-satisfaction bringing a grin to her face. Liam's guitar rang out again, the sound carrying through the open windows of the empty house as Ellie leaned complacently against the counter, bottle in hand. It was enough just to hear him. She could stand in the kitchen alone and imagine he was only hers.

Several songs and half a bottle later, she wandered through the darkened front room, her books of essays still littering the coffee table. She ended up at the bathroom sink, splashing water onto her flushed face, willing herself to return to the party. Liam's bath towel hung on the back of the door. She couldn't resist lifting it to her face to pat it dry. As it touched her skin, her stomach dropped.

You've done this exact thing before.

Oh God, the smell of him! It had brought on the strangest sensation. Déjà vu? She stepped back from the towel, stunned. She wasn't drunk, and yet…

No, but you're exhausted. Sleepless.

A sharp knock at the door startled her.

"Ellie, it's me," Marta called through the barrier. "You almost done?"

Ellie answered by opening the door.

"Becca just got called out for some horse with colic, whatever that means. Can you give me a ride home later?" she asked hopefully. "I don't want to ask Megan," she added with a smirk.

"I wouldn't force you to do that," Ellie joked. "Although maybe I should."

An awkward silence fell between them.

"I'm sorry," Marta finally said.

"For what?" Ellie tried for nonchalance.

Marta pursed her lips in a "do I really have to explain?" expression.

"I am happy for you and Becca, if that's what you mean," Ellie conceded. "I really am, Marta. I was just surprised, that's all. My sister is an amazing person—so smart and empathetic. You're…"

"Lucky to have her?" Marta finished.

"Well, yeah, I guess," Ellie answered, unsure.

"That's what I figured you'd say," Marta admitted, just the slightest bit defensively.

"That's not fair, Marta. Have I ever judged you?" Now Ellie was defensive. "Have I ever tried to change you? Given you unsolicited advice? Condescended?"

"No," Marta answered.

"Then why would you—"

"Because she's your sister," Marta interrupted.

"And she loves you as you are, Marta," Ellie insisted. "Just like I do! And she will cherish you!" She smiled warmly, looking her best friend in the eyes. "As you deserve to be."

Marta couldn't answer. Her emotions forced her eyes back toward the ground.

"The two women I love most in this world have found one another! What could make me happier than that?" Ellie asked with sincerity and then pulled Marta into a comforting embrace. "Can we still go dancing though?" she whispered into Marta's hair with a laugh.

"Yes," Marta answered lightly. "Maybe I will actually dance next time."

"That's something I would love to see." Ellie laughed. "Novel idea. Dance when you go dancing."

"Hell, I've already gotten on a horse for Becca! Dancing would be no big deal." Marta chuckled.

"You're in love," Ellie stated.

"I am." Marta's face beamed with the admission. "I am for the first time in a very long time. And this feels different. It feels…"

"Healthy?" Ellie asked.

"Yeah. Yes! That's a perfect description." Marta was filled with childish excitement. "It's not like Lilliana. It's not crazy and toxic. Becca brings out a side of me I didn't even realize existed. Or maybe she just makes me want to be the best, calmest me I've ever been. Do you get what I mean?"

"I can sense a difference in you," Ellie agreed.

"But do you understand what I mean about someone bringing out the best in you as opposed to being in love with someone who brings out your worst side? Like Lilliana, who I thought I couldn't live without? She made me crazy with jealousy and self-doubt. We lived together; we partied together. We did everything together, but I always felt so alone. It's not like that with

Becca. She challenges me to be better. I want to live up to the person she believes I am."

"I do get it." Ellie turned her face toward the sound of Liam's guitar, a sharp pain squeezing her chest. *I understand completely. Thank God there is happiness somewhere, even if it's not meant to be mine.*

"Let's go back out," Marta urged. "I'll give up my seat next to Liam for you." She smirked knowingly. Ellie kept her face impassive, in fear that any show of emotion might lead to a torrent of tears.

She allowed Marta to lead her back outdoors, where small collections of people had begun to branch off from the larger group. Liam still sat on his perch, quietly strumming random cords, his ambling fingers picking out notes, lost in his own thoughts, solitary and pensive amid the conversations going on around him. He watched Ellie's approach with mild, curious eyes, a small, welcoming smile turning up the sides of his beautiful mouth. He looked tired. *Or sad?* Ellie took the seat next to him as Marta settled on a log at his other side.

"You look quite content," Liam commented to Marta with a nod.

She answered with a broad, genuine grin, so full of innocence that Ellie barely recognized her pugnacious, indignant friend, a girl in metamorphosis. "Ahh, what love can do to you," Liam mused, almost to himself.

The three sat in silence for a while, watching the students begin to split into smaller groups and then coalesce, pair up, and eventually retreat to their cars, two or three at a time, to continue their partying elsewhere or finish their evening in a foreign bed.

"This party was a great idea, Liam. The food looked like it turned out well." Ellie attempted small talk.

"Did you eat, Elizabeth?" he replied without looking up from his guitar.

"No," she admitted. "My stomach…" She let the words die in her throat. He knew she hadn't eaten, and he also knew why.

And yet, he still thinks you don't mean what you say ("Take me.")

After the last few students stopped on their way out to say thank you to Marta and Liam, Marta popped up from her seat.

"You look worn out, Liam. Let me straighten up the kitchen for you," Marta offered.

Ellie couldn't resist a spontaneous chuckle. "My God! Who has possessed my best friend? You're going to clean up the kitchen instead of kicking back and lighting a joint?"

"No one said I wasn't going to smoke while I clean, Ellie." Marta winked and then set off for the kitchen, leaving Ellie and Liam alone by the waning light of the bonfire.

Ellie watched passively as Liam set his guitar down at his feet, freeing his hands. Expressionless he took her left hand into his right, weaving his strong fingers through hers, the absence of her wedding ring obvious to them both. Without removing his steady gaze from the flames, he possessively covered their entwined fingers with his left hand, the gesture forcing Ellie, heart beating wildly, to move in closer. She ventured to set her head on his tense shoulder, which softened at the moment of contact, the position almost eerily natural.

This is what is meant.

"Liam—" Ellie began.

"I know." He stopped her, shutting his eyes very slowly. A breath in, a breath out, and then he fixed his gaze once again on the fire.

Ellie molded to him, complacent just to be near.

Don't ever let go of me.

*B*y the time Ellie dropped Marta expectantly at the doorstep of Becca's townhome, the wind had shifted, forcing heavy clouds across the sky to obscure a once luminous moon. Suddenly the night was black with the threat of storms.

Ellie lay in bed, watching the cool wind force her bedroom curtains into a manic dance. There was no moon to mark the passage of time, only complete darkness and the sound of branches swaying rhythmically, rustling leaves, to lull Ellie to sleep.

Liam.

She drifted in and out of half dreams, a slow torture, rolling onto her back for air, embracing a pillow, kicking off the sheets, wrapping herself back up in the bedspread.

Liam.

There was no sleeping. His hands were at her shoulders, her breasts, her abdomen, between her legs.

I want you inside me. I am yours. Take me. I give myself to you.

He rested his warm hands against her but would not enter.

Her eyes burst open again. *Dammit!* Even in a dream, there was no closure. She couldn't have him. Rolling onto her stomach, she hugged the pillow to her face, trying to remember his scent.

Liam.

A crack of thunder rang through her bedroom, so close it shook the mirror, sending stray earrings sliding across the smooth wooden top of her dresser. The fuzzy gray of the room hinted at morning. Ellie lifted her head slightly to look at the clock. Sure enough, 5:00 a.m.

Maybe he will be waiting for you at the top of the hill.

The thought was enough to pull Ellie up to a sitting position. Maybe he would be! Now that they were speaking, had reached some sort of truce—were no longer pointedly avoiding each other—maybe he would be waiting for her!

Another crack of thunder, so loud it reverberated inside her chest cavity. The curtains whipped up into the room and then floated gracefully back toward the wall. She couldn't get her running clothes on fast enough. Within minutes, she had brushed her teeth, pulled her disheveled hair into a ponytail, and was lacing up her running shoes.

She ran out the front door to a chorus of thunder, some near, most still in the distance. the ominous promise of a disgruntled sky. The storm hadn't quite hit yet, but it was coming. And quickly.

She flung open the front door of her house, sprinting down the drive.

She ran. Not away from the storm. But toward Liam.

She ran. The storm gaining on her with every footfall.

When she reached the top of the hill, her hopes were dashed. He wasn't there. Just the trees and the wind and Ellie and her desire.

("Go to him!")

And before she knew it, her legs had chosen their own route, right up to Mrs. Dobb's gravel drive and then down the flagstone path toward the house, around the back to…

Ellie stopped.

Liam.

He stood before her in the far back of the yard, bare chested, arms and face flushed with exertion, forcefully shoveling ash from the fire pit into the garden, working out some inner angst, sweat beaded on his chest and neck, his hair damp and curling.

Like a ghost, Ellie emerged slowly from the tree line, into the wide-open space of the clearing, long, lose pieces of hair waving wildly. She floated steadily toward the garden as if carried on the wind.

Liam looked up from his work, surprise widening his eyes.

For a moment, both stood motionless, the universe momentarily stilled.

"I am yours," Ellie swore over the wind.

Liam let the shovel fall softly to the ground.

"I am yours!" Ellie demanded, stepping in toward him, placing her hands on his slick chest, head upturned.

Say something!

His strong hands were suddenly at her back, pulling her toward him, arms enveloping her as he leaned in toward her mouth, a slow, soft kiss growing deeper and more urgent. One arm held her tightly in place as the other removed her ponytail holder, freeing her hair to the wind as he gripped the back of her head. His hand traveled down her neck, her shoulder, down her back. Hard, cold drops of rain began to pelt them from above.

E. J. Densmore

Both Liam's hands now grasped her shoulders as he reluctantly pulled his mouth away. "Inside," he ordered. Sudden, furious sheets of rain chased them to the back door, heralded by black clouds and the constant flash of lightning. By the time they reached the screen door, their clothes were soaked through.

Just inside the door, Ellie turned to face him. Driven by the greed of lust, her hands madly reached out, groping his shoulders, his biceps. She stood on her toes to reach his lips and then pulled his mouth to hers again, kissing him voraciously. He obliged, pressing her up against the wall, angled in, hands splayed on either side of her so she could explore the length of his tensed arms, every muscle of his torso, his back, the ridges of his spine.

His tongue slowed as he tasted her lips, as if he were eating a plum, savoring the sweetness. Gradually he pulled his mouth away.

"Slowly," he instructed Ellie. "I've waited too long for this."

He traced the side of her face with one finger and then ran it down to the hollow of her neck, resting it between her breasts at her racing heart. "Come in here with me," he instructed with a playful tug at the center of her sports bra. As he turned to lead Ellie toward the bathroom, she gasped.

His broad, muscular back was covered from shoulder to waist with a mosaic of tattoos, so intricate and varied that the images were difficult to decipher at first glance.

"Liam!" Ellie managed. She ran her right hand down the length of his back. He stopped momentarily to let her gawk in surprise and then turned to face her questioning eyes.

"My grief tattoo," he explained, reaching down to her waist to peel off her wet tank top. Lifting it over her head, he balled it up and threw it to the bathroom floor. "Undress. I'm going to bathe you," he ordered. "If you are mine, I want to know every inch of your body, Elizabeth, just like I know every inch of your mind."

He sat on the side of the claw-foot tub, his own bare feet black with garden mud, the bottom of his Levis soaked through with soil and rain. As the hot water rushed from the faucet, the bathroom disappeared in a fog of steam. Liam fixed a patient gaze on the woman before him.

"Take off your clothes."

Ellie obediently pulled off her sports bra, exposing her breasts, light-brown nipples puckering under the weight of Liam's stare. Every nerve in her body became alert, blood rushing to all her extremities, throbbing madly at the apex of her thighs. She watched his eyes travel her body, inspecting her an inch at a time.

Touch me!

She boldly shimmied out of her soaked pants, stepping forward over them toward Liam, his face now only inches from her abdomen, the small strip of hair between her legs. She was completely bare before him, exposed.

"Goddess, nymph, perfect, divine," he whispered in genuine awe.

"Quoting Shakespeare?" Ellie laughed, taking one of his hands and placing his forefinger inside her mouth. She began to suck softly.

"You are so beautiful." Liam caught his breath. His head fell back for a moment, lost to the sensation. "I see what you're doing!" he said finally. "Get into the tub. I want to learn every curve of you, Elizabeth." He stood, a tower above her, allowing her space to slip into the tub.

The bathroom lights flickered as thunder cracked overhead, and then the electricity hummed loudly and fell dead. Rain and wind beat furiously against the roof, the window pane. Then Liam disappeared for a moment as Ellie submersed herself in the steaming water, reappearing with a lit candle that he placed on the back of the toilet. Kneeling beside the tub, he dropped his long forearms into the water.

"I am going to wash you with just my hands," he explained, starting with Ellie's left leg. He gently lifted her pointed foot out of the water, propping it onto his thigh. Lathering the bar of soap under her arch, he lovingly slid his fingers between each of her painted toes. Ellie leaned her head back against the lip of the tub, hair trailing over the back, as she studied his intense face. He seemed to be memorizing her with both his hands and eyes, so focused he appeared almost in a trance.

She realized she was holding her breath again when he slid his hand further up her flexed calf to her knee, and then to the inside of her thigh. She sucked in air.

"Liam!" she begged, grabbing the sides of the tub.

His eyes, heavy with want, raised momentarily to her face. "Patience, Elizabeth. I am just getting started," he said huskily. He ran the soap back down the length of her leg again and then placed her foot back into the water. Reaching for the other leg, he repeated the same routine—heel, toes, calf, thigh...inner thigh. This time his fingers found their way between her legs, softly caressing, teasing and then slipping inside her.

"Liam!" she cried out this time, grabbing his hand to force it in further.

"I will never tire of you calling out my name," he said softly. He moved his fingers out gently and then in again. Ellie's hips and hand joined in the same rhythm, pushing his fingers deeper.

"You are so ready for me," Liam whispered.

"Take me," Ellie begged, opening her eyes to see him biting down on his lip.

"Not yet. Be still!" he commanded, pulling his hand away. Ellie's arm fell limply into the water, exhausted from the tension of her arousal.

"Close your eyes and feel my hands on you," Liam instructed her. "Be present. Stop anticipating what I'll do next and just experience it."

Ellie sucked in air again and let out a long, deep sigh. She shut her eyes, trying to relax her face, untense her abdomen.

"Good," Liam said, encouraging her. "Keep taking long, slow breaths. You're going to need that runner's stamina for me, Elizabeth," he promised. Then his hands were on her again, running up the sides of her hips, over the top of her taut abdomen, cupping her breasts. Ellie sucked in air again, resisting the urge to guide his hands, willing herself to remain still. *Be present.*

His soapy hands felt slick on her chest as he gently explored the soft skin, playing his fingers over her nipples, rolling them, pinching slightly, just enough to raise them to his palms as he rolled his hands over them. He splashed water onto her chest, rinsing her clean. For a moment, no contact, and then his warm, wet mouth devoured her left breast, his other hand kneading the right.

Ellie's back arched up from the tub as she cried out in surprise. Her reaction made Liam suck harder.

"Oh, God, Liam!" she grabbed his head.

He moved his face across to the other breast, running his tongue over the right nipple, letting it harden in the cool air.

Be still. Complete warmth again as he covered the right breast with his mouth, his tongue tasting, circling, sucking. Ellie groped his massive shoulders, looming tensed above her.

Be present. She forced herself to keep her eyes shut, to absorb every detail: the warm water splashing against her abdomen, the drumming of rain against the window, Liam's warm, wet mouth on her breast, the thick, curly hair of his bent head in her right hand, the swollen throbbing between her legs. She was simultaneously in heaven and hell, so aroused the pit of her stomach twisted in agony.

His warm mouth retreated. Ellie kept her eyes shut but knew Liam had pulled out of the water and stood, blocking the soft glow of the candle.

"Stand up and turn around," he ordered over the thunder.

Ellie did as she was told, placing her hands against the tiled wall, her backside facing out. Liam breathed in sharply.

"You are perfect, Elizabeth." His hands started their exploration at the back of her thighs, rounding the smooth flesh of her behind to the narrowing of her waist, up under her arms to cup her breasts from behind as he forced her head to the side with a nudge, burying his face in her neck. Kissing her slowly behind the ear, down the neck to her right shoulder, he pulled her back against his bare chest, one hand holding her breast, the other hand reaching between her legs, slipping inside of her as she felt his rock hard arousal against her backside, his warm, wet kisses on her neck.

"I want you," he whispered into her ear. Pressing her body into Liam, Ellie moaned in agreement. She let her head fall back against his chest, arms limp, relishing every sensation, the power of his presence. Suddenly he took her by the shoulders, turning her to face him. Without a word, he directed her by placing her eager, trembling hands on the zipper of his bulging jeans.

His green eyes met hers with anxious passion, daring her to break his stare, but she couldn't. He owned her, body and soul.

I'll do anything for you.

She ran her hands over the outside of his pants and then slowly pulled down the zipper, reaching gently inside to find the immense size of him, rock hard, smooth-veined skin. She gripped his shaft, easing him out of his clothing as he helped by pushing his pants to the floor. Now he stood in front of her, all six-feet-two of him, an Adonis, beautiful, flawless. Broad, well-defined shoulders, triceps, lined abdomen, a light-brown patch of hair trailing from his heart to the place Ellie desired most.

He stepped into the tub, pulling the plug out of the drain with his foot and starting the shower. The warm spray covered them both as Liam pulled Ellie close to him, leaving her long, brown hair matted in curls around her nipples. Liam moved the hair with a gentle forefinger, leaning down to take Ellie's breast into his mouth again.

"Let me wash you," she begged, groping his shoulders.

Complicit, he handed her the body wash. She started by washing and rinsing both their hair. Now she could explore! The mosaic. She angled Liam slightly to reach his shoulders and back. In the dim light of the bathroom, obscured by the pelting water of the showerhead, the intricate details, and much of the wording woven into the complicated mural of tattoos was still garbled. Ellie soaped up her hand, running it along his spine as if she were restoring a painting, desperately trying to follow the patterns, make sense of the imagery. In the very center of Liam's back was the central image, so artfully intertwined with the others that, at first, it wasn't obvious. And then...a black horse. In the center of his back—a beautiful, black horse.

You've been here before.

Liam turned to face her, an obvious distraction.

"I think I'm clean." He laughed.

"Not yet," Ellie whispered slyly. She took the body wash into her hands, soaping up his chest, running her hands over his nipples, down his torso to his perfect erection, the size of which amazed her. She couldn't resist herself. Rubbing and rinsing it, she leaned down to take it into her mouth, slowly at first and then greedily, lips pressed forward, hands assisting in the exploration.

"Oh my God, Elizabeth." Liam gasped in ecstasy. His reaction was a lightning rod to her arousal. *He is mine!* She couldn't stop herself, madly groping his tensed legs, his behind, sucking harder and harder.

"Slow down!" he ordered. "I want you on the bed. I want to watch you."

She took one last, long pull with her mouth and then released him, getting to her feet. He reached between her legs again as she stood, covering her mouth with his, his tongue strong and demanding. "Get out and let me dry you off."

Liam, glistening beautifully, tiny rivulets of water running sensuous trails over his perfect body, shut off the shower and then stepped out after Ellie. He grabbed a towel and began to dry her, gently at first and then firm and quick over her nipples, hardening them to the rough touch of the towel. Every nerve in Ellie's body stood alert, watching him look at her. He quickly ran the towel over himself, leaving his hair a blissful, curly mess on top of his head, causing him to look a man half his age. Grabbing the candle with one hand and Ellie by the other, he crossed the hall to the tiny master bedroom, the four-poster bed and antique floor mirror swallowing up most of the space. The mirror was a mere three feet from the end of the bed.

"Stand here," he told Ellie. He stood her in front of the floor-length mirror. "I want you to see how perfectly we fit together." She watched her own strange image, unrecognizable—this middle-aged woman morphed by her lust, appearing curiously younger, hair wet and matted against her chest, alert, upturned nipples, plump with arousal. Then Liam's form behind her, arms enveloping her shoulders, his hands running the length of her body, covering her breasts. His head fitted into the crook of her neck, kissing her softly as she leaned her head to the side.

"You were made for me," he whispered into her ear.

He turned her around, kissing her passionately as he guided her to the side of the bed, laying her down and slowly lowering himself onto her, the weight of him heavenly—their naked chests, skin to skin, sublime.

"I need you inside me," Ellie pleaded, looking Liam intensely in the eyes.

"I've always been inside you, Elizabeth," he whispered heavily, pressing down, the head of him just parting her slowly and then sinking all the way into her. Filling her. Deeply.

Ellie cried out.

"You are mine." He pressed his pelvis into Ellie's groin and held and then released and then pulled out.

"Don't stop," she begged.

"Just be present, Elizabeth," Liam told her, leaning down to kiss her deeply and then plunged into her again, her body willingly taking in his massive girth. She grabbed his tensed behind in an effort to hold him to her, her hips grinding frantically.

"Don't leave me! Just…keep…" Ellie struggled to speak. The feeling was too exquisite.

"Watch," Liam ordered, turning her head to the mirror.

Liam leaned over her, his flexed arms up on his elbows, her tiny, anxious legs a triangle as he thrust into her over and over. In the mirror, she watched him push in and pull out, taking her just as she had commanded him to do the night before.

I am yours.

She closed her eyes now. *Be present.* She allowed her body to answer his naturally, slowing when he slowed, losing herself in his deep, slow kisses. Then groping madly at his shoulders, his hair, his back when he quickened his thrusts again.

Suddenly he rolled her on top of him as he lay on his back, using his strong hands to guide her hips up and down, up and down the length of him. He pulled her forward, taking her nipple so forcefully into his mouth, sucking so hard, it undid her.

"Oh, God, Liam! Oh, God!"

He thrust up again and again twice more and then let out the most lovely sound Ellie had ever heard— savage, soulful. The sound of Liam Curran satisfied.

She crumpled into a heap on his chest, tears streaming from her eyes.

Fourteen

"Carpe diem, quam minimum credula postero."
May you not inquire - for to know is a sin - what
end the gods have given to me, to you, [...]
May you be wise, strain your wines,
and within a short time
you shall withdraw your long-
lasting hope. While we speak,
envious life will have fled: seize the day,
trusting as little as possible in the future.

—QUINTUS HORATIUS FLACCUS,
"ODE I–XI"

Rain still drummed steadily against the roof, but the dim, gray light of the bedroom gave no hint of time. Was it morning, afternoon? Dusk? Ellie's mind tried to make sense of where she was as she gradually awoke from the depths of a blissfully dreamless sleep, feeling more rested than she had in weeks.

Where am I?

As she struggled to come to, she found her leg intertwined in Liam's as he lay on his stomach, her right arm draped heavily over the hieroglyphs of his cryptic back, rising and falling ever so slightly with the force of his steady breath. She didn't dare move. If he awoke, this perfect moment would be over, this waking in Liam's bed, tangled up in him completely. Could she burrow into his skin, use his body like a shield, be covered by his chest and arms forever, protected, safe?

He can't protect you from yourself, Ellie.

She crushed the thought.

Be present.

Right now. In this moment: bliss.

She ran her hand lightly over his back and then scooted herself just slightly away, allowing her eyes better focus on the puzzle of tattoos. The central image, the black horse, reared up on its hind legs, surrounded by patterns of lighter colors that resembled either flames or bursts of light (meant to be sunshine?). Certainly the images, like any art, could be interpreted differently, but the initial mood of it didn't feel like sunshine to Ellie. The horse's mane trailed down ominously, swirling into blue and gray clouds skirted by mountains, sea, a red-haired mermaid. A large scythe at his left shoulder blade, an obvious symbol of death. And tiny foreign words woven into the waves, bursting from the flames.

Ellie leaned in closer. Were the characters Greek? She strained to make any sense of the words when finally she arrived at the final line as it wove its way through the labyrinth of imagery: Carpe diem, quam minimum credula postero. Latin. *Seize the day, trusting as little as possible in the future.* Her face grew hot with emotion.

Taken in context with the dark imagery, the message wasn't meant to be inspirational. It was a portrait of Liam broken. Liam cynical. Liam in despair. Ellie felt her throat constrict, reaching out to trace the letters with her forefinger. A tattoo that size would have taken many sittings, countless hours, even months to complete—a grief tattoo indeed—the external pain temporarily masking the internal.

"It's quite something, isn't it?" Liam asked quietly, startling Ellie.

Of course he had awoken when she touched him! Why was she so surprised? He could sense her, knew her thoughts, movements, even before she did.

"What happened to her?" Ellie asked bravely as she continued to trace the path of Latin.

"Katherine was thrown from a horse," Liam answered in a whisper.

A dozen questions competed for a voice, but instead, Ellie wisely waited, silently.

"She actually hated horses," he continued. "She was afraid of them. The day she was killed, I forced her to go riding with me. We were on holiday in the Caribbean, and we were galloping down the beach when…"

"Your horse went into the water, but hers got spooked and threw her," Ellie finished his explanation matter-of-factly, surprising even herself.

How do you know this?

She didn't know how she knew. She just did. She had a perfect, distinct picture in her mind, so clear it was as if she'd been there.

Liam rolled over to face her, his eyes narrowing momentarily and then softening.

"Yes," he confirmed. "Her neck was broken instantly. That same neck I'd thought about breaking myself several times."

Ellie gasped in surprise, bringing her hand up to her mouth suddenly.

"That trip was a last-ditch effort, really, to save our marriage. We'd been separated for six months already. That very morning we'd been fighting. I don't even remember about what. It had gotten to the place where we fought about every little thing. I made her get on that horse out of spite, Elizabeth. And when she died, I carried that guilt with me for a very long time," he spoke softly as he ran his hand over his face, rubbing the pressure out of his eyes. "So the tattoos—all of them—were my own self-imposed punishment, a medieval self-flagellation of sorts." He laughed ruefully.

"It must have taken a very long time to complete the entire back," Ellie remarked impersonally; she was unsure how to proceed, how much to pry.

"On and off for about a year and a half," Liam explained. "It wasn't as if I had any plan. The tattoo was a constant work in progress. Any time the grief was too extreme, I'd have an artist add more. The work is pretty varied since I was abroad that entire time, traveling wherever I could climb. I took a leave from the university, at their urging, and found myself all over Europe and Asia, trying to make sense of my life."

Ellie touched the soft brown hair of his chest tenderly, smoothing her hand over his nipple. He grabbed her hand to kiss it.

"You're still so afraid to ask." Liam smiled. "Keeping traits from a Victorian past."

"What do you mean?" Ellie laughed.

"Elizabeth, I can sense your trepidation. Ask me what you will." He lied down on his back, placing his hands behind his head.

"Well, in that case," Ellie exclaimed, straddling him playfully. She leaned down to kiss him, her slightly damp hair creating a dark canopy over them as she thrust her tongue into his mouth aggressively. He answered by pulling her body into his, his strong arms and warm, soft hands embracing her, caressing the bare skin of her back.

Settling on top of him, she pulled her mouth away. "I want to know how you really ended up here, Liam Curran. I want to know how you found your way to the wilds of Wisconsin from the depths of the far East!" Her hips moved naturally to the rhythm of her own passion, steadily increasing with the sensation of Liam's growth beneath her.

"You're no innocent, Elizabeth, are you?" Liam teased, running his hands over her breasts. He rolled her nipples between his thumb and forefingers.

"I never claimed to be." She smiled lasciviously, reaching back to cup him in her hands as she continued to grind up and down. Both their breathing increased as the movement continued.

"You spent an awful lot of time playing coy, Elizabeth. Time we could have spent doing this!" he tried to tease. She had wrapped her hand around him, now fully erect, rendering him momentarily speechless with pleasure. He let out a small, encouraging groan.

"I didn't trust you," Ellie admitted. "You took me forcefully on that library table and then disappeared for days."

"I know." His eyes shot open. In one swift move, he knocked her to the bed and was on top of her, tensed arms supporting the weight of his body above her. "Do you trust me now?" he asked passionately.

"Should I?" Ellie played.

He grabbed both her knees suddenly, forcing her legs up to her chest, as he ran his tongue slowly down her abdomen right to the center of her, plunging deep and wet. Ellie's legs went slack, her stomach and jaw clenched as she sucked in air. His tongue circled repeatedly as he used his lips and teeth to gently taste her, stopping only once to ask, "Do you trust me?"

"Yes, Dr. Curran! I trust you!" she answered sarcastically through gasps for air. His mouth became more forceful as his fingers joined in, accompanying his tongue, entering her slowly at first and then more roughly. Finding the perfect spot, he began to suck. Hard.

"Oh, God, Liam!"

"Do you trust me?" he asked again, his fingers demanding an answer.

"Yes, I trust you, Liam. Yes! Yes!"

Immediately he reclaimed her with his mouth, sending her back arching off the mattress, fingers gripping the sheets. She exploded into an ear-piercing climax, her cries of ecstasy muffled by the driving rain.

"You're not done yet," Liam told her as he climbed back up the bed to lay behind her, draping his long arm over her, his hand smoothing her hair from her cheek and turning her chin upward to meet his face. Swollen and sensitive, she ached from the luscious feel of his throbbing erection against the back of her leg. God, she couldn't get enough of him.

"Why did I come here?" he asked her without waiting for an answer. His salty tongue was already inside her mouth, urgent with need as she grinded into him slowly, seductively. His arm pulled her into him forcefully, holding her back to his chest as they spooned, perfectly fit together.

"You came for me," Ellie said huskily.

"I did," Liam whispered into the back of her neck. "I came here to find you, Elizabeth." He positioned himself to enter her, using his free hand in front to guide himself in gently. Slowly—oh, so slowly—he moved...almost undetectably but for the sublime feeling of him filling her up. The sensation of complete fullness.

I belong to you. Take me.

She couldn't control the reaction of her body, which seemed to move of its own free will. Her hips circled madly against his pelvis and abdomen, forcing Liam to restrain her with his arm.

"You can't be still, can you?" he bit her shoulder lightly. "Let me be inside you. Let me..." he struggled for control over his breath. "Let me live inside you, just...for a moment."

Ellie caught her breath and consciously stilled the motion of her hips.

Be present.

Prying Liam's hand from around her waist, she licked the tips of his fingers and then kissed them gently, finally taking his forefinger into her mouth. She began to suck harder and harder until she felt him stirring inside her, the movement of his hips, and then mirroring the intensity of her mouth.

Soon he was freeing his hand in order to pull Ellie into him as he pounded against her back, emptying himself into her with a loud bellow. She followed directly after him, blinded by the raw intensity of a second climax.

Still spooning, Liam gathered Ellie into both his arms, covering her completely with his body, just as she'd imagined.

I could stay like this forever.

"Why did you come here to find me?" Ellie asked quietly without turning around.

"That's a long story," Liam answered. "Are you sure you're ready to know?"

"I think I've proven that I'm ready." Ellie laughed tiredly.

"Carpe diem, quam minimum credula postero," Liam recited in the loveliest Italian accent, stopping decisively as if that answered the question completely.

Ellie looked back at Liam with questioning eyes.

Go on!

"I had that transcribed on my back not long after Katherine died. That last line was actually one of the first tattoos. 'Seize the day!' I kept thinking. Seize the day: as in 'you better seize the day because time is short—you better live it up because like Katherine, you might die young!' So I traveled to places as foreign to England as I could find. And I drowned my sorrows in liquor and women, attempting to 'seize the day,' if you will. It really was a shallow, bitter mantra I repeated over and over to myself to try to justify my indulgent, avoidant behaviors."

"You were heartbroken." The words came from Ellie's mouth more as a statement than a question.

"No," Liam answered ironically, an audible ring of true shame present in his response. "I wasn't heartbroken at all. Just broken."

A long, pensive silence fell over them as the hypnotic cadence of rain drummed against the roof. The bedroom was shrouded in shadow, timeless and still, as the two laid naked on the bed, entwined in one another, surrounded by a mess of white, cotton sheets.

"Eventually I ended up in Nepal," he continued, finally, "really just to climb Everest. I had decided that if I could climb to the highest point on earth, then I could do anything, including overcoming the pain I felt." He released Ellie so that he could prop himself on his elbow in order to face her.

"The problem was—I was so blinded by my own self-pity that I couldn't even identify my true emotions in order to heal. One minute, I was angry with myself, angry with Katherine for dying. The next I was horribly depressed; I believed that I had killed my wife. I was certain I was cursed—certain I would never be loved by anyone ever again."

Ellie touched his face compassionately.

"The truth was that Katherine and I hated each other at the end. We were poisonous to one another, each bringing out the most hateful qualities in the other. And I was just as much to blame as she was…I was just as much to blame."

He ran his fingers thoughtfully over Ellie's chest, tracing the shape of her breast, up over her nipple, an absentminded tenderness.

"The fact was that I had wasted Katherine's life. Her existence with me was short and unhappy, and I felt responsible for that. And my guilt was made even worse by the fact that on some level, I was…" He paused.

Ellie waited compassionately.

"On some level, I was relieved," Liam choked out and then fell silent while he carefully chose his words. "Relieved that I didn't have to fight with her anymore. Relieved that I didn't have to try to love someone I no longer loved. Relieved that I didn't have to continue the act. Relieved maybe to finally be alone to figure out who the hell I was."

The words, so precisely chosen, stung Ellie. He meant for them to resonate, deep inside that festering wound that Ellie bandaged with mock ambivalence, her own unhappy marriage. A long, intentional pause was his obvious invitation for her to speak.

"I know what you felt, Liam. Obviously my own marriage is a farce," Ellie offered.

It was not enough.

"Why have you stayed with Alec all this time?" Liam pressed.

"I've stayed for my son. Why else? Isn't that reason enough?" Ellie asked without defense. "And besides, what else is there?"

"Who knows what else there is? You've just given up," Liam answered passionately.

"I thought we were talking about why you came to find me."

"This *is* why I came for you," Liam insisted. "Don't you see?"

"No," Ellie admitted with frustration, "I don't understand."

"When I attempted to climb Mt. Everest the first time, I failed. And that's when *you* found *me*! That was the beginning of my spiritual awakening."

Ellie watched as Liam's face became more animated and passionate as he grew absorbed in the storytelling. She wondered what version he had told his students. It certainly wasn't this one.

"On the first climb, weather conditions had defeated us. Too much wind and barely any visibility. Honestly I hadn't enough mental fortitude to push myself. The

Sherpa I'd hired for the climb was this wonderful, wise older gentleman, devoutly Buddhist. He knew about Katherine and why I had come to Everest. He knew I was a mess. When we failed to reach the summit, he told me I wasn't yet ready. He told me to find my path and come back when I was stronger. I didn't understand what the bloody hell he was talking about, but I felt like that climb was the only passage to my salvation. I had to make it up there!"

"So you obviously did what he said. You made it to the top eventually," Ellie said.

"I did," Liam continued. "I went down to Kathmandu. Spent a few weeks sleeping in. Reading. Touring monasteries and temples. I immersed myself in the local culture as much as I could. Instead of soothing myself with liquor, I began to meditate on my own. It just happened naturally, like I was finally really ready to stop self-destructing. Being surrounded by the abject poverty that I saw every day there, people in the villages burning bodies and letting the ashes wash down river toward the women bent over their daily wash loads—other women using the water for cooking. Suddenly it made my life seem ridiculous. What did I know of suffering when compared with that?

So one night, I was in the lobby of my hotel and I happen to overhear two people speaking perfect English with British accents! I was so overwhelmingly happy that I rushed over like a fool and introduced myself! It turned out this gentleman and his wife were literature professors from Manchester on holiday for their tenth wedding anniversary. I ended up having dinner with them in the hotel that night and mentioned how desperate I was for reading material. My Internet service in Katmandu was spotty at best, and English magazines or newspapers were so sparse. No worries, Evelyn, the wife, told me. Before I retired that evening, she brought me three well-worn journals, one of which was a copy of *The Antioch Review*, featuring an essay by the very notable Dr. Elizabeth Purnell!"

"The essay on elegies." Ellie sighed. He had told her this once before, but as was her instinct, she had brushed it off. Protected herself from having to explain the circumstances of that essay.

"Yes." Liam's eyes flashed brilliantly. "For years, I wondered at the perfect timing of that essay. What bizarre coincidence. I no longer believe in happenstance. I know your words were meant to reach me."

"I wrote that essay around the time you published *American Mask*," Ellie explained. "When I found out this spring that you were coming to the university for a debate series, everyone in the English department gave me such a hard time about not being familiar with your work. Didn't I remember the acclaim your book had? Hadn't I read *American Mask*? But that year of my life was a blur; Jordan had just been diagnosed with diabetes and…well, he was the only thing I cared about. I didn't know what was going on in the outside world."

"Ironically the public success of that book was over-shadowed by the personal failure of my marriage," Liam explained. "Katherine died not long after the book's publication, and then, of course, I faded into obscurity. It would seem that you and I endured the greatest challenges of our lifetimes simultaneously. Just continents away. But then, by some divine plan, you wrote that essay!"

"I didn't know what else to do," Ellie choked out. The memory of Jordan's brush with death lived just under the surface. The smallest mention, like a scratch, sent a fresh wave of despair.

"You thought he was going to die?" Liam asked, already knowing the answer.

"I did," Ellie admitted, her throat constricting. "And I felt so guilty for all the time I had spent worrying about trivial shit. Why had I left him to go back to work? Why couldn't I have given him a more perfect life?"

"And that became the basis of your essay," Liam said with conviction.

"Yes!" Tears threatened the corners of Ellie's eyes. She felt relieved to finally articulate what had been buried mute within her for so long. "Isn't it really what we all feel when someone dies? Guilt? Why didn't I spend more time with this person? Why didn't I confide more in this person? Why didn't I tell this person I loved him more often?"

Liam took Ellie into his arms, smoothing her hair.

"I read your essay that night, Elizabeth, even as I struggled to see by the dim light of the crappy night-stand lamp. And literally it brought me to tears. It was the most poignant, beautifully written essay I'd ever read. And your claim that anyone with true faith would not write an elegy went to the core of my personal dilemma. My grief was due to my lack of faith, my lack of trust in perfect order. The belief that everything is as it should be."

"The essay was written out of my own grief, Liam, not any strong spiritual convictions of my own," Ellie admitted. "If anything, I was angry when I wrote that."

"You don't think I know that?" Liam laughed gently.

"I made a deal with God that I would never ask for anything again for as long as I lived if Jordan could just recover," Ellie whispered, her face flush against Liam's chest. "So maybe, really, that's the reason I never left my marriage."

"Do you think that's how it works?" Liam asked, somewhat amused.

"I don't know," Ellie murmured.

"The truth spoke through you, and yet you ignored your own words!" Liam exclaimed. "You will never find peace until you accept that you can't control the events of your life. Your guilt comes from the belief that you have willingly done wrong—chosen wrong—messed up somehow, when in reality, everything is exactly as it should be."

"All of that suffering we did?" Ellie asked.

"Life *is* suffering." Liam smiled gently. "That is the first noble truth. But life is also perfection. And beauty!" His eyes flashed brightly. "'I thank you God for most this amazing day: for the leaping greenly spirits of trees and a blue true dream of sky; and for everything which is natural which is infinite which is yes.'"

"Liam!" Ellie laughed. "Who could argue with a man that quotes poetry so easily? No wonder you're so convincing," she teased. "Who is that?"

"E.E. Cummings. Lovely, isn't it?"

Ellie sighed, "It is. Almost as lovely you, Dr. Curran. I just wish I found comfort in that."

"That's why I've come for you," Liam explained, taking Ellie's lips and kissing them softly. "Unbeknownst to you, your own writing, so raw, so honest, led me on a path to my own enlightenment. You may believe that it was just coincidental, but I don't. It was destined. Your ideas transformed the message on my back, Elizabeth. Carpe Diem, 'seize the day,' came to mean 'be present in the now.' Not 'live it up because I fear my inevitable death.'"

He kissed her again, chastely. It was more than she could bear.

He came here for you. He came here to find you.

Ellie deepened the kiss, running her hands over Liam's chest. He was so warm and hard. Before she knew it, she was beneath him again, feeling the pressure of his heavenly weight.

"Do you want me to make love to you again?" he breathed silkily.

"Yes," Ellie managed to say before Liam gently entered her. Once again, she was overcome by comfort and euphoria, a feeling of completion.

You love him.

She held Liam to her, burying her face in the crook of his neck, deeply breathing in the delicious scent of him.

She *did* love him. Oh, God! She did. His ironic smile, the curls in his sideburns, the shift of his accent when he was angry, the sound of his voice when he sang, his easy, disarming laughter, his animated green eyes, the curve of his lower back, the way his presence illuminated a room.

I love him.

How did this happen? How?

"Liam," Ellie whispered into his ear as he moved his hips ever so slowly, pushing himself just slightly out of her and back in again, caressing her insides patiently, lovingly. "I believe you."

"I know, my darling," Liam answered, taking her mouth. His tongue slipped in to find hers, a kiss so intense, Ellie couldn't determine where she ended and

Liam began. They dissolved into one another—mouth, arms, hands, hips, a single heart beating in sync as they reached climax together.

For some time afterward, they both lay quietly spent, basking in each other's satisfied glow.

"I'm starving," Ellie announced finally.

"You are?" Liam popped up on his elbow enthusiastically. "That's wonderful news! By the feel of your hipbones, I can tell you haven't eaten all week. Let me feed you!"

"I'll let you do anything you want." Ellie grinned. It was true too.

"I'll keep that in mind." Liam smiled mischievously as he rolled out of bed and slipped on a pair of briefs that he grabbed from his dresser.

"Oh, don't cover that perfect body of yours," Ellie begged.

"If I don't, we'll never get any food cooked, Elizabeth. I would just be inside you for the rest of the day. Maybe forever. Maybe I would never leave you!"

If only that could be true.

Ellie just laughed in agreement. She hurried to find a small throw to wrap around her nude body so that she could follow him into the kitchen. Even a second away from him seemed unfathomable.

"Come with me." He beckoned. "I don't dare let you out of my sight. Like a dream, you may vanish into thin air!"

"Sometimes I feel as if you can read my mind, Liam," Ellie admitted.

"You're cold. Come here," he said, opening a drawer and pulling out a long-sleeved Henley. He helped Ellie into it as she lifted her arms, allowing him one last look at her exposed body. His gaze was both sensuous and familiar, imbuing her with a sense of confidence and acceptance that she'd never known before. Was it really only hours ago that Liam had first appraised her nude body? It seemed like the most natural thing in the world to stand before him naked.

Once she was covered, he drew her close to him, shrouding her in his embrace. Kissing her forehead, he asked, "What would you like to eat?"

"Whatever you want to make me, Dr. Curran. Surprise me."

"OK." He smiled. "I know just the thing."

Taking her by the hand, he led her to the kitchen and instructed her to sit at the counter as he poured her a glass of orange juice.

He caught her glancing at the clock.

"Do you have to be somewhere?" Liam asked, only partially joking. Ellie's heart sank.

No, not right now. Not yet.

It was 3:00 p.m.

"Not until tomorrow night, I suppose," Ellie answered honestly. No more hiding from him. She would try to be as direct as she comfortably could.

"That's a long time off," Liam observed. "Be present now."

"I am," Ellie promised.

"Shall I get rid of all the clocks?" he joked.

"I would have you still time if you could, Liam. Let's just be stuck forever in right now!" Ellie replied sentimentally.

Liam reached under the cabinet for a mixing bowl, smiling radiantly at Ellie's words. Taking out eggs, flour, milk, he set to work creating something for the skillet. "You know," he mused, "before I could Google any images of you, I imagined your beautiful face exactly as it looks now."

"How's that?" Ellie asked, brushing her hair from her face.

"Happy," Liam answered as he continued his measuring and stirring. "I envisioned this tragic brown-haired goddess before me developing a light in her eyes. Much like the light I see now." He continued talking as he rummaged through the refrigerator, pulling out fresh blueberries. "Of course, there was never anything in your writing that gave me any clues to your physical description. Perhaps I just created a vision of you from what I knew of your father and his photos."

"So did you Google me much?" Ellie asked with a laugh.

"Yes. Probably even more than you Googled me!" Liam teased. "I thought your face was going to burst into flames when I caught your computer open in Chicago."

Ellie laughed outright, clasping her hands together. "Yes, I was checking out your wife, I'm ashamed to admit."

"Well, I was terribly flattered. The most disinterested, possibly coldest woman on earth was showing some interest finally!" Liam laughed.

"I'm not cold," Ellie denied, feeling slightly offended.

"I'm only joking, Elizabeth! I know you're not cold. You forget I am also a student of Avery Vaughn."

"I didn't forget, Liam," Ellie answered. "How did you find her anyway? How did you figure out that Avery is me?"

"Ha! Another event that was meant!" Liam winked. "*I* didn't find Avery Vaughn. She found *me.* Just as Elizabeth Purnell and the essay on elegies found me."

Liam turned away from Ellie to start the burner on the stove, the mural of his back and broad shoulders fully exposed. How quickly it seemed all their secrets had been revealed. That tattoo. Ellie never would have guessed.

"A few months after I returned to England, I was teaching a class on twentieth-century American poetry, and one of my students actually wrote an essay about your father. The thesis? I'm not making this up—the thesis was that this mysterious Avery Vaughn, Internet phenom, was a student of James Lawson! And then he speculated over whether or not she was a mistress, what with the admissions your father made in his writing." Liam turned to gauge Ellie's reaction.

"Yeah, Avery is student of sorts." Ellie laughed ironically, shaking her head. "Oh, the things I learned from my father."

"This student's paper actually compared Vaughn's and Lawson's poetry side-by-side, citing several descriptions, metaphors, phrasing similarities, and syntax that was nearly identical. And then, of course, there was this constant reference to a river, the description of which was so identical to both poets that they had to be related somehow."

"Well, it's difficult to write originally when your authentic voice is so deeply influenced by your parents, I suppose," Ellie commented. "Of course I sound like my father. We all sound like our parents."

"That was my theory exactly!" Liam exclaimed triumphantly. "My student had stumbled onto something, but he didn't quite grasp the whole truth. Maybe he didn't know James Lawson had a daughter who, like him, was an English professor. But I knew immediately you were Avery Vaughn. After I'd read your essay in Nepal, I had developed this reverent gratefulness toward you, and I was almost obsessive about reading everything you'd ever published in an effort to find out more about you. Imagine the joy I

E. J. Densmore

felt at my good fortune when your poetry happened to find me!"

Ellie sat quietly at the counter, silent with humility. Writing had always been an exercise in self-preservation. To think that her words had actually influenced others, inspired them!

And then, there was the story her poems told. She shifted uncomfortably in her seat.

"Oh, Elizabeth, don't," Liam told her gently. "I see your expression darkening." He shut off the burner and walked around the island, leaning down to kiss Ellie tenderly. She placed her hands at his waist, sliding her fingers just inside the waistband.

"I thought you were hungry!" He laughed as he pulled away. "We will never eat at this rate! Stop tempting me!"

"Fine! Finish cooking." Ellie allowed him to return to the stove where she could watch him again.

Within minutes, he set before her a perfect plate of three small blueberry crepes sprinkled with powdered sugar.

"How…" formed on Ellie's lips, a look of such surprise, alarm almost, that Liam stepped back.

"You don't like crepes?" he asked, perplexed.

"I love crepes, Liam," Ellie answered softly, an overwhelming sense of familiarity seizing her. "This was my father's apology dish. Whenever he would return from one of his episodes, he would make Becca and me as many blueberry crepes as we could eat. We would stuff ourselves until we were sick." She took a small, cautious bite, rolling it around in her mouth, savoring the taste.

"I make no apologies today," Liam said, his eyes softening. "I hated traditional English breakfasts as a kid. Have you ever had black pudding?" He laughed.

"No," Ellie answered between bites.

"Blood sausage. It's as foul as it sounds. My mother would make me crepes instead, much to my father's ire," Liam explained. He watched Ellie eat with intense satisfaction. Picking up his own plate, he leaned against the counter next to her to eat.

"My father stopped cooking us crepes after my mother accused him of learning the recipe from one of his French mistresses," Ellie confided. It was a memory that had been buried deep in the recesses of her psyche until just now.

"Did your parents fight much?" Liam asked.

"No. Never. I just happened to overhear that in passing. My mother preferred to wear him down with her snide comments, her passive-aggressive ambivalence," Ellie explained bitterly.

"And yet, they're still married," Liam noted. "Why do you think that is?"

"Love?" Ellie wondered doubtfully.

"Perhaps," Liam replied. "How can we say what is meant between two people? What lessons they have to learn from one another. Perhaps staying in an unhappy relationship is a lack of faith," Liam suggested, taking another bite of crepe without looking away.

"How so?" Ellie challenged.

"It is the ultimate resignation. The acceptance that there is nothing more fulfilling or life affirming waiting for you than your current situation. The belief that there is no greater happiness to be found," Liam explained.

"That might be true," Ellie agreed. "But it could also be a different sort of faith—an undying belief that you can still recapture the dream."

"And what dream is that?" Liam asked skeptically.

"The dream you have of ideal love when you're young. Before you've ever been hurt or disappointed. The dream you have before you're jaded. When the world 'seems to lie before you like a land of dreams, so various, so beautiful, so new.' The dream that you will marry your soul mate and have babies and live happily ever after," Ellie concluded with a rueful laugh. "Certainly you must know that type of faith, Liam. After all, you stayed married to Katherine long after things had disintegrated. You even tried one last time to patch things up by taking a trip together."

"Yes, and now I am looking at this from a completely different perspective," Liam gently insisted. "Things appear much different now that she's gone. I know now how limited our time is in this life, and that Katherine and I should have let each other go much sooner."

"You didn't have children," Ellie added, getting at the true heart of the matter. "Here's the paradox, Liam: the more a person loses faith that the dream is attainable for him- or herself, the greater the belief that he or she can craft and control the dream for his or her children. And most of the time, that means staying married, maintaining the charade for the sake of the child's happiness."

"How did that work for you? Being the child of a charade?" Liam countered.

"I'm still not sure if it *was* a charade." Ellie laughed. "I guess Maggie and Jim Lawson have done a stellar job of confusing me…or, like all children, maybe I have chosen to see only half-truths in regards to my parents. I don't really know whether or not they love each other or hate each other. Maybe there's a fine line between the two."

Liam quietly pondered what Ellie had said as he scraped the last of the blueberries into his mouth. "I suspect you gave up your faith in the dream long before you married Alec," he mused finally, still standing so close to Ellie that the soft hair of his legs brushed her knees.

Ellie felt her cheek twitch just ever so slightly. He was referring to Dylan.

"I guess I probably did," she admitted, the limited memory of her heatstroke experience on the apartment floor appearing like a hazy nightmare. Now that she was nearly forty, she felt a fierce instinct to protect the memory of her twenty-five-year-old self, that sweet, ignorant fool! Ellie envied that younger self, the girl who still believed the world was a land of dreams. A girl full of hope (Her parents be damned! She was sure her marriage was going to be different. Life for her would be different!)

"Dylan Ross?" Liam asked, setting down his plate. Pushing Ellie's legs apart with his free hands, he moved to stand between them as he pulled Ellie forward. "He was not the one, Elizabeth."

"I know, Liam. I just regret that I let him crush my soul and send me on a trajectory toward disaster," Ellie lamented.

"No, you didn't, Elizabeth. Everything that happened was part of what was meant. And it sent you on a trajectory toward me," he insisted.

Ellie smiled weakly, turning her head upward to look into Liam's sincere eyes.

"I don't suspect Avery Vaughn would accept a doomed fate so willingly." Liam snickered. "Why hasn't she been allowed to make any decisions?"

"Ahh, that Avery." Ellie laughed. "She has only a voice, but no true power. I suppose she's only reactive, not proactive. I would say at this stage of my life, most major decisions have been made."

"Nonsense!" Liam argued. "Avery has all the power. You just have to stop hiding behind her."

Ellie didn't respond, instead letting the air settle between her and Liam. Why didn't Avery make the decisions? Well, she was a loose cannon, that's why. Should Ellie ever truly unleash Avery Vaughn, there might be no reigning her back in. Avery was the embodiment of chaos, Ellie unchecked, pure emotion, the type of rage and grief and disappointment that was just too painful to face head on. No one could be that honest without some sort of emotional breakdown *(like Daddy)*.

Being here with Liam was "Avery" enough.

"You already know why I can't be Avery," Ellie finally responded.

"Because that would mean admitting your true feelings, your failures, to the world. And admitting you are human makes you feel weak. Makes you feel as though you've lost control of your life," Liam said, rattling off his theory.

"Yes," Ellie admitted. "Avery is the guise that allows me to be honest, to speak freely."

"But the people to whom you are speaking don't know to listen. Dylan. Alec. Your parents," Liam argued. "And the greatest irony is the fact that the control you think you have is falsely perceived. None of us have control."

Ellie stood up suddenly, throwing her arms above her head. "I admit it! I am Avery Vaughn! Otherwise known as Elizabeth Lawson Purnell! I have no control of my life!" she yelled into the air mockingly.

Liam grabbed her head, his tongue insistently entering her mouth.

Instantly they were a frenzy of hands as he swiped the plates off the counter, sending them crashing to the floor. He lifted Ellie onto the island, madly groping at her shirt to reveal her erect nipples, taking one into his mouth as he freed himself hastily from his briefs. Before Ellie could even reach out to touch him, he entered her urgently, passionately, with a loud, low moan of ecstasy.

"Stop mocking me, Elizabeth! You want to give up control, don't you?" Liam demanded.

"Oh, God, Liam!" Ellie cried out in pleasure as she tried to catch her breath. "This is the only way I can."

He smiled slightly, deviantly, as he pulled out and then slammed back into her. "That's fine, Avery Elizabeth." He moaned. "You don't have to pretend anymore. You don't have to hold back. You were made for me. Just be."

"Liam…" Ellie gasped as her words died on her lips. She fell back against the counter as he held her by the waist, pulling her into him over and over again. She would relinquish her "perceived" control and simply be present in the moment, immersed in the sublime pleasure of a rough, raw screw on the kitchen counter this rainy day, thunder crashing all around.

Liam's shuddering climax was followed by Ellie's long, loud finish and a round of uncontrollable laughter as she hugged him to her with legs wrapped around his back.

"Are you trying to teach me a lesson in letting go, Dr. Curran?" Ellie teased hoarsely. All the hard breathing and screaming out were wearing on her vocal cords.

"Yes, and you're a fine student," Liam mumbled from the place on her chest where his head had fallen postcoital. He kissed a path up to her mouth, settling gently there for several minutes. "Let's stay nude all weekend, shall we?"

"Whatever you wish, Liam," Ellie whispered, once again feeling bittersweet.

She knew this couldn't last.

Fifteen

"We both step and do not step into the
same rivers. We are and are not."

—Heraclitus

For once, the weather that bittersweet weekend delivered everything the forecasts promised—lightning, winds, horizontal rain. It kept the forest surrounding Mrs. Dobb's cottage, quiet, the wildlife tucked in its nests, the sun banished, the college students holed up in their homes, their dorms, the streets empty, the world temporarily still. It also kept Liam and Ellie locked in one another's arms, blissfully separated from the outside world, suspended in time, every sublime minute alone, a gift. As planned, they had spent the two days barely dressed, confiding every minuscule detail of their lives, Liam playing guitar, stopping only to eat occasionally before they continued to make love in every room of the house.

"Must you go?" Liam had leaned against the jamb of the bedroom door, shirtless, boxers hanging low on his hips, running his hands through his disheveled hair, impish wisps winging out near his lovely ears. The sight of him tugged at Ellie's heart. He knew the answer even as he asked it.

Beg me to stay! (Even though she wouldn't—couldn't). The thought of Alec and Jordan pulling into the driveway to find her gone—missing all weekend—was still a greater fear than walking away from this happiness. She left Liam with one last long, passionate kiss, committing the smell of him to her memory, the taste of him heavy on her tongue.

"I'll wait for you in the morning, then," he promised at once when she didn't respond. He refused to walk her to the door. It seemed too much for him to let her go.

And so they met to "run" every morning the following week, which turned out to be very short runs indeed, beginning at the top of the hill where Liam waited for Ellie, a mile from her home, and always ending in Liam's bed. These early-morning trysts ensured that they had some time alone together each day, enough time to make suffering through their public act, maintaining their professional personas at the college, almost bearable.

"Do you want to actually run this morning?" Ellie asked Liam the next Saturday when she knew they had a bit of extra time; she had used Thursday's debate as an excuse to be gone all day, "preparing" for it in her office.

"I'd rather make love to you instead." Liam laughed quizzically, pulling Ellie into him to kiss her passionately, boldly exposed on the open county road.

"We have time for both!" Ellie promised, pressing her body receptively against Liam, answering his need. She grabbed his hand.

"Very well," he said, giving in and following her resumed pace, down the hill and around the bend, a different route than they used to take (back when they actually ran).

They jogged for some time, half a mile or so, before Ellie led Liam off road into a dense pine forest. When she glanced up to assess his reaction, a smirk played across his face.

"You seem to know these woods quite well, Elizabeth. Where are you taking me?" he asked.

"You'll see!" She grinned with satisfaction. She continued jogging through the trees carefully, Liam following close behind.

At some point, they encountered a fence and slid carefully through its slats. Slowing their pace to a walk, both caught their labored breath as their bodies adjusted. Ellie had run them hard. Within moments, Liam became vaguely aware of a very distinct sound, one which grew increasingly louder the farther in they walked: running water.

Suddenly the trees opened up, early-morning sun reflected up from the ground, a million blinding beams pulsing rhythmically.

The river!

A wide grin broke across Liam's face, answered by Ellie's pleased expression. He understood.

"Your fabled water," Liam stated, moving forward toward the gentle flow. This patch of the river was narrow and slow moving, more a stream with its bed exposed, scattered outcroppings of rocks creating an easily navigable path across. Liam approached the water, slowly, reverently, the light engulfing him as he left the shade of the forest to stand on the bank. Ellie followed and then stopped abruptly.

A peculiar, unidentifiable emotion overtook her, some weird sense of nostalgia, as if Liam had walked here with her a thousand times. And yet, as she watched curiously while he leaned down to scoop water onto his flushed face, he appeared as if he had been transplanted here suddenly, an alien, foreign to this scene, a bright, shiny oddity visibly out of place, obscenely conspicuous on the bank. Did he really belong to this spot?

"Why did you bring me here?" Liam asked gently. He walked back toward Ellie, brushing a stray hair from her face.

"I needed to see you in this place," she answered, struggling to articulate her motivations. "It makes you real...It makes you fit into the schema of my life, I guess. Maybe I brought you here because I need you to understand."

Liam waited patiently, a spark of sympathy in his eyes.

"This is where I came to be alone as a kid," Ellie explained. "Back then, this river represented hope. Possibility. The beauty of nature. I used to ride out here all the time by myself to be alone. I'd stop and let my horse drink. Sometimes I would write. Meditate on life's great questions at age twelve!"

Liam smiled compassionately.

"My father, as it turned out, came out here too. During one of his episodes—those times when he would separate himself from our family, locking himself in his library for weeks—I happened to catch him sneaking out. When I saw him late one afternoon, my first reaction was to yell to him. To jump off my horse and run to him and throw my arms around him. But he wasn't himself. He was absorbed in melancholy, so depressed, he seemed to be wandering the woods aimlessly. I stopped my horse and watched him as he undressed and bathed in the river, cleansing himself of sadness or shame or whatever fucked-up emotions kept him from being with us."

"Did you understand why he came down here?" Liam asked almost soothingly.

"Not really," Ellie admitted. "I had a sense that the river was some sort of purifying ritual, but I didn't truly get it until I read his poetry as an adult." She kicked a stone absently as her eyes surveyed the opposite shore. "My dad had this obsession with Nietzsche's theory of 'eternal return.' You know, the question of whether or not our actions continue on in perpetuity or whether we live once and every action is gone—lost forever—once it occurs. He still muses in his writing over whether or not what we do matters wholly or not at all. When we were kids, he loved to quote Heraclitus to Becca and me."

"In between quoting Whitman!" Liam laughed.

"Yeah." Ellie laughed bitterly in return. "He would always say, 'You can't step twice into the same river.' As if that was supposed to give us permission to do whatever we pleased without repercussion. As if it gave him permission too."

"And did it?"

"I don't know," Ellie lamented. "Even then, I knew it was all bullshit coming from him. Almost like he was just trying to convince *himself* by saying those things to us—like repeating over and over 'You can't step into the same river twice' was some sort of mantra meant to erase his infidelities. Like that made it all OK." Ellie sighed heavily, rubbing her face in thought. "I grew to hate this river because I knew he came down here to try and wash himself clean. But bathing in this water didn't make it all OK; a person's actions don't just wash away, Liam. Everything my father did left an indelible mark."

She walked farther down the shore, away from Liam and then turned suddenly to face him. "And now, here I am with you. How am I any different?"

"Is that what you believe?" Liam smiled sadly.

"I don't know what I believe!" Ellie cried out in desperation.

"You're still imprisoned by your father's thinking, tortured by the same ignorant assumption that you have control of the universe somehow, that you can craft your own destiny, and so need to carry around guilt for any misstep. How exhausting it must be to calculate every single action one makes so as not to 'mess up,'" Liam argued. "Sure, your actions affect others, but it's your intent that weighs heavily on your karma. Do you liken our relationship to your father's affairs?"

"I don't know," Ellie admitted.

"Exactly, Elizabeth," Liam continued with fervor. "You *don't* know. You have no idea why your father acted the way he did. And it's not your place to know. I never lived your life, but I'm a student of your father's poetry, and I say unequivocally that your father's affairs and our relationship are not the same." He swayed suddenly, putting his hand up to his face.

"Are you all right?" Ellie rushed to him with concern. As she reached out to grab him, his arm felt dry and impossibly hot. He leaned into her arms weakly, remaining silent. "You're burning up, Liam!" her voice cracked with alarm.

Gradually he knelt down at the riverbank, removing his shirt to submerge it in the water. The black horse on Liam's back reared up toward the late July sun.

You've been here before.

Ellie loomed over him helplessly.

As he looked up at her from the bank of water, reflected light created a blinding halo around his crimson face. "Rid yourself of any doubt, Elizabeth. I came here for you, and now I know it was the right thing to do."

Taking the wet shirt from him, she wrung it onto his back and neck, sending tiny rivulets over the weaving Latin. He stood slowly, negotiating his balance.

"Are you OK?" Ellie asked with concern. "You're so hot."

"You're abusing me by running me all over the countryside. I'm fine." He waved his hand dismissively at her. "Had I not sought you out, you'd be traversing these back woods, regretting the steps of your life ad infinitum. Now this is what you can live over and over instead," he demanded, pulling her face into his and kissing her deeply.

Every muscle in her body relaxed at his scorching touch. He was right. (In that moment, he was right.) Nothing else mattered.

"I love you!" Ellie cried out wistfully. "Oh, God. I love you stupidly, Liam Curran, with 'my childhood's faith'!"

Liam's eyes blinked slowly as he sighed, absorbing the full weight of her words before he replied.

"I have always loved you, my darling. I will love you eternally."

"You're sure you can handle me, Dr. Curran?" Ellie whispered playfully into Liam's ear during John Long's introductions. They sat next to one another at a long conference table underneath the dancing leaves of three massive cottonwood trees in the center of the university quad. A light wind blew the corners of the linen cloth that had been laid across the table. Liam had arrived at their debate with only a blank pad of paper and a pen.

Ellie had brought a stack of notes and the scent of their lovemaking still heavy in the folds of her skirt.

When he had cornered her in the empty lecture hall just a half an hour before, she had accused him of trying to distract her.

He had only laughed. "I am just trying to heighten your understanding of the novel, Elizabeth. A firsthand account of *The Scarlet Letter*, if you will. You can be Hester!"

She had laughed in return, but just the slightest bit uneasily. She *was* a Hester of sorts (or so she believed), and he was going to challenge her on it openly. She knew it. But not until he made sure he claimed her roughly against the back wall of the darkened auditorium.

"I am quite well enough to handle you, Dr. Purnell," he answered in a clipped voice, her married name sticking in his throat. He did look better, healthier than he had all week. Less feverish.

She smiled back at him knowingly. He was ready for a fight, and she could probably guess which one: he wanted her to leave Alec.

And he knows if he uses literature as a metaphor—if he does it in front of an audience, you will have to listen to his arguments.

What's to argue? I would follow him to the ends of the earth—if only circumstances were different. Besides he may have professed his love to me, but he never asked me to run away with him.

"As per Dr. Curran's suggestion," John Long said, continuing the introduction, "the debate tonight will focus on the American classic *The Scarlet Letter* by Nathaniel Hawthorne. American literature of the Romantic period is Dr. Curran's area of expertise."

"It is, Dr. Long," Ellie replied, "but since Dr. Curran was so shamefully beaten at our last debate, I thought it only fair to give him first choice of subject matter in this one." The audience burst into surprised laughter, accompanied by John Long's stunned face. Obviously this informal tone was not the one her humorless boss had expected the debate to take. Liam laughed openly at Ellie's taunting, pleased with her unabashed familiarity.

Shit! You're supposed to be acting professional. Stop flirting.

Too late. She spotted Marta and Becca in the audience, two rows from the front. Marta had her hand over her mouth.

Consciously straightening up in her seat, Ellie clasped her hands formally in front of her on the table.

"Dr. Purnell did most graciously allow me to choose the topic of this debate," Liam answered. "I have indeed written several essays on Hawthorne. For this debate, I presume she's actually read some of my work in preparation for it." He winked almost imperceptibly, a small smirk playing across his face.

Touché!

Over the last eight weeks, Ellie had, in fact, read everything Liam had ever published. Obsessively. If she couldn't be physically near him, she could live inside his head. Pore over his words, memorize them. Hold his books to her chest. Trace the lines of his beautiful face on the glossy back cover of his publications. Google him impulsively, a lovesick school girl. She was not the researcher he was, turning up papers from his days in undergrad, but she had scoured every book of essays he'd ever penned. She was now, unequivocally, an expert in Liam Curran.

"I'd prefer to think of this debate as more of a panel discussion, albeit a very small panel," Liam explained. "Let us call this a 'discussion,' as that word seems more intimate and less contentious." He emphasized the word "intimate," touching Ellie's hand briefly. Her cheeks flushed crimson for a fleeting moment.

Stop! I can barely sit still next to you! You're giving me away!

"Very well," John Long agreed. "Would you like to begin, Dr. Curran?"

"Absolutely," Liam replied after Ellie nodded consent.

As Liam launched into an explanation of the novel's plot, Ellie absently scanned the audience. Roughly sixty people, mostly English professors and students, a much smaller crowd than the first debate drew, sat under the tent that had been set up. She spotted her father a row behind Marta and Becca, sandwiched between Megan and one of Liam's foreign-exchange students.

No Maggie Lawson this time.

Mom worked an excuse to get out of this one! Figures.

The sun gradually moved behind the trees, casting long, wistful shadows over the crosswalks. But for the cherubic sound of Liam's voice, the university quad seemed eerily still. Ellie's heart ached suddenly. Summer would be ending soon. What then?

She sighed heavily when, out of the corner of her eye, a flash of red caught her attention. A shifting movement to the left of Megan, two people over. Jordan's soccer jersey.

Jordan?

Sitting next to Jordan, hands clasped rigidly in his lap, was his father. Alec! His eyes locked with Ellie's.

No nod. No smile. His impassive face stared directly at her, unaltered.

Ellie's heart rattled madly in its cage.

Oh my God, why is he here? He didn't tell me he was going to come! He never comes to these things.

She feigned a smile at him. Still nothing. Alec looked from Ellie to Liam and back again, observing, calculating, sizing them up.

He knows.

"And do you agree with this?" John Long directed the question at Ellie.

Her head snapped toward him, "I'm sorry, Dr. Long, could you be more specific?"

Liam laughed easily, leaning back in his chair, "Elizabeth, he's asking you whether or not you agree with my theory on Hester Prynne. Have you not been listening?" he teased.

Elizabeth?

Ellie felt the color drain from her face. It was too informal. It was too familiar! Now Liam really *was* giving them away. Under the weight of Alec's acid stare. Oh, God! How was she going to play this?

"I'm sorry, Dr. Long," Ellie said, attempting her most professional voice, refusing to turn toward Liam. "Could you explain the context of the question?"

John Long looked flustered and confused; what was she asking him to do?

"I'll explain," Liam offered tersely, sensing that she had pulled away.

Liam knows damn well that Alec is watching us both. He wants him to know!

Instinctively Ellie faced Liam now, unexpectedly beholding a placid face. Only the annoyance in his voice and a slight twitch in his jaw betrayed him. From this position, the red of Jordan's soccer jersey framed Liam's head, almost blinding her. And there, next to the angry red of the jersey, no more than five feet away, seeming to hover in the air over Liam, was the equally red face of her husband, boring holes into both of them.

Ellie's stomach lurched.

"Dr. Purnell," Liam said, resuming the formality, "my argument regarding Hester Prynne has always been the opposite of most critics. I consider her somewhat weak for not standing up to her husband, Roger Chillingsworth. I don't read her as the heroine of the novel."

Ellie smiled feebly.

So that's where you're going.

She searched Liam's eyes for some mercy *(Go easy on me!)*, but there was none.

"I disagree, Dr. Curran." Ellie managed to find her voice. "While Hester is deeply flawed, I think her actions show nothing but strength. How can you argue that she is not truly heroic when she denies her own happiness by refusing to reveal Dimmesdale, her lover? She does this only for him—in order to protect him from public scorn."

"Or she refuses to reveal him because it's easier just to carry on with her life as it is. Accept her fate, bear the burden herself. Never strive for what is possible," Liam ardently leaned into the table toward Ellie. The audience winced with surprise.

"How is misery and loneliness easier?" Ellie shot back.

"Indeed?" Liam asked sarcastically.

Indeed?

Ellie scrambled to deny his claim. "Hester Prynne accepts her fate, Dr. Curran. She accepts her responsibility in the affair and chooses to wait for Dimmesdale to be ready to confess on his own time."

"Yes, but how is that heroic, Dr. Purnell? How is that not just plain foolish? At the end of the novel, everyone finds out that Hester and Dimmesdale had the affair anyhow, and then he simply dies. Look at all the time she wasted!" Liam argued.

Ellie scanned the audience as they sat breathless and engaged. Her father sat back in his chair with his arms folded over his chest. She didn't dare look toward Alec and Jordan, strangling the insistent urge.

"She had Pearl, her daughter, to think of too," Ellie countered quietly.

"Of course." Liam snickered with condescension.

"Why do you dismiss that stance, Dr. Curran? Is it so impossible to believe that a mother might endure misery on behalf of her child?"

"Not impossible to believe at all, Elizabeth. The irony is that Pearl knows all along who her father is! It makes no sense for Hester to simply wear the scarlet letter and endure the public scorn when Pearl knows about the affair all along! Her mother is not protecting her at all!" Liam's usually calm voice began to rise with frustration. "Children are much more intuitive than we give them credit for. Consider how Hester's misery affected the happiness of her daughter. When the reader approaches the novel from that angle, Hester does not seem very heroic, does she? It's only when Hester and Dimmesdale admit their affair that Pearl is able to live a normal, happy life." He paused for effect. "You know—the truth shall set you free."

Ellie's brow furrowed with confusion; he was being so antagonistic. This was obviously no longer a debate over the novel but about the two of them. About Alec and Jordan. Could she continue the charade? Did it matter?

Probably not.

Any fool in the audience could sense the heat between them.

And Alec was no fool.

At the end of this debate (unlike the first), Ellie purposely stayed put, too fearful to move from the front table until all the handshaking and congratulations were dispensed. It was reverse avoidance.

(Always repressing or avoiding something, aren't you?)

Two professors from the junior college had attended, waiting to speak with Liam, offering a merciful distraction as Ellie looked on. By the time the small circle of Liam's fans had dispersed, everyone else in the audience had left, even her father.

Thank God.

"Interesting 'discussion.'" John Long snickered. "So much for it not being contentious, Dr. Curran." Ellie smiled feebly in response as Liam folded his arms across his chest in challenge. "The audience seemed enthralled, though." Long backed off. "There is certainly a dynamic between you two," he commented ambiguously as he turned away. "Good night."

He left Liam and Ellie standing alone under the cottonwoods, the low, gray light of dusk weaving around the buildings of the quad.

Exhausted, Ellie headed toward the doors of the liberal-arts building.

"Have you nothing to say?" Liam called after her.

"What do you mean?" she asked without turning around.

He caught up to her with two easy strides of his long legs. Grabbing her arm, he spun her around to face him. She couldn't disguise the despair in her eyes.

"Don't look like that!" Liam implored. "Do you want to continue hiding forever?" Pulling her into his arms, he stroked her hair with his hand. Ellie was vaguely aware that they stood exposed in the university quad, in an obviously intimate embrace, but what difference did it make now? Surely everyone had already figured it out. And anyhow, wasn't adultery part of her genetic code? People here had probably expected this of her all along. The professor daughter of Dr. Robert Lawson involved in an adultery scandal was...well, poetic!

She allowed herself to drink in Liam's scent before pulling away. In silent frustration, she led him into the building, up the stairs, and into her office where she gently closed and locked the door behind them both.

Privacy.

Finally.

"So?" Ellie spun around to face Liam. "What would you have me do?" she begged under her breath.

"What do you want to do?" Liam asked calmly.

"No! That's bullshit, Liam! Don't answer my question with a question. Why did you call me out publically? Again!" Ellie insisted in a harsh whisper. All the lights were off in the building, but who knew if anyone still lurked in one of the offices—if anyone was present to hear.

"I didn't call you out, Elizabeth. I did *not* stand up and announce, 'I love Elizabeth Lawson aka Avery Vaughn! Alec Purnell doesn't deserve her!'" Liam yelled out with a sarcastic flourish of his hand.

"Shhhh!" Ellie admonished him.

"I won't shush! I *won't* shush!" Liam refused loudly. "I ask you again—what do *you* want, Elizabeth?"

"I want to be happy!" Ellie cried. "I just want to be happy."

"And are you happy here, married to a neglectful alcoholic? Are you happy here in this town you returned to after college, lost and broken? Are you happy living in your father's shadow? Are you happy perpetuating this lie for your son?"

"You already know the answer to that," Ellie answered indignantly.

"Do I?" Liam asked. "I know what Avery says. But what she says and what Elizabeth does are two very different things. I am inclined to believe that you quite enjoy your suffering. Just like Hester Prynne." He raised his hands in mock surrender. "Be a victim forever then, Elizabeth, or change your current situation. At the risk of sounding trite, sometimes things have to get worse before they can get better. The lessons you don't learn now you are bound to repeat in the next life."

He stepped in toward her, so close that Ellie had to crane her neck to look up at him. "My intentions were to force your hand, Elizabeth. Now you have to face Alec. Now you have to face yourself and all your excuses for staying. What will you do?"

"I just want to be with you, Liam!" Ellie grabbed his chest roughly through his shirt. "I just want to stay here with you. Right now. I just want to be here right now."

"So be with me, then, Elizabeth!"

"Make love to me," she demanded, frantically unbuttoning his shirt, two buttons at once. It was the only answer.

Sighing heavily, he let his arms fall slack. At the last button, she slipped the linen over his shoulders, down his back, dropping it on the floor at his feet. Exposed, his perfect, muscular chest and abdomen, a sculpture in front of her.

"This won't solve your dilemma, you know?" Liam whispered into Ellie's hair as she reached for his zipper. A small gasp escaped him as he closed his eyes momentarily, lost in the sensation of her desperate fingers on his growing erection.

"I don't care," Ellie answered between soft kisses on Liam's chest. Her hand worked him partially out of his jeans. "I am being present, Liam. Isn't that what you always tell me?"

"Convenient for you to say when you're avoiding something, Elizabeth," Liam answered huskily as he pushed forward gently, forcing Ellie to sit on the end of her desk. In a moment, he had worked her skirt around her waist and had his long, nimble fingers inside her panties. He paused to kiss her chastely.

"Now you're teasing, Liam," she scolded him breathlessly.

Without breaking his gaze, he slid his fingers into her.

"Take off your blouse, Elizabeth," Liam ordered. "If you want me to make love to you, I want to do it properly."

"Even on a desk?" Ellie asked almost giddy with desire.

"Even on a desk," Liam answered seriously. "I want to see you. All of you." He slid her panties down her tensed legs and over her heels, dropping them to the floor as she unbuttoned her blouse, exposing her camisole. "Take that off too," he demanded. She peeled the straps from her shoulders, sending the silk camisole in a cascade over her nipples into a pool at her waist.

Liam ran his hands admiringly over her breasts, smoothing the skin, tenderly tracing the lines of her torso with his fingers. Then he lowered Ellie's back to the desk, pulling her legs around him. Bending over her slightly, he slowly eased into her, lingering deliciously before sliding partially out again. Ever so slowly, he filled her again. And again. Silently. Deeply.

With their eyes locked, Liam continued his slow, sensuous rhythm, lovingly smoothing Ellie's hair from her face. She was transfixed in his gaze, some intensity she couldn't quite place, and suddenly she found tears streaming from the sides of her eyes and into her hair. It was sorrow Ellie saw reflected back at her, Liam's emotions intuitively mirrored in her.

"Why couldn't I have met you twenty years ago?" Ellie lamented, reaching up to wipe away her tears. Liam pulled her up toward him, forcing himself so deeply into her that he filled her completely.

"You've known me eternities, Elizabeth," he whispered into her ear. "That's what I've been trying to get you to understand." He kissed her passionately as he held her to his chest. "Everything has occurred exactly as it was meant. Everything is as it should be."

"Then why..." She let the words die on her lips. She just wanted to feel him in her, around her, covering her in his warmth, protecting her. She grabbed his neck, his face, pressed her lips against his, forcing her tongue inside. Placing both hands around her waist for control, he buried himself into her again and again. Within seconds of one another, they both cried out in climax, not mindful of anyone overhearing.

"Liam?" Ellie asked quietly into his shoulder, the weight of him on top of her, still inside her, comforting and sublime. He made a move to lift himself to his elbows, but she held him to her.

"Yes?" he answered, staying put.

"I have never loved anyone like I love you."

"I know, Elizabeth," he whispered, a voice almost full of despair. "I just need you to love yourself that way too. I need to know you are going to be OK."

"I'll be OK, Liam," Ellie promised, kissing his shoulder. "I'll deal with Alec. Whatever happens, I'll deal with it."

Liam insisted on walking her to her car, but Ellie refused. She needed a few minutes alone to gather her thoughts, to calm the panic that had begun to rise from her queasy gut to her chest.

What are you going to do when you get home? What if Alec confronts you?

What if he doesn't confront you? Are you going to begin the conversation? What will you say?

"So, Alec, I've fallen in love with someone else." God, that sounds so simple. So juvenile.

Fairly trivial compared to fifteen years of marriage, for sure.

Bullshit. It's not trivial. Every fiber of my being believes that I was meant to fall in love with Liam. This man studied my writing for years and then came all the way from England to find me! No one has ever known me as well as he does. This is what is meant.

Ha! Is that how you'll explain it to Alec?

How can I ever explain this to anyone? I just know it to be true. I can just feel it. This was all meant to happen.

And what will you tell your son?

Ellie's stomach twisted violently in protest. What *would* she tell Jordan? Was she really prepared to leave her life?

Hugging herself with wet palms, she wandered toward the office window, absently looking out onto the university parking lot. Maybe she could just get into her car and drive away, jam the gas pedal so hard into the floor of the car that it would take flight, into an alternate universe where no one ever had to make difficult decisions.

If only.

Unconsciously avoiding the potentially volatile return home, Ellie continued to watch her car blankly, daydreaming of escape, when she became aware of movement at the far end of the lot. Into the ugly yellow circle of fluorescent light cast by an adjacent street lamp emerged a figure. An older man. Who looked just like her father.

Daddy!

With a quick, purposeful stride, he headed toward the end of the lot. Ellie's eyes scanned the pavement. Where was he going with such determination? Then she spotted his car parked farther down, obscured by a tree and an SUV.

What is he still doing here?

More movement. Behind him. A girl racing up to catch him. A young girl, long, blond hair trailing behind her, hands pleading with him as he stopped and turned to her, hands grabbing his face and pulling it toward her mouth.

Megan?

Megan!

Oh my God, Daddy! Megan? Oh my God! No!

Ellie's hands shot up to the window as she pressed her face to the glass in disbelief. Surely she was not seeing this! Surely this was some fucked-up hallucination, the cruelest of coincidences. Momentary hysteria caused Ellie to laugh out loud as she watched the scene unfold under the makeshift spotlight.

Initially her father hesitantly returned the kiss, but then passion forced him to draw Megan into an embrace, holding her hair in a fist, as he pulled her to him possessively. Ellie turned away, overwhelmed with a child's embarrassment.

The feeling was quickly replaced by rage and bitter sarcasm.

James Lawson, you dog! You still have the ability to charm the panties off your young admirers. This girl is nearly forty years younger than you! Who would have guessed?

Ellie whipped her purse off the desk, leaving her office door ajar as she fled down the hall.

Daddy! You are a con! You don't love anyone but yourself. You bastard.

She slammed through the doors of the liberal-arts building, her eyes madly scanning the parking lot. They were gone.

An engine started.

James Lawson backed up slowly and then exited the parking lot at the opposite end. He was in the car alone.

Ellie ran for her car. She would follow him— wherever he was going, she would follow him.

It didn't take much effort to catch up to Jim Lawson's car.

You might have the sexual prowess of a college boy, but you still drive like an old man, Daddy!

Lost in some delusional afterglow, her father had no idea he was being trailed. Even when Ellie's car instinctually steered itself onto the long gravel driveway of her childhood home, past the stables, past the arena, past the solemn, secretive oaks that lined the entry, James Lawson seemed unaware. Ellie fantasized about ramming the front of her car into his back end, sending him flying through the windshield, but she controlled her anger with short, jagged breaths.

Unbelievable!

Still oblivious, he quietly entered the house through the front porch as Ellie skidded loudly to a gritty stop and slammed her car into park.

"Daddy!" she yelled as she flew from the car. "Daddy!" She couldn't help herself. For a moment, Ellie envisioned her behavior the same as Megan chasing after him, the same sense of desperation in Megan's movements as she chased him to the parking lot. Was he trying to leave Megan too? What had he done to *her* head? Had he damaged that young girl like he'd damaged Ellie?

She tore up the steps, flinging open the front door of her parents' house.

"Ellie." Her mother stood in the center of the living room.

Maggie Lawson's tone stopped Ellie dead in her tracks. Just twelve inches inside the door. Ellie knew the tone intimately, but her mind scrambled to make sense of its use in this situation. It was an admonishing tone. The tone her mother took just before Ellie received a punishment. Ellie's eyes searched the room. Her father stood just on the other side of the kitchen island. On the other side of her mother.

"Daddy!" Ellie called over her mother's shoulder in challenge. "I saw you!" she accused breathlessly. "I saw you with Megan! Tell mother what happened! Tell her!"

Her father stood motionless, only a hint of shame playing across his face, but still he said nothing.

Ellie moved a step further into the room, but her mother held her ground. "Why are you blocking me?" Ellie turned on her mother. "Why are you protecting him? Do you think I'll scratch out his eyes for fucking my assistant?"

"Elizabeth Ann Lawson, don't speak about your father that way."

"Mom, are you not hearing me? He has been having an affair with a girl! A child, practically! A child, Daddy!" she yelled over her mother into the kitchen at him.

"Megan is no child, Ellie." Her mother laughed.

Ellie stopped immediately, her brow drawn together in confusion—Maggie Lawson was laughing disdainfully.

Not crying. Not screaming at her husband. Not distressed.

("Megan is no child, Ellie.")

Why is she laughing?

The sick light of realization nearly blinded her. "Oh my God, Mom. Did you know about this?" Suddenly Ellie couldn't breathe.

"Ellie, this is none of your business," her mother insisted sternly. "Jim, go to bed, honey."

"No, Jim, don't you dare go to bed!" Ellie yelled, pushing past her mother to charge into the kitchen. Ellie lunged at her father, palms opened, pushing him squarely in the chest.

"Are you fucking crazy, Daddy? Megan is only twenty-six years old! I have to work at that university! What is going to happen to my job when this gets out?"

Maggie Lawson, strong as ever, grabbed her daughter by the shoulders from behind, holding her back from her stunned father.

"Say something!" Ellie screamed.

"I'm sorry, Elizabeth," James Lawson stammered, hanging his head. Maggie Lawson flung Ellie aside and then once again stood protectively between her daughter and her husband.

"If I were you, Ellie, I'd be more concerned about how *your* behavior is going to affect your job," Maggie Lawson scolded. "From what I've seen and heard, you don't have much room to judge your father."

The blood rushed to Ellie's face.

"That's what I thought." Her mother snickered, seeing Ellie's reaction.

"Don't you *dare* make this about *my* behavior, Mother!" Ellie cried. "This isn't just about my job; it's about Daddy playing head games with this girl. You should have seen her run after him tonight. Heartsick. In love."

"Oh, bullshit," Maggie Lawson replied with a snort. "Your father is an icon. That woman and all the others were just like groupies. Only worse. They were all supposedly educated women, book smart but stupid about reality. The reality was that your Daddy is just a man. A man who suffers from manic-depression. A brilliant writer but just as weak as the rest of us. *They* are the ones who are guilty for putting him up on some pedestal—like his celebrity made him invincible. Those fools all deserve their heartbreak. You father has always loved his family over everything else, even his writing. Even his mistresses."

"So all these years, you've known?" Ellie asked incredulously. "All this time, you've allowed him his vice, and that's supposed to be love?" Her voice rose sharply. "*This* is love?" she yelled at her father.

"Who said anything about love, Ellie? Marriage is about responsibility. What would *you* say love is, Ellie? A twenty-six-year-old girl chasing after a sixty-five-year-old man after meaningless sex? Staying married for forty years. Raising a family. Building a life. That's as close to *love* as you're ever going to get."

"Oh my God, Mother! Listen to yourself! What sorry bullshit! *I* would say love is expecting someone to keep a fucking promise! Whether that is to stay faithful or to stay sober. Making a vow to someone and keeping that promise!"

"Like *you've* stayed faithful?" her mother chided.

"I *did* stay faithful to Alec, Mother. Trust me, over the years, there was at least one other man I could have slept with over and over, but I never acted on it. Do you know why I never cheated? Do you know why I didn't leave years ago?"

"Enlighten me, Ellie."

"Because I'm just like you!" Ellie laughed irrationally, throwing her head back, a touch of hysteria making her momentarily dizzy.

"All this time, I've been so afraid I was going to turn out like Daddy—that I was going to lose touch with reality somehow, like I was going to fucking lose it, go nuts, lock myself in a room for weeks the way he used to, but that could never happen! I have inherited your complete lack of passion, Mother! Your complete lack of faith that there is anything greater than this! I have inherited your ability to deny, to repress, to simply resign. *To resign!* To lay down and die this slow death. To believe there is no greater happiness in the world than a loveless marriage."

Maggie Lawson shifted her feet, looking down with disinterest.

"You once told me…What did you say? I want to get the words just right. Something to the effect of 'don't expect so much.' Remember that? When Alec and I were in counseling, you told me not to expect too much from marriage. Allow him to drink, to be gone, to do whatever he wanted since he had given me a son and a nice house!"

Maggie Lawson folded her arms, still unmoved by her daughter's rant.

"But you know what, Mom? You didn't have to give me that advice. My entire life, I'd already learned that lesson through your example."

Run! Save yourself while you still can!

Ellie turned to leave and then spun back around. "You're a disgrace." She sneered, pointing her finger hatefully at her father. Neither parent moved to stop her.

Her feet pounded down the steps of the porch, kicking up stones all the way to her car until she stopped abruptly, violently emptying the contents of her stomach.

Sixteen

Farewell! thou art too dear for my possessing,
And likest enough thou know'st thy estimate:
The charter of thy worth gives thee releasing;
My bonds in thee are all determinate.
For how do I hold thee but by thy granting?

—SHAKESPEARE, SONNET LXXXVIII

Ellie gripped the steering wheel, white-knuckled with steely resolve. Careening down the black county road toward home, she knew what had to be done. (She knew what had to be said.)

I will not be like my mother. I cannot continue to live a lie, to let my life gradually fade away—a hazy, gray ambivalence.

How fortuitous the evening had been, this turn of events. Just hours before, she had sat nervously between Liam and Alec, her son looking on, unaware of the drama, as she grappled with her guilt. Now, after confronting her mother and father, she saw everything with perfect clarity! She knew now, beyond a shadow of a doubt, that she could no longer perpetuate this charade of a marriage.

Everything is as it should be.

(And this is what is meant.)

And even so, her stomach somersaulted at the prospect of confrontation. How would she talk to Alec without Jordan knowing (overhearing)?

Oh, please, Ellie. Do you think that Jordan really doesn't know? ("Children are much more intuitive than we give them credit for.")

The errant thought saddened her. How much did Jordan already know? About Alec's drinking. About Liam. About living in a house without tenderness. How fucked up was he already?

No. There is still time! I can make this right! I can make him see there is more to life than just this. Jordan doesn't have to end up like me, repressing all emotion, hiding from confrontation, giving up all hope.

Suddenly hot tears of regret streamed down her face. She wiped them away quickly in a strained effort to see the road. God help her; whatever decisions she had ever made with regard to Jordan's happiness and emotional well-being now seemed foolish and near-sighted. Maybe staying with Alec (not giving up on "the dream") had been the wrong thing to do all along. If only she could see into Jordan's future and know that he would turn out OK, that his life would be all right.

Maybe then, she could stop obsessing. Maybe then she could stop feeling so crushed by guilt.

A sharp ding from her purse made her jump.

A text.

Against her better judgment, she dug her right arm into her bag, trying to control the swerve of the car with her left.

From: Jordan
Need you at home!

Ellie's heart thumped erratically against bone, her right foot pressed to the floor.

Oh no! Jordan! Oh God, are you OK?

By the time she threw the phone back onto the seat, she could already see the lights of her house through the dense forest of trees lining the street. On two wheels, she took the turn into the long gravel drive, barreling up to the house and screeching to a halt.

There was Jordan, his face illuminated by the glow of his cell phone, sitting calmly on the front porch steps, staring into the screen as if he had just hit send.

Ellie slammed the car into park and swung open the door, running toward her son with hysterical alarm.

"What's wrong, sweetheart? Are you OK?"

He stood to meet her as she threw her arms around her not-so-little boy.

"I'm fine," he answered, pulling gently away. "It's Dad."

The words barely registered when the scream of machinery split the air, setting the hairs on Ellie's neck on end. Her mind scrambled to make sense of the ear-piercing sound.

The chainsaw!

"He's in back," Jordan explained, indifferently. He sat back down on the steps, resuming his video-game play.

Ellie's jaw clenched in apprehension as she tore past him into the house, foolishly following the sound. The sonic whine of the chainsaw was momentarily accompanied by a frightening crash that shook the entire house. Something very heavy had just hit the roof on its way to the ground. She ran out the patio door just as the chainsaw sputtered. Stopped. Sputtered. Then once again roared to life, crescendoing into a deafening screech.

"It's dying!" Alec yelled into the thick summer air as he worked. "It's dying!"

"Alec!" Ellie waved her arms up at him frantically.

He teetered on an unsteady ladder, chainsaw in hand, amputating the limbs of their beautiful maple. Already, an obscene pile of branches littered the cement, covering all the benches, the ground, the deck furniture. The tree looked as though a tornado had ravished it from the bottom up.

"Stop cutting the tree! Stop! You're killing it! " Ellie implored. "Alec!"

But he couldn't hear her; he was drunk.

The chainsaw still fired up, Alec struggled to the top of the ladder, wielding his weapon precariously outward, swinging at a branch just out of reach. The chainsaw snagged the branch violently, sending it whipping toward him, just enough to catch him squarely in the chin. Ellie instinctively jumped back in self-defense as the branch catapulted to the ground, sending Alec, the ladder, and the chainsaw close behind.

Everything smashed against the earth with a thunderous boom and one last protesting cry of the chainsaw. Then, complete silence. Ellie stood frozen. Stunned.

"It was dying," Alec mumbled, a deep gash near his mouth smearing his face with blood, some demented clown.

Ellie ran to him, freeing him of the ladder. He struggled to move.

"Stay put, Alec!" she ordered, more out of duty than sympathy. She couldn't sort her emotions. Anger? Disgust? Pity? Human decency forced her to take care of any human being in peril. Even him.

"Can you feel your limbs? Is your head bleeding?" Ellie asked calmly, trying to assess Alec's injuries.

"I tried to save it, but it was dying, Ellie. I tried, but it was dying," he slurred.

"Just stay awake, Alec. I'm calling an ambulance."

She dialed 911 and then went out front to tell Jordan that Aunt Becca would pick him up. That would be her next call.

~

There was a quiet, persistent shame in being the wife of an alcoholic. Even on the verge of leaving Alec, the sting of association still assaulted Ellie as she endured the thinly veiled looks of amusement on the faces of the emergency-room staff. (Obviously this jackass in bed one had done it to himself.) What a story they would have to cackle over when they went on break ("Did you see the imbecile who got wasted and decided to saw down the tree in his backyard? The dumbass fell off a ladder and broke his arm and ribs. He's lucky he wasn't hurt worse! Serves him right.") Somehow being there, sitting mute at his bedside, appearing the dutiful wife, implied she was complicit, enabling, forgiving. Really, nothing could be farther from the truth.

He wasn't always like this! Ellie felt the urge to explain, to defend suddenly. But what was the point? The urge to defend Alec was less about protecting him than it was about protecting her own ego, and she knew it. By defending him, she had justification for staying married all these years, when really, there wasn't any justification.

Fine. I'm a doormat. Is that what you all think? Is that why you smirk?

Fuck these people! What do they know anyhow?

Ellie sat up straighter in her chair. What *did* these people know? Suddenly she got up and walked toward the door, nervously peeking her head down the hall. The last thing she needed was to run into one of her students (most likely also drunk) in the emergency room. She left the door open, just a crack, and tiptoed to her seat. Shame won out over indignation. It always did. That was the problem.

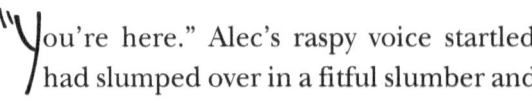

"You're here." Alec's raspy voice startled Ellie. She had slumped over in a fitful slumber and now struggled to come to, working out a crick in her neck with a hand still half asleep. The emergency room was eerily silent in the dim, uncertain light of dawn.

"You're here."

For a moment she debated how to respond. The remorse in his voice actually tugged at her heart.

Stop it! You know the routine—the morning-after contrition. He gets wasted, says or does something stupid, and then the next day, he apologizes for it, tries to make it better. But there is no going back now! This time is different. This time, it's about what you've done, too.

Her stomach did a nosedive. It was true. This time it was not just about Alec's drinking but about her and Liam.

Alec's bloodshot eyes fluttered open, fixing on Ellie's uncertain face.

"I'm sorry, Elle," he choked out.

Nothing more.

A standoff of sorts. What should she say?

"I'm sorry too, Alec," Ellie replied, the admission of guilt running freely from her eyes now.

She *was* sorry. Sorry that she had used Alec fifteen years ago as a rebound to get over Dylan. Sorry that they had rushed into marriage. Sorry that "the world which seemed to lie before her like a land of dreams" when she was in her twenties turned out to be anything but "various" or "beautiful" or "new." She was sorry that her son had an alcoholic father, and there wasn't a damn thing she could do to stop it. She was sorry years of marriage counseling never fixed anything.

The only thing she wasn't sorry about was Liam.

"You sent me a text," Alec continued in a voice strained with emotion.

"What do you mean?" Ellie asked, wiping her face.

"You accidentally sent me a text meant for someone else. I was laying in bed the Saturday morning after our party about a month ago—you know, when the investors were in from Texas—and I got a text from you saying, 'I missed you this morning!'" Alec explained.

Ellie felt nauseous. That was the text meant for Liam—the text she thought he purposely ignored!

"At first I thought you were flirting with me! But how ridiculous a notion was that, Ellie? When is the last time you said or did anything affectionate toward me? I tried to figure out why you would say you missed me when you'd just gotten out of bed to run an hour before...and then it dawned on me that you meant to send that text to someone else!"

Ellie sat motionless, her face neither confirming nor denying his conclusion. She was unsure of his mood and feared how the conversation might escalate in the stillness of the hospital. God, she longed for the solitude of her home, where they could have a real, honest conversation without the anxiety of being overheard.

Don't be stupid! You're probably safer here anyhow. Alec isn't drunk anymore. He won't make a scene.

"So I suspected it's this British guy you're working with. I mean, he tries to embarrass me at my own party the night before. Tells me, in front of my friends and employees, that I should read my wife's writing, like I don't even know my own wife. What sort of a dick does that?" Alec shook his head almost woefully. "But it got me to thinking that maybe I really *didn't* know my wife. That maybe I didn't know what my wife was capable of. Maybe I really didn't know my wife at all."

Ellie finally spoke. "Maybe you never showed any interest in knowing your wife, Alec."

"Maybe I didn't, Ellie. Maybe I was just too afraid to look stupid," Alec conceded, almost in a whisper.

"Maybe I've known all along that you were way out of my league and that I could never get to the core of you. I swear to God I have tried though! What more could I have done all these years? Haven't I given you everything you needed, Ellie? Haven't you had a perfect house, an expensive car to drive? Haven't you always been able to buy the nicest clothes and travel whenever you felt like it? Hasn't our son had a comfortable life?"

"Hasn't our son had to be raised by an alcoholic, Alec?" Ellie shot back, just a bit louder than she would have liked. She lowered her voice, "Haven't I begged you for years to stop drinking? Haven't we gone to counseling and yet nothing has ever changed?"

"Ellie, you gave up on me years ago," Alec replied without passion. He seemed to have no fight left in him, just self-pity.

"I did," Ellie admitted. "I did give up! Why do you think we never had a second child, Alec? I completely gave up on you after Jordan got sick because you weren't there for me! I was all alone! Every time I wanted your comfort, every time I needed you, you had some excuse to be gone."

"Ellie, I thought providing for you would be enough. Giving you and Jordan all the things you needed to be secure," Alec explained.

"All the material things, Alec. None of the emotional things. No interest in my work. No interest in my writing," Ellie lamented.

"How could I know?" Alec defended himself. "You have always been so fucking closed off, Ellie. So independent. How was I to know you needed me?"

"Are you kidding me?" Ellie shook her head. "I practically begged you to be present."

"To be present?" Alec's face scrunched up in confusion.

"Yes! At the beginning of our marriage, when Jordan was still young, before he got sick. Back when I still longed for you. I practically begged you to be present!" Ellie tried to explain, realizing Liam's words now poured out of her naturally like indoctrination. "I begged you to spend time with us when you came home from work or from business trips—to do things with us instead of disappearing to your mother's to drink. Isn't that what we always talked about in counseling? Even before your mother died, I wanted you to stop drinking all night and sleeping all day."

"I was working, Ellie," Alec insisted, the same old argument.

"Bullshit, Alec. That's always been your excuse. You weren't *always* working. You begged me for years to just stay home and be a wife, but I had no husband to be home for. All that independence you think I have— that was misconstrued. It was actually loneliness. I didn't know any other way not go insane, so I just shut myself down."

"Why, Ellie? Why did it have to come to this?" Alec questioned regretfully.

"Maybe I finally accepted you would never change, Alec. I finally gave up hope that by some miracle, you would stop drinking and be the person I needed you to be."

"I could never be that person, Ellie. I could never be the person you needed me to be. Maybe that's why I never stopped drinking."

"Were you so unwilling to try, Alec?" Ellie asked sadly.

Maybe he was right, though. Maybe he never could have been the person Ellie needed him to be.

He could never be Liam.

"You never loved me the way you love him." Alec's sullen eyes searched Ellie's face for confirmation. "Am I right?"

She blushed a deep, hot crimson.

"I thought so." Alec could barely speak. For a moment, he put the hand of his good arm up to his face. "Any fool sitting in the audience last night could have figured out there was something going on between the two of you," Alec said finally. "It wasn't the cuteness at the beginning, though, Ellie. All that 'Dr. Curran' and 'Dr. Purnell' bullshit you two tried to pull off, like you had some totally professional thing going. Like you didn't know each other or something. That crap isn't what convinced me. It was when you got so angry at him. That's when I knew for sure. Whatever you two were arguing over—the character in the book and her kid. He couldn't understand your point of view, and it infuriated you. I could see it in your jaw! That's when I knew. You would only bother to get that angry at someone you..." his voice broke off.

A deep, inexorable regret filled Ellie's chest cavity with the weight of an anvil.

The dream was dead.

Now openly estranged, husband and wife sat silent for some time, the strange, intrusive sounds of the hospital gradually returning as the morning light began to peek through the vertical blinds.

"I don't regret marrying you, Alec," Ellie offered genuinely. "I don't regret Jordan."

"I know, Ellie," Alec answered, his tone almost consoling. "At the very least, I saved you from returning to that asshole, Dylan Ross."

Ellie cringed at the mention of Dylan's name. She was surprised that Alec even remembered who he was; surely it had been ten years since they'd even spoken of Dylan Ross. "Yeah, he was a manipulative prick," Ellie answered absently.

"I'll say," Alec agreed. "Manipulative right up to the present. Two days ago, I get this letter he sent to our home addressed to Liam Purnell. I thought, 'Who the hell is Liam Purnell?' So I opened it, and it's this note written to me on Ross Accounting letterhead... saying how 'lovely' it was to run into us at the opera in June. He and his wife would love to have us out to Chicago again sometime, blah, blah, blah. It was bullshit, of course. I knew right away that you must have run into Dylan while you were there with Liam Curran, and he was just selling you out." Alec laughed bitterly. "I guess in the end, you must have broken Dylan's heart too, getting knocked up by me! Seems a lot of trouble to get back at you after all this time."

"Alec…" Ellie managed to get out, shock almost paralyzing her. "Nothing happened with Liam that weekend."

Alec raised his hand to stop her. "It doesn't matter now, does it?" he asked rhetorically, rolling over to face the wall. "I love you, Ellie," he said softly. "I love you enough to let you go, if that's what you want. You deserve to be happy. We both do."

Ellie's mouth began to form a protest and then stopped.

"Ellie, don't beat yourself up too much about it," Alec offered. "You weren't the only person in this marriage to be unfaithful."

"Don't, Alec." Ellie stopped him.

It was too pathetic now, this complete obliteration of the dream, the promises they made to one another when they married (for better or for worse).

Promises are shit.

Whatever he was about to admit, she didn't want to know.

"I was lonely too, Ellie," Alec explained. "I've been lonely too."

Ellie stood at the front window of their cavernous home, full of all the meaningless material items they'd amassed over the years. How futile it had been to try to fill the emotional void with new furniture or expensive window treatments, marble and mahogany—all just Band-Aids. Now that Ellie watched Alec in the driveway, stubbornly struggling with a casted arm to lift his suitcase into the trunk of his car, it was even more obvious how ineffective hiding behind their money had been. All the things they owned had never brought her peace.

"We should take some time and figure out what to tell Jordan," Alec had said before he left. "I'm going to move out for a while. Give you some time and space."

"Where are you going to go?" Ellie asked, surprised by her concern. "What about your arm?"

"Don't worry," Alec had assured her. "I have someone to help me."

Now she watched him pull slowly away and found herself confused and alone, wandering into a kitchen engulfed by strange angular shadows, late-afternoon reflections of the sunset maple's mutilated branches.

What should she do? Take a shower? Eat something? Surf the TV channels? No! She couldn't sit. Should she laugh hysterically or cry? The life she had known (had hated?) just ended. Now what was she supposed to do?

Run. Run and save yourself while you still can.

Tearing up the stairs to her room, Ellie shed her dress frantically and then kicked the knotted ball of it into the corner. In no time, she had redressed in shorts and laced up her running shoes.

Run.

She flew out the front door, down the drive, already at a sprint when she got to the road, headed for the same route she had taken every morning since the end of May.

Liam!

After the first half mile, she slowed her pace, suddenly apprehensive. She needed more time to sort her thoughts. Why was she running so quickly toward Mrs. Dobb's cottage? What would she say to Liam once she saw him?

I am yours now! Forever! I love you! I love you! I love you!

She really *had* been in the present with Liam; up until right now, she really hadn't considered any future other than this moment. Now that she knew her marriage was over, what did she want from him?

Don't be ridiculous! You know what you want...what is meant. You want to be with him. You want to be his.

But is that what he wants?

Of course it is! Of course that's what he wants.

"Liam!" she called into Mrs. Dobbs's house breathlessly as she flung open the screen door. Classical music played softly from speakers somewhere in the house.

"Liam!" Ellie called, but no answer. An open bottle of red wine sat on the counter next to a half-empty glass, a colander of damp vegetables in the sink. A cutting board and knife set out, ready to use.

Ellie searched the rooms of the house before exiting through the back door toward the yard. Perhaps he'd gone into the garden to gather more food for dinner.

"Liam!" Ellie yelled out again.

"So urgent!" a quiet, amused voice came from beneath the tree to her right. She had run right past him.

"Liam." She smiled once she spotted him cross-legged beneath the shelter of a hickory. "What are you doing out here? It looks like you were in the middle of making dinner."

"I was," Liam admitted. "I suppose I got distracted. The wine. The sunlight. Too beautiful an afternoon to ignore. Something beckoned to me. I came out to watch the garden grow!" From where he sat beneath the tree, he had a perfect view of his plants. The merciless rays of an August afternoon engulfed the garden, nearly setting it aflame, bees and butterflies hovering contentedly through the greenery.

A wide, placid grin spread slowly across Liam's face as he surveyed Ellie's usual disarray, hair in a matted, sweaty mess of exertion, excitement. "I thought you might come," he said finally.

"I left Alec!" Ellie blurted, the words in her own ears sounding simple and ridiculous. Certainly it was more complicated than that.

Liam patted the ground next him, inviting her to sit.

She straddled his lap instead, taking his face into her hands, pulling his mouth to hers. Liam laughed initially at her urgency but was soon overcome by Ellie's frantic hands, the depth of her kiss, her labored breathing.

"Whoa, slow down." He laughed again, grabbing her hands to steady her, but his body beneath her responded immediately.

"I need you, Liam!" She unzipped his shorts, sliding her hand around him. The feel of his arousal, the smell of him, thick with soap and the outdoors—his warmth ignited Ellie's desire. "I need to be lost in you."

"Shall I make love to you right here then?" he asked between kisses.

"Yes!" Ellie insisted.

"Very well." Liam obliged. "Stand up."

Ellie did as she was told so Liam could slide her shorts gently off. As she lowered herself back down to sit on top of him, he guided himself into her slowly, lovingly, intensely watching her face as her tension morphed into ecstasy. He fingered the straps of her tank, tracing the outline of her shoulders and then ran his hand back up along the line of her jaw. She turned her head to kiss his hand as minute movements of her hips brought them rhythmically closer together.

"I love you, Elizabeth," Liam whispered into her hair, pulling her closer to him, one arm around her waist, the other wrapped around her shoulders. "I am so relieved." He thrust upward to meet her several more times, hitting just the right spot inside to send her spiraling into climax around him, followed by a guttural gasp, the feeling too intense to release sound outward, an implosion that sent pins and needles to her fingers and toes.

Liam held Ellie to him, her head melded to the crook of his neck, her small arms, the folded wings of an origami bird, beneath his protective embrace. Motionless. Perfect. One body. One soul.

"Were you finished?" Ellie looked up suddenly, realizing her own selfishness.

"I am fine," Liam assured her, smoothing her hair.

"What's wrong?" Ellie asked looking into his ashen face. Liam's green eyes shone with the threat of tears.

"I am just so relieved, Elizabeth," he said again.

"Relieved?" she asked as he rolled her to the ground, gently pulling out. He quietly helped her slide her shorts back up and then propped himself onto one elbow next to her in the soft grass beneath the shade of the tree.

"Yes, I'm relieved that you chose to leave Alec. It means my decision to come here was not in vain. Just promise me you won't go back."

"Why would I go back?" Ellie asked, genuinely confused. "I want to go with you! I want to be with you!" She reached up to kiss him and found his face was wet.

"I won't be leaving here," he told her.

"Why not? You're not going back to London?"

"No, Ellie. I won't be going back to London." Liam shook his head slowly.

"Why? Why would you stay here?" Ellie couldn't understand what he was saying.

"I'm dying, Elizabeth."

She tried to joke, her heart erratic in her chest. "We're all dying, Liam."

"Ahh, you've learned well, Elizabeth. That *is* something I would normally say." The sides of his mouth lifted in some form of a smile, but it didn't reach his eyes.

"What are you telling me?" She sat up abruptly, eyes blinking madly to clear the stars that had suddenly appeared in her peripheral vision. Through the blur of her panic, she could barely focus on his face.

"It's OK." He sat up, grabbing her shoulders. "It's OK."

"What do you mean you're dying?" Ellie cried, her eyes wide with fear.

"I have cancer, Elizabeth. I beat it once, but it returned. This time, the doctors gave me only a thirty percent chance of survival. I left chemotherapy treatments three months ago to come here."

"Then maybe you still have a chance!" Ellie suggested hopefully. "Maybe you can still beat it! Maybe it's not too late to return to your treatments!"

"No, Elizabeth, I know I'm dying, and it's OK," Liam explained softly, kissing her on the forehead.

She pulled away angrily. "How can you say it's going to be OK? You just gave up! Why didn't you try to get better? Why did you have to come *here*?" She wept. "Why did you have to come here, Liam? Why couldn't you try to save yourself? Why?"

He grabbed Ellie as she struggled to free herself, but finally she gave in, crumpling into his arms, convulsive sobs wracking her body. They huddled awkwardly in the grass, the animallike wail of Ellie's weeping violating the calm of the surrounding pine forest. Liam cried silently with her, allowing himself finally to admit his sorrow. If only they had had more time. In this life.

"Why, Liam?" Ellie cried quietly into his chest. "Why did you stop chemotherapy to come here?"

"I followed Avery Vaughn's writing for years, piecing together the events of your life, watching you fall further and further into hopelessness. I was afraid I would die without ever finding you, Elizabeth. I couldn't take that chance, so I left."

"So you basically chose to die," she said, weeping.

"I chose to save you instead." Liam squeezed her more tightly, kissing the top of her head. "I chose to save you, Avery, like you saved me once. That is why I came."

"Oh, Liam, no," Ellie whimpered regretfully.

"Seeing you that first time in the hall of the liberal-arts building, full of fight and fear—I knew immediately you were my destiny. Just being near you confirmed any doubts I had about the perfect order of the universe." He let out a long, ragged sigh, still attempting to comfort Ellie by cradling her head at his chest.

"I don't think you really understand yet, Elizabeth, but I hope one day you will. Maybe you'll take the same journey I took to discover the truth, *your* truth. Leave this town finally. Travel the world. Climb a mountain! Work toward your own enlightenment. Right now, this all seems horrible, but it's what is meant, Elizabeth. Everything is as it should be. This moment, right here, right now, under this tree…you in my arms. This is what is meant. Your words in that essay on elegies that found me in my darkest hour, lost and alone in Katmandu… that was no coincidence. That was all meant."

"Why couldn't we just have more time, Liam?" Ellie lamented. "Why couldn't *that* be meant?"

"We have had eternities together already, Elizabeth. Our souls are permanently knit, inextricably bound. You are born for me over and over, each new life we enter into. Who knows how many lives we've already lived together? Don't you see? I *had* to come here! I had to redeem myself for not freeing Katherine. Maybe freeing you balances that karmic debt."

"I don't want to be free!" Ellie cried. "I just want to be with you, Liam."

"You *are* with me, my darling." Liam stroked her face and then leaned down to gently kiss her salty lips. "If I hadn't come for you, Elizabeth, how would you know to look for me in the next life? Death is not the end."

"Can't I just keep you now?"

"You can be in the present, Elizabeth. You can be in this moment right now. We still have right now." He tilted her chin up tenderly to look into her face. "Stay with me?" he implored.

"I would never leave you, Liam! Never. I am yours forever."

Seventeen

The smallest sprout shows
there really is no death,
And if ever there was it led forward
life, and does not wait at
The end to arrest it,
And ceas'd the moment life appear'd.

All goes onward and outward, nothing collapses,
And to die is different from what
any one supposed, and
luckier.

—WALT WHITMAN, "LEAVES OF GRASS"

Liam Charles Curran left this world as gracefully and unassuming as he had once existed in it, lying in the arms of his lover on a brilliant, sunny Wisconsin Sunday, late in the month of August.

E. J. Densmore

His parting gifts consisted of a basket of ripe to-matoes and several bunches of freshly cut herbs with a note he addressed to Joe Dobbs and signed "With love, your Mother."

The other was a sealed envelope "for my Elizabeth," which he had hidden inside the cover of her book of essays. Ellie had found it, of course, only days after he died, poring over his belongings in a haze of grief.

It was too much, this last gift to her, his last words. Once she opened it, she would have nothing of him left to anticipate, so she only clutched the unopened letter to her chest, carrying it with her into bed where she remained for days, rolled into a ball on her side, facing away from the door.

"Take this." Becca handed Ellie a sleeping pill on one of her and Marta's many visits. They would sit on the end of the bed quietly or stand vigil just outside Ellie's bedroom door, both wisely saying nothing. Just watching. Waiting.

You are Daddy. You are just like him, locked up here in your room, avoiding life, avoiding pain.

Then Ellie would see Liam shaking his head in dis-approval ("Stop, Elizabeth!"), and her subconscious would end its berating.

Hours, days, weeks, she waited for the pain to numb, for the panic and the loneliness to subside, but the only relief from it came in the form of medication.

The bottle.

Becca had foolishly left the bottle of pills perched on the nightstand, just within Ellie's lazy reach.

Maybe you should just swallow them all. Finally you could get some peace.

Maybe she would!

Maybe she would.

She scooted herself toward the nightstand without lifting her head from the bed. Maybe she would just hold the bottle in her palm for a bit. Turn it over and over in her hand—Liam's letter clutched in one, the pills in the other.

She reached out finally for the bottle when a knock at the door startled her.

Instinctively pulling in her guilty arm, she stilled completely, an animal in self-defense.

Pretend to be asleep.

She didn't want to talk to anyone.

The knock came again, a bit louder.

"Mom," Jordan's worried voice called softly into the room. Ellie's swollen eyes sprang open. She couldn't turn him away.

"Jordan," she managed to whisper, her voice the crackle of a dried leaf. She slid the letter beneath her pillow and attempted to sit up against the headboard. The worried expression on Jordan's unexpectedly mature face told her she looked as horrible as she felt. When had he suddenly become a man?

"I had a dream," he told her as he sat on the side of the bed next to her. "I had a dream about you last night. It was totally crazy!" He laughed for a minute and then seemed to remember his concern. "You were riding Whisper, I think. Only it wasn't Whisper. Some black horse. You know how dreams are—everything is like something you know in your real life, just a little twisted and different. It was like that. And you were riding through the snow. Climbing up like it was a mountain or something, Mom. But you were happy. And I was happy to see you happy."

His bottomless, brown eyes were so full of trepidation, it made Ellie's eyes well with shameful tears.

"So I got to thinking, maybe this is the answer." He handed her a small blue book.

Her passport.

"I'm so sorry, Jordan," Ellie choked out, taking the passport from him.

"It's OK, Mom. It's all going to be OK. I think this is…" He paused as if searching for just the right words, his face earnest with concentration. "I think you should use this. I think this is what is meant."

Epilogue

My Dearest Elizabeth,

No more hiding behind Avery.
And for God's sake, no elegies!

Search for me, my darling.
I am everywhere.
Waiting.

Eternally yours,
Liam

"*Antielegy*"

If Whitman's infamous kid were to
wave that fistful of green grass at me,
begging an answer to the

mysteries of life and
death,
I'd say,
"Stop plucking Dr. Curran's hair!"
(After all, he is everywhere.)
underfoot.
Laughing in the leaves,
an echo through the
"leaping greenly spirit of trees" or
floating in the
"blue true dream of sky."
Forget the cavernous sinkhole
of my chest—
he lives there too.
The persistent pulse in my thumb,
the exhalation of lungs.
Liam,
I am lost
But will not mourn you.
I will not say good-bye.

—ELIZABETH LAWSON

www.ingramcontent.com/pod-product-compliance
Lightning Source LLC
Chambersburg PA
CBHW021833010726
47493CB00005B/1373